ACCLAIM FOR LOUISE JENSEN'S
THE SISTER

"I couldn't put [it] down until I had answers! ...I wasn't sure which characters to trust and which to not trust ...A five-star book that would make a fantastic summer read!"
—Steph and Chris's Book Review

"One of those books that you can't stop thinking about even when you're not reading it! ...The tension never seems to drop for one second! ...An absolute treat, albeit a scary one, to read! Highly recommended!"
—Books and Me!

"Hooked from the first page till the end ...A gripping tale for fans of *I Let You Go* and *The Girl on the Train*. A must read."
—Berlitz Chile

"I was left gaping ...You cannot help but speed read through this novel. You have to know what happens."
—Aloha Reviews

"I was hooked on the story from the word *go*."
—Hollie in Wanderlust

ACCLAIM FOR LOUISE JENSEN'S
THE SURROGATE

"This novel was paced perfectly and I actually finished it in one day because I couldn't put it down ...So addictive! *The Surrogate* is a five-star novel that is a 2017 must read! I am already looking forward to reading what Louise Jensen comes out with next!" —Steph and Chris's Book Review

The Gift

ALSO BY LOUISE JENSEN

The Gift

LOUISE JENSEN

GC

GRAND CENTRAL
PUBLISHING

New York   Boston

Copyright © 2016 by Louise Jensen
Cover design and art by Henry Steadman. Cover copyright © 2020 by Hachette Book Group, Inc.

Grand Central Publishing
Hachette Book Group
1290 Avenue of the Americas, New York, NY 10104
grandcentralpublishing.com
twitter.com/grandcentralpub

Originally published in 2016 by Bookouture, an imprint of StoryFire Ltd.
First Grand Central Publishing edition published in trade paperback in March 2020

First Mass Market Edition: December 2020

Grand Central Publishing is a division of Hachette Book Group, Inc. The Grand Central Publishing name and logo is a trademark of Hachette Book Group, Inc.

The publisher is not responsible for websites (or their content) that are not owned by the publisher.

The Hachette Speakers Bureau provides a wide range of authors for speaking events. To find out more, go to www.hachettespeakersbureau.com or call (866) 376-6591.

LCCN: 2019951951

ISBN: 978-1-5387-1341-9 (mass market)

Printed in the United States of America

OPM

10 9 8 7 6 5 4 3 2 1

For Callum, Kai, and Finley
You will always remain my proudest achievement.

The Gift

Later

Run.

It's dark. So dark. Clouds scud across the charcoal sky, blanketing the moon and stars. Dampness fills my lungs and as I draw a sharp breath nausea crashes over me in sickening waves.

My energy is fading fast. My trainers slap against the concrete and I don't think I can hear footsteps behind me anymore, but it's hard to tell over the howling wind.

I steal a glance over my shoulder but my feet stray onto soft earth and I lose my footing and stumble, splaying out my hands to break my fall. The side of my face hits something hard and solid that rips at my skin. My jaw snaps shut and my teeth slice into my tongue flooding my mouth with blood, and as I swallow it down, bile and fear rise in my throat.

Don't make a sound.

I'm scared. So scared.

I lie on my stomach. Still. Silent. Waiting. My palms are stinging. Cheek throbbing. Rotting leaves pervade my nostrils. My stomach roils as I slowly inch forward, digging my elbows into the wet soil for traction. Left. Right. Left. Right.

I'm in the undergrowth now. Thorns pierce my skin and catch on my clothes but I stay low, surrounded by trees, thinking I can't be seen, but the clouds part and in the moonlight I catch sight of the sleeve of my hoodie, which, unbelievably, is white, despite the mud splatters. I curse myself. Stupid. Stupid. Stupid. I yank it off and stuff it under a bush. My teeth clatter together with cold. With fear. To my left twigs snap underfoot and instinctively I push myself up and rock forward onto the balls of my feet like a runner about to sprint. Over my heartbeat pounding in my ears, I hear it.

A cough. Behind me now. Close. Too close.

Run.

I stumble forward. I can do this, I tell myself, but it's a lie. I know I can't keep going for much longer.

The clouds roll across the sky again and the blackness is crushing. I momentarily slow, conscious I can't see where I'm putting my feet. The ground is full of potholes and I can't risk spraining my ankle, or worse. What would I do then? How could I get away? The wind gusts and the clouds are swept away and in my peripheral vision a shadow moves. I spin around and scream.

Run.

CHAPTER ONE
Now

Every Tuesday, between four and five, I tell lies.

Vanessa, my therapist, nudges tortoiseshell glasses up the bridge of her nose and slides a box of Kleenex toward me, as if today will be the day my guilt spews out, coming to rest, putrid and toxic, on the impossibly polished table between us.

"So, Jenna." She shuffles through my file. "It's approaching the six-month anniversary—how do you feel?"

I shrug and pick at a stray thread hanging from my sleeve. The scent from the lavender potpourri irks me, as does the excess of shiny-leaved plants in this carefully created space, but I swallow down my agitation as I shift on the too-soft sofa. I can't keep blaming my medication for my mood swings, can I?

"Fine," I say, although that couldn't be further from the truth. I have so many emotions waiting to pour out of me, but whenever I'm here, words tie themselves into knots on my tongue, and however much I want to properly open up, I never really do.

"Have you been anywhere this week?"

"I went out with Mum, on Friday." It's hardly news. I do it every week. Sometimes I can't understand why I see Vanessa at all. I've completed the set number of appointments I was supposed to, yet still I arrive on the dot each week. I guess it's because I don't get out much and I do like my routine, my little bit of normality.

"And socially?"

"No." I can't remember the last time I had a night out. I'm only thirty but I feel double that, at least. I wasn't up to socializing for ages afterward and now I prefer to be at home. Alone. Safe.

"Emotionally? Are things settling down?"

I break eye contact. She's referring to my paranoia, and I don't quite know what to say. At almost every hospital appointment the cocktail of drugs I am taking to stop my body rejecting my new heart is adjusted, but anxiety has wrapped itself around me like a second skin, and no matter how hard I try, I can't shake it off.

"The urge to..." she consults her notes, "run away? Is that still with you?"

"Yes." Adrenaline pricks my skin and the underarms of my T-shirt grow damp. The sense of danger that often washes over me is so overwhelming it sometimes feels like a premonition.

"It's not unusual to want to escape from your own life when something traumatic has happened that is difficult to process. We have to work together to break the cycle of obsessive thoughts."

"I don't think it's as simple as that." The fear is as real and solid as the amber paperweight that rests on Vanessa's desk. "I've been having more..." I'm not sure I want to tell her but she's looking at me now in that way of hers, as if she can see right through me, "...episodes."

"Are they the same as before? The overwhelming dizziness?" She lifts her chin slightly as she waits for my answer, and I wish I'd never mentioned it.

"Yes. I don't lose consciousness but my vision tunnels and everything sounds muffled. They're getting more frequent."

"And how long are these episodes lasting?"

"It's hard to say. Seconds probably. But when it happens I feel so ..." I look around the office as though the word I am looking for might be painted on the wall, "...frightened."

"Feeling out of control is frightening, Jenna, and it's understandable given what you've been through. Have you mentioned these episodes to Dr. Kapur?"

"Yes. He says panic attacks aren't unheard of on my medication but if all goes well at my six-month check he can reduce my tablets and that should help."

"There you go then. And you're due back at work..." she glances at her papers, "...Monday?"

"Yes. Only part-time though. At first." Linda and John, my bosses, have been more than generous with the time off they have given me. They're friends of Dad's and have known me most of my life, and although Linda said I shouldn't feel obliged to return I've missed my job. I can't imagine starting afresh somewhere new. Somewhere unfamiliar. I'm nervous though. I've been away so long. How will it feel? Being normal again. I'm jittery at the thought of mixing with people. I've got too used to my own company, being at home, filling my time. "Puttering around," Mum used to call it; "hiding myself away," she says now, but in my flat the jagged unease I carry with me isn't quite so sharp. But life goes on, doesn't it? And if I don't force myself to start living again now, I'm afraid I never will.

"How do you feel about going back?"

My shoulders begin their automatic ascent toward my ears but I stop them. "OK, I think. My parents aren't keen. They've been trying to talk me out of it. I can understand that they're worried it will be too much, but Linda has said I can take it slowly to start with. Leave early if I get too tired and go in late if I've had a bad night." I've always had a good relationship with Linda, even if she hasn't visited me in the past few months. She doesn't know what to say, I suppose. No one does. The fact I nearly died makes people uncomfortable.

"And the donor's family? Are you still trying to contact them?"

I shift in my seat. Over the past few months I have poured my thanks into letter after letter that was rejected by my transplant coordinator. I'd inadvertently revealed too much. A clue about who I was, where I live. But without those details it all seemed so cold and anonymous. Eventually I paid a private investigator to find them and wrote to the family directly. It cost a small fortune just for their address but it was worth it to be able to express how grateful I am and how much their act means to my family, without filtering my words. I wasn't going to bother them again and never expected to hear back but they replied straight away, and seemed genuinely pleased to have heard from me. I know Vanessa won't like what's coming.

My mouth dries and I lean forward to pick up my glass. My hand trembles and ice cubes chink and water sloshes over the side and trickles onto my lap where it soaks into my jeans. I sip my drink, conscious of the tick-tick-tick of Vanessa's clock, discreetly positioned behind me. "I'm meeting them on Saturday."

"Oh, Jenna. That's completely unethical. How did you trace them? I'm going to have to report this, you know."

My face flames as I study my shoes. "I can't tell you. I'm sorry."

"You know contact isn't encouraged." Disapproval drips from every word. "Especially this early on in the process. It can be incredibly distressing for everyone, and it could set you back several stages. A simple thank you letter would have sufficed but meeting—I just..."

"I know. They've been told exactly the same thing, but they want to meet me. They do. And I need to meet them. Just once. It feels as though someone else is inside of me, and I want to know who it is. I have to know." My voice cracks.

"It's become almost an obsession and it's not healthy, Jenna. What good will it do you knowing whose heart you have?"

The colors in the painting behind her, something modern and chaotic, swirl together and the gnawing agitation inside me grows.

"It would help me to understand."

"Understand what?" Vanessa leans toward me like a jockey on a horse, pushing forward, sensing a breakthrough.

"Why I lived and they died."

* * *

There's an indent in my chocolate leather couch marking the place I've spent too many hours. There might as well be a sign, "GIRL WITH NO LIFE LIVES HERE." I light a berry-scented candle before flopping down in my usual spot. I always feel so drained when I've been to see Vanessa, and I'm never sure whether it's from the emotions that bubble to the surface when I sit in her immaculate office, or the effort of keeping them inside.

From the coffee table, I pick up my sketchbook. Drawing

always relaxes me. I stream James Bay through my Bluetooth speaker and as he holds back the river I tap-tap-tap the pencil hard against my knee, staring at the bland walls as I wait for inspiration to hit. I've been meaning to decorate since Sam moved out nearly six months ago. Make the flat my own. Cover up the magnolia with sunshine yellow or rich red: bold colors that Sam hates. It's not like he's coming back although I know he'd like to. He never wanted us to split up but I couldn't stand the look of sympathy in his eyes whenever he looked at me after my surgery, the way he fussed around asking if I was all right every five minutes. I didn't want him to be stuck with someone like me, "helping me through" as though we're old and there's nothing more to life. Cutting him free was the kindest thing I've ever done, even if my stomach still twists every time I think about him. We're trying to be friends. Texting. Facebooking. But it's not the same, is it? I add decorating to my mental list of things to do that I'll probably never get around to. The days when I had to take it easy have passed but I'm stuck in a rut I can't get out of and, truth be told, I'm scared. Despite the hours of physio and the mountain of leaflets I was sent home with, there's a hesitancy about my movements. An enforced slowness. My body is healing well, my doctor says, but my mind doesn't seem to believe it, and I'm terrified I will push myself too hard. That something will go wrong, and what would I do then? I picture myself lying on the floor. Unable to reach the phone. Unable to move. Who would know? I pretend to Mum I'm fine living alone. I pretend to everyone. Even myself.

What can I draw? I flick through the pages of my pad. Initially there is image after image of Sam, but lately my drawings have become darker. Menacing almost. Forests with twisted tree branches, eyes peering out of the gloom, an owl with beady eyes. I sigh. Perhaps Vanessa is right to be concerned about my mental health.

My mobile beeps. It's a text from Rachel, and I know without opening it she'll be asking what I'm doing later. I'll tell her I'm having a night in and to have a drink for me at the pub. It's our weekly routine, like Punch and Judy. The same every time even though sometimes you itch for a different ending. *I could go*, I think to myself but then I bat the thought away. It seems fruitless to try to fall back into the same habits. I'm not the person I was before, and besides, people treat me differently now, never quite meeting my gaze, not knowing what to say. I'll see Rachel at work on Monday.

Nearly six months ago, someone died so I can live. My world has become so small it sometimes feels as though I can't breathe. Who was it that died for me? I squeeze my eyes tightly closed but the thought still juggernauts toward me and I don't know how to make it stop. I shiver and cross to the window. The breeze blowing in is freezing but I am grateful for the fresh air. I have been home for weeks now but the heavy smell of hospital seems to have embedded itself into my lungs, and whatever the weather I always have the windows cracked open. I peer out of the slatted blinds into the dusk and a chill creeps up my spine. A shadow shifts in the doorway across the road, and the urge to run I told Vanessa about swamps me. My breath quickens but the street is still. Quiet. I slam the window and close the blinds and am cocooned by the dim light in my living room. My world is shrinking; my confidence too.

Back on the sofa, my hands are shaking too much to hold the pencil steady. *I'm safe*, I tell myself. So why don't I feel it?

CHAPTER TWO

Ten months ago, we'd both been ill. A virus had rocketed around Sam's office, and I'd come home from work one day to find him huddled on the sofa, duvet draped over him, a pile of scrunched-up tissues on the floor. Radiators belted out heat, and I'd thrown off my coat and jumper.

"I think I'm dying, Jenna," Sam croaked, stretching his arm toward me, and I'd laughed but as I took his hand it was slick with sweat, and I pressed my palm to his forehead. Despite the fact his teeth were rattling together with cold, he was burning up.

"Man flu." I'd grazed my lips against his hot cheek. "Be back soon."

I'd dashed out to the late-night pharmacy and stocked up on cold medicine and aspirin, and at home I warmed through chicken and sweetcorn soup. A couple of days later my throat stung, eyes streamed, and I shivered so furiously I bit my tongue. We stayed in bed for days. The air grew thick and sour as we binge-watched box sets, volume blaring to drown out hacking coughs. We took it in turns to shuffle to the kitchen, slow and purposeful, like zombies, and fetched snacks we couldn't swallow, drinks we couldn't taste. It was such a relief to feel better. To hoist open the sash windows and let the cool breeze sweep away the stench of ill health. Under the shower, hot needles of water peppered my skin and I believed the worst was over.

Sam's strength returned day by day, but mine didn't and after about a week I felt so exhausted I was napping in the car during my lunch break, falling asleep on the couch as M&S ready meals blackened in the oven. At night, I'd wake gasping, trying to force oxygen into my lungs, and I'd stick my head out the window and gulp fresh air, wondering what was happening to me.

"I've booked you a doctor's appointment," Sam said one day. "Five o'clock. No arguing."

I was too drained to protest. I sat in the GP's waiting room, the fug of illness stale and oppressive. The doctor barely listened to my symptoms before he scratched his salt-and-pepper beard and told me what I was experiencing was completely normal and I just needed to rest. He reassured me that my energy would return.

Three weeks later I barely had the strength to get out of bed. I hadn't been to work in over two weeks.

"This doesn't seem right to me," Sam said as he stood over me, his face etched with worry. "I've booked you an appointment to get a second opinion. I'll be back to pick you up at lunchtime."

Later that morning I'd hefted myself out of bed and was shuffling to the bathroom when I stopped to scoop the post up from the doormat, and that was the last thing I remembered. Apparently, Sam found me on the hallway floor, lips drained of color, and I was rushed into hospital, sirens blaring, blue lights flashing.

The next few months were a blur. On one level, I was aware of what was going on around me. I had viral myocarditis, which had aggressively attacked my heart function; and a transplant was my only option. Sam was permanently curled up in a ball in the chair next to my bed. Mum plastered on her bright, happy smile and visited every day. Dad paced around the room, hands in pockets, head bowed. The beeping of the machines was the last thing I heard at night and the sound I woke up to in the morning, wondering where I was until I inhaled. There's nothing quite like the smell of hospitals, of disinfectant mixed with decay; hand gel mingled with hope. I was too weak to read, and I couldn't focus on the TV.

"Kardashians or soap stars?" Rachel would ask as she read aloud from the gossip magazines, but I'd drift in and out of sleep and never could quite keep up with who was divorcing who, or which actress was currently too fat. Too thin. It all seemed so trivial, the things we used to laugh about in the pub, but I was grateful for her company. None of my other friends came to see me.

Before indistinguishable meals arrived on rattling trolleys Mum would prop me up against pillows. I never equated the fact she could hoist me up in bed with the amount of weight I'd lost. She'd cut soft hospital food into small pieces and I'd swallow them whole, too exhausted to chew. What must have run through her mind? Memories of the chubby toddler I was, strapped into my white plastic highchair, mouth open wide like a baby sparrow. How did she cope? I never saw her cry, not once. What no one told me was the doctors thought it was highly unlikely a heart would be found in time. I was dying. The transplant lists were flooded, and although I wasn't well enough to go home, I wasn't a priority either. How do you prepare for the worst? I can't imagine. And I ache when I think of what they must have gone through: Mum, Rachel, and

Sam sitting around my bed, fingers laced together, as they prayed to a God they didn't believe in. Dad, helpless and frustrated, visited every day but never stayed for long, and when he spoke there was an edge to his voice as if he was permanently furious, and he probably was. You don't expect to watch your only child fade away in front of you, do you? Time was interminable: doctors consulted, nurses fussed, and notes were made until, one day, a miracle happened.

"We've found a heart," Dr. Kapur announced.

The heart was a perfect match but there was no celebration as I was prepped for surgery; everyone painfully aware this gift of life only came to fruition through another family's grief.

The trolley wheels squeaked as I was rolled down the corridor, harsh overhead lights so white it was as if I could be sucked into their brightness and transported to an afterlife I desperately wanted to believe in.

I didn't think it was possible to feel any worse, but when I woke two days afterward in intensive care, I felt so ill I almost wished I'd died. Fluids were fed through tubes in my arm, and my chest drain felt as heavy as lead.

One day, by the side of my bed, Sam dropped to one knee, and at first I'd thought it was through exhaustion. I'd reached for the buzzer to call for the nurse when I noticed the black velvet box resting on his palm. A ring—oval sapphire surrounded by sparkling diamonds—inside.

"This isn't the romantic setting I'd envisaged, but marry me? Please?" he'd asked.

"Sam?" I didn't know what to say.

He had lifted the ring from the box and held it toward me. I ran my finger over the stone, which was as deep a blue as the ocean.

"It was Grandma's. She wanted me to start a new tradition. Passing it down along the family."

I swallowed hard. My head battling my heart.

"I can buy another if you don't like it?"

Sam looked uncertain, younger than his thirty years, and it took every ounce of willpower not to cry. I curled my fingers to stop him sliding the ring on. I knew I'd never want to take it off.

"I can't marry you," I whispered. "I'm so sorry."

"Why not? We've talked about it before."

"Everything is different now. I'm different."

"You're still you." He stroked my cheek with such tenderness it was all I could do not to fall into his arms. Despite my unwashed hair, my stale breath, he gazed at me as if I was the most beautiful woman in the world. It tore me apart to look into his eyes and see worry reflected from the place lust once sat.

"I don't want to be with you anymore, Sam." I forced out the words that hurt more than the scalpel that had sliced through my skin.

"I don't believe you, Jenna."

"It's true. I'd been having second thoughts about us before all this."

"It's just because you're ill . . ."

"It's not. I've been having doubts for ages. I'm so sorry."

"Since when? Everything was fine before."

Before. Such an innocuous word but there would always be a divide. Before and after. A glass wall separating the things I could do then with the things I couldn't do anymore.

"Jenna, be honest. Do you love me?"

I was at a crossroads. Truth or lies.

"I don't love you, Sam." I chose lies. "I'm so sorry." It

was the right thing to do. For him. Sam began to speak but I couldn't meet his eye. I twisted the starched corner of the bed sheet between my fingers and willed myself to stay strong. He would be better off without me.

He put the ring back in the box, and I jumped as he snapped it shut and crossed the room, his shoulders slumped. I longed to call him back and tell him, of course I loved him, but the words were shackled to my tongue. He hesitated in the doorway and I bit the inside of my cheek hard to stop myself crying his name, my mouth full of metallic blood and regret, and as he carried on walking, my gifted heart and guilt pulsed away inside of me.

* * *

Four weeks after my transplant I was discharged from hospital. Mum picked me up.

"Where's Dad?"

She ignored the question. She had settled me into the back seat of a taxi showing as much care as the new fathers leaving the maternity wing, clutching car seats cradling newborn babies, and dreams of a perfect future. Mum clicked my seatbelt into its holder despite my protests that I could do it myself and shook out a cotton-wool-soft plaid picnic blanket, placing it over my knees.

"My daughter's had a heart transplant. Please drive slowly," she said.

"Blimey." The cabbie twisted the dial on his stereo and the music grew fainter. "You're a bit young for that, love, aren't you? Kids! Always a worry, aren't they? I've got three myself. Grandkiddies too."

The taxi rumbled forward, and the traffic light air freshener swung from the interior mirror, its smell sickly sweet. We'd crawled along at a snail's pace—Mum not flinching at the cacophony of horns demanding we speed up—toward the three-bedroom bungalow I'd grown up in.

"Paint It Black" began to play: the Rolling Stones were one of Dad's favorites, and over the music Mum chatted to the driver about what a mild winter it was so far. I closed my eyes, resting my heavy head against the window, slipping off into sleep. The vibrations from the engine made my cheeks tingle.

The sound of shouting roused me. Hard, angry voices climbing in pitch. Dazed I started to push myself upright, forcing open my eyes when the car lurched forward, its wheels gathering speed, and I was thrown back in my seat. Dizzying blackness engulfed me as my head lolled and cracked against the window.

"No. No. No!" A woman's terrified screams rang in my ears and fear raced through my bloodstream.

The brakes screeched. Glass shattered and there was the feeling of flying, my skin burning, bleeding, as shards of glass sliced into my flesh.

My hands flew upward to cover my face, and then came stillness. Silence. Music? I splayed my fingers and peered out. I was still strapped in my seat. The cabbie's head bobbed up and down along to "Paint It Black." Mum was telling him how a hard frost was predicted for the coming weekend.

I scrutinized my palms, turning my hands over. No blood. I'd been warned to expect a myriad of side effects with my medication, and as I tried to analyze what happened my head felt fuzzy and I wasn't sure if I'd imagined the whole thing. The lull of the engine teamed forces with the medication and I rested my head back once more and stared blankly out of the window for the rest of the journey. I must have been dreaming, mustn't I?

CHAPTER THREE

I have been home for weeks but I still find it unsettling living alone. The slightest noise wakes me and I lie stiffly in the middle of the bed, head fuzzy, panic tight around my throat like a cord. I clutch the duvet to my chest until I identify the sound. It's usually a car door slamming or the neighbors coming home late, and I force my hands to unclench and think happy thoughts, like Vanessa said. Sam slips into every memory. I miss him with each and every breath I take.

I drag a brush through my tangled hair and squirt vanilla perfume onto my wrists. Outside the bedroom window the sky has transformed from muted pastels to cornflower blue. It is going to be a gorgeous day but the sunshine doesn't dispel the blackness I feel inside. Today I'm going out. A squealing of brakes outside makes me jump. Mum waves from a taxi, and I shout that I'll be down in a minute. In the hallway, I pull open the front door, pausing in the doorway—there's nothing to be afraid of—before stepping over the threshold.

"Have you taken your medication?" Mum asks before I have properly shut the car door or fastened my seatbelt.

"Yes." You wouldn't think I was thirty, sometimes.

"This is nice, isn't it? I've got a surprise. Two, in fact."

The taxi indicator click-click-clicks right and we pull into the traffic. I pop a breath mint on my tongue letting the minty zing settle my nervous stomach.

"Want one?" I offer the pack to Mum.

"No, thanks." She smiles but it looks forced and I notice how pale she is. The fine lines that spider her eyes have deepened.

"Everything OK, Mum?"

She stares out the window as if formulating her words before she speaks.

"I've got something to tell you." She can't meet my eye but she slides a hand over to grip mine. "I've decided to file for divorce."

"Mum! No!"

The taxi driver cranks up the volume on the radio but I don't care if he's listening or not. I still can't quite believe my parents separated shortly after my surgery. "You can't just give up on thirty-five years of marriage. Does Dad know?" I had been hoping they'd sort it out after some time apart.

"Not yet."

"I still don't understand why you split up?"

"It's complicated."

That's all Dad will say whenever I ask him, as if they've carefully rehearsed the words together. "This can't be what you want."

"It is. I'm fine on my own," she says but the gray hairs poking from her scalp, the deep grooves carved into the bridge on her nose, tell a different story.

"Is it my fault?" They seemed so happy before. I can't imagine the pressure they were under fearing I might die.

"Not everything is about you, young lady."

Her tone is brisk and she does seem together but I'm not reassured. Since I've been sick there's been an incalculable emotional cost to us all and the joy of my recovery has been tempered by the sorrow of Mum and Dad falling apart. Me and Sam unraveling.

"We're here now anyway." She fishes a twenty pound note out of her purse as the cab pulls up outside the Masonic Hall. I release my grip on the door handle and as I step out of the car I flex my fingers, allowing the blood to flow freely, as I wonder what we are doing here.

* * *

A cluster of girls, Smarties-colored skirts and bangles, are heading into the hall, and above the stone doorway a banner flaps in the breeze, "Mind, Body, Spirit." I suppress a groan.

"I know you don't go in for all of this but Vanessa recommended meditation, didn't she? For your anxiety? I thought this would be a good place to look into it," Mum says. Her face is glowing with anticipation.

Before I can answer, feet thunder up the steps behind me and I lurch forward with a whimper as my shoulder is knocked, raising my hands to my head to protect myself.

"Jenna." Mum gently takes my hands in hers, lowering them. "You can't go on like this. You're not yourself. You're on edge all the time. I just want you to be happy again. Start to live."

"I want to." Emotion threatens to overcome me. "I'm so grateful for this second chance, really I am. But . . ."

"It's overwhelming, I know. But if you're going back to work on Monday, and you know I think it's too much, you need to find something to help you relax, and you're taking so many tablets already. Let's just take a look inside for some natural alternatives, shall we?"

"Yes." My voice sounds uncertain, and Mum links her arm through mine and together we walk inside.

I jump as the sound of a gong being struck rattles my skull. The hall is crammed with trestle tables that wobble and creak under the weight of silver jewelry, and piles of books that all have "life changing" on the cover.

Keeping my lips clamped together I rifle through brightly colored clothing hanging from a metal rail. The air is fogged with incense, and the smell of sandalwood is cloying. A long skirt with an elastic waist catches my eye and I pull it out and hold it up against me. The fabric swishes around my ankles. I am in desperate need of some new things to wear. My diet is the healthiest it's ever been, but I've put on nearly two stone. At my last check-up Dr. Kapur said it's my medication and a small price to pay for being alive, and I felt ashamed I'd even mentioned it. I don't think I can pull off tie-dye though. I'm usually always in jeans. Last year I'd tried to be adventurous but Rachel fell apart laughing when I tried on wet look leggings in Topshop, and I smile at the memory, wishing she were here.

Mum is squinting as she studies the program.

"There's a psychic medium in room two. Shall we have a look?"

I can't think of anything worse but I know it will make Mum happy so I agree. It can't do any harm, can it?

* * *

Room two has a piece of white A4 paper tacked to it with "DO NOT DISTURB" scrawled in blue pen. I lean against the wall as Mum instructs me not to tell the medium anything too personal. The door swings open and a girl, who I think is around twenty, bounces out, smile stretched across her face.

Mum squeezes my hand; her palm is hot and sticky, and I worry she's taking this too seriously. I hope Gypsy Lee or whatever she calls herself will be kind.

The room is bright. The lady beckoning us in can't be much older than me. Her hair a swishy honey bob. Baby pink butterflies are dotted across her cream blouse. I'm disenchanted. I'd been expecting something more atmospheric. Candles. A crystal ball. Tarot cards at the very least.

"Please. Sit." She gestures to the seats with her sharp acrylic-nailed fingers. "I'm Fiona."

Mum and I exchange a glance, and I know she's wondering if we should give our real names. I stifle a giggle remembering how Rachel and I once uncovered our porn star names by combining the name of our first pet with the road we grew up on. Silky Queen was mine, while Rachel's was Misty Manor.

"First time?" Fiona asks.

"Yes." Mum gives me "the look." The one all mothers have, and I pull myself together. "I'm Daphne, and this is my daughter, Jenna."

"Nice to meet you both. I'm a psychic medium. Do you know what that is?"

"You communicate with the departed?" Mum says, and I can't help rolling my eyes.

"Not entirely. I tune into the energy of people or objects using intuition but I'm also guided by the spirit energy surrounding you. Who wants to go first?"

"We're just here for Jenna." Mum shrugs off her cardigan and leans forward. "I'm fine."

Fiona closes her eyes briefly before studying me with an intensity that makes my cheeks burn.

"You've had an upheaval lately?"

I nod—I'm not impressed. Hasn't everyone had some kind of upheaval? "A loss?" I press my lips together; I don't want to give anything away and I'm determined not to mention Sam's name.

"You've been ill," she states, and I suppress a sigh as I think most people have had a cough or cold recently. A headache at least. My mind wanders, musing how soon we will be finished and what we might have for lunch. This is all so vague.

"Jenna, were you one of a twin?"

I look at Mum in surprise. "No, at least I don't think so?"

"Did you ever have reason to believe there was more than one fetus?" Fiona directs this to Mum.

"No. Never," Mum says.

Fiona frowns. "I'm definitely sensing two energies. A split. You often find that in identical twins. It's almost as if two personalities are battling here."

My new heart thuds inside my chest. "This other energy," I ask. "Is it male or female?"

"It's definitely feminine," Fiona says.

I lean forward in my chair. Could she be talking about the donor? But that's ridiculous, isn't it? I chew my lip as I try to decide whether I should tell her about the transplant.

"Could it be Nana?" Mum asks, and I slump with disappointment.

Of course. It will turn out to be a grandparent who has passed. I berate myself for momentarily buying into the idea Fiona has any special gift.

"No," Fiona says. "It's younger. Stronger."

"Who is it?"

Outside the window, darkened clouds block the sun, turning day to night, and I shiver.

Fiona leans forward and grasps my hand, and I feel a static shock and my fingertips tingle. I try to pull away but she tightens her grip, bright pink nails indenting my skin. As she touches me, my vision begins to mist and the room fades away until I'm shrouded in darkness. Where am I? There's shouting. My heart is pounding. Sweat trickles down my face. A shadow looms toward me and there's a sense of being shaken. I'm scared. So scared. Something very, very bad is happening and I'm not safe. I swallow the acrid taste of my fear and take a deep breath to calm myself but a metallic smell floods my nostrils. There's a flash of red. Blood. A scream builds inside me but Fiona wrenches her hand away, and I'm back in the Masonic Hall. My chest is heaving with fright as I struggle to speak. I wipe my damp palms on my jeans.

"Are you OK, Jenna?" Mum has a worried expression on her face and she reaches out and touches my arm. "You're trembling all over."

"What was that that just happened?" My voice shakes. "It felt so real."

"Darling, I don't know," Mum says. "You just seemed so out of it and—"

"She's asking for your help," Fiona interrupts.

"Who?" I'm close to tears now. Am I going mad? What have I just seen?

"You must learn to listen to what she tells you." Fiona pats my hand, and I flinch as she touches me again but nothing happens.

"I don't understand..."

There's a tap at the door and two girls enter the room. "Sorry." They hesitate when they see Mum and me.

"It's OK. I'm done here," Fiona says. "There's nothing more I can tell you, Jenna."

"But who . . ."

"The connection I felt is gone. I really don't know anything else." She sounds apologetic and I want to ask more questions but the girls are hovering by the table now, waiting for us to leave. My legs are trembling so much it's an effort for me to stand. "Be careful, Jenna," Fiona's voice follows me out of the room.

"Let's find somewhere you can sit," Mum says linking her arm through mine. "I don't know what on earth she was talking about. She seemed like a bit of a charlatan. Sorry, darling. I just wanted her to give you something to look forward to. Talking about being careful! Take no notice."

We reach the bottom of a flight of stairs.

"Sit here, darling. I'll get you some water," Mum says. "You look so pale."

I sit on the bottom of the stairs and close my eyes as I try to make sense of what just happened. My heart jumps in my chest, hard and fast. A second energy. It couldn't be . . . could it? I press my palm against my ribs and my new heart seems to thump *help-help-help*.

CHAPTER FOUR

As me and Mum leave the Masonic Hall I'm still reeling from my encounter with Fiona. It all felt so real: the sense of being shaken, the blood, the shadowy figure. During the episodes I'd told Vanessa about, usually everything goes black. This one was different. Like looking through a kaleidoscope. An image that was there one second and gone the next. One twist and it all falls away leaving fragments that don't quite make sense on their own.

Discomfort slithers along my spine as I think of the "second energy" Fiona talked about, and my head throbs as I try to make sense of it all. As much as I don't believe in mediumship of any kind I can't deny what I felt. I'm unnerved and tired.

"We can go home if you want to, Jenna?" Mum's voice breaks through my thoughts and I force myself to smile. I know she's planned something else and I don't want to disappoint her.

"I'm fine. I can't wait to see what you've got in store next." I hope she doesn't pick up on the flatness in my voice.

"It's a surprise. We're nearly there. You'll be able to

have a sit-down," she says, and I know I can't fool her. She can tell how exhausted I am.

It doesn't take too long before Mum pushes open a glass door of what used to be a bakery. The smell of chemicals hits the back of my throat as we step inside the hair salon, all glossy black tiles and chrome fittings.

"I've booked us hair appointments. My treat."

"There's nothing wrong with my hair."

The receptionist with the swinging bleached blond bob raises an eyebrow skeptically, and I feel my face heat as I wonder when I last washed it.

"It's got so long. You need to look smart for Monday, if you're still going back to work?" There's an edge to Mum's voice as she says this.

I understand she's worried but as much as I sometimes feel I'd like to I can't hide away in my flat forever. My statutory sick pay has run out and although Dad has said not to worry, he'll take over my rent, he's already paying Mum's bills, and I know he can't afford it, despite his assurances he can. You only have to look at the awful bedsit he's living in to see how stretched he is. Besides, I love being a veterinary nurse, and I'd been heartbroken when the doctors advised me against being around animals at all for the first few months after surgery. There was a risk of infection from the pets, particularly cats, that could prove fatal. I added it to the long list of other things I initially had to avoid: crowds of people, driving, sex. Not that I have a car, or have anyone to have sex with, but it felt like a loss all the same. That said, my rejection drugs have been gradually reduced, with Dr. Kapur pleased with my progress, so it's back to normal. My new normal anyway. He agrees the psychological benefits of being back at work will outweigh the potential risks, now infinitely smaller than they once were.

"Yes, I'm still going back. Linda will look after me," I say, and Mum purses her lips together. I know she thinks no one can look after me quite like she can. "A trim would be good. Thanks, Mum." I twirl long mousey strands around my finger. The ends are quite split and it's so much thinner than it used to be. I shrug off my coat and hold my arms out, mummy-like, as a black gown is cloaked around me.

The basin digs sharply into my neck as I tilt my head backward and my jaw clenches. Warm water floods my ears and cools as it trickles down my collar but I confirm through gritted teeth the temperature is OK; "Yes, I'm comfortable." The water stops and firm fingers massage my scalp. The shampoo is zesty—lemon, I think—and it feels so good to be touched I almost groan out loud, and my tension melts away.

In front of the mirror the hairdresser tugs a comb through my hair. In the chair next to me Mum dunks a digestive into a coffee.

"Just a trim then?"

Flashes of red flit through my mind. A feeling of lightness I haven't felt before urges me forward. It's almost as if since hearing Fiona talk about a second energy I don't feel quite so alone anymore. I imagine there's someone whispering just outside my consciousness, and I somehow feel a little braver.

"I've changed my mind," I reply. "Can I try something completely different?"

* * *

The back of my neck is cool without a curtain of hair blocking out the breeze, and I can't help staring at my reflection in every shop window we pass, hardly able to believe it's me. As soon as we get home I stand in the hallway, gazing into the gilded mirror I'd bought at a yard sale.

"You look good." Mum stands behind me.

"I don't know what possessed me," I say, twisting my head left to right, tugging the hair in front of my ears as if I can somehow make it longer.

"It's certainly a bold choice for someone who's never dyed their hair before, or had it short, but you look good. Younger."

I'm hardly old anyway, but I know what she means. The strain of the past few months is etched onto my face but the pixie cut suits me.

"Tea?" she asks.

"Please." I breathe in as she squeezes past me and heads toward the kitchen.

There's the whoosh of water as she turns the tap and the kettle clicks on. I hear her opening the fridge to pull out the carton of milk I know she'll sniff to check it's OK.

I can't stop staring in the mirror. The new red color of my hair has warmed my skin tone. The purple bags under my eyes aren't so prominent. Raising my hands to my head I smooth my hair against my scalp with both palms; it's so soft. My fingertips tingle as though charged with electricity and panic mounts as I begin to feel the way I felt with Fiona. Detached from reality, almost. In the mirror, my image begins to blur and dizziness hits. This can't be happening. Not again.

Darkness. Screaming. Pain.

The sense of fear hits me so hard and fast I feel a band has been tightened around my lungs, restricting my breathing. The sense of danger is suffocating. In an instant, the feelings dissipate and I'm once again in my hall, leaning heavily against the wall as though I would fall without its support. *I'm safe*, I tell myself, but I don't feel safe. It's as though Fiona has triggered something inside me, and my skin crawls with the thought. I breathe in slowly and deeply but the screaming I'd heard in my mind seconds earlier lingers, along with the sense of panic. My secondhand heart thuds against my ribs, and I press my fingers against it. Who did you belong to?

"Let go of your obsessive thoughts," Vanessa had said last Tuesday.

But what if they won't let me go?

What then?

CHAPTER FIVE

"Seven, eight, nine, ten: coming, ready or not."

My eyes spring open and I seek flashes of your ruby red sundress but I can't see you. Daddy said we mustn't go too far so you must be nearby, but you're smaller than me and can squeeze into places I can't. I crunch gravel underfoot as I run. A small, sharp stone slips between my toes. I hobble over to the giant wooden owl and sit on the dusty earth; his outstretched wings shielding me from the hot yellow sun. I unbuckle the strap of my jelly sandal and toss the piece of gravel back onto the ground.

Seagulls flap across the cloudless sky, screeching their hunger, and my stomach growls as a boy runs past clutching a hot dog, leaving a trail of fried onions and ketchup behind him.

The heat makes me cross, and I trudge over to the hedge and stand on tiptoes to peep behind it but you're not there.

There's a constant thwack of metal clubs hitting balls, and I jog over to the mini-golf course. The coins Daddy gave me for two ice-cream cones jangle in my pocket and I can almost smell the Cadbury Flake, feel the coolness of the ice cream as I push the chocolate down to the bottom of my cone with my finger. Saving the best till last.

I scan the course of impossible ramps and obstacles, searching for a small figure with a messy ponytail and scabbed knees. If I don't find you soon, I'll have to call your name and then I'll lose, but it will be worth it to be able to buy our ice-cream cones.

Over the crashing waves in the distance, and the squeals of children in the playground, I hear it. A cry. I turn my head slowly, ears straining, trying to block out the background noise. There it is again. A cry. Your cry. I know exactly where you are. I sprint over to the wooden hut that stores golf clubs and balls, drop to my hands and knees. The hard ground presses against my bare skin, and dry grass tickles my shins. I look underneath.

"Found you!" I stretch out my fingers and you slip your smaller hand inside mine, and I help you to your feet. Mud smears your face. Tears streak your cheeks.

"You were ages." You sniff hard. "I didn't think you'd find me."

I crouch down and pull out the tissue from the pocket of my denim skirt and I help you blow your nose.

"Of course I was going to find you," I say. "I promise I will always find you."

CHAPTER SIX

Hazy light begins to flood my bedroom. I curl onto my side, hugging my pillow, staring out the window as the sky transforms from mauve to gray to blue as the sun slowly rises. My sleep has been fitful. Vivid dreams are a common side effect of the prednisone I'm taking but as I brush my hand against the sole of my foot I almost expect grains of sand to tumble onto my crumpled sheets. The cry of seagulls, the aroma of hot dogs; both still sharp in my mind.

After showering I rub cocoa butter into my skin, my fingers tracing the paper-thin scar on my chest. Ed Sheeran sings "The City," and I stifle a yawn as I sit in front of the mirror, dabbing Touche Éclat over the black half-moons that hang under my eyes.

The song playing through my phone cuts out as Dad rings and I put him on speaker.

"I thought you were popping round yesterday to pick up the books I've got of Linda's so you can take them in on Monday?"

"Sorry, Dad, it slipped my mind. I had a busy day with Mum."

"How is she?" he asks.

"She's fine."

Dad huffs out air, and I can picture him sliding off his glasses and rubbing the groove on the bridge of his nose. It's almost as if he wants to hear she's not managing without him, that she's desperate to have him back, but I can't fill him with false hope.

"Why don't you ask her yourself?"

"It's not that simple."

"It is that simple if you still love her. Do you still love her? She's mentioned divorce, Dad! You should sort it out before it's too late." My voice has risen.

There's a long pause before he changes the subject.

"Jenna, I understand why you want to go back to work on Monday but I'm worried it will be too much for you. It seems too soon. Why don't you come and work at my practice? I could keep an eye on you, and you could leave whenever you feel tired without worrying."

"I'll be fine. Linda and John will look after me. It's only part-time." We must have had this conversation a million times. I check my watch. "I've got to go," I say.

"Are you going somewhere nice?" He sounds hopeful.

"Rachel's coming over." I hate lying but my stomach throngs with nerves at the thought of meeting my donor's family, and I can't deal with my parents' emotions today on top of my own. Just like Vanessa, I don't think they'd approve.

* * *

The bus trundles through the city and gathers pace through country lanes. Outside the window, sheep chew emerald green grass, and herds of cows stand in a field so distant they look like the size of Dalmatian dogs. It looks idyllic outside, but the interior of the bus smells of cheap perfume.

It's so hot. I start to worry there's not enough air, and I close my eyes and let my thoughts drift as I try to calm my breathing. I think once again what the donor might have been like. In his letter, Tom, the man I wrote to, referred to her as "my daughter" in his reply so I know it's a female heart beating inside me. I can't wait to find out more about her today.

A screeching of brakes jars me back to the present and a silver convertible skids around a hairpin bend drifting into the path of the bus. I take a sharp intake of breath as our driver blasts his horn and yanks the steering wheel. I am buffeted left to right as we veer onto the grass verge, and as my head thuds hard against the window my stomach floods with fear. My surroundings fade away and it's as though I've been transported somewhere else entirely. There's the sensation of fingers grasping my arms, shaking me, and I whimper.

"It's OK, we didn't hit anything. Are you hurt?" a voice soothes and suddenly I'm back on the bus, blinking at the sun streaming through the grubby window. An elderly man is looking at me with concern while the other passengers grumble about idiot drivers. My breathing is ragged. I've had another episode, and I wish I'd brought Mum with me. *I'm OK. I'm OK. I'm OK.* I remind myself Vanessa said it's just my medication causing anxiety but that doesn't make it any less real. Any less frightening. For the rest of the journey my head throbs, and I imagine I still feel hands around my arms, fingertips pressing hard into my skin.

* * *

The bus grinds to a halt in a well-maintained street of bay window detached houses set back from the road. Google Maps tells me it's a twenty-minute walk, and I alight the bus wanting to burn off some nervous energy. The breeze carries the scent of freshly cut grass. The warmer weather has encouraged cars to be washed, borders to be dug. Daffodils and bluebells poke through the earth.

The GPS on my smartphone tells me to turn right, and as I head away from the main road the houses gradually get smaller and shabbier and closer to the pavement. The sun doesn't seem to be shining quite so brightly anymore. An empty crisp packet blows across the road like tumbleweed, coming to rest in a gutter littered with cigarette butts. As I reach number thirty I wonder whether the donor lived here too, in this almost derelict house I'm standing before.

There must have been a path here once. Flashes of gray stone are visible beneath weeds of epic proportions that have forced their way through the cracked concrete. Yellowing net curtains cover grimy windows, wooden frames, and chipped paint. I trample down nettles and jab the doorbell. I can't hear a tell-tale chime so I press it harder with my thumb. There's a crashing coming from the house next door, a deep voice swears, and a small boy runs outside, crusted snot under his nose, congealed food stains on the front of his grubby gray T-shirt. I smile. He sticks two fingers up at me, and I feel my face burn. I turn back toward the front door and rap so hard my knuckles sting.

The door creaks open. The lady that stands before me is gray with grief; deep lines of worry are carved into her face. Stringy, blond hair falls over her shoulders.

There's a beat. We both stand transfixed by the other. The urge to hug her is so powerful I thrust my hands in my pockets.

"Hello. You must be Amanda?" I say but I don't need to ask. I know it's her. "I'm . . ."

"Oh my god." She covers her mouth with her palm and steps backward, shaking her head. Her eyes widen and she slams the door shut.

CHAPTER SEVEN

The boy next door roars with laughter as I stand with my mouth hanging open. I'm too shocked to move. I stare at the closed door: at the patches of bare wood visible beneath the red chipped paint, at the rusted number thirty that isn't hanging quite straight. There's a smell of blocked drains making my stomach roll, and I snap my teeth together biting my tongue. My mouth floods with blood and humiliation. I have spent weeks imagining this day. Our first meeting. The picture in my mind never included a small boy hopping from foot to foot, his hand forming an "L" shape that he holds against his forehead as he chants, "Loser, Loser." I have never felt so small or insignificant before.

Feeling my cheeks burn red I fish around in my pocket and pull out a crumpled-up scrap of paper with the address. This is definitely the right house. What should I do? The door creaks open again. This time a man with dark brown hair and ruddy cheeks steps forward.

"Jenna." He offers me his hand to shake. It's damp and warm. "I am sorry about Amanda. I thought getting her to answer the door might help her feel in control. She's been so nervous about meeting you, but it was a shock; it's the hair, you know?"

My hand flutters to the back of my neck. I have no idea what he's talking about, and I am about to ask but he speaks again.

"I'm Tom, anyway. But you already know that. Come in. Please."

My heart hammers against my ribs as though it recognizes Tom's voice, and I step inside. Hot tears inexplicably prick the back of my eyes and I swallow them down.

"Come through."

There's a strip in the center of the carpet that is flat and crusty and darker than the rest. The pile trampled with years of traffic. And as I walk down the hallway it occurs to me that I am following the footsteps of my donor. Placing my feet where she has placed hers, and I am overcome with the enormity of it all.

The lounge is stifling. Sun streams through the window and a smell of cooking lingers. Amanda is swamped by the huge floral armchair she sits in.

"I'm sorry, Jenna. About before," she says, but she can't seem to look at me. Tom, on the other hand, doesn't stop staring.

"Tea? I can make a pot?" Tom asks.

"Please." The room is so stuffy I'd prefer a glass of water but I am conscious that, for Tom, the ritual of boiling the kettle, steeping the tea, might bring a sense of normality to this situation. He heads toward a doorway at the back of the lounge. I grasp my cotton scarf and tug it away from my throat so I can breathe a little easier, but I don't remove it, as if the layers that cover my scar can hide the reason why I'm here. Stupid really. It's not as if they'll ever forget.

I wish I'd brought a gift: flowers, chocolates, anything to break the ice. I'd thought about it, of course. But I didn't want to appear insensitive. Nothing could compare to the gift they have given me; but now, being here empty-handed feels rude. I clear my throat, and Amanda jumps at the sound, as if she'd forgotten I was there.

"Tom won't be long. Make yourself comfortable, Jenna," she says and her voice is so soft I daren't move while she's speaking in case I don't hear her.

"Thanks." I put my bag on the floor and gaze around the room. Magnolia has been painted on woodchip wallpaper and is grubby with age. A flat-screen TV stands in the corner, coated by a thick layer of dust. Underneath the window sits a large Chinese vase. A smeared glass coffee table rests its gilded legs on a faded jade and gold patterned rug. The furniture seems solid. Expensive. Not what I'd have expected from the outside of the house. There are several small oil paintings dotted around the walls.

"These are gorgeous." I cross to one and lean forward to get a closer look. Two girls are holding hands as they stand on the ocean's edge kicking at waves that shimmer under a butter yellow sun. Droplets of water spray into their laughing faces to remain suspended there forever.

"They are very good. Are they all by the same artist?" I study the next one. A seagull is mid-flight and beneath him a small girl is crouching on the sand, covering her chips with her chubby hands as she stares at the bird.

"I painted them," Amanda says.

"You're very talented. I've always wanted to paint but I've never really had the space in my flat for an easel. I sketch though." I want to ask whether her daughter painted too but I don't know how to broach the subject without distressing her even more than she already is. "I'm not this good though." My voice, louder than I'd intended, seems to bounce around the room and sounds as unnatural as I feel.

On the shelf above the gas fire is a silver trophy surrounded by photos. My stomach lurches as I draw closer to the sea of faces staring back at me. Is one of them her? My donor?

My eyes are drawn to a Victorian frame next to a photo of Tom holding a fish aloft in the air, fishing rod propped next to him, and I pick it up. It's heavier than I expected, and it takes two hands to hold it steady. Two girls beam into the camera, arms looped around each other's necks. The girl to the left has a pixie cut, her hair dyed crimson. My hand flutters to my hair. No wonder Amanda got such a shock when she opened the door and saw me.

"Is this your daughter?" I ask although I already know the answer.

"Yes. That's Callie," Amanda says.

"Callie." I taste the word on my tongue. How did you die? The room is hot and stuffy but the hairs on my arms prick up and I can't stop myself shivering.

CHAPTER EIGHT

"Who's that with Callie?" I study the second girl in the photo. Her hair is long and ash blond. As I examine her face I feel a tug of familiarity but I don't think we've met.

"That's Sophie. Our younger daughter."

"Is she here?" I look over my shoulder, half-expecting her to appear.

"No." Amanda's voice wobbles. "We lost her too."

"I'm so sorry." I carefully place the picture back onto the shelf. My T-shirt is sticking to my skin, and I tug it away from my stomach. It feels as if the air has been sucked from the room, and I don't know how Amanda can stand the heat in her cardigan. She must have lost the ability to feel, in every sense.

We sit in awkward silence, and the lump that rises in my throat feels so solid it's almost as if I could reach in and pull it out. There's a rattle of china and I spring to my feet as Tom walks into the room, cups and saucers—balanced on a silver tray—chinking together.

"Jenna, please. Take a pew. Make yourself comfortable."

He smiles and I think it's genuine. More genuine than the one I offer in return. I'm almost desperate to leave, to run away from these people I'm at a loss to know how to comfort.

"Help yourself," Tom says as he scoops up a sugar cube and plops it into his tea. "Biscuit?"

"Thanks." I take a piece of shortbread, clutching it tightly between my fingers, but I'm too anxious to eat it and as it begins to crumble I place it on my knee. I lick the sugar off my fingertips while I try to quell my rising panic. This is awful. I've never been good at small talk and I don't want to skirt around the reason I'm here, but I don't feel I can dive straight in either. My eyes bounce around the room as I fidget in my seat.

"Whose is the trophy?" I point to the gas fire.

"That's Tom's." Amanda's response is immediate, and I think she is grateful we are not talking about Callie yet. "He won it at golf."

"My dad played golf for years." He'd meet up with John on a Saturday afternoon. Mum and Linda would sometimes go shopping. Dad's clubs are still in Mum's garage, and I wonder if he misses it. I wish he'd start playing again but I suppose breakups do that, don't they? Fracture friendships. Force people to take sides.

"I was a late starter," Tom says. "I had a heart attack three years ago but I didn't really change my lifestyle. I stupidly thought I was too young for long-term heart problems but then I had a second heart attack and it was touch and go for a while. The doctors didn't think I'd pull through. Callie and Sophie were terrified. Sophie used to interrogate me on what I'd eaten and drunk every day; she lived in constant fear of me dying."

"We all did," interjects Amanda.

"I know. But I made changes. I gave up booze and cigarettes and I took up power walking and playing golf but

I didn't enjoy it as much as the fishing me and my older brother Joe used to do. You can't beat sitting next to a river but that doesn't get you fit, does it? It's hard to stick to a regime if you don't enjoy it. Not like Amanda and her yoga. She used to get up at six every day to do her routine. I don't exercise anymore."

"You should. I couldn't bear it if anything happened to you, Thomas." Amanda looks stricken.

"I'm not going anywhere." He reaches across the arm of the sofa and tenderly brushes her hair away from her face. "You're stuck with me." The gesture is so simple, so intimate, my chest tightens.

"Golf is a strange game," Tom says. "Walking for miles after a ball. But it was good to get out of the house. I'd spent so much time laid up, resting. I felt disconnected from the world. Amanda said I needed a hobby. Something to occupy me. I was at a bit of a loss without the business to run; my brother Joe stepped in when I was sick. It was supposed to be temporary but I never did go back. I needed to stay stress free. I had my orders." He shoots Amanda a smile as he says this.

"What was your business?" I am glad Tom is so talkative.

"I sold car parts. My father, Colin, was a scrap metal merchant. I wasn't born into money. Not like Amanda. Her parents were horrified when we started dating; not that they ever warmed to me. They live in Florida now. I suppose I wasn't exactly a catch. I was brought up on a council estate. My mum was a cleaner and my dad was a scrappy. Still, Amanda saw something in me, didn't you, dear?"

"I still do. You're a good man."

"I used to sell insurance but when my dad passed and left the yard to me and Amanda, and the house and money

to my older brother Joe, I thought I might as well give it a
go. It folded after Callie died. No one had the heart to carry
on with it. You might meet Joe later. He's popping in to
drop off Amanda's repeat prescription. He's a godsend. I
don't know what we'd do without him."

Amanda's brow furrows and as she sees me watching
her she says: "It was awful when Thomas was ill. I was
beside myself when the doctor said I should prepare for the
worst. When Thomas came home I drove him mad with my
fussing."

"That's what Mum was like. Spraying everything with
Dettol so I didn't come into contact with any germs. I can't
imagine the strain when someone you love is so sick."

"I found it difficult to cope." Amanda tucks her hair
behind her ear. "Thomas had always taken care of everything and suddenly it was all down to me. I didn't even
know which day the recycling bins went out. I had to mud-
dle through the best I could."

"You did a great job holding everything together," Tom
says, but Amanda gives a small, sad shake of her head.
"How did your parents manage?" she asks.

"It drove them apart, I think. They ended up separating
when I was ill."

"I'm sorry," says Amanda. "Do you think they'll sort
things out?"

"I hope so."

"Maybe they just need a break now you're on the
mend?" Tom says. "Once I was better, Sophie took off for
weeks, traveling. She needed to unwind. It's heartbreak-
ing that we never were as close again. She spent more time
with her boyfriend than us, but I suppose she had to grow
up and distancing herself was part of that. We all cope in
different ways, don't we?"

"I suppose so." But I know there's more to my parents' breakup than they are telling me.

"So you're a veterinary nurse and you live in the city center?" I am grateful Tom has changed the subject. "It's been a comfort to find out you're so close. The hospital was horrified we'd received a letter from you directly. They advised us not to meet but I think—"

"I don't care what they say." The words burst out of Amanda. "With you here I feel like part of Callie is with us. In this room. It's incredible." The atmosphere is charged with emotion and as Amanda locks eyes with me I've never felt a connection like it before. Instinctively I reach for her hand. She starts to cry, and I can feel my cheeks are wet with tears too.

"She saved your life. Our little girl," Tom's voice cracks.

"I had all these things I wanted to say." I wipe my eyes with my fingertips. "But now I'm here . . . Thank you. It just doesn't seem enough but I'm so incredibly grateful. My parents are too. It's such a selfless thing to have done. I can't imagine . . ."

"I couldn't bear the thought of another set of parents feeling like we felt. I wanted to do the right thing. Make the right choice." Amanda pulls her hand away and tugs a tissue from her sleeve. We sit in silence as she blows her nose while I fumble around for the right words. Any words. The clock ticks. Amanda blows her nose, but at last Tom speaks.

"Callie lived in the city too. It's such a coincidence."

"My mum says there are no such things as coincidences. Things are meant to be or they're not. She's a great believer in fate. Or she was. Before . . ." I trail off, aware of how tactless I sound. Fate or not, some things will always remain incomprehensible.

"Do you have any siblings, Jenna?" Tom asks.

"No. I'm an only child but I always wanted a little sister to look after." I wince as my eyes flit to the photo of Callie and Sophie. I've said the wrong thing again, but Amanda's a little more animated as she tells me: "Callie always wanted a sister too. She was so protective of Sophie, always getting her out of trouble. Sophie would get stuck at the top of a slide or get lost in the supermarket and Callie was always there for her. They were so close, weren't they, Thomas?"

"Peas in a pod to look at them but personality-wise they couldn't have been more different. There was such a bond between them it was lovely to see. Joe and me were the same growing up. He used to do everything he could to look after me when we were young; our parents worked such long hours. He still does, I suppose. Callie was the same with Sophie."

There's a pause and I swallow hard before speaking. "Do you mind me asking how Callie died?"

The air thickens and movements slow as Tom clatters his cup onto his saucer. Staring at his lap he curls his fingers into his palm, and I hold my breath as I wait for him to answer.

CHAPTER NINE

"Callie died in a car accident," Tom says. Amanda's face crumples from within as though her cheekbones have been removed, and she begins to rock back and forth on her chair.

"Do you want a lie-down, Amanda?" Tom asks and when she nods, too distraught to speak, he gently cups his hand under her elbow and eases her to her feet.

My mind is a riot of thoughts and emotions. Part of me wants to ask Amanda to stay, to reassure her we don't need to talk about Callie, but the desire to find out more burns hot and bright and eclipses the words I know I should say. Instead, I watch as Amanda shuffles toward the door—Tom's arm wrapped around her waist as she leans into him—and I listen to the slow thud of footsteps as they traipse up the stairs.

While they are gone, I dash over to the window and yank aside the stiff net curtains before pushing against the window until it opens with a pop. I breathe crisp, fresh air as though I've resurfaced after swimming underwater.

The ceiling above me creaks, and Tom's footsteps thud back down the stairs.

"It gets a bit much for her," he says, coming back into the room, his arms full of photo albums, which he piles on the floor, where they topple and slide. Loose photographs are strewn over the threadbare carpet. I drop to my knees and scoop up a smaller version of the photo on the mantelpiece of Callie and Sophie. I am transfixed by it.

"We got a few done of that one to pop into Christmas cards," Tom says. "Would you like one?"

"Thank you." I tuck it carefully inside my purse before turning my attention back to the other photos. My chest is tight as I study the pictures of the short life laid out before me. It seems an age before Tom speaks, but when he does his words are slow, as heavy as lead.

"We'd been to the wedding of the daughter of our old neighbor. Amanda and me, and Callie and Nathan."

"Nathan?"

"Callie's fiancé. Lovely chap. They had been together for five years. We thought she was too young to move in with someone but he really looked after her. He was so protective. They picked us up in their car that night, and I noticed they didn't say much on the journey. They were quiet all night too, not that we could hear each other over the rubbish the DJ was blasting out. Grime, I think Callie said it was called. Not our cup of tea, that's for sure. It was a relief when they turned down the volume for the hog roast. Amanda and I were hungry but Callie and Nathan said they'd wait for a bit. When we got back to the table they'd gone, and at first I thought they'd be on the dance floor. It was only when the DJ cleared it for the happy couple's first dance we realized they weren't. I don't know how long they'd been gone. We checked the toilets before going outside to see if they'd stepped out to get some fresh air, but their car was missing. I tried ringing them both but neither picked up. That's when I got worried. It wasn't like Callie to leave without saying goodbye." Tom's face creases in pain. "I never saw her again."

"So the accident..." I stumble over my words. Conscious I might sound insensitive. "It happened on their way home?"

"No. When we couldn't get them by phone we got a taxi to their house. There was no car but the light was on. Nathan answered the door. He said he'd come home in a taxi because he had a migraine. 'I'm not surprised; the music was that loud,' I said. He'd left Callie the car, as she'd said she wanted to stay with us. He called her but she didn't pick up for him either."

"What did you do?"

"Nathan was panicking. He wanted to go and look for her but I told him to stay put and ring any of Callie's friends he could think of—that Sara and Chris she talked about from work—and the hospitals. He didn't have the car and someone needed to be at their house in case she turned up. We got the taxi to take us home. 'Perhaps they've had a row and Nathan's not telling us,' I said to Amanda. 'We'd better stay at home in case she comes to ours.' We didn't know who else she'd have turned to. At school, she had loads of friends but since she'd been with Nathan she didn't seem to go out much on her own. They were always together. Superglued, I used to say."

"Did they argue much then? Callie and Nathan."

"God, no. I had never heard him raise his voice, and I didn't think they'd fallen out, but they were so quiet all evening, and we were trying to make sense of it, you see. Think of all possibilities." He pauses and when he speaks again his voice is quieter. "When the phone rang my blood ran cold. I just knew it wouldn't be good news. It was the

hospital. Callie had been found on a grass verge at Woodhaven. The car had crashed into a tree. She'd gone . . ." His
voice cracks. "She'd gone straight through the windscreen.
She was barely alive when we got to the hospital." He
presses his fingertips against his eyelids as though he's trying to force an image away.

"Woodhaven? Is that where the wedding was?" It is
about forty miles away. Me and Sam had driven through
it once on the way back from the coast. We had stopped
for a cider at a thatched pub on the village green, its garden packed full of wooden benches and brightly colored
sunshades.

"No. The wedding was in the opposite direction. She
had no reason to be in Woodhaven. It's not as if it was on
the way home."

"Couldn't Nathan throw any light on it?"

"He was inconsolable. And just as confused as us. The
police asked us about Callie's state of mind. As if she might
have driven into the tree deliberately." The color drains
from Tom's face. "She wasn't wearing a seatbelt, you see.
Can you imagine anyone feeling so low they'd do that?"
He's visibly shaking now. " 'Not our Callie,' we said; she
was happy. We'd have known if she wasn't, wouldn't we?"

"Of course." I reach out and touch his arm.

"I wondered if she swerved to avoid something. Some
sort of animal that had run in front of her. That would
be typical Callie. Never wanting to hurt anything. There
weren't any skid marks but the police said that's not
unusual when roads are wet."

Tom opens a brown leather album and flicks to the back
and slides out a photo. He passes it to me. "This is Nathan."

I hold it at the edge before resting it on my palm, conscious of my sticky fingertips. Nathan is the epitome of tall,

dark, and handsome, and as I look at his chocolate eyes, his curly hair, I feel a fluttering deep in my stomach. In the picture, Nathan and Callie are standing on a lawn sprinkled with snow. Behind them is a tangle of plants and bushes, dotted with color, despite it being winter. Callie's cheek is pressed against Nathan's chest as she gazes adoringly at him.

"Are you still in touch with him?"

"No. He was completely devastated. Afterward, I spoke a bit harshly to him if I'm honest. I insisted he must have known Callie wasn't with us. I practically accused him of lying. Everything got muddled with all the questions the police were asking." Tom shakes his head. "I didn't mean it; I know how much he adored her but emotions were running high. I was looking for someone to blame, I suppose. It was awful. We didn't speak at all at Callie's funeral, and he didn't come to the wake. I apologized afterward. We had a cup of tea a few months ago when he dropped her things off but it was really awkward. He was like a son to me as well, before . . ." Tom's words wobble with emotion.

"They look happy together."

"They were. He thought the world of her. That was their first Christmas together."

"Where was it taken? It looks lovely." I flip the photo over but there is nothing scribbled on the back.

"It was taken at home. It was lovely. Callie used to do our garden. She loved being outdoors. Amanda and I were never green-fingered."

I look toward the small stone courtyard, visible through the patio doors.

"Not this home, obviously." Tom notices my confusion. "We used to live in the city center too. But after Callie, when the business went under, we couldn't keep up the mortgage payments and we had to move here."

"I'm so sorry." I can't believe how much they have been through this past year.

"There are worse things to lose than money." Tom touches my arm. "And we do OK. We have a policy from my insurance days that provides a small income, and we had some savings. We get by for now but fifty is too young to retire really, isn't it? I'd like to go back to work if I could find a job that isn't too stressful, but I'm considered a dinosaur at my age. I don't like to leave Amanda on her own either. She's so fragile."

Tom takes back the photo, and I turn to the first page of the album. Callie and Sophie, much younger this time, pose on golden sand. The sea sparkles behind them and a burnt orange sun beats down. The sisters could be twins. Shimmering blond bobs and jade green swimming costumes.

"They loved the beach. Sophie couldn't swim but she liked to paddle. They'd bury me in the sand every year."

The next picture could easily be lifted from a greeting card. Mum, Dad, and two gorgeous teenage daughters pose in front of a Christmas tree. White fairy lights glow and silver decorations hang symmetrically from its branches. Callie and Sophie are holding out a plate of gingerbread men.

I can see from the picture that Tom hasn't changed much. He is a lot thinner now and his smile doesn't reach his eyes anymore, but you can tell it's him. I have to bring the photo closer to my eyes and scrutinize it before I'm certain it is Amanda. Her face in the photo is fuller, smoother. Her hair rich with honey and caramel highlights. Around her neck, a pendant shaped like a star catches the light; rubies and diamonds sparkle as brightly as Amanda's smile. When she'd answered the door, I thought she must be in her fifties but I think she must be at least ten years younger than I'd thought. Grief has sucked the life from her.

The last photo in the book is Callie and Nathan. Nathan is wearing a lemon cravat and a cream carnation button-hole and Callie is elegant in a long red sequinned dress that should clash with her dyed crimson hair, but somehow doesn't. They're sitting at a round table. An elaborate floral display stands in the center but it's Callie's face that draws my attention. I look up at Tom in surprise.

He sighs. "Her poor face. It's not very flattering, is it? She'd walked into a cupboard at work earlier. She would have deleted it if she'd seen it but it was the last one we took of her."

"This was taken the night she died?"

"Yes."

In the picture Callie is angled away from Nathan and her forehead is creased as she stares into space, either lost in thought or looking at something the camera can't see. Her makeup is thick but it doesn't disguise her black eye or the angry bruise that covers her swollen cheek.

CHAPTER TEN

"Callie never regained consciousness, you know," Tom says.

The sentence sits between us. It could so easily have been my dad reciting those words about me. I look Tom straight in the eyes. "What you did. Signing the donor consent form..."

"It's what she would have wanted. Honestly, Jenna." He touches my arm and squeezes and a feeling of warmth spreads through me. "It's a comfort knowing Callie saved your life. Really. And I think you being here will do Amanda good. Might shake her out of her blackness a little. More than those blasted pills the doctor gives her anyway. They seem to make her constantly exhausted, but don't seem to lift her mood at all. She never talks to anyone, and she never goes out. Meeting you though and knowing that a part of Callie lives on..." He pats my hand. "I'm glad you came."

"Me too," I say, and I am.

"I'd best check on Amanda." He crosses the lounge, no longer with the purposeful strides he had earlier but with small, slow steps, dragging his heels as though there's something else he wants to say, and as he reaches the door he turns, leaning back against the frame. "It's the not knowing," he says quietly. "All the questions. At night, Amanda's knocked out by her medication, but I lie there and I wonder why. Why did they leave the reception? Why was Callie in Woodhaven? Why wasn't Nathan with her? We talked about it once afterward, Nathan and me, as we were arranging her funeral. He cried and said I had to let it go or it would drive me crazy but I couldn't cry. I was so bloody angry. I know he's right. Knowing won't bring her back, but if we had the answers." He raises his palms to the ceiling as if the answers might drop into them. "If we understood why she died." He shakes his head. "I never knew what the blasted Americans were on about when they talked about closure but—Sorry." He toes the carpet.

"No need to apologize."

"It's just that Amanda won't talk about it. Can't talk about it. She says knowing won't bring any peace. Nothing will except Callie coming back and that can't happen. Maybe she's right. I don't know. It's just so bloody agonizing. The not knowing. I even went through her iPhone when Nathan brought her things around looking for...I don't know what I was looking for. Maybe she'd just fancied a drive. I'll never bloody know, will I?" The corners of his mouth downturn and for a horrible minute I think he's going to cry but instead he bends and picks up an invisible piece of thread from the floor. I watch his defeated shoulders slink into the hallway, and I wish more than anything I could help but I'm at a loss to know what to do. What to say.

* * *

"You never think you'll have to do it. Bury your own child." The statement tumbles from Tom's mouth as he comes back into the room, as though he can't contain the words anymore.

"It's not right, is it?" I begin to answer but he starts to talk again as he sits.

"The church was packed. Funerals for the young always are, I suppose. Amanda wanted it to be family only. Intimate. Neither of us wanted to make small talk afterward but word gets around, doesn't it? In the end, I'm glad so many came to pay their respects. Her colleagues. Even some of her old school friends had heard. I thought she'd lost touch with most of them after she got serious with Nathan but there were so many people. We didn't recognize all of them, not that I could tell you who was there now, it all passed in a bit of a blur really. We played 'I Have a Dream' by Abba. It was Callie's favorite song. Not many came back to the wake at the pub and those that did only stopped for one drink. It was a relief when the last person left."

"I can't imagine how you felt." I have only been to one funeral, my nana's, and that was when I was small. I have never forgotten the chill of the church. The smell of beeswax.

"It was such a godawful day. When we got home, someone had broken into the house. Completely ransacked it." The muscles in his cheek tic. "The police said it's common. Can you believe it? There are people who make a career of targeting properties when they know the occupants are at funerals. There are some sick bastards in the world. Amanda was distraught. We were moving anyway and we decided it was the right time to pack up and leave the city. A fresh start. But memories? Well, they follow you wherever you go, don't they?"

"I'm so sorry. Did they take much?"

"The cash we kept in the safe. Jewelry. Amanda had some lovely pieces. There was a star we commissioned made of rubies and diamonds that was worth a bomb, but it didn't seem important at the time. Possessions you can replace. People..."

We fall into silence. In the distance a dog barks. Tom stifles a yawn. The sun has shifted around the back of the house, and a warm golden glow breaks through the grime-coated patio doors, pooling over the sofa where he sits, silent now. In the sunlight, his scalp is visible through his thinning hair. His skin appears looser. Paler. He looks older than when I'd arrived, somehow, and my heart goes out to him. Losing two daughters. I can't imagine, and although I want to ask what happened to Sophie, he has clearly been through enough for one day. I stand.

"I must make a move. Can I use your bathroom or will it wake Amanda?"

Tom straightens his spine and stretches his neck. "She's had a pill. It would take an earthquake to wake her. It's the door opposite the top of the stairs."

* * *

Upstairs, I creep past what must be Tom and Amanda's bedroom. It's cloaked in darkness and a sour smell exudes from the open door.

"No. No. No," Amanda murmurs, and I instinctively go to her.

In the shadows, I see her collarbones jutting out under her nightie, and she looks even thinner than she did downstairs, swamped in her cardigan. It seems she's only woven together by threads of grief, and as she thrashes her head from side to side I worry she'll soon unravel. Soothing her with words she cannot hear I brush away the damp hair that sticks to her hollowed cheeks.

It's hard to tear myself away from Amanda but eventually I tiptoe back out onto the landing. As I glance in the next room I notice it is full of boxes. The walls are pale pink and a bunny rabbit border is peeling off in several places. Lilac curtains that don't quite meet in the middle hang at the windows, but they're so thin they don't block out the light. The last occupants must have had a baby girl, and I can't imagine how Amanda and Tom can bear to come in here. It must bring back so many memories. On top of one of the boxes is a doll and I wonder if it was Callie's or Sophie's, and although I know I should carry on to the bathroom, I'm drawn toward it. I touch its wiry hair, rough beneath my fingers.

My hand hovers over the cardboard box. I really shouldn't snoop but I can't help opening the flaps.

"Are you OK up there?" Tom stage-whispers. The stairs creak with his steady footfall.

I dart into the bathroom and stand with my back against the door, breathing hard. I can't believe I've almost been caught poking around in Callie's things.

The doorbell rings, and Tom's footsteps grow fainter, and I flush the chain and run the taps. I'm halfway down the stairs when I hear angry whispers coming from the lounge.

"She can't find out," Tom almost hisses, and I freeze, hovering mid-step.

"You know how I feel about it," a man replies, his words coated with resentment.

"What's done is done. It's too late for regrets." Tom's voice is firm.

My bag is in the lounge, I can't exactly slip away, and so I exaggerate my steps as I descend, warning them of my impending arrival.

The room falls silent as I push open the door and Tom steps away from the man he's squared up to.

"Jenna," he says evenly. "This is my brother, Joe."

The man swings around and as he glares at me I feel my skin crawl with a million invisible ants.

CHAPTER ELEVEN

"I must go," I blurt out, skirting around Tom and Joe. I pick up my bag from the floor and loop it over my shoulder.

"Jenna, I'm so glad you came." Tom takes both hands in his. "Now, you must let Joe drive you home. It's such a long way on the bus and you're looking really tired."

"It's fine, I don't—" I step toward the door.

"No. Really. He only came to drop off Amanda's repeat prescription. You don't mind, do you, Joe?"

There's a pause as Joe studies me, and there's nothing to hear but the ticking clock before he eventually says: "Of course. You'll have to direct me though."

"I don't really know the way from here." There's no way I'm admitting to having Google Maps on my phone. I don't want to sit in awkward silence with Joe in the car. "It'll be easier on the bus."

"I think there's one of those satnav thingys in one of the boxes of Callie's upstairs. We bought her it for Christmas," Tom says. "I'll nip and fetch it. I need to check on Amanda again anyway."

"No, please . . ." but he's gone, and my stomach tightens as I wonder whether he will notice I've opened a box and

I try to remember whether I pushed the flaps back down again. Lost in thought I jump as Joe speaks.

"I don't know how much you heard. Before." He gestures toward the lounge door, and as his stare penetrates me I can't help telling the truth.

"Someone said 'she can't find out.' I wasn't eavesdropping." My tone is defensive. "It's none of my business."

"We were talking about you," Joe says, and I am momentarily thrown.

"Tom didn't want you finding out I didn't agree with you coming here. He didn't want you to feel uncomfortable. It's just ..." He glances at the floor before raising his head. "I wasn't keen, I have to be honest. When I heard ... you know. The thought of Callie being all cut up. I was furious when Tom got your letter. It felt really selfish you contacting them, without their consent, especially when they are so deep in grief."

"I am so sorry." I sit down heavily on the sofa and drop my head into my hands.

"It seems to have given him a lift though. Hearing from you. Growing up, I always tried to protect Tom, and I've felt so helpless watching him go through this. It feels like I've failed as a big brother," Joe says. "When Tom received your letter it was easy to direct some of my anger toward you."

"I just wanted them to know a bit about me and my family, make the letter more personal. We're all so grateful. I hoped it might help you too. In some small way. I didn't think ..."

"It's not always easy to put yourself in someone else's shoes, is it?" The cushion I am sitting on shifts as Joe sits next to me. He smells of cigarettes. "I only thought about what we were losing, not about what some faceless person could possibly gain, but now I've seen you it's hard to believe you wouldn't be here without Callie, and I feel really proud of her. She was so kind. It's what she would have wanted."

"Thank you."

"You're welcome." His graciousness leaves me with a heaviness that feels a little like shame and I don't know what else to say. I am glad when Tom returns.

* * *

I'm twisting around in my seat, waving goodbye. Tom is standing on his step getting smaller and smaller, and I don't turn around until he is out of sight.

Joe's car is old and tired. An "I'D RATHER BE FISHING" bumper sticker peels from the back window. The interior is littered with McDonald's bags and I kick one away, scrunching it against the footwell to give myself more room.

"You'd think I'd know better, with Tom's heart attack, but it's the easiest option, sometimes, when you're on the road. Feel free to chuck stuff in the back."

He cracks open both windows and air streams in diluting the stench of stale smoke and fries. I press the button on the Garmin satnav Tom had pushed into my hands as we left, but nothing happens. There's a charging wire and I push it into the cigarette lighter. The battery light on the side of the unit flashes green.

"It's too flat," I say.

"I'm OK for a bit. There's a pocket map in there if we need it."

Joe nods toward the glovebox, and I pull the handle.

"Jelly Babies?" I lift out the bag of sweets.

"I used to take the girls out a lot when they were young.

Tom worked long hours and Amanda was fraught with two small children and no money to amuse them. We'd drive into the middle of nowhere and fly kites and have races up hills. There was always a packet of Jelly Babies in the car that I'd produce whenever the inevitable 'are we nearly there yet' questions started. Over the years I seem to have developed an addiction to the red ones. Not very healthy when you spend as much time in the car as me."

"What do you do?"

"I sell cleaning products to chains of hotels and large organizations. It's as boring as it sounds but it's not easy finding a job when you're classed as middle-aged. After the business folded I wanted something less stressful. I'm told where to go every day and what to say. I don't have to think but I do hate being away from Tom so much. He's so busy looking after Amanda he doesn't look after himself. If I had my way we would both sit by the river all day fishing, but you can't make a living from that, can you?"

We make small talk until we glide down the service road onto the dual highway. As we pick up speed Joe presses a button and the windows whirr closed, and I smooth my hair down.

"Can I ask you a question about Sophie?" I form my words as carefully as I can. "Did she die recently?"

"Die?" Joe looks at me in surprise. A car horn blasts to our right and his head snaps back to the road, and as he jerks the wheel sharply I fall against the door. We narrowly avoid being hit.

"Sophie isn't dead!"

"Sorry. Amanda said 'we lost her too.' I assumed..." I can feel my cheeks burning. "I'm so sorry, I thought..."

"Sophie's in Spain with her boyfriend. She was on holiday when Callie had her accident. I had to break it to her over the phone but she said she couldn't handle the funeral and needed some space to process what's happened. We all thought she'd be back by now."

"Isn't she in touch with them?"

"No one has heard a word from her."

"Tom says she's disappeared before?"

"Yes. After Tom's second heart attack she couldn't cope and took off for weeks. She sauntered back in the door one day as if nothing had happened. It'll be the same this time, I'm sure. She'll come back, she always does. I do wish she'd get in touch though. I'm not sure where we go after this roundabout."

I press the power button on the Garmin again and this time it switches on. It doesn't take long to navigate the options. Buried in one of the submenus is "previous routes." I glance at Joe, he's leaning forward as he drives, concentrating deeply on the road ahead. Overcome with a desire to find out more about Callie I touch the screen. Where did she like to go? The last known destination is dated days before Callie's accident. I press "go here" and a map image is displayed. I zoom in. Burton Aerodrome. It's in the middle of nowhere, and I know it well. For a time, when I was young, we had a German shepherd called Fox. She came from a rescue center Dad had been called out to. Elderly, malnourished, and partly bald, she was timid around humans but aggressive around other dogs. Dad was asked to put her down but he'd brought her home instead. Every evening after work Dad would bundle Fox into the back of his car and drive out to the airfield. It had been deserted for years and was so remote there was little risk of bumping into another dog walker.

What could Callie possibly have been doing there?

CHAPTER TWELVE

My flat is warm. A garlicky smell from last night's lasagna hangs in the air. I clatter my keys onto the kitchen table and heft open the sash window, sticking my head outside to wave goodbye to Joe as his car crawls along the road. My head thumps with pent-up tension. It's been a harrowing day. I'm home. I'm safe. Joe disappears around the corner and before I even take off my coat I sit at my kitchen table, turning my laptop on, blinking at the brightness of the screen as it whirrs to life.

Callie Valentine. That's whose heart beats inside of me. Already I can't stop thinking about her.

In the Google search bar, I type Callie's name along with "CAR ACCIDENT" and the date it happened, almost compelled to discover every single detail I can. It strikes me if I am this desperate for information how utterly wretched Tom and Amanda must feel with so many unanswered questions. I could help them. The thought pops into my head unbidden. My fingers slip away from the keyboard and I lean back in my chair. *It's the not knowing.* Tom's words are sharp and pointed in my mind. What if I could find out why Callie left the wedding, and was alone in a car, miles from home?

Reading the online news report of the crash I don't learn anything new. Callie wasn't wearing a seatbelt at the time of impact. The roads were wet and driving conditions poor. It was ruled an accidental death and no other cars were involved.

I skim through Callie's social media. There are no privacy settings on her Facebook account. She's laughing in her profile picture, displaying straight, impossibly white teeth. She looks a million miles away from the pale, frowning girl photographed at the wedding. Her posts are infrequent and mundane, her photo albums full of pictures of her and Nathan. He is tagged as Nathan Prescott, and now I have a surname my fingers fly over the keyboard. A thumbnail of Nathan pops up, somber in a shirt and pinstriped tie, dark eyes staring directly into the lens. He's ridiculously handsome. His bio says he's an accountant at Nash and Rogers. I yawn. My thoughts are jumbled and I'm squinting now with tiredness. Where do I even start trying to uncover what happened that night? All at once it seems impossible to even try, but I can't give up. I can't let Tom and Amanda down before I've even begun.

It might help to write things down. Since I've been taking medication my memory has been cloudy and I'm often confused, easily losing my train of thought. I pull a new sketchbook from the cupboard and I draw a box and write "CALLIE" inside in black felt tip. I draw a line to a smaller box and write "NATHAN." I used to create mind maps when I was studying for my exams, a way of untangling my thoughts. I'm at a loss to know what to do next when I remember her last known destination was Burton Aerodrome; it seems a strange place to visit. I Google it and the most recent report, and that was months ago, states planning permission for a new housing estate had been declined as the land was classed as a conservation area.

I take colored pens and add squares containing facts I know. Callie at the wedding. Nathan leaving early. Burton Aerodrome. The accident. I already know from Tom and Amanda that Callie was a dental nurse and I uncover an old newspaper report, which is accompanied by a photo of a group of girls, perfect smiles and jet black tunics, holding up a giant check for five hundred pounds. It says the staff at Callie's dental surgery had taken part in a fun run to raise money for Cancer Research, and I add the details to my mind map. When I've finished, I stick it to the fridge with the magnetic letters I used to spell out messages to Sam with, and I sit and stare at it for so long the white spaces between the boxes disappear. Shadows creep into the kitchen. A cold breeze drifts through the open window and goose bumps spring up on my arms. I pull the window shut. Outside the moon shimmers silver and is reflected in miniature in the water that pools in the bottom of the washing-up bowl. I swoosh the water with my fingertips and the ripples snatch the image away. The sound of my mobile ringing breaks through my thoughts, and I wipe my fingers dry before picking up my phone.

"Hi, Rach."

"Are you home?"

"I've just this minute got in," I lie. I'd forgotten I had promised Rachel I would call her the second I got back. "Have you had a good day?"

"I've been stuck in all day. I'm skint and Liam has the chance of a residential trip at school, so that's something else to fork out for." Since Rachel's mum left, her dad has been too drunk to hold down a job for long and Rachel has shouldered the responsibility for her brother. "Anyway," she says, "how did it go today? Are you OK?"

"I'm fine. They aren't though. Tom and Amanda. Her parents. Callie's parents. That was her name. Callie. She was only twenty-four." Words torrent and I take a breath.

"Well, no," Rachel cuts in. "They wouldn't be fine, would they?"

"I know but I hoped seeing me and knowing part of Callie lives on might comfort them."

"I'm sure it does in some way but they've lost a daughter, Jen. Not a lot is going to help with that. Only time."

"There is something I think might help." I tell Rachel about the circumstances surrounding Callie's death. "If I could find out why she left the wedding and where she was going it might bring them some closure."

"Closure?" I can hear the skepticism in her voice and I can almost tell she's raising an eyebrow.

"I don't mean they'll forget her. But it's the not knowing. That's what Tom said. It keeps him awake at night. It seems odd, don't you think? Her disappearing like that?"

"Not really. We don't know anything about her. I'm sure if there was anything strange it would have been investigated at the time."

"But listen." I read from the newspaper article online. "Callie was driving without a seatbelt on. Who does that?"

"She did." There's a pause. "Look, Jenna. Why are you Googling her? You've met her parents and said thank you. Isn't that enough? For months, you've been obsessing ..."

"Hardly obsessing ..."

"You've talked of nothing else, and you said once you'd found out whose heart you got you'd be able to move on. Put it behind you."

"I know but ..."

"Look. I know how hard it's been. I do. And these past few months without work, without Sam to occupy your time, it must have been easy for you to become fixated on the donor, but things are changing now, aren't they? Getting back to normal. You're starting work again on Monday and there will be lots to occupy your time."

"But I feel I owe them."

"You owe it to yourself to live a normal life. Besides, how can you possibly find out what happened?"

"I thought I'd ask Nathan. Don't you think it's strange he said he didn't know where she was? He must have. Say she ran away because of him?"

"Thousands of people have rows; it's not a big deal."

"But her face was so bruised. What if he hit her?"

"And this is what Callie's parents think, is it?"

"No. They say Callie and Nathan were really happy together and they never argued but..."

"There you go then. Just drop it, Jen. It's not as if you know where he lives anyway, and if he was responsible for her bruises then he's dangerous and you shouldn't be anywhere near him."

"I've already found out where he works."

"Christ," Rachel snaps and I feel my earlier excitement begin to ebb. "Are you just going to walk up to him and say: 'You don't know me but I have your fiancée's heart, and could you please tell me why she left the wedding on her own?' He'll probably tell you to piss off. I would." There's a beat. "Look." Her tone softer now. "Why don't you talk it through properly with Vanessa and see what she thinks?"

"She'll say it's a bad idea."

"Probably because it is." There's the sound of beeping in the background. "Sorry, Jen, that's the smoke alarm. I've got to go before that brother of mine burns the house down. Honestly, you'd think making beans on toast would be easy. Promise me you'll forget this and move on? Promise me, Jenna."

But I can't promise and so I don't say anything, and the line crackles with static and disappointment before Rachel ends the call.

Feeling low I pull a tub of salted caramel ice cream out of the freezer and I yank open the cutlery drawer. Nestled with the knives and forks is the wooden spoon Sam used to pretend was a microphone as he sang along to Ed Sheeran's "Kiss Me" as he cooked his signature dish—his only dish—of beef chili. It was our song. Was Callie as happy with Nathan as I was with Sam? Whatever Rachel thinks, I know on Monday I'm going to meet Nathan. It can't do any harm, can it? After all, if he were dangerous, Tom and Amanda would know. Wouldn't they?

CHAPTER THIRTEEN

Rain pitter-patters against the window drawing me from sleep. Callie is the first thing on my mind, thoughts jostling for my attention before I have even opened my eyes. Rolling over, I check the time. It's not yet eight. Sunday stretches before me with endless hours to fill. It's far too early to ring Rachel; I've always been an early riser but she never surfaces before eleven at weekends. I think of our phone conversation last night, and the frustration I had heard in her voice still stings, and I'm not sure whether I want to talk to her today. Meeting Tom and Amanda has stirred up so many emotions, things I thought I'd got over. Rachel has never felt the crushing weight of loss, and I am pleased she hasn't, but that means there is sometimes a divide between us. The things we can talk about and the things we can't.

I throw back the covers. It is chilly. I slip my feet into fluffy socks before crossing the room. I slide the wooden box out from the bottom of the wardrobe and place it on the bed. Sitting cross-legged on the mattress I wrap my duvet around my shoulders like a cape. It's so quiet. I open up iTunes and set the music onto shuffle. The Goo Goo Dolls sing "Iris," and I place both hands on the lid of the box, but I still don't feel ready to open it. I'm never ready to open it. Instead, I run my fingertips over the ornate carvings of the elephants that adorn the box. Confronting the past is the best way to step into the future, Vanessa says, but what if I'm not ready to let go?

My phone begins to buzz and a photo of Sam flashes up, and I think it's because I'm feeling so lost and alone I answer it rather than diverting it to voicemail, as usual.

"Hey," he says, and the sound of his voice snatches my breath away. I try to keep our contact to text or messenger. Hearing him is so bloody hard.

"I thought you'd be awake. What you doing?"

"Nothing," I say.

"I wanted to check how it went yesterday."

"OK," I say but the catch in my voice betrays me.

"Shall I come around? Do you need to talk?"

"No." Having him here, in the space we once shared, would be unbearable. We don't speak for a moment. I hear him breathing. Remember the time when I'd lie in this bed with his arm around my shoulder. My head on his chest. The rise and fall. "Sam," I say. "There's somewhere I want to go. Will you please take me?"

* * *

I'm hovering in the porch, shielded from the rain. Sam's cherry red Fiat turns into the road and I dart toward the curb, feet splashing through puddles, hood pulled over my head. My body molds itself into the passenger seat I've sat in a thousand times before. My legs stretch out, my feet in the footwell, and it seems the seat hasn't been moved since I last sat here. The floor is littered with discarded plastic wrappers from the humbugs that Sam always crunches when he drives. The smell of mint has embedded itself in the interior. We don't speak, as if Sam senses I'm not quite ready to talk about yesterday, but the silence is comfortable, familiar, and after a quick stop we're here.

Thunder rumbles and lightning illuminates the church in front of me. The churchyard is empty. The light rain of this morning is now torrential and the sky a mass of darkened clouds. We trudge between the gravestones. There's a smell of rotting leaves, and the bushes rustle with an unseen animal. My trainers are soaked, and the bottom of my jeans cling to my legs. Sam is carrying the silk flowers we'd called into the supermarket to buy, and as I suddenly stop he walks into me.

"This is it." The headstone is black and shiny. "*Callie Amanda Valentine*" etched in a swirling font. This is where she rests, and as I think of her body lying there, her heart inside of me, my knees buckle and I sink onto the wet grass, overcome with the enormity of it all. Sam lays down the flowers and steps back, resting his hand on my shoulder. My fingers trace the inscription—"*Once Met, Never Forgotten*"— and although I never met her, I know I will think of her every single day for the rest of my life, this girl who gave me a second chance.

I blink back tears that threaten to spill down my cheeks.

"I won't let you go," a man's voice whispers, but it isn't Sam and there is no one else here.

From out of nowhere I have the sensation of being pushed. I'm falling. Panic grips me and I stagger to my feet. I'm stumbling, running, desperate to get away, and as an arm snakes around my waist, forcing me to stop, I spin around and lash out.

"Jenna!" Sam's face swims into focus, and I cling onto the front of his raincoat, and he envelops me in his arms. I press my nose against his neck and breathe in his familiar spicy aftershave. He doesn't let me go until I've stopped shaking.

* * *

"What happened back there? You looked terrified." We're sitting in Sam's car and I'm huddled in his bottle green fleece.

"I don't know. I felt…strange. It's happened before. Vanessa thinks my medication is too strong but Dr. Kapur says he won't reduce it again until after my six-month check-up. It's nothing to worry about," I say with a confidence I don't feel. I'm shaken to the core but I don't know what else to tell Sam. How could I hear a voice? Feel hands pushing me? Be swamped with fear one minute and it's gone the next? Sometimes it feels as though I am going mad.

"It might be worth another chat with him. You look really pale, Jen. Do you want me to come to the hospital with you?"

"No," I say, even though I do.

At first, after the transplant, I thought things would go back to normal. We nearly had enough saved for a deposit on a house. We'd have the three children we'd talked about. That was in the early days. The days I'd thought a new heart meant a new life, but the doctor shook his head and told me if I wanted to stay alive there'd be no future swelling of my belly. No kicking of miniature feet against my skin. No tiny person with Sam's eyes and my hair wrapping their small fingers around mine as they guzzled milk. Sam said it didn't matter, of course, but when he mentioned adoption I knew he still longed for a family.

Statistically the survival and recovery rates for heart

transplant patients are improving all the time, but even though I know them all off by heart I still Google them endlessly. Searching for a new miracle story. Someone who has defied the odds and is still alive after ten years, fifteen, twenty. The knowledge I might not be here in five years' time is always at the back of my mind. I bury it under "aren't I luckys," and "there are always exceptions," but five years seems impossibly short and yet sometimes longer than I dare hope for. How can I adopt a child knowing I might not be around to see them grow? Sam says we can still be a family of two but that would almost feel as though I've trapped him. He has the chance to meet someone new. Have children. And I want, more than anything else in the world, for him to be happy.

But today, it's easy to wish things were different. Cold rain drips off my hair and trickles down my cheek and he leans forward and wipes it away with his thumb. My skin tingles. "I worry about you." His lips brush mine, warm and soft. His breath smells of mint and despite myself I entwine my fingers in his hair and kiss him back before I come to my senses and push him away.

"Sam..."

"I know." He leans back in his seat. "Friends." He twists the key in the ignition and the engine roars to life, and in his eyes, I watch his hopes die.

CHAPTER FOURTEEN

My stomach is full of the sandwiches you'd made for our romantic picnic. I have the best boyfriend ever. Overeating has made me drowsy. I can hear your soft snores as I try to drift off too. There's a buzzing around my ear and I stir. I'm hot and sticky; one arm is covering my face, the other flops against my side. It's an effort to open my eyes. The sun beats down from a blue and cloudless sky. Everything seems too bright. Too vibrant. It's the kind of picture-perfect summer day that makes strangers smile at one another and agree nobody will need an umbrella today. Give it until the end of the week and they'll all be grumbling the garden is too dry, the flowers are curling and browning. Why on earth is there a hosepipe ban when June was torrential?

I flap my hand making a half-hearted effort to shoo away the bee. My weight has shifted and I'm not comfortable anymore. I wriggle my bottom, trying to find the indent I made on the ground before. The picnic blanket moves with me; it's stuck to the bare skin on the back of my thighs.

I tense my calves, flex my feet, and stretch my toes. My coral toenails look really summery. I should have painted my fingernails too but they always chip so easily. My feet splay out to the sides as I relax my muscles. Corn pricks the soles of my feet. A stream bubbles to my left. We'd stood on the rickety wooden bridge earlier, shaded by the giant willow tree, and played Poohsticks. I'd won, and you'd pretended to sulk.

"I never lose," you'd said, making your voice growly and cross before you pressed your mouth hard against mine, crushing my body against yours.

I smack my dry lips together as I listen to the trickling water. The cool box is out of reach and I'm too hot to move. I promise myself five more minutes and then I'll have a drink and a paddle. I think I doze because the next thing I know my skin is burning, and a headache pounds behind my eyes. A film of sweat coats my body. There's the sound of a tractor in the distance and I hope the farmer isn't heading this way.

My elbow digs into the ground as I try to lever myself up, but a shadow is cast and your weight presses down on me, skin as sticky as mine. Hot hands run up my body, fingers ease inside my bikini top. My nipples harden and I groan.

"It's too hot for that. Get off," I protest even though we both know I'm easily swayed. Who could say no to you?

"How about this?"

Something moist touches my bottom lip and I stick out my tongue—strawberry—the sweet smell reaches my nostrils and I salivate as the fruit is pulled away.

"Feed me," I demand, opening my mouth wide like a baby bird, and the soft berry is placed gently on my tongue. I roll it between my back teeth and bite. The juice floods my mouth and trickles down my throat. I can't remember ever feeling quite so happy.

The brightness of the sun makes my eyes water. I squint;

I've left my sunglasses on the top of the fridge again. I can't see your features; you're nothing but blackness hovering in front of a white-hot sun but I feel you. Oh, how I feel you.

I chew, swallow, and lick my lips.

"Another strawberry, baby?"

I wonder if you want some. If you'll eat them off my naked body like last time. "Please." I'll never have enough. I crave them almost as much as I crave you.

"Do you want me?" Warm fingers trail up the inside of my thigh.

"Always."

"Forever? You know I'll always look after you."

"Let me think about that. Forever is a long time," I say but I smile to show I'm joking.

"You're stuck with me whether you like it or not." Your fingers seek out my ribs, and I squeal as you tickle me, and I'm laughing as I push you off and spring to my feet.

"Only if you can catch me," I shout over my shoulder as I run, giggling, as you begin to follow me.

"You can't get away from me!" you call, and in that moment I wonder why I'd ever want to.

CHAPTER FIFTEEN

My first day back at work and I'm already exhausted before I start. Last night in bed I couldn't settle. I was awake in the early hours cuddling Sam's fleece that I had still been wearing when he dropped me off. My mind tried to replay the events in the churchyard like a DVD on a loop but as I tried to recall the details they became as opaque as a childhood memory, and I'm not sure now whether I imagined the whole thing. Sleep when it came was disturbed and when I woke I couldn't believe I'd dreamed of bloody strawberries. I've always hated them and the taste clung to my tongue long after I'd woken.

Chewing spearmint gum I stand in front of the veterinary surgery at 7:45 a.m. and it feels like the first day back at school after the summer holidays. There is a fluttering deep in my gut as I think about stepping inside but coming back is the right thing, I think. If I didn't do this, what would I do? Who would I be?

"Jenna!"

Hands grab my shoulders and my heart springs into my mouth.

"You coming in or what?" Rachel grins. Her face, round

and freckled, looks delighted to see me, and I follow her swinging brown ponytail through the glass doors. Inside, disinfectant stings my nostrils, and I begin to relax. I can't imagine why I thought it would all be so different. I'm the one who has changed.

"So you didn't answer my calls yesterday." Rachel waggles a finger in front of her face as if she's cross, but I know she isn't really. She's the last person to ever hold a grudge. "How are you?"

"I'm good. Really well." It's not a lie; physically I'm fine, but she narrows her eyes, and I know she doesn't believe me.

"And what we talked about Saturday? The donor? Have you thought any more about what I said?"

"Her name was Callie," I snap but am instantly apologetic. "Sorry, Rachel. I didn't mean . . ."

"It's OK, Miss Moody Pants. I know you'll be back to your sweet-natured self once your medication is reduced. In the meantime," she sighs theatrically, "it's a hard job being your best friend but someone has to do it, don't they?" She shakes her head sadly, and I shove her shoulder, and all of a sudden there's nowhere else I'd rather be.

"So now you're back at work there's no excuse to miss the pub quiz anymore. No one else is quite the font of knowledge you are when it comes to the arty stuff that no one else gives a toss about."

"I'm sure you've done well in the crappy pop music round."

"Better than the depressing singer/songwriters you listen to." She feigns a yawn, and a laugh bursts from me. It's been such a long time since I heard the sound I self-consciously clap my hand in front of my mouth.

"How's everything been here?" We've hardly talked about work at all since I've been off.

"Nothing's changed, except Linda's been really stressed out and snappy. John's hardly coming in at all and it's tons of extra work for her."

Linda and her husband, John, own the practice but John semi-retired last year and it will be odd not seeing him every day, cracking jokes. Raiding the biscuit barrel in between consultations.

"She's even started buying plain digestives instead of chocolate ones, now John's not coming in. Can you imagine? It's almost staff cruelty. I'll have to hand you back your senior veterinary nurse crown. You can lead the revolt."

"Not yet. I'm sticking to part-time hours for a while."

"That's good." Rachel beams. "I've got used to the extra money each month." Her eyes widen. "Oh God, Jenna. I didn't mean good that…" she falters. "It's just, with Liam and everything."

"It's OK. Really. I understand, and if you're ever short you know you can ask," I offer, but I know she won't. She's too proud.

We automatically fall into our default roles. Rachel switches on the ventilation unit, and I fire up the desktop, flick through the CDs, and push the button on the ancient CD player, and the lid creaks open. Some things never change.

"Abba?" Rachel shimmies across reception and raises an eyebrow as "Mamma Mia" starts. "Who are you and what have you done with Jenna?"

"I just fancied something uplifting."

"Says the girl who once said she'd rather slit her wrists than listen to Swedish pop?" She twirls around and hip-bumps me before she grabs a pen, holding it in front of us, and we sing into it as if it's a microphone.

I feel happier than I have in ages.

"Someone sounds pleased to be back." Linda click-clacks across reception in her heels and hugs me, and I feel the bumps of her spine beneath her clothes. She's lost so much weight and the dark circles under her eyes make her look paler than usual.

"Are you OK, Linda?"

"I should be asking you that."

"I'm fine."

"John sends his love. He'll pop in later in the week and see how you've settled back in." Linda and John never had children, and John's always had a soft spot for me, showering me with sweets when I was small, and as I got older, pressing five pound notes into my hand whenever they came around for dinner. He's softer than Linda but I love working for them both.

"You mustn't overdo it today, missy. I'm not convinced you should be back at all." She studies my face. "If this is too much we both understand. Don't feel obligated to be here."

"I don't. I'll be OK if I build up gradually."

"If you're sure? We're keeping Kelly on for the time being. She's eager to stay permanently so don't worry about leaving us short-staffed."

I haven't yet met the temporary nurse who has been filling in for me. Rachel says she's lovely, but then Rachel thinks everyone is.

The bell tinkles as the front door opens and the first patient of the day rockets through the door, claws scratching and panting heavily.

"Johnson!" I can't resist dropping to my knees to fuss the boxer dog who slides backward as he tries to gain traction on the sterile white tiles.

"Lovely to see you back, Jenna."

"Thanks, Mr. Harvey. Is Johnson OK?"

Mr. Harvey bought Johnson after his wife died, and although the dog has proved to be a real handful, he's stopped Mr. Harvey's son crying himself to sleep every night.

"No disaster for once. Just his boosters today."

Mr. Harvey signs the consent form, and Rachel leads Johnson to a consulting room as he jumps up, trying to catch his red fabric lead in his mouth.

There's a steady stream of patients all morning—I'd forgotten how busy it gets—and I'm glad of a break when Linda sticks her head out of her office and asks me to make drinks. Heaping spoons of coffee into mugs and adding splashes of milk, I lean back against the kitchen counter. The kettle gurgles and spits and above the noise I hear the phone ringing, and I scoot back to reception to answer it, but by the time I get there it has stopped. Back in the staff-room I tip water into the mugs and distribute the drinks. I am on my hands and knees in front of the fridge wiping up milk that has seeped from its carton when Kelly sloshes her coffee down the sink and swills out her mug. Rachel follows with her and Linda's drinks.

"Trying to give us diabetes?"

"What's up?"

"They're full of sugar."

"I didn't . . . I don't remember. Sorry. This has been more tiring than I'd thought," I admit.

"If you want to leave early I'll cover you," Kelly offers.

"Thanks." We head back to reception and I gather my things together. "I'll just hang on and say hello to Mrs. Bainbridge. She has Casper, her Jack Russell, booked in at twelve." He's such a sweetie. So is Mrs. Bainbridge. It's hard to believe it's nine months since I've seen her. I have missed our chats. She had sent me flowers and a get well card via Linda, and I want to tell her how touched I am she'd thought of me. I know she can't really afford flowers on her pension. Several times I've paid the excess on her insurance policy for Casper's treatment, without Linda knowing.

The bell tinkles and we both look toward the door. The smile on my face freezes. My stomach floods with anxiety as Casper scrambles toward me, panting hard, his pink tongue lolling to the side. Sweat pricks my armpits and my vision tunnels. Mrs. Bainbridge stands in front of me, and I can see her lips moving out of the corner of my eye but I can't rip my eyes away from Casper. From the saliva spilling from between his needle-sharp teeth.

"Jenna?" Kelly's face looms toward mine.

I can hear my name but it's as if I'm underwater. I press my palms against the front of my desk and wheel my chair backward and run to the loo. Nausea swirls and I scoop cold water into my palms and splash my face before pulling out a rough blue paper towel and dabbing my skin dry. In the mirror my reflection stares back at me, bright red hair and haunted eyes. Why am I so scared of Casper? He's a third of the size of Johnson, and anyway, I love all dogs.

A fist thuds against the door. "You all right in there, Jen? Kelly said you looked terrified."

"Fine thanks, Rach," I call, but I'm not fine at all. My legs are shaking so hard I sink down onto the lid of the toilet and drop my head into my hands. What's happening to me? Since seeing Fiona, the medium, on Friday these ephemeral feelings that swamp me, snatching my breath and accelerating my pulse, are becoming darker. More frequent. There's an almost constant unease gnawing at the pit of my stomach. I can't stop thinking about this second energy, and I've never believed in stuff like that before. I'm not sure I do now, but still. Something has changed, and I don't mind admitting I'm scared of it, this foreboding that's ingrained itself into my being. What does it mean? I'm not in danger, am I? And in my mind I think I hear a scream, short and sharp. But I can't be sure.

CHAPTER SIXTEEN

My eyelids are glued together with sleep and I prize them open and yawn. Napping in the daytime always leaves me feeling sluggish. The sun is still bright outside, shining through the slatted blinds that cover my lounge window, casting tiger stripes on my laminate floor. My body is stuck to my leather sofa and, as I peel myself to sitting, I drop my head in my hands remembering what a disaster my first morning back at work has been. Stumbling into the kitchen, my bare feet sticking to the tiles, I fill a glass with lemon squash, slouching against the sink as I drink, letting the sourness chase away the last whispers of tiredness. The swirling lines of my mind map catch my eye and I stare at it transfixed, ignoring my buzzing phone. It will be Mum or Dad stressing about how my first morning back went. I did text them both when I first got home to reassure them it went well but they won't be placated until they've actually spoken to me. The way they fuss you'd think I'd been mountain climbing. If I call them they'll realize straight away something is wrong, particularly Mum, and I can't face them knowing I fled the surgery in tears after my encounter with Casper. I can't face the "I told you it would be too much" conversation that would inevitably follow.

Shaking thoughts of the Jack Russell away I sit and pull my laptop toward me, and I download various images of Callie from her Facebook page and send them to the wireless printer in my hallway. The printer whirrs and churns and spits them out, and I stick the photos to my fridge with the magnetic letters: When it's full, I Blu-Tack them to the walls: Callie cross-legged on a carpet of green, face shining with happiness, a daisy chain looped around her hair; Callie and Nathan, unaware of the camera, staring deeply into one another's eyes; Callie, sitting in the middle of Tom and Amanda, glasses brimming with fizzing champagne raised into a toast. Underneath each photo I write captions on Post-it notes so I remember where and when they were taken. Where did you disappear to that night? I trace the outline of Callie's face with my finger. Her clear and perfect skin glows. My spine straightens as though strength has flowed into my bones and, standing tall, I suddenly feel strong. No longer disempowered by illness but I have a sense I can actually do something. Make a difference. Purposefully, I pick up my mobile and, punching in the number of Nathan's office that I'd written on my mind map, I make a call.

* * *

Outside Nathan's office the sun glistens on hot tarmac, and the air is heavy with the stench of exhaust fumes. Leaning against a tree trunk I ensure I'm shaded by its boughs; the immunosuppressants I'll always have to take leave me vulnerable to skin cancer but I'm going to embrace the English Rose look this summer. I don't take my eyes off the door to the building. Nathan's secretary had told me on the phone that he finishes work at six. As I wait, feeling alone and exposed, anxiety dampens my clothes. I don't make eye contact with anyone. In my head I run through the script I've prepared, but even to me the words sound forced and contrived. At six o'clock people begin to stream out of Nathan's office. Men loosen ties and roll up sleeves as women bunch cardigans into handbags. I flinch whenever someone brushes against me as they hurry by, and I press myself harder against the tree. Bark scrapes against my bare shoulders causing my skin to sting. By quarter past my legs ache. The frequency with which I check my watch doesn't make the time go any faster, and by half past I'm hot and tired and close to giving up. I think perhaps I've missed him. The traffic is constant, engines rev, and stereos blare from open windows, and a dull ache has formed behind my temples. I'm about to go home when the door swings open again and there he is. Nathan. Beige mac looped over his forearm. Tan leather briefcase swinging in his opposite hand. I inhale sharply at the sight of him as a bolt of recognition shoots through me. My legs move without conscious volition as though there's an invisible cord tugging me toward him. His strides are long, black shiny brogues slapping against the pavement, and I have to half-run to keep up with him.

The high street is teeming with people scurrying home to enjoy the sun before it disappears, and I'm knocked and jostled. It's too crowded and I lose sight of Nathan. My blood whooshes in my ears as I fight to stay calm. Clenching and unclenching my fists I try to recall Vanessa's advice by noticing how fast I'm breathing and attempting to slow it down. My anxiety increases. I can't remember whether I am supposed to breathe in for the count of three or five or whether that's exhaling, and I feel utterly useless as I fight to control my panic. Stepping into a doorway I crouch down and try to make myself as small as possible. Breathe. One, two, three. My head jerks upward as a bus hisses fumes as it releases its brakes, its wheels turning as it pulls away from the curb. I stare into its windows as it passes but I can't see Nathan. He could be anywhere. It feels hopeless that I'll find him again now and after the long wait outside his office to have lost him is sickening, but if I'm honest, underneath the disappointment is relief. My head feels thick and my thoughts jumbled. Dry-throated I look left and right searching for somewhere to buy a bottle of water. There's a Co-op down the street, and I clamber to my feet, continuing to breathe deeply as I cross the road. After this I'm going home.

The shop is packed. There's almost a Christmas-like mania as customers shove their way to the shelves, grabbing the last of the burgers to barbecue, tutting because there are no bread rolls left. The air-conditioning is a stark contrast to the glorious sunshine outside. I stand still at first, welcoming the feeling of my blood cooling and calming, but before long my arms are covered in goose flesh and I pick my way toward the fridge. As my emotions start to settle, I begin to think about dinner and I look around to see if there's anything I fancy. At the end of the fruit and veg aisle are punnets of fresh strawberries, plump and red, and saliva floods my mouth. Even though I normally hate them I feel compelled to peel back the cellophane, and I pick the largest fruit up by its stalk, dangle it over my open mouth before sinking my teeth into the soft flesh. The sweetness explodes into my mouth, and I close my eyes as juice trickles down my chin.

"You look like you're enjoying that."

I snap my eyes open and he's there. Nathan. Sound

crescendos around us and then fades. I can't stop staring at him. My hand twitches with an almost magnetic pull to reach out and trail my fingertips along the stubble on his jawline. Does he feel it too? This connection. I wipe my mouth with the back of my hand.

"I couldn't resist. I will pay for them."

His laugh is low and belly deep. "I wasn't judging you. I knew a girl who used to do that." His head tilts to the side as he studies me. "You remind me of her. I think it's the hair."

My hand touches the back of my neck. It's still strange to feel the exposed skin.

"Strawberries were her favorite; she ate them all the time. She said they were a natural teeth whitener too. Not that she needed her teeth whitened being a dental nurse." He runs his fingers though his hair, thick and curly. "Sorry. I'm babbling. But Callie used to do that. Eat the strawberries that we were supposed to be buying for a picnic as we walked around the shop, and I'd have to go back for more."

Callie. Picnic. Strawberries. My dreams. They can't be of Callie, can they? I think back to the painting at Amanda's. The girls on the beach in my dream. Callie and Sophie? In front of me, Nathan is asking, "Are you all right?" his brow furrowed, but I can't seem to move my mouth, to smile, to talk. "A second energy," Fiona said. Callie? It's impossible. Despite the air-conditioning I am boiling hot as emotions tumble, all tugging for my attention. I am floating above my body, almost touching the hot white strips of lights. Noise fades. Silence screams. I'm spinning and turning and my vision is shrinking and shrinking. I'm Alice disappearing down the rabbit hole until there's only a pinprick of light and then, nothing.

* * *

Shoes. I'm surrounded by feet. Trainers, skyscraper heels, and flip-flops. Strawberries are scattered around me like confetti. My senses roar back into life and I sit up blinking, grasping the bottom of my top and tugging it down, conscious the rolls of flesh around my waist might be on display.

"Here." Nathan scoots down next to me and untwists the cap from a bottle of Evian. The label is soft and damp with condensation.

I croak my thanks and gulp greedily as the crowd disperses.

"You must have overheated outside. You've caught the sun."

"Probably. I missed lunch today too."

A spotty shop assistant glares at me—even though his name badge says he's "HAPPY TO HELP"—as he picks up whole strawberries, mops the ones that have been splattered on the white tiled floor. It looks like a crime scene, and I shiver, drawing my knees up to my chin and tucking my arms around my shins.

"Look. I know you don't know me but I only live around the corner. Would you like to come back to mine? I can offer you some food and call you a cab when you're feeling better?" Nathan proffers his hand and pulls me to my feet. I sway, and his arm curves around my waist, and I lean into him as though I've done it a thousand times before.

"It's kind of you but . . ."

"No buts. I can't let you go home in this state. I'd never forgive myself if you fainted again crossing the road or something."

"I could always call my dad. I'm sure I could wait here until he comes."

The assistant vigorously cleaning around us runs the mop over my feet so the water trickles over my toes, exposed in sandals, and they become sticky with disinfectant.

"Sorry," he mutters, although he is grinning as he says it, and I don't want to remain here a second longer.

There's no way I'd ever usually go home with a stranger, let alone stay for dinner, but I am feeling sick. Besides, it's not as though Nathan is a stranger, is it? Not really. And I did want to talk to him. But an image of Callie's bruised face looms into my consciousness, and I hesitate. What if Nathan is dangerous?

"If you feel happier calling your dad I'll wait with you until he arrives."

His brow is wrinkled with concern, and I brush my doubts aside. How many people are kind enough to stop and help a complete stranger?

"Thanks, but I'd like to go back to yours," I say.

Back to Callie's, I think.

Back to mine, beats my heart.

CHAPTER SEVENTEEN

My feet seem to know where they're going as I walk beside Nathan: left at the traffic lights, right at the church, pause and cross the road. Nathan's voice is low and comforting, but I can't understand what he's saying. I can't understand what's happening to me. Strawberries? I've always hated strawberries. The dream I had of the picnic flits across my mind. Am I going crazy? Callie's heart aches inside my chest. Could it be irrevocably tied to Nathan's? But that's ridiculous, isn't it? A heart is just an organ.

Somehow I know we're here. There's a sense of home. And everything feels so surreal it's almost as if I'm drunk. We slow and pause together at the end of the driveway while Nathan holds up his raincoat in one hand and pats each pocket to locate his keys. These houses still have the new-build look about them even though they have probably been here over twenty years. Red roof tiles, and not a chimney in sight.

Nathan pushes open the gate that creaks and unlocks the glossy black front door that has a silver knocker, and I follow him into the hallway that holds the lingering smell of washing powder. There's a giant print of the Eiffel Tower at night in a glossy black frame.

"Make yourself at home." Nathan strides down the hall. It only takes him four steps to reach the kitchen. "Tea?"

"Please." My fingers trail along the buttermilk walls as I follow him, and I rub the gloss white doorframe that leads to a cloakroom. I can't stop touching things. Wanting to feel the solidity beneath my fingertips, if only to convince myself this is not a dream.

In the kitchen Nathan pulls mugs from the cupboard and fetches milk from the fridge.

"Sugar?"

"No thanks."

Nathan digs a spoon into a caddy and heaps white granules into my drink, stirring as they sink, and I wonder if he's heard me but before I can speak he glances at me and adds another half teaspoon.

"I know you said no but it's good for shock. Sugar. You still look really pale. Let's get you sat down. Shall we sit in the garden?" Nathan's already hooking open the back door.

I'm desperate to see the rest of the house but he hands me a box of chocolate fingers. "Take these outside and get something in your stomach. I'll sort out some proper food in a bit."

The garden's beautiful, its borders a riot of color, and I remember Tom telling me how much Callie loved gardening. I lean against the fence, sipping my drink, while Nathan grapples with a large green umbrella, angling it so the table falls into shade.

"Are you OK to grab the seat cushions from the shed?" he asks.

The heat in the shed is stifling, but it still smells of damp and earth. Garden tools hang from the wall, mud stuck to the prongs of the fork. Stacked at the far end are bags of compost and lime, and there's a shelf crammed with gardening books and packets of seeds. I spot the cushions half-hidden under a tarpaulin. I tug them and dislodge a flowerpot and as it tips over I see a glint of silver, and the biggest spider I've ever seen skitters across the floor. I shriek as I bolt outside.

"You OK?" Nathan takes the cushions from me.

"Spider," I say, and I edge toward the corner of the garden as Nathan bangs the cushions together. Dust rises and falls.

"You girls. Scared of everything." He smiles.

"Not everything," I say. "Is your girlfriend scared of spiders?"

"I don't have one. Callie. My fiancée. She died a few months ago."

"I'm so sorry." And I am.

"Thank you," he says. His face is closed as he drags the chairs over to the table, and I can see he doesn't want to discuss Callie. Part of me is relieved. It's difficult to know where to start and my head is still pounding with the effort of analyzing everything that's happening.

There's a yapping from the garden next door, a small dog by the sound of it.

"Bloody thing, I can't stand it," Nathan says. "He belongs to the new neighbors. Callie would have a fit if she were still here. She hated Jack Russells with a passion. She was bitten by one as a child and terrified of them ever since. Funny, because she loved big dogs but she couldn't go near a Jack Russell, even if it was on a lead."

The garden tilts and sways—images pulse: Mrs. Bainbridge, Casper—his needle-sharp teeth—Callie—the fear I felt at work. I stumble toward the back door.

"Just nipping to the loo," I say. I need to collect my thoughts.

In the cloakroom, I perch on the lid of the toilet. Callie was terrified of Jack Russells. In the surgery, could I have felt her fear? It sounds crazy. I press my palm against my forehead. I'm hot. The sun is fierce outside and I reassure myself the heat is making me irrational or my medication is making me paranoid, but I know it's more than that. I'm feeling what she felt but how can that be?

Nathan taps on the door jarring my already jagged nerves.

"Are you OK, Jenna?"

"Just a sec." I fumble for the lock—my hand won't stop shaking—and I open the door not knowing quite what to say.

"I'm sorry. It was stupid to take you outside in that heat when you've already fainted. You look so pale. You're not going to keel over again, are you?"

"No, I'm fine. Really. I just felt a little light-headed. I should probably go."

"Wait until you've eaten, at least, and you are feeling better. I'll rustle up a bolognese. We can eat in the dining room. It'll be nice to use it again."

I hesitate. I do feel awful, and I did want to speak to Nathan.

"Sorry. Am I being bossy? Callie said I could be sometimes. I mean well though. Honest. I'd be glad of the company," he says, and as he smiles I know I'll stay.

"OK. Thanks."

* * *

"How did you meet her? Callie?" I'm sitting on a kitchen stool crunching on a piece of the pepper Nathan is chopping for the pasta sauce.

"In a bar. I was on a night out with some lads from work.

She was waiting to be served and laughing at something her friend had said. The sight of her took my breath away. She was the most beautiful woman I'd ever seen. Her friend went to the toilet and this sleazebag sidled up to her and started trying to chat her up. You could tell he was a chancer. Drunk so much he couldn't stand straight." He frowns at the memory. "She turned away, and was obviously trying to brush him off, but he didn't get the hint. I'll never forget her face as I strode over, put my arm around her, and kissed her cheek. 'Sorry I'm late, darling,' I said, and he got the message and staggered back to his mates. She called me her knight in shining armor and that was it."

"Love at first sight?" It had been a slow burn for Sam and me. We'd been friends for ages before we got together.

"She was everything I wanted. Sweet, gorgeous, and kind. Too kind." He slices the top from another red pepper.

"Can you be too kind?" I often think the world's not kind enough.

"Sometimes you have to learn to stand up for yourself, don't you?" His tone is soft but he is gripping the knife so hard his knuckles bleach white. He scrapes the vegetables from the chopping board into a saucepan, meat and garlic and herb tomato sauce already simmering, and my stomach growls.

"Let's go and sit in the lounge while that cooks through," Nathan says.

The lounge is immaculate. Furniture, shiny and white. A large cream deep-pile rug lies between the caramel leather sofa and the coffee table. At the far end of the room is another door, which I assume leads to the dining room. Over the mantelpiece, in a silver frame, is a large photo of Callie. She's standing on a rickety wooden bridge over a bubbling stream. She's laughing. Her arm is outstretched, fingers splayed open, and a small stick tumbles from her hand.

My dream. It's as though the bones in my legs have disappeared as I sink onto the sofa.

"It was her birthday," Nathan says from behind me but I can't tear my eyes away from the image. "She loved playing Poohsticks. We didn't have much money at the time for an elaborate day out. She said she was thrilled with a surprise picnic though."

I know she was. I want to tell him about the dream, the feeling of being utterly loved and utterly happy, but how could he understand? It sounds impossible. It is impossible. I'm dreaming about things that have never happened to me. That have only happened to someone I've never met. I press my hand against my chest and feel the thump, thump, thump of Callie's heart inside of me.

And that's when I know with absolute certainty. A heart is not just an organ. The heart stores secrets and lies. Hopes and dreams. It's more than a muscle. I know it is.

The heart remembers.

CHAPTER EIGHTEEN

"Read these." I wave a wad of A4 paper toward Vanessa, creased from being stuffed into my bag. Last night when I got home from Nathan's, I'd spent hours Googling, printing off page after page of true-life stories, Blu-Tacking some of them to my wall among the photos of Callie. The magnolia paint in my kitchen is barely visible anymore.

"Jenna, I understand you believe there is such a thing as Cellular Memory..." says Vanessa.

"It is a thing." I spring to my feet, hands balled into fists by my sides. "There are many scientists and doctors, and these are growing in number all the time, who support the theory memories can be stored in the neurons of the heart and transferred to the recipient. New science is testing the theory that the heart is involved in our feelings. It has already shown the heart has intelligence."

"But it's not actually proven that Cellular Memory..."

"It is proven that memory itself is distributed throughout the neural system, and the heart's nervous system contains around 40,000 neurons that communicate with the brain. If you transplant a heart you are also transplanting these neurons." I'd stayed awake half the night filtering facts, trawling through medical jargon, trying to understand. I continue: "There was a paper published in Austria by the Quality of Life Research that documented that twenty-one percent of heart transplant patients who were part of the study experienced a change to some degree. Twenty-one percent! That's huge."

"Please sit down." Vanessa's tone never changes. She may raise an inquiring eyebrow and look over the top of her glasses in that way of hers that makes you question everything, but her voice is always the same.

I ignore her and stride over to the window.

"How are you finding being back at work?"

"You can Google it too." I'm determined not to let the subject drop. "Cellular Memory is . . ."

"Jenna, I can't . . ."

"You won't." I spin around to face her. "Please. Just read the medical journals. At Honolulu University, Hawaii, the School of Nursing carried out research and they documented that all of the heart transplant patients who were part of the study changed in ways that were parallel to the donor's history, not just their tastes either, their sensory experiences too. There are thousands of real-life cases online as well where people receive an organ and it changes them."

"Of course it changes them. It gives them a second chance of life."

"Of whose life? Theirs? Their donor's?"

"It's not possible that . . ."

"There's a case where a British woman woke after her op speaking fluent Russian. She's never been to Russia. The donor was Russian. Another where a boy found he could play piano, as good as any concert pianist—he'd never tried an instrument in his life. I'm not making this up." This morning I'd silently recited the facts to myself over and over, knowing I needed to present them calmly to have any hope of being taken seriously. Instead, I trip over my words in a rush to get them out. My voice is too high and too fast.

"I'm sure you're not making it up, but scientifically . . ."

"Scientifically it's impossible that a teenage girl can receive a transplant and get behind the wheel for her first driving lesson and drive like Lewis Hamilton. Her donor was a racing driver." It sounds ludicrous, I know, but I desperately want Vanessa to believe me. I sink back onto the sofa. "Look." I calm my voice. "It's not only massive changes for people. It's small things too. Craving food they never ate before, listening to new music, reading in different genres. If recipients meet the donor's family, they often find out that the new things they are trying were the donor's favorite things. Scientists are taking it seriously, why can't you?"

"But tastes do change. And it's only natural that being given a second lease of life would lead to wanting new experiences. To live as much as possible. Trying new books and music is part of that."

"But there's strange dreams, memories of things that haven't happened, yet they all turn out to have happened to the donors."

"People experience the same things all the time without knowing it. Not many experiences are brand-new."

"I felt such a bond with Nathan. Like we were connected somehow."

"And he felt this too? This connection."

At Nathan's house, I'd been in a daze during dinner as I twirled spaghetti around my fork, and I'd left as soon as he'd cleared the plates. We hadn't swapped numbers, and I'd sent him a Facebook friend request this morning but he hasn't responded. Tom and Amanda haven't been in touch either. These people I feel tied to have let me go so easily. Is it all in my head? I ignore Vanessa's question and press forward.

"What about my episodes? The fear? The panic? The things I think I can see? It's like they've happened before. What if they have, but not to me? To Callie? It's a possibility, isn't it? I'm not going mad, am I?"

"You're not mad, Jenna, but you have been through an incredibly harrowing experience and you're on very strong medication. Your mental health has suffered. Understandably so. We've talked about relaxation, haven't we?"

I ignore her question. "What about my dream? Playing Poohsticks on the bridge. The picnic."

"I think everyone has played Poohsticks at some stage. It's probably an old memory resurfacing from when you were small."

I didn't have sex in a cornfield when I was small, I think, but I can't tell her that part of my dream. It's too embarrassing.

"So why would I have remembered it now? Just before I met Nathan?" No matter what Vanessa says it doesn't make sense.

"Who knows? There are lots of things that can cause the subconscious to nudge something back to the conscious mind. A smell. A sound. A feeling."

"It's too coincidental." I lean forward, pulling the sleeves of Sam's green fleece over my hands, resting my elbows on my knees that jig up and down.

"That's often how memories are recalled. Subtly. Have you ever seen one of Derren Brown's shows? He uses triggers to coax the mind in a certain direction. He knows what people are going to say and do because he's engineered their response. Planted visual and auditory stimuli. It's not unlikely that your memories were triggered the same way."

"But I don't think they are my memories. I think they're Callie's. The dreams when I'm on the beach with another little girl—I think that's Sophie. Her mum had paintings on the wall of girls on a beach. The picnic. The man. That must be Nathan."

"Let's suppose for a minute you are dreaming Callie's memories." Vanessa's face is neutral, and I know she is humoring me. "What does she feel? With this man? This little girl?"

"Happy."

"Would you consider the possibility that your deep-rooted guilt with regard to Callie's death could be manifesting in your dreams? Showing you she had a happy life to help ease your conscience?"

I think about this for a moment; it does seem plausible. "But it feels so real. I believe she's trying to tell me something but it's so muddled. The dreams are happy but the snippets of memories that flash when I am awake are so dark. She was scared of something. Or someone. I'm sure."

"Do you feel scared, Jenna? Not Callie. You."

"Sometimes."

"And the dreams you are having. Let's take the one of you playing on the beach. How did that make you feel?"

"Less lonely," I admit. Growing up I'd always wanted a sibling. "And..." I trail off. My face flushes as I think of some of the other dreams I've had with the man in them. I don't want to tell Vanessa that I can still feel his warm fingers on my skin when I wake and my body burns with the desire to be touched. Could it be just my subconscious whispering to me? Cellular Memory seemed so real to me an hour ago. Now I'm not so sure.

"Are you lonely?"

"No. Yes. A bit, I suppose."

"The world can seem a scary place when you're already feeling alone. All of the emotions you're feeling are entirely yours, Jenna. You have to own them in order to move forward. You've been through a very difficult time. You nearly died. Your relationship with Sam broke down. Your parents have separated. Any one of those incidents on their own can cause severe stress. All of them together, it's no wonder you're fraught."

"But Callie . . ."

"Becoming fixated on Callie is not going to help you. My heart goes out to her family, it really does," Vanessa says. "It's very commendable donating organs but you need to find a way to make peace with what's happened. Callie would have died anyway, whether she donated or not. This . . ." She taps her pen against my notes. "This is why we try to discourage any contact other than a thank-you letter. It's too emotional. For everyone. I strongly advise against having any more contact with her family. I don't want to sound uncaring but you're my main priority, Jenna. You have to put your own emotional well-being first."

"But my picnic dream . . ." I'm wavering now. "I couldn't stand strawberries before I had that dream. Now I can't stop eating them."

"Tastes change as we get older. I used to parcel my Brussels sprouts in a tissue and hide them in my pocket but now I love them."

"It's hardly the same thing."

"I'm not a dietician, but cravings can be triggered by hormone imbalances and deficiencies. Your body knows what it needs. Strawberries are a healthy choice and not something to worry about."

"But . . . listening to Abba."

"Now that may be something to worry about." Vanessa winks at me to show she's joking and then puts her clipboard and pen on the table in front of her. "Sorry, Jenna. The session has flown past. I know you're concerned and I do take it seriously. Journal your thoughts, make a note of anything else you think is strange, and bring it along next week. We'll go through it together. In the meantime, please try to relax."

She stands, and I know I'm not going to find the answers I need here. She doesn't believe me. But something's happening to me and I'm determined to find out what.

As I turn to walk out of the door she says: "Let Callie go, Jenna."

But what if Callie won't let me go? I want to ask. But I don't. And an icy chill brushes against the back of my neck.

CHAPTER NINETEEN

As I leave Vanessa's office I am deep in thought. She doesn't believe me. And now, I am doubting myself. Last night, as I'd read up on other recipients' accounts, I'd been so certain tissue could retain memory but like Vanessa said, I suppose we are all on the same medication. Could we be experiencing similar side effects? As I step off the curb to cross the road, brakes squeal and a horn blasts. I'm frozen in place as a man sticks his furious red face out of his car window and yells, "Watch where you're going, you stupid bitch," as he swerves around me. Suddenly, a middle-aged woman yanks me back onto the path.

"Are you OK, dear?" she asks.

Panic rises as she continues to hold my arm. The feeling of being restrained hitting like a punch as though it has happened before. Did this happen to Callie? Or am I delusional? I pull away from her grip but I can't breathe properly. There's not enough air. Everything seems too bright. Too loud. My underarms prickle and I'm hit by a desperate need to get away. I feel alone. Utterly, hopelessly, irrevocably alone, and there's only one place I want to be.

* * *

Sam's car is outside his mum's house. He's been staying here ever since we split up. I hover outside the garden gate, my fingers gripping the cool metal latch, but I don't lift it. I haven't seen Kathy since Sam and I separated, and I'm not sure what sort of welcome I'll get.

A thumping on the window draws my gaze upward. Harry, Sam's half-brother, waving from his bedroom, and the nerves I feel at being spotted are dampened by a flood of relief that I can't just go home now.

The front door swings open. Sam, wearing his suit trousers, sleeves of his white shirt rolled up, and I know his tie will be stuffed in his jacket pocket. He can't have been home long or he'd be in T-shirt and jeans. His big toe pokes through his black sock, and I feel a tug of sadness as I realize if things were different I would have been his wife, looking after him, darning his socks. Chiding myself for romanticizing I try to pull myself together. I've never darned anything in my life.

"Hey you," he says.

"I've brought your fleece back. I know it's one of your favorites." I fiddle with the drawstring toggle at the bottom but I don't make any move to take it off.

"Do you want to come in? Say hello to Mum?"

I hesitate but I'm yearning for a semblance of normality, even if it's only for an hour, and I step inside. I'm barely through the door when Harry torpedoes himself into my arms. Resting my chin on the top of his head I inhale the scent of his lemon and lime shampoo.

"I've missed you, Jenna."

"I've missed you too."

"Then you should have come to visit."

"I should. Stupid, aren't I?" Stepping back, I pull a face and he giggles. Harry is only seven and was the result of Kathy's brief relationship with a younger man who hasn't wanted anything to do with her or his child.

In the kitchen, Kathy is on her knees, twisting the dial on the oven and pressing the ignition button, and there's the whoosh of a flame. My stomach rolls as she stands and faces me. I tense as I wait for her reaction, but although exhaustion is imprinted onto her face and there are creases around her eyes that I'm sure weren't there a few months ago, she looks genuinely happy to see me.

"Stopping for dinner?" Kathy asks as though it hasn't been months since I have seen her.

"I'd love to."

"Roll your sleeves up then, girl." She grins and it's like old times. Harry measuring out orange squash into glasses; Kathy rummaging through the freezer pulling out random bags of things that might make up a meal. Smiley face potatoes and toad-in-the-hole. Sam opens a can of baked beans, and I hold a frozen chocolate gateau over a bowl of warm water, hoping it will defrost a little quicker. "Hungry Like the Wolf" blares out of a radio that's always tuned to a "hits of the '80s" station. It feels like home. As we squeeze around the tiny kitchen table it occurs to me I haven't thought of Callie once since I got here and there's a flash of guilt as I realize it's a relief.

We chat through the meal and after we've eaten the edge of the gateau—the middle is still ice—Sam washes up, and Harry tells me he's now collecting Lego Star Wars and he thunders upstairs to fetch his models.

Kathy and me move into the lounge. She yawns. Tendrils of hair have escaped her ponytail and she tucks them behind her ears. "Harry wants to meet his dad," she tells me.

"Oh." I'm not quite sure what to say. She's never talked about him to me before, and Sam almost never mentions him; if he does, he calls him "The Tosser."

"It had to happen, of course, but the odd question has turned into an almost constant demand."

"What are you going to do?"

"I thought it only fair I text him, loser that he is, and let him know his son was asking questions. I thought I'd test the water but he didn't reply and he stopped paying maintenance shortly after. He used to always let me know when he was going to stick some cash through the letter box—he doesn't do banks." She makes quote marks in the air with her fingers. "He was always careful Harry wasn't around to spot him. I don't think he ever thought Harry might want to meet him. Maybe he's done a runner."

"Have you called him?"

"Yes. For weeks, the number rang and rang and now it's disconnected. I've had to take on extra cleaning work to make up the money. I'm knackered."

"What have you said to Harry?"

"What can I say? I can hardly tell the truth. His dad was just a stupid fling. He didn't want a baby. He acted like a child himself. I've seen him in the past driving around in a convertible with a girl practically young enough to be his daughter in the passenger seat. They stopped at a red light and he snogged her face off. I felt like telling her she could do better. To his credit, at least he'd always provided financially for Harry, even if he didn't want a relationship with him. But now ..."

"Isn't there an organization that collects child support? Have you contacted them?"

"There's no point. He's always said he's self-employed.

An entrepreneur. If there's no employer to collect from there's little they can do."

Before she can say any more Harry staggers into the room, arms laden with models, and I sit cross-legged on the floor to admire them all and help rebuild the pieces that fell off as he carried them down the stairs. Harry's beaten me at Dr. Who Top Trumps three times when I tell him it's time for me to leave.

"Can I come and see the animals at work again, Jenna? *Pleeease!*" Harry wraps his arms around my legs.

"Is that OK?" I ask Kathy.

"Of course."

"Sunday morning?" I know we've got a couple of weekend stays booked in.

"Lovely. I'll see you then."

"I'll drive you home," Sam says.

"It's OK. I'll walk." I can't risk being in the car alone with Sam again. Kissing him. It isn't fair. To either of us.

On the doorstep, we stand awkwardly before leaning forward and giving each other a one-armed hug, trying not to let our bodies touch.

I step outside and I'm alone again. The clouds blacken and scud across the sky. There's a bite in the air and I'm glad I have forgotten to give Sam his fleece back.

* * *

I'm halfway home when the heavens open and I'm pelted with cold, fat raindrops. Inside the flat I scoop an envelope from the doormat and carry it into the bedroom, pull Sam's sodden fleece over my head, peel off my jeans, dropping them in the overflowing laundry basket in the corner of my bedroom. Sitting on the corner of my bed I rip open the envelope that arrived in the post.

Dear Jenna,

*Thank you so much for coming to see us. We knew
of course a piece of Callie lived on but meeting you
has made it real somehow. Our daughter saved a
life and we feel immensely proud of her. We both felt
such a bond with you.*

*Next Saturday will be Callie's birthday. I suppose
I should say would have been, shouldn't I? I'm not
sure if I'll ever get used to that. We didn't want to
put you on the spot by asking you this by phone but
we will be going to lay flowers on Callie's grave
first thing and we'd really like it if you could join
us later in the day to celebrate the life of our little
girl. It would make all the difference knowing that
a part of Callie is there with us.*

*Yours,
Tom and Amanda*

By the time I've read the letter twice I'm shivering. Pulling
open my wardrobe to find some dry clothes I can't help taking out the wooden box and cradling it to my chest. How do
Tom and Amanda cope with the loss they've experienced?
The box is closed, the wood is thick, but I don't have to
open the lid to see what's in there. I do that every time I
close my eyes. What would Sam say if he knew what was
inside? I can't imagine. Kneeling, I carefully put the box
away, covering it with one of my scarves.

Another evening in. On the kitchen table I line up my
tablets the way I'd once have lined up shots, and I swallow the first dose of the ridiculous number of pills I need

to make sure I stay alive, washing them down with a glass of tepid water. Callie stares at me reproachfully from her photos that cover the walls. I don't know what to think. I'd been so sure before I talked to Vanessa that this heart—her heart—must feel some of the things she felt.

It's hard to settle. In the lounge, I light a coconut candle, which always conjures images of lying on a golden beach, trickling hot sand between my fingers. Ben Howard sings "Only Love." I'm sketching as my thoughts run free, my fingers flying across the page almost of their own accord, and as I glance down at the paper I am shocked to see I have drawn a girl, her knee is raised, and her opposite arm, bent at ninety degrees, is thrust forward as though she is running. She's twisting her head to look behind her and on her face is a look of absolute horror. That isn't what has shocked me though, it's the fact the girl looks just like me.

CHAPTER TWENTY

I push the lollipop stick and feather into the turret. A flag of sorts. Pebbles mark the windows and the doors. There are loads of other kids on the beach but I think our castle is the best. Sand flies everywhere as you dig a moat, landing in my eyes, my mouth, my hair.

"Stop it," I say.

"Stop what?" you ask, rocking back on your heels.

I glare at you but I can't keep a straight face. Your body blocks out most of the wooden owl behind you but it looks as though his wings are sprouting from the sides of your body. You look like an angel with your long blond hair shimmering in the sun, and I giggle as I grab my bucket.

"Let's fill up the moat. Last one to the sea's a loser."

I hang back, giving you a head start. Your legs pump furiously, bucket in one hand, spade in the other, and as your feet splash into the ocean, I am right behind you.

The ice water slows me down, and I lick saltwater from my lips, laughing at the shock on your face.

I bounce on my toes and curl my knees up to my chest, submerging myself in the not-quite-blue sea. My hair fans around my shoulders, and I allow myself to fall backward, starfish out my arms and legs, and float. Water roars in my ears, and I feel detached from everything as I focus on the clouds. I can see a dragon, a pig, a castle.

I lower my legs, feet flailing until they touch the seabed, gritty and slimy, and I turn to you.

"Try it," I say. "It's like being a fish."

You shake your head. You've always had a fear of getting your face wet, even in the bath, and when Mum washes your hair, you wear goggles. You can't swim and won't even try.

I stand behind you and squeeze my hands into your armpits.

"Lay back," I say.

"I'm scared," you whisper.

"Don't be scared. I'll catch you. I'll always catch you."

CHAPTER TWENTY-ONE

The weather is foul. It hasn't dried up overnight and the clouds are still gray and swollen. As I walk to work freezing raindrops gust into my face. I wipe my eyes with my fingertips and they come away dark where I've smudged my mascara, and I can't help thinking about Callie's black eye. Was it really caused by walking into a cupboard at work? A thought occurs. I could find out by visiting the dental surgery she worked at and asking the staff. Water has pooled by the side of the road and a car speeds past, instantly saturating me. Irritated, I switch my thoughts to something happier. The beach dream I had last night with the two little girls. Despite the science Vanessa throws at me I still secretly believe it is Callie and Sophie, and thinking of Callie's happier times lifts my bad mood.

Pushing open the door to the surgery I'm thrilled to see John in reception with Linda.

"How's retired life?" I ask as I step forward to give him a hug, but the expression on his face stops me.

"Jenna. Can we see you in the office, please?"

Dropping my bag, I follow John. Linda shuts the office

door behind us before bustling around the desk to her chair and sinking into it with a sigh.

"After you left yesterday we had a complaint from a Mr. Freeman." John stands behind Linda resting his hand on her shoulder but she shrugs him off.

"Who?"

"He's just moved to the area. He rang with an emergency. His cat had been run over. He was told there weren't any appointments."

"Who did he speak to?" We have a policy of including our names when we answer the phone.

"He said he spoke to you, Jenna, and that he was very distressed he couldn't be seen but you told him it wasn't our problem and put the phone down."

"Me?" I lean forward in my chair. "He said he spoke to me? I've never heard of him."

"Are you sure?" John says. "Linda tells me you've been very...distracted."

"Positive," I say. The medication might make me forgetful but it doesn't make me rude. "You believe me, don't you?"

There's a beat before Linda says: "He may have misheard the name. Let's not dwell on it then," but as I get up to leave she can't meet my eye. We all know that Jenna doesn't sound remotely like Kelly or Rachel and it stings that they might not trust me. This job is the thread linking me to my old life and if it's severed I really don't know what I'd do.

"Perhaps it was Kelly pretending to be me?" I haven't time to filter the words that spring from my lips.

"And why would she do that?" There is no trace of the usual warmth in John's voice.

"To get me into trouble? You said she wanted more hours?"

Linda looks at me with an expression on her face that looks like sorrow. "Kelly's a lovely girl. Jenna, we're worried about you. You're so preoccupied. Even when you're here it seems your mind is somewhere else."

"Sorry. I'll be more careful. I promise."

Linda and John exchange a look before John says: "Back to work then, but if there's anything you need to talk about, anything we can do to help you, you know where we are." And as I leave their office, pulling the door behind me, their voices are low and muted and I know they're talking about me, and as I pass Kelly in the corridor I can't help glaring at her.

* * *

The next time the phone rings I am extra polite as I answer.

"Hello, Jenna," says a voice that is warm and familiar. "It's Nathan. I wanted to check you were OK? After Monday? I've been kicking myself for not taking your mobile number and I'm hopeless on social media, but I remembered where you worked. Hope you don't mind me calling?"

"No. I'm fine. Embarrassed but fine."

"I was wondering..." I hear the tremor in his voice. "I remember you saying you don't work Fridays and I'm owed some hours. Would you like to meet for a walk along the canal?"

I hesitate, but only for a second.

"Yes."

* * *

The flame on the Yankee Candle glows orange and the flat is soon fragrant with cinnamon. Lifting the cushions off the sofa one by one, I thump them to plumpness, wanting everything to be perfect when Rachel arrives. She used to come around once a week while Sam was bowling but that petered out after I fell ill. I've missed it.

Often during our girls' nights in we'd binge-watch trash TV. Picking apart *Don't Tell the Bride*, screeching at the groom's choices. Tonight, the TV will remain blank and silent. There's such a lot to talk about, it's not always easy to snatch time to chat at the surgery. I scroll through Spotify trying to find something we'll both like, settling on Ellie Goulding. "Anything Could Happen" drifts out of the speakers and I sing along as I straighten the rug.

When the doorbell rings I rush to answer it, enveloping Rachel in a hug as though I hadn't left her at work only hours before. Her hair is shower damp, the smell of the surgery replaced with the sweetness of pear shampoo.

"Sorry." She thrusts a carrier bag toward me and bottles chink together. "It's Aldi. I'm too skint for Tesco—how depressing is that?" But she smiles as she steps through the door. Nothing brings her down for long.

"You needn't have brought anything." But I'm glad she has. I'd meant to call into the supermarket on the way home but I'd forgotten. "Go and make yourself comfortable in the lounge and I'll bring some drinks in."

I don't realize Rachel has followed me into the kitchen until I hear her say: "What the fuck, Jenna?"

Her bag thuds to the floor as she stands in the middle of the kitchen, turning 360 degrees, her mouth hanging open in shock as she takes in the photos of Callie, the scribbles on my Post-it notes, the sheets of information about Cellular Memory.

"I know it's a mess." I empty the carrier bag of the bottles she's brought, rosé wine for her, sparkling elderflower for me, and I take two glasses out of the cupboard. "But there is a logic to it." Pulling open a bag of sea-salt crisps I shake them into a bowl, and I can't resist popping one into my mouth.

"This..." She stares at me as I lick salt from my fingertips. "This isn't normal, Jen."

"Having someone else's heart transplanted into your body isn't normal, Rachel. You know I wanted to find out what happened to Callie. For Tom and Amanda?"

"Yes. But..." She gestures toward the pictures.

I've never known her lost for words before, and I feel annoyed that she's being so judgmental. She stoops in front of the fridge, studying the swirling lines of my mind map. I wait for her to speak.

"Christ," she says, finally, straightening up, and I grab my drink from the worktop and sticky cordial splashes over my fingers.

"Come through," I say, picking up the crisps and striding from the room.

In the lounge, Rachel sits heavily on the chair and gulps from her glass, draining it in seconds before glugging more wine.

"Callie's fiancé, Nathan, rang me today."

I can't wait to tell her I'm meeting him on Friday, but I wait for her flurry of questions.

Instead, she quietly says: "Jen, I think you need to talk to someone."

"I was hoping to talk to you, tonight." My enthusiasm for having her here begins to wane.

"I mean someone who deals with...well, in mental health. Vanessa?"

"I'm not mad." Hurt she thinks I might be. I haven't even told her yet about the episodes I'm experiencing, and loneliness wraps itself around me like a cloak as I know I won't be able to now.

"I don't think you are mad." She speaks slower than usual as though choosing each word carefully. "But you've been under a lot of pressure: the operation, Sam, returning to work."

"Work is stressful." I clutch at the opportunity to steer the conversation onto a subject that isn't Callie, or my state of mind. "What do you think of Kelly?"

"She's lovely. Young, of course. But eager to pitch in with whatever needs doing."

"I think she might be trying to get me sacked."

The disbelief on Rachel's face says far more than her words ever could. The gulf between us widens. The sense of loss is jagged and raw.

"Forget I said that," I quickly say. "Shall we watch some TV?"

Turning off the music I aim the remote control, channel-hopping until I find an old episode of *Say Yes to the Dress*. We watch in silence, crisps untouched, as the bride squeals in delight at a delicate heart-shaped pendant and bracelet set. Sam bought me a bracelet just like it one Valentine's, and I carry it around in the zipped pocket of my handbag every day so it's always close to me. Now I wear a medical ID bracelet, and I miserably fiddle with the clasp. When the program ends barely an hour later Rachel stands to leave.

"Are you working tomorrow?"

"Just for the morning," I say.

"And afterward? Will you speak to Vanessa? For me?"

"I'll think about it," I say but I've got no intention of ringing Vanessa tomorrow afternoon. I'm going to call into Callie's dental practice and meet her colleagues. I am determined to find out whether the bruise on Callie's face was really caused by her walking into a cupboard at work, or if there is another explanation.

CHAPTER TWENTY-TWO

We shelter under the wing of the giant wooden owl. Fat raindrops bounce off the gravel and fog hangs low in the sky blanketing the steely sea.

"Ready?" I ask, and I pull the hood of your raincoat over your head and tighten the cord under your chin so the howling wind outside doesn't force it back down.

We hold hands as we sprint toward the arcade, sandals splashing through puddles, the bottom of our dresses soaking wet. Inside, I unzip your coat and you shake your head like a dog and droplets of water cascade over the machine nearest the door.

"That one." You point, and I press a handful of coins into your palm and watch as you slot a ten pence piece into the machine. I curl my hand around the cold metal lever and steer the giant metal claws left and right, back and forward, until you squeal and clap as they hover above Piglet. The crane shudders as it lowers, and you clap your hands with excitement as Piglet is lifted by his feet, and I am triumphant. Just as he is nearly ours Piglet slithers from the grasp of the claws and tumbles down to nestle with the other unobtainable prizes. You burst into noisy tears.

I placate you with fluffy pink candyfloss, and while you pull bits off with your fingers and stuff it in your mouth I go to the kiosk and swap all my pocket money for a cuddly toy. I tell you I've won it just for you. You flash a smile and wrap your arms around my waist and tell me I always make things better for you. Always. And I promise I always will.

CHAPTER TWENTY-THREE

"Earth to Jenna." Linda waves her hand in front of my face and I start. I'd been thinking about Callie again.

"Sorry. Did you say something?"

"The insulin I asked you to order in for Casper—where is it?"

"Isn't it in the stockroom?"

"I couldn't see it. Did it definitely come?"

"It must have." But I don't remember seeing it. "Kelly?"

Kelly turns. She's restocking the shelves with the plastic dog chews molded into grinning mouths.

"Did you take delivery of the insulin?"

"No."

I push my chair back. "I'll go and check. It must be here somewhere. Perhaps Rachel has moved it?" I haven't seen her all morning, and I think she might be avoiding me after last night.

Kelly slides into my seat as I stand up, and taps the keyboard. "I'll check the order system."

"Do you have a log-in?" I begin to recite mine.

"I've got my own." She frowns at the screen. "I helped

with the orders when you were off. There's no record of insulin being requested this week."

"I'm sure . . . I'm sorry." I cover my hot cheeks with my palms.

"Not to worry, I'll give Greenacres a call and see if they've got any spare," Linda says but she doesn't smile and there's an edge to her voice.

I don't blame her. I'm making so many mistakes lately. A couple of days ago the medication I'd left in one of the treatment rooms for the kitten with intestinal parasites was double the dose of his weight. I could have killed him, and I am filled with horror whenever I think of it.

"Don't worry, Jenna. I can go and collect it." Kelly smiles brightly and I shoot her a look.

Linda thinks she's so bloody perfect. But is she? It's not hard to delete an order on the system. Suspicion flows through my veins causing my blood to heat, my muscles to tense. Is it really me making all the mistakes? My mind is filled with gaping black holes where my memories should be. I wish I'd talked about it properly with Rachel last night.

The bell tinkles as the door opens and a lady steps inside, dragging a reluctant poodle on a lead. The dog plants his feet on the floor, throws back his fluffy white head and howls, and I feel like howling with him. Checking my watch, I see there's another hour to go before I finish at lunchtime, and the sounds of the surgery grow fainter as I drift off back into thought.

* * *

It doesn't take long to reach the dental surgery where Callie worked, and as I walk through the car park I notice how expensive the cars are: a black BMW, a silver Mercedes, and a bright yellow sports car that looks as though it could be a convertible. I wonder whether dentists earn more than vets.

Pushing open the heavy front door I'm hit by the smell of cloves, and I hear the muffled buzzing of a drill. I used to dread the dentist when I was small. I had a filling once and was so terrified of the injection I'd shake each time I got the reminder for my annual check-up. The amount of blood tests I've had now I barely notice each time sharp needles penetrate my skin.

The reception is stark white with a glossy green rubber plant towering in the corner. A toddler kneels on the floor pulling toys out of a blue plastic box, squealing with delight as he finds Thomas the Tank Engine.

"Can I help?" I'm so transfixed by the whiteness of the receptionist's teeth I forget to speak until she repeats the question.

"Yes. Sorry. I'm not a patient here yet but my regular dentist is on maternity leave and I wondered if anyone could squeeze me in here today. My gums bleed a lot and I'm really worried."

"I'll have a look but I think we're pretty busy." She cups her hand over the computer mouse and shakes it and her screen springs to life. "Is there no one else at your surgery that could see you?"

"They're all busy. I want to register here anyway. My cousin used to work here and I've heard such good things."

"Really?" She looks up. "Who is your cousin?"

"Callie. Callie Valentine." I can hardly believe what I'm saying.

"Oh my god. I'm so sorry. I'm Sara. I was quite good friends with Callie. Did she ..."

"Sara!" I remember the photo I'd found online and I

hazard a guess. "You did the fun run with her for Cancer Research?"

"Yes!"

I breathe a sigh of relief.

"We were all so shocked to hear what happened. Look, let me ask Chris. He's on his lunch break but I'm sure he'll see you. He had a real soft spot for Callie." She pushes a piece of paper and a pen across the desk. "Fill in these forms so I can register you as a patient."

"Thanks." As she speaks on the phone I scan the posters on oral hygiene stuck to the walls but the words seem to blur into one. What am I doing? Lying. I'm bound to get caught out.

"He's on his way down," Sara says, and seconds later footsteps pound down the stairs.

A man around my age wearing a white lab coat bursts into reception.

"This is Chris," Sara says.

"Hello," I say, and after a few awkward moments he says: "You look like her. Like Callie." There's a catch in his voice. He's staring at my hair as though committing every strand to memory. I shift my weight from foot to foot, uncomfortable under his scrutiny.

"Not really." I raise my hand and touch my head. "It's the red hair. It's very distinctive. Thanks for seeing me without an appointment. It's really good of you. I don't know if Sara explained . . ." I'm gabbling. Filling the silence between us.

"Yes. You're worried about your gums. Come on up and I'll take a look." He turns and I follow him up the steep stairs and into his room, where I drape my bag and jacket over the coat stand in the corner.

I ask if I can use the loo before we start. I splash my face with cold water. I'm unnerved and I'm not sure if it's his reaction to me, or being in Callie's workplace that's making my breath come a little faster, my cheeks feel a little warmer.

Back in his room, Chris gestures toward the huge black chair and hands me a plastic apron to cover my clothes.

"Were you close to her? Callie?" I ask, desperate to fill the silence.

"You're her cousin?"

"Yes." I falter. "She talked about you. Of course . . ." I trail off and tie the apron straps around my waist as I gaze around the room, shiny white and chrome. There's a corkboard hanging from the wall, a jumble of photos and postcards pinned with multicolored tacks. In the center is a photo of Chris and Callie, cheeks pressed together, smiling at the camera.

"Work barbecue." Chris follows my eyeline. "So how long have your gums been bleeding?"

"A few months." I tell him what medication I'm on but I don't say what for.

"That's usual, I think, but you did the right thing calling in. It's better to be safe than sorry, isn't it?"

I sit down as Chris snaps on plastic gloves. The chair whirrs as it tilts back, and as Chris picks up a stainless-steel instrument, which glints in the glare of the overhead light, I close my eyes and stretch my mouth wide open. I am conscious of a dribble of saliva that trickles down my chin. Sharp metal scrapes against my teeth and pokes my gums, and I try to concentrate on the radio in the background. It is tuned to a classical station.

"I think the bleeding is an inevitable side effect of the drugs but everything looks good otherwise. Make another appointment for six months and we'll keep an eye on it."

The chair whirrs again and I'm sitting upright, blinking at the brightness and swooshing pink liquid around my mouth and spitting into a stainless-steel bowl that gurgles and hisses. Chris pulls off his gloves and drops them into a wastepaper bin by his feet.

"I'm sorry about Callie. I was very fond of her. We all were."

There's a tap at the door.

"That's my next patient," Chris says, and I'm disappointed I haven't been able to ask him any questions.

"Thanks for squeezing me in," I say.

"You're welcome. See you again."

Downstairs, I rummage through my bag for my purse and wait while Sara bags up an orange toothbrush with a lion on the handle and a tube of toothpaste with strawberries on it for the toddler I saw on my way in.

"Look. Doggie." The little boy points at his sticker of Scooby-Doo, and I tell him I didn't get a sticker, that he must have been a really good boy, and he beams in delight.

"How did it go?" Sara asks me once they leave.

"All good," I say. "Sara, do any of the staff here live in Woodhaven?"

"Goodness. No. That would be a bit of a trek over here, wouldn't it? Why do you ask?"

"It's where Callie had her accident. We're not sure why she was there. We're desperate to find out."

"I've no idea. Sorry."

"Is there anyone who might know? We don't really know her friends; you know what it's like with family. You don't always share everything. Who did she hang around with?"

"Just Nathan, I think. We used to tease about it a bit, in a friendly way, but it was sweet. The way they were always together. He often dropped her at work and picked her up if their schedules matched. 'Wish I had a man like that,' I said more than once."

"How did she seem to you? In the days before she died?"

"Let me think." Sara screws her face up. "She was off sick on the Monday. Some sort of bug. Nathan rang, wanting to speak to her, so it must have come on suddenly after he left for work if he didn't know she was at home. When she came back she looked awful, really pale. She had a black eye too. She said she'd slipped getting out of the shower. 'You shouldn't be here,' I said. 'You'll only pass it on and I don't want to be throwing up for my birthday next weekend. If I catch it, I'll kill you.' " She lowers her gaze. "If I'd known she was going to . . . Well, I'd never have said that."

"It's just an expression. Please don't feel bad. She'd hate that," I say, as if I really knew her.

"She wouldn't go home. She was too conscientious. She never liked taking time off. I made sure she didn't do too much that week and I made a bit of a fuss of her. I even brought some homemade soup in but Nathan came and met her for lunch every day so she never got to have any."

Like Tom, Sara seems to think Nathan really looked after Callie but it almost sounds a little obsessive to me.

"I'm sure she appreciated the thought."

"I hope so." Sara sniffs. "Anyway, how are her parents? Sophie?"

"Tom and Amanda are coping as best they can but Sophie's not here. She's been in Spain for months but no one has heard from her."

"I suppose Sophie getting away is not a bad thing considering."

"Considering what?"

Sara's face colors. "She used to drink in the Prince of

Wales; you know the pub on Green Street? Didn't you know? She went a bit off the rails. Callie wasn't happy about some of the crowd she was hanging out with."

"I'll pop in there on my way home and see if anyone has heard from her. Thanks."

"Hang on a sec, I've remembered something." She turns and rifles through a drawer and when she turns back to me she passes me a clear plastic bag containing a chunky Nokia mobile phone. "I found this when I was clearing out Callie's drawer. She had an iPhone so it wasn't her current one. It hardly seemed worth bothering her parents with. It's such an old handset, it's probably been there for donkey's years. It doesn't switch on anyway. There were some Kit Kats too but I ate them. Is that terrible? We used to share."

"She wouldn't mind." I'm beginning to believe I really did know her.

I take the phone. Even though Sara has told me the battery is flat I can't help pressing the button, but the screen remains dark.

As I leave the surgery, clutching the phone against my chest, I am conscious of eyes burning hot into the back of my head and I turn and look up at the consultation rooms. Chris's shadow looms in the window.

CHAPTER TWENTY-FOUR

After leaving the dentist I call into the Carphone Ware-house and pick up a charger for the phone Sara gave me, but rather than going straight home I head toward the pub Sophie used to drink in, hoping to catch the crowd calling in for an after-work drink. Someone must have heard from her. Imagine how delighted Tom and Amanda will be if I can contact Sophie and convince her to come home.

The Prince of Wales looks as far removed from royalty as you can get. The chipped and faded sign depicting a crown creaks in the wind and the single-paned windows vibrate with the sound of heavy rock music. Motorbikes line up against the curb like soldiers, shiny chrome and slick black seats. It's still early. The sky is peppered with smudges of indigo and gray as the moon and sun occupy the same space. I peep through the cracked glass panel in the door; the pub is surprisingly busy for the time of day. I take in the row of silver tankards hanging above the bar but when there's a roar I step back hurriedly, my ankle turning in the process, but the door remains closed. As I peep inside once again I notice the TV hanging from the far wall, silently showing a football match while a couple of guys jeer at the screen.

"You going in or what?" I jump at the growling voice behind me and stutter my apologies, standing aside and letting the man push past me into the pub. As the door swings open the smell of stale beer rushes toward me. I follow the customer inside, my ankle throbbing as I walk.

It might be my imagination but as I stand at the bar it seems the chatter in the pub quiets. There's a chill on the back of my neck as though someone is standing beside me, softly breathing, but as I swing around no one is there. My hand is shaking as I pull a ten pound note out of my purse and wait for the barman to notice me. The thwack of pool balls behind me makes me jump and all at once everything seems loud. Too loud. Coins clatter from a fruit machine and sweat trickles between my shoulder blades. The urge to run away, back to the safety of my own flat, is all-consuming, and I don't notice the barman standing before me until he slams both palms down on the bar.

"You deaf or something? I am talking English, right, Neil?"

The guy on the stool to my right sniggers. "Yeah. I understand you, Steve."

I open my mouth to speak but my words are stuck to the dry roof of my mouth.

"Do. You. Want. A. Drink?" Steve asks.

My face is burning now but as I think of Tom and Amanda my sense of unease pales into comparison against their loss. I can do this. I lick my lips and swallow hard.

"Lemon and lime." I look him in the eye. "Please," I add as he doesn't move.

"And do you want a straw with your lemon and lime?"

I start to answer but Neil twists his head to look at me and says: "Perhaps she wants a cherry and an umbrella," and I know they're laughing at me. The hope I'd felt that I could find some answers here seeps from my body, sapping the strength from my muscles as it leaves. I scrape a stool toward me and sit.

My drink is banged on the bar in front of me and it spills over the side of the glass. Steve's stare is challenging, almost daring me to say something. Lowering my eyes, I pick up a beer towel to mop up the puddle but the material is hard and crusty and I drop it and wipe my fingers on my jeans. My lemonade is flat and warm but the zing from the lime revitalizes me. I straighten my spine and raise my head, pushing my drink back across the bar.

"I'd like some ice."

There's a beat and then a ghost of a smile flickers over Steve's face. Neil roars with laughter and drags his stool closer to me, bringing the ice bucket with him. He stinks of oil and stale smoke, and I suppress the urge to recoil.

"I've not seen you here before?" Neil unzips his black hoodie and shrugs it off. His hands are filthy and dark hair springs from the pale skin on his forearms. He lifts the lid on the bucket and scoops up ice cubes with his fingers, and I try not to grimace as he plops them into my drink. Pushing the thought of the dirt under his nails out of my mind I smile gratefully and pick up my glass, even though I can't bring myself to take a sip.

"I've just moved here," I lie. "My friend used to drink here. So I thought I'd try it out."

"Oh?" He raises his pint of ale and sips. A frothy mustache covers his top lip, and he wipes it off with the back of his hand. "Who's your friend?"

"Her name's Sophie."

"I don't know anyone of that name. We get lots of girls in here."

"Hang on." I remember the photo Tom had given me, and I take it out of my purse and show it to Neil.

"That's Sophie, on the left. Do you know her?"

"No. And I've drunk here for years." His expression is unreadable as he stares at me, and I shift uncomfortably, bracing my feet against the floor as my bottom slides across the wooden stool. I start to put the photo back in my bag but he plucks it out of my hand.

"Steve," he hollers. "This girl is friends with someone called Sophie, who apparently used to drink here." He dangles the photo between his fingers. "You've been here longer than me. Do you know her?"

"Nope," Steve says without even turning and looking.

"So where is she? This friend of yours?" He leans toward me as he speaks. His breath reeks of onions.

"I don't know." His scrutiny is making my skin crawl. "She's not really a friend."

"But you carry a photo of her around? She must be quite important to you? You look a bit like her sister." His tone has changed now as he studies me.

"How do you know Callie is Sophie's sister if you don't know her?" I challenge.

"You must have said."

"I don't think I did." I try to replay our conversation in my mind, but I've been so nervous already the details are sketchy.

"Are you calling me a liar?" Any pretense of friendliness is gone as he stares at me, eyes narrowed.

"No. Of course not." I grab the photo and open my bag but my hands are shaking and it slips from my grasp and the contents spill over the floor. Crouching down I slap my palm over a tampon that's rolling away, wishing the ground would open up and swallow me.

"You're from Forest Gate? Not very local then?" Neil has opened my purse and is reading my ID.

"That was from before I moved," I lie as I snatch it back from him and stuff it into my bag, rising. "Is there a toilet here?" Perhaps I can slip out of a fire exit.

He jerks his head toward the back of the pub, and I rush toward the darkened doorway, the soles of my shoes sticking to the wooden floor with each and every step.

I can't see another way out and so I push my way through a chipped door marked "LADIES." The toilets are pungent with chemicals. Bright pink liquid sloshed down stained toilet bowls. The opaque window above the ring-stained sink is cracked open, and I lean toward it, desperate for fresh air.

Shadows move outside and there's a scuffle. The sound of something being slammed against the wall. I hardly dare move as I hear a man pleading: "I'm sorry. I can get it. Please don't—"

There's the sound of a thump. A cry. Another voice, deeper this time.

"You'd better. You know what will happen if you don't, and you don't want to leave your kids without a father, do you? Imagine how they'd feel if you had an accident."

And I think of Callie driving without a seatbelt and my blood runs cold. I know I have to leave the pub right now, but how?

Peering around the door leading to the bar I can barely hear the sound of the jukebox over the whooshing of blood in my ears. The stool Neil was sitting on is deserted; his empty pint glass rests next to my full lemon and lime but his hoodie is draped over the stool. Is it him I heard around the back? I dart toward the front door, ignoring the call of Steve behind me: "Don't you want your drink, princess?"

Outside, a couple of men loiter, cigarettes in hand, smoke curling into the air, and I shiver as I feel their eyes on me. I half-run down the road, my ankle pulsing with pain. Night is quickly drawing in, the sky turning to inky blue, and only every other street lamp is lit. It's a long walk home and I hesitate when I see a bus stop, but I feel exposed standing still. The threat I'd heard outside the toilets fills my head, "we could make it look like an accident," and the circumstances of Callie's crash bounce around my mind but I shake them away. The weather is turning, a mist descending, and as I walk I wrap my arms around my ribs in an effort to keep out the biting wind that stings my cheeks and numbs the tip of my nose. I'm only wearing a light jacket and a cotton scarf with sunflowers on it; I'd forgotten how unforgiving spring evenings can sometimes be. Cars rumble slowly past, headlights slicing through the gloom. The hairs on the back of my neck prickle as I think I'm being watched, and I swing my head around but there's no one to be seen. Increasing my pace, I stride along the street. Behind me there's a noise I can't identify and I stop. My heartbeat is pounding in my ears. I twist my head from left to right. The glow of a TV flickers through net curtains, and the thought someone is so close is comforting and I berate myself for being so paranoid. I'm toying with the idea of ringing Sam when there's a shuffling from behind a parked car. Adrenaline heats my body as I strain my eyes, waiting for a movement. Everything in my peripheral vision fades away and there's nothing to see but blackness. But then there's a shift. A shadow. And I turn and run. Feet pounding along the pavement.

It's not too far home now but I'm breathless by the time I reach the crossing. I jab the button but I don't wait for the lights to change before I race across the road. It's quiet as

I hurry across the park. In the pond, the ducks have tucked their heads under their wings. There are no toddlers chucking crusts into the murky water. As I pass the play area there's a creaking, and I freeze. What was that? The wind gusts again, and I realize it's a swing moving as though a ghost child is playing in the deserted playground.

I rush forward, cutting across the grass, adrenaline masking the pain in my ankle. Moisture seeps into my canvas shoes. Away from the path it's darker now but I know I'm almost at the gates. And then I hear them. Footsteps. I stop and turn. It's quiet. My fists are so tightly bunched my nails cut into my palms. A rustling in the bush. An animal, that's all. I push forward and there it is again. The clump-clump-clump of feet on concrete.

"Hello?" I swing around in a circle, holding my breath. Over the sound of my heartbeat pounding in my ears I think I hear the footsteps again, and I run. Pelting toward the gate, my messenger bag bumps against my thigh. My lungs are burning with exertion and from the freezing air I'm gulping. I'm back on the path now and so very nearly there. My shoes are sopping wet and the heels slide on the path but I don't slow down. Another couple of minutes and I'll be home. But as I hurtle toward the gates I'm yanked back. Something has snagged my scarf.

Or someone.

CHAPTER TWENTY-FIVE

The sensation of being restrained accelerates my fear, and clawing at my scarf with both hands I scream, muscles tensed, waiting for the feel of hot breath on my neck, hands on my throat, but there's only the sound of cotton ripping. My scarf is caught on the branch of a tree, and I wriggle free and run through the gates, almost crying with relief. I'm nearly home. Turning into my street I unzip my bag and fumble for my keys but I'm shaking so violently they fall from my grasp with a clatter. Behind me there's a cough. A male cough. And I'm shaking as I scoop up my keys.

The communal door to the flats is always unlocked, and I push it so hard it bangs against the wall and springs back, hitting me on the cheek. I clamp my teeth, biting my tongue.

Swallowing my blood, I take the stairs two at a time, and by the time I reach my door I'm trembling so hard I can't get the key in the lock. The outer door at the bottom of the stairs slams. Has someone else followed me through it? I struggle with the key again. The bottom stair creaks. Is it the floorboards settling or is someone there? I can't keep still, jigging up and down as I jab the key forward once more, and this time it slides into the lock. I twist it, there's a click, and I fall through my front door, slamming it behind me.

My legs are no longer willing to support me, and I slump to the hall floor, sitting for the longest time, feeling the adrenaline slip away, listening to my own juddering breathing, the strains of rap music from the flat above.

When I feel calmer I stand but my legs still feel shaky, and I wobble toward the kitchen window as though the floor is made of sponge. Outside, the street lamps are shrouded in mist rendering much of the street invisible. There's nothing to be seen. But that doesn't mean no one is out there.

The light is dim as I switch it on, but as the energy saving bulb shines brighter and brighter, the photos of Callie Blu-Tacked to my walls become clearer. I stand in front of one of Callie I'd pulled from Facebook. She's kneeling in front of a baby pink rose bush, secateurs in hand. *What happened to you?* Taking a red felt tip, I add the Prince of Wales to the mind map on the fridge and curve a line connecting it to Sophie. Is the pub significant? It's like staring at a dot-to-dot picture that doesn't quite make sense if you miss one of the numbers.

I plug the mobile phone Sara had given me into the charger I'd bought at the Carphone Warehouse but it still won't switch on. Sitting at my table I hit the space bar on my laptop to wake up the screen. It's quiet save the sound of my fingertips clicking on the keyboard. I Google "SOPHIE VALENTINE" but I can't find anything immediately relating to Sophie, and on Facebook there are thousands of people with that name. Instead, I try "THE PRINCE OF WALES" pub and its address and dip in and out of articles, the TripAdvisor reviews that would put anyone off visiting, and then I find something of interest, an archived news report:

The severely beaten body of a man in his early thirties was found this morning by joggers in the park near the Prince of Wales public house on Green Street. The man was reported missing by his yet unnamed girlfriend at around 9 a.m. after she was unable to reach him on his mobile, which was found smashed up at the scene. Police were on their way to speak to her when the call came that he had been located. His injuries are critical but are not thought to be life-threatening. Officer Phillip Denby stated that the man was last known to have been drinking in the Prince of Wales, and had called his girlfriend when he set off at around 10:30 p.m. but never arrived home. The police are urging anyone with information to contact them immediately on the number below...

The words I'd overheard at the pub settle like a weight on my chest: "You don't want to leave your kids without a father, do you? Imagine how they'd feel if you had an accident."

The communal door downstairs slams, and I jump. Was that someone going out or coming in? I wait, curling my fingers into fists. There's no footsteps on the stairs, no movement from the flat above me. A sense of disquiet washes over me and ever so slowly I stand, lifting my chair rather than pushing it back so it doesn't make a sound. In the brightness of the kitchen all I can see as I look out of the window is my own worried face reflected back at me.

Uneasy, I return to my laptop and open up another archived newspaper report, dated a few days after the one I've just read:

Police yesterday arrested local man Neil Cartwright (pictured) at the Prince of Wales Pub on Green Street on suspicion of an alleged assault. Cartwright has been previously

questioned in relation to intent to supply a class B drug and
has served several sentences for burglary.

Enlarging the grainy image, I study the man in the photograph. His head is turned slightly to the right as though
he's talking to the man standing behind him who is even
more out of focus, but it's definitely him. The same Neil I'd
spoken to earlier. Who is he and how did he know Callie
and Sophie were sisters?

There's a bang, but this time it doesn't come from downstairs. Somebody has thumped on my front door. My heart
leaps into my mouth. I'm not expecting anyone. My world
has shrunk so much since my surgery there's only a handful of people who would call round, and they would all ring
first to make sure I'm up to it. The knocking comes again,
louder this time. Impatient. I don't dare move. Can hardly
breathe. Holding myself perfectly still I wait but then a horrible thought occurs to me. Did I lock the door? I screw my
eyes up, remembering my relief as I burst into my hallway,
slumping to the floor, clutching my bag and my keys. Shit. I
didn't lock it. I know I didn't.

There is nothing stopping whoever is out there getting in.

CHAPTER TWENTY-SIX

Picking up my key ring I creep down the darkened hallway toward the door, wincing as my keys chink together. Stretching out my hand I slip the key into the lock and twist, holding my breath, but it's already locked. I must have done it automatically. I'm just stepping backward when the letter box rattles open and eyes shine through the slot.

"Callie? Are you there? It's me. Chris."

It takes a few seconds to register the name. The voice. Callie's colleague.

"Chris?" I flick on the light and unlock the front door and crack it open. He's wrapped up in a black overcoat and still somehow smells faintly of the dental surgery.

"What are you doing here?" I am ready to slam the door shut if I need to. "Did you follow me?" I remember I'd told Sara as I left the dentist that I'd be calling into the pub. Was it Chris who followed me home from the Prince of Wales?

"What? God. No. I took your address from your registration form. Sara found this in reception after you left." He holds out the bracelet with hearts that Sam had bought me. "She thought it might be yours."

"It is." I stretch out my hand. He drops the bracelet into my cupped palm, and I curl my fingers around it. I was sure it had been zipped in the compartment in my bag but I suppose it could have slipped out when I pulled out my purse.

"It must have fallen off when you paid. I thought as you're on my way home…"

"How did you get here?" It sounds like an accusation rather than a question.

"I drove. Look. Sorry, Callie. I didn't mean to upset you."

"Jenna. It's Jenna," I snap.

"Sorry, sorry, it's just so…It's the hair." He begins to back away. "Sorry," he says again as he turns and thumps down the stairs.

I slam the front door and pull the chain across before dashing toward the kitchen window and flinging it open, straining my ears for the sound of a car starting, but the street is quiet. Dark. And I can't hear anything at all.

* * *

The phone is now charged enough to switch on and I find it isn't as old as Sara had thought. The flurry of texts and calls are dated just before Callie died. As I read the text messages the hairs on my arm stand on end.

There's only one contact listed. It's a number. Not a name. And all the calls and texts are to and from that person, and I scan through them.

> *"I tried to meet you but he followed me."* Callie says
> in one of them.
> *"Be careful."* is the reply.

"Can U get away?"
"No. He's watching everything I do."

"I need you."
"I know. I'm trying. Give me some time. It's not easy."

"Come now."
"He's following me."

There's a flurry of incoming texts dated the night Callie died, but no replies from Callie were sent.

"Thought you'd be here by now?"
"I've tried ringing you. PICK UP!"
"Where are you?"

Who was Callie texting? Was she having an affair? I have to know. Almost without thinking I dial the number in the contact list on Callie's phone, making sure I withhold my own number. It rings and rings and just when I am about to give up there's a click. The sound of a breath. I stay still. Silent. Waiting for them to speak first. There's something in the background. Something familiar but I can't quite place it. I close my eyes. What is it? That noise?

I rub my forehead as though I can make an image appear to accompany the sound, like a genie in a bottle. The breathing on the other end of the phone becomes ragged and there's the soft sound of a throat clearing but I can't tell if it's a man or a woman.

"Hello," I say at last, unable to wait any longer. There's a whirring in my ear as the line goes dead, and I try calling again, this time from Callie's phone, but a robotic voice tells me the mobile is currently switched off. What now?

* * *

The kitchen is in darkness except for the green glow of the clock on the hob. It's 1:00 a.m. and my eyes are burning with the need to sleep, but I can't tear myself away from the window. I've been kneeling for so long on the wooden chair I usually sit on to eat my breakfast, the pins and needles in my feet have faded into numbness. The walk home from the pub has unsettled me, and I can't stop thinking about Neil. Each time I think I'll go to bed something outside catches my eye. A shadow lurking behind a parked car, a shape shifting in a doorway. The night is still. Mostly silent, except from the hum of my fridge, but every now and then a sound pierces the air: the yowling of a cat, the thrum of a car in the distance. I'm clinging to Callie's mobile phone as if it's driftwood, my mind racing. Who was watching her? Are they watching me? I look up and down the street but I can't see anyone.

At last I uncurl my body and stumble as I try to stand, stamping life into my dead feet. Too tired to clean my teeth I douse my pillow with lavender oil to help relax me, and fall into bed, but as I wait for exhaustion to claim me I wonder yet again if the front door is properly locked, if I am really safe. I get up and rattle the handle and check the bolt is across but I don't feel reassured. Someone followed me. I know they did. In bed, I toss and turn until I click on my bedside lamp and a golden glow fills the room and, at last, reassured by the soft light, I close my eyes.

Sleep, when it comes, is fitful. Faces looming toward me: Chris, Neil, Nathan. Callie crying for help. When I wake in the early hours I reread the texts on Callie's phone. Someone was watching her, following her, and panic pinballs in my chest as I think that now they might be following me.

CHAPTER TWENTY-SEVEN

Sweat trickles in between my shoulder blades. It is early Friday morning but already the police station is overly warm. I've been sitting in reception for nearly an hour now. It is harshly lit and oppressive, and I feel the gray walls are sliding toward me, the ceiling crushing down. The hard, plastic chair I am sitting on is bolted to the floor, and I clutch the seat to stop myself from leaving as I breathe in the same stale air.

Callie's phone is tucked inside my bag. It's the only evidence I have that someone was watching her. Following her. If she was having an affair the person following her could be Nathan but I think of how kind he was to me when I fainted and it is hard to believe he could be the cause of Callie's fear. I don't know if I am doing the right thing, coming here. The thought of a police car turning up at Tom and Amanda's, an officer standing solemn in their sweltering lounge informing them Callie's death is now being classed as suspicious, breaks my heart. Could I be making things worse?

I can't think clearly. The constant noise is jarring; phones ring, doors slam, and radios crackle with static. The man sitting next to me has barbed wire tattooed around his neck, and his clothes stink of smoke. The way his knee jiggles up and down as he flicks open his Zippo lighter before clicking it shut over and over again grates on me.

The door to my left buzzes and squeaks open and a policeman who looks too young to be here calls: "Jenna McCauley?"

I stand and nod. "I'm Jenna."

"I'm PC Hodges, if you'd like to follow me?" He strides down a seemingly endless corridor.

The soles of my sandals squeak on the dirty white lino as I struggle to keep up. By the time I'm shown into a small room I'm breathless, and I sink gratefully on a chair.

"You said you had some information for us, regarding a suspicious death?" PC Hodges's pencil hovers over his pad, and I'm momentarily thrown.

"Doesn't someone else need to be in here?" I ask. "Another policeman?"

"We're not formally interviewing you, Miss McCauley."

"But you record everything?" I look around. There's nothing but blank walls and a small rectangle window that's so high there's only clouds to be seen.

"You've been watching too much TV. This is just an informal chat. Let's start with your name and address."

His pen scratches on his notebook as I recite my details.

"And whose death are you here about?"

"Callie Valentine."

"Is she a relative of yours?"

"No."

"Do her family know you are here?"

"Not exactly."

"She was a friend of yours?"

"Sort of."

"Sort of?" He raises an eyebrow.

"Yes," I say, more firmly this time. I tell him about Callie's accident. "But I don't believe it was an accident." PC Hodges's face remains impassive as I tell him about my visit to the pub, the conversation I'd overheard. "And I have this." I slide the phone over the table almost triumphantly, and he picks up the handset, making notes as he scrolls through the texts.

"And this was found in her place of work?"

"Yes."

"But you're not certain it was hers?"

"It was in her drawer. Look, can't you just run the number through a computer? It's proof."

"Proof of what? It's not always that simple, Miss McCauley. If this is a pay-as-you-go phone it will be almost impossible to trace. Even if this phone did belong to Miss Valentine it doesn't mean her death was suspicious. Wait here."

He leaves the room and the door bangs shut behind him, and I get up and pace around, doing circuits of the impossibly small room, feeling like a rat in a cage.

Much later, I've drained the water in the white plastic cup I was given that crumpled under my grip and I'm sitting again, my head in my hands, when PC Hodges slides back into his seat.

"It seems we investigated Callie Valentine's death at the time and it was ruled as accidental."

"I know but..."

"Her family and friends were spoken to. We were very thorough."

"But the phone—"

"We'll look into it." He holds out the handset to me.

"Shouldn't you keep it? For evidence?" I'm insistent now.

"At this stage it isn't reason to reopen an investigation, but as I said we'll look into it and be in touch if anything else comes to light. In the meantime, please feel free to pop back in."

"But I got a really strong feeling that…" I raise my voice.

"Unfortunately we need more to go on than feelings, Miss McCauley." His sarcasm stings. "I'll see you out." PC Hodges presses the mobile into my hand and strides toward the door, yanking it open, and just like that I am dismissed.

* * *

Outside the station I sink onto the cold steps, the dampness seeping through my jeans. The sun is breaking through the clouds but it's still chilly, and I wrap my arms around my legs, resting my chin on my knees. The warm bloom of embarrassment I'd felt in the station has dissipated. The expression on PC Hodges's face was much like the one on Rachel's the other night. No one believes me, and I don't know what to do next. I'm due to meet Nathan at the canal at two, and I'm at a loss to know whether I should go or not. At the sound of a car door slamming my head jerks up. On the opposite side of the road is a row of shops, and parked in the lay-by is a bright yellow sports car. I've seen that car before, but it takes me a second to remember where from. The dentist's car park. Is it Chris?

There's no one in the car, and my feet tap-tap-tap their anxious rhythm on the pavement but I fight against my natural instinct to run. Fueled by the skepticism I've just encountered I march across the road. I'm going to confront Chris. Ask him what the hell he's playing at. Leaning against the hood of the car I try to act far more casual than I feel, breathing deeply through my nose, trying to unfurl my fists. The door of the chemist swings open, and a lady with long brown hair frowns as she steps outside.

"Excuse me. Do you mind not leaning against my car?" she snaps, and I stutter apologies as I step away from her.

My mind and body feel detached from each other and my head swims. I reach out a hand and steady myself against the wall as though I can stop myself floating away.

Is it all in my head? The engine of the yellow car I'd been so sure was Chris's thrums, and I am angry. Scared. Confused. I am everything but certain of my own thoughts. I know I can't go on like this, and leaning against the rough brick I make a call.

"Please help me," I beg.

CHAPTER TWENTY-EIGHT

Vanessa tells me it is nice to see me and asks me to take a seat. She doesn't ask why I implored Beverley, her receptionist, to fit me in. Thunking my bag onto the floor I sink into the sofa. Vanessa slides a box of Kleenex closer to me, as if this might be the day she breaks me. I can't stop my knees jiggling up and down while I fight to put the things I am desperate to tell her into some kind of order. Vanessa sloshes water from a jug into two glasses, and I take a sip, grateful for its coolness. I'm sweating and shaking after running all the way from the police station. My head thumps and each time I inhale the lavender from her potpourri, the band around my forehead tightens.

"Thanks for seeing me in your lunch hour. I really appreciate it." My voice is flat and I fall silent again.

"How are you, Jenna?"

I open my mouth to speak but a sob bursts forth instead. Vanessa sits silently as I help myself to the tissues I never thought I'd need. I wipe my eyes and blow my nose, but every time I try to talk my breath catches and the words get stuck in my throat.

"Take your time," Vanessa says and I nod, embarrassed I can't seem to pull myself together.

At last, my shoulders stop shaking, and Vanessa passes a brown wicker bin over the table and I drop my balled-up tissues inside. "I don't know what to tell you." I gaze out of the window at the rolling clouds, not wanting to meet her eye.

She doesn't ask any questions, and I know it's a ploy. She thinks if she stays silent for long enough I'll fill the space between us with words but I honestly don't know where to start. She'll think I'm crazy, and I'm beginning to wonder if I am.

"I think something bad happened to Callie." I twist my head back around to face her but her expression is impartial. "And I don't know what to do about it."

"What do you think happened to Callie?" she asks.

I tug another tissue out of the box and twist it round and round in my fingers.

"I think she was scared. I think someone hurt her. I've been to the police station but they didn't take me seriously. I think she might have been..." I hesitate, not wanting to say the word aloud. Not wanting to even think it. "I think she might have been murdered," I whisper and I brace myself for her reaction.

Vanessa doesn't gasp. She doesn't even register surprise. Instead she asks in that neutral tone of hers: "Why do you think someone hurt Callie?" and I feel wrong-footed. I'd expected more of a response.

"I've been trying to find out what happened that night—for Tom and Amanda, you know? So they can stop being fixated on why Callie left the wedding, and grieve properly." As I say the word "fixated" I think Vanessa's eyebrow raises a millimeter but I can't be sure. I push forward.

"It's harder than I thought. At first I thought Nathan had hurt her. I feel so much fear and I think it's her fear. I dream about a man a lot, always the same one, but I never see his face. I'm sure it's Nathan though."

"And in these dreams? The man is hurting Callie?"

"No," I admit. "The dreams are happy, but there's lots of dark feelings when I'm awake. I think they are Callie's memories but I can't figure them out. When I met Chris I got a really strange feeling..."

"Who is Chris?"

"Callie's boss, at the dentist's surgery." This time Vanessa's lips purse but I can't help telling her everything. How I'd thought it would help if I found out where Sophie was in Spain so Tom and Amanda could contact her directly. I recount my experience at the Prince of Wales pub, and it's a relief to let it all out. By the time I've finished I half-expect Vanessa to be leaping to her feet, insisting we call the police right away. But instead, she pushes her glasses back up the bridge of her nose with one hand while she scribbles notes into my file with the other, and while I wait for her to finish writing I speak again.

"I did some more research. Into Cellular Memory. There's a documented case where an eight-year-old girl received the heart of a ten-year-old murdered girl and she had horrifying nightmares of a man murdering her donor. The dreams were so traumatic and so detailed her psychiatrist and mother notified the police and they gathered enough evidence to find the murderer and convict him."

Vanessa looks up and I think I've piqued her interest but she says: "I can't comment on that, Jenna, but I can tell you what you're experiencing is a completely normal reaction."

"Thinking someone has been murdered is normal?" I can't see how she can convince me of this.

"Are you familiar with Secondary Traumatic Stress—STS—Jenna?"

"No."

"It occurs when an individual, you, in this case, hears about the firsthand trauma of another. The risk is greater among women or those who have unresolved trauma issues themselves. You fit into both categories. The guilt you feel over receiving Callie's heart, coupled with the empathy you feel toward Tom and Amanda and your helplessness to ease their suffering, has resulted, I believe, in Secondary Traumatic Stress." Vanessa sips her water before continuing. "The symptoms range from feelings of hopelessness and despair, anxiety, to unwanted thoughts, reliving traumatic events even if you weren't there at the time, and nightmares."

"But I was followed home; I'm sure of it. I feel so unnerved almost all of the time. Like someone is watching me."

"Heightened sensitivity and excess vigilance can sometimes be part of the symptoms of STS. It would be quite easy to believe someone is following you, even if they aren't."

"I'm not imagining everything though." I refuse to believe it's all in my head.

"I'm not saying you are imagining anything, Jenna. Everything you are thinking and feeling is very real to you. But I believe STS, combined with the medication you are taking—and we know a side effect of prednisone, for example, can be paranoia—is contributing to irrational thoughts. Your preoccupation with Callie's death is a way of manifesting these symptoms. Do you really believe if there was any suspicion it would have been ruled an accidental death? You said yourself the police investigated the accident thoroughly and ruled out anything suspicious."

"But Tom and Amanda think there's something strange."

"They're bound to. It's a coping mechanism. Accidents are too random. They are too difficult to process. It's natural to want to find a reason why. Nothing makes sense otherwise, do you see?"

I think about this for a minute. "I suppose I can understand they are trying to make sense of it. But Secondary Traumatic Stress doesn't explain everything, does it? The mobile Sara gave me at the dentist's and the messages on it—they're real. I'll show you." I rummage in my bag and pull out the handset. Vanessa turns the phone over slowly in her hands as though she's never seen one before.

"How do you know this is Callie's?" I am asked for the second time today.

"Sara found it in her drawer at work."

"But where's the proof that it was Callie's phone? The texts don't mention her name, do they? You know Callie had an iPhone that her parents now have. A patient could have left this in reception, and she put it in her drawer to deal with it later. I've got a box full of lost property in my cupboard. Hasn't anyone ever left anything in the vet's?"

Only a few days ago I'd found a baseball cap in reception and I'd stuffed it into my drawer in case the owner came back to reclaim it, but I don't share this; instead I change the subject. "But the pub? I definitely heard a man say 'we could make it look like an accident,' I know I did."

"That pub is notorious for small-time crooks. It's teeming with them. You don't know who it was you heard talking outside and it isn't somewhere you should be going, especially on your own. You have no proof Sophie or Callie knew Neil." And there it is again, that word that's stopping everyone taking me seriously. Proof.

"But he knew they were sisters," I protest.

"Perhaps a natural assumption if they look similar, but are you sure you didn't mention it?"

"Yes." But I've hesitated too long before answering. I'm not completely sure and Vanessa knows it.

"Look, Jenna. There's nothing I can see to demonstrate anything untoward happened to Callie, or Sophie."

As she says this I am left with a heavy feeling. I've never considered anything might have happened to Sophie. "Do you think Sophie's OK? It seems so strange she hasn't been in touch."

"Sophie has been through a traumatic experience. Her big sister has died. It's not unusual to need some space and distance to deal with grief. I'm sure she'll be back in contact with her parents when she's had a chance to process everything. You said she'd disappeared before when things got too much?"

"Yes." I chew my lip, my mind tick-tick-ticking as I try to make sense of what Vanessa is saying. Every explanation she's come up with is plausible. Maybe more plausible than my theories; is it all in my head? I just don't know anymore. I try one last time to convince her. "Callie left the wedding...Nathan too. Tom says it wasn't like her at all not to say goodbye."

"They could have had a row. Thousands of people do. Look, Jenna," Vanessa puts down her notes and leans forward, "if I thought there was a smidgen of doubt that Callie's death was anything other than an accident I'd be morally bound to report it, but I don't see any evidence of that. I really don't."

"But I've been feeling so strongly Callie wants me to do something." I think of my kitchen, plastered in photos of Callie and mind maps, but I'm not so certain anymore. I don't know what I'm doing half the time. "Vanessa, at work, I've been making mistakes, forgetting things. Could this be part of it? This Secondary Traumatic Stress thing?"

"Absolutely."

"Can it be fixed? Can you make it go away?" My voice is small.

"We can work together. Keep talking. When are you next due for a medication review?"

"It's my six-month check next week."

"All being well your medication should be reduced again. That should make a difference too. You're not alone, Jenna." And she reaches out and squeezes my hand, and for the second time that day tears escape, but this time I'm crying with relief.

* * *

Feeling positive I step out of Vanessa's office into the bright afternoon sun and slip on my sunglasses over my tired eyes. As I'm walking along the almost empty street I resist the urge to swivel my head around to check whether anyone is following me. Vanessa's explanation about Secondary Traumatic Stress causing paranoia and irrational thoughts has put my mind at ease somewhat, although I'm not entirely convinced that Cellular Memory doesn't exist. There's too much research to just dismiss it. But I do accept the phone could have been anyone's, and it seems that Callie's death was properly investigated. The smell of freshly baked bread wafts from the open door of a bakery causing my stomach to growl. Checking my watch, I see it's past one thirty. I'm due to meet Nathan at two, and I think I'll still go, and have one last try to at least find some answer for Tom and Amanda, or even better, Sophie's address.

Footsteps pound behind me on the pavement, drawing closer and closer, and my shoulders tense but I don't look around. There's nothing to be afraid of. My pace is quicker now, but I tell myself it's because I don't want to be late, not because I am nervous. The back of my neck is hot; it's the heat of the sun, I know, not someone's eyes burning into me. I replay the conversation with Vanessa in my head, reassuring myself my fear is not real, but behind me the clatter of pallets being dropped slices the air and my stomach muscles tighten. I can't help swinging around, and I think I see someone wearing a black hoodie, despite the heat, darting into the bakery as I catch sight of him or her. My breath quickens and I don't know why. There's nothing to be afraid of. Is there?

CHAPTER TWENTY-NINE

Clouds of midges hover over the sun-speckled water of the canal. Nathan's not here yet, and while I wait I sit on a slatted bench, stifling yawn after yawn. A narrow boat with orange flowers painted on the side drifts lazily past, the smell of bacon wafting across the water. I watch as it stops at a lock. A gray-haired woman and a yapping Yorkshire terrier alight the boat while a man in a flat cap stays on board. A movement on the bridge catches my eye. A shadowy figure. I can't make them out in the brightness of the sun, but it seems they are looking straight at me. Despite Vanessa's reassurances I am edgy as I stare back at them but when they raise their arm and wave and step forward I see it's only Nathan, and I slowly exhale in relief.

"Nice to see you again," Nathan says as he joins me, kissing me on the cheek as I stand. "I have something for you." He swings the rucksack from his shoulder and pulls out a bottle of water. "So you don't overheat again," he says and I laugh, instantly at ease.

Making small talk, we walk. The sunshine has brought out families and the towpath is teeming with toddlers on scooters, children on bikes. Dogs strain against leads, desperate to jump into the water.

"Look!" Nathan stops. A brood of ducklings bob up and down struggling to keep up with their mother as she paddles through the water at an alarming rate.

"Oh, that little one's getting left behind." I point.

"Let's slow her down." Nathan reaches into his rucksack again and produces a bag of bread.

"Here." He hands me a crust, and I break it into small pieces before tossing them into the canal where they float on the top of the murky water. The duck weaves toward them, her babies close behind as we watch the bread being gobbled up before the family swim away, disappearing behind reeds.

Nathan stuffs the empty bag into his rucksack. "Ice cream?"

"I'd love one." I sit on a bench as Nathan queues at the kiosk, thanking him as he returns with a cone, ice cream swirled into a point, chocolate flake sticking out like a flag.

I swirl my tongue along the edge of the cone as Nathan bites into his ice cream. He winces.

"Brain freeze?"

He nods, curling his lips over his teeth.

"Press your tongue against the roof of your mouth," I say. "Harry's always rushing his ice-cream cones. It helps generate heat. It really works."

A few moments later he's ready to talk. "That did help. It's a sign of getting older, isn't it? Not being able to bite into anything too cold." He nods toward a young boy chomping away on a Fab lolly, hundreds and thousands of sprinkles scattering over the grass. "When I was his age, I used to bite on lollies just like that. Who's Harry?"

"So you're still in touch with Sam's family?" He frowns after I've explained.

"Yes. I didn't see them for ages after…after me and Sam broke up but I can't imagine not having Harry in my life. Do you still see Callie's family?"

"No." His reply is curt but I push him to elaborate.

"Why not?"

"They didn't want to see me after the accident. Too painful, I suppose."

"Did she have any brothers? Sisters?" I watch a brilliant blue dragonfly dip toward the water as I ask, not quite able to look him in the eye. The deceit doesn't sit well with me.

"She had a sister, Sophie, but I haven't seen her since before the accident. She couldn't handle it. Didn't even come to Callie's funeral to pay her last respects. Sent a wreath as though that made up for it."

"Does she live close by, Sophie?"

"I've no idea where she is."

I take a deep breath. "And Callie's accident. What happened?"

Nathan breaks the remainder of his ice-cream cone into pieces and tosses them into the water.

"She was driving and ran into a tree. It was a terrible night. The roads were treacherous."

"That's awful. Where was she going?"

"Does it matter?" His tone is terse. I feel I am interrogating him but it has to be done, for Tom and Amanda's sake. I try again.

"I just wondered if she'd been on her way to meet you?"

"No." His voice breaks and he leans forward and drops his head into his hands, and I feel guilty for pressing him.

"You must miss her very much." I reach out and squeeze his arm. "You were together a long time, weren't you?"

He straightens his spine and huffs out air. "Five years. Not that it counted for much in the end. I didn't get a say."

"In what?"

"In anything. Where she was buried. She'd have hated the church service. She wanted to be cremated and her ashes scattered near the ocean. We talked about it once after watching a film where someone died young. Her parents even allowed her to be cut up. Imagine that. Slicing out parts of her and handing them out as though they're bits of meat from the butcher's counter."

"You don't agree with organ donation?" My voice is sharp.

"It's not natural, is it? Doctors playing God." He thrusts his hands deep in his pockets and leans back on the hard wooden support. "She was, well, she was just so perfect, beautiful, you know? And to think of her not being whole. It's not right."

"I can't imagine how hard it must be for you. But she must have saved lives."

"I know. She'd have liked that. I just can't bear the thought of her not being Callie anymore. And I should have had a say. We were going to get married. Tom and Amanda were handed the pen and the consent forms, and I didn't even get asked my opinion. I remember when it was all over and the nurses handed Tom Callie's belongings; he passed them to me as if all I was good for was holding her things. I crushed them so tightly to my chest I thought my ribs might snap. I was so bloody angry."

We sit in silence. I don't know what to do. I don't know what to say, and I wonder whether I should just go home. Tom and Amanda will come to terms with everything eventually, and Nathan's still grieving. My detective work doesn't seem to be getting me anywhere.

I clear my throat, and Nathan twists to look at me.

"Sorry. This wasn't how I planned the day. Talking

about my ex, but I feel comfortable with you, Jenna, in a way I don't usually feel with people," he says and I wonder if he feels it too; this invisible thread that binds us together.

"It's OK. Really."

"No it isn't. Hungry? I can make it up to you with food." He stands and reaches out both hands and pulls me to my feet. "There's a great pub and it's not too far."

* * *

Conversation flows easily over dinner. I feel I've known Nathan forever and I suppose, in a way, I have. Each time I mention Callie or Sophie, Nathan changes the subject, and after a while it's a relief to talk about the mundane: TV, music. I'm surprised to find I'm enjoying myself, and I wonder if he is too.

There's a change in the atmosphere as our plates are cleared, and as we both reach for the bill our hands brush and there's a spark. Nathan asks if I'd like to go back to his for coffee. I feel a pang of longing and I tell myself it's only because I am feeling Callie's feelings. I try to think of Sam, but as we leave the pub I can't feel anything except the heat of Nathan's hand through my jacket as it rests on the small of my back. I can't help wishing he were touching my skin.

* * *

At Nathan's I sit on the end of the sofa with my feet tucked under me, feeling completely at home.

"Wine?"

"Not for me, thanks." The warm flush of alcohol would settle my nerves but it's strictly off limits after my transplant. "It gives me migraines," I lie. Telling people I never drink always causes them to eye me suspiciously, and leads to a multitude of questions.

"That must be rough. A girl at my office gets migraines. I've never had one, thankfully. I'll make some tea."

Alone, I try to recall why Tom said Nathan had left the wedding. Wasn't that a migraine? Or did he feel sick? I scrunch up my eyes but the memory dances just beyond my fingertips and I can't quite reach it.

When Nathan sits back down he's so close our thighs press together, and I'm hot and cold and excited and terrified and everything but thirsty, but that's OK, my hand's shaking too much to pick up my drink anyway.

"Can I ask you something personal, Jenna?"

My hand instinctively flutters to my chest, making sure my scar is covered. "Yes."

"Are you still in love with Sam?"

The question hits me like a punch in the gut and I open my mouth to say no, but the word sticks to my tongue like peanut butter and I can't spit it out. Instead I shake my head but I don't know if I've convinced Nathan any more than I've convinced myself.

Nathan crosses the room, bends, and fiddles with the silver iPod that rests on a Sonos Dock. Laid-back folk music fills the air, and my feet begin to tap a rhythm as though they've heard the song before.

"Do you get lonely?" Nathan asks, picking up the conversation where he'd left it.

I think of the times I've lain on the bathroom floor feeling as though I might die. The nights I've woken up, pressing my hands against my chest, checking my heart's still beating, terrified it will stop. The dark and chilly evenings curled on the sofa alone.

"I'm OK on my own," I say but my eyes fill with tears and my voice breaks, and I hate myself for feeling so vulnerable.

Nathan stretches his arm around me and strokes the back of my neck until my skin feels so hot I think it must surely be burning his fingers. I'm stiff at first. Awkward. But I allow myself to lean into him. He's not Sam but there's a familiarity about him that makes my body ache. It's been so long since I have been touched. We sit still at first. Silent.

"Jenna," he whispers, and I twist my head to look at him.

I'm scared and excited, and as he leans in to kiss me I pull back, not sure this is what I want. I touch his face. He leans in again; his lips brush mine, and I am lost. He pushes me back until I'm lying on the sofa; my hands twist in his hair, and his tongue thrusts into my mouth. His hands are everywhere and my body is screaming out for this but as he tugs at the button of my jeans my ecstasy plunges into terror. Is my heart strong enough? Will I die? I bat his hand away and try to sit up but he kisses me again and begins to unbutton my blouse. I can't let him see my scar, and I slap my own hand over my buttons to block him but I can't stop kissing him. Can't seem to tell him it's too much. Too soon. I'm not ready. I was never meant to like him but I want this so badly my hips rock up. I tug his shirt from his jeans, feel the warmth of his skin. I count the beats of my heart as Nathan rolls my nipples between his thumb and forefinger. I stop counting as he trails kisses down my neck and by the time his hand snakes his way inside my jeans my initial whimpers of fear morph into cries of passion, and I no longer care that my heart is galloping. I gasp and part my legs and feel myself falling, falling, falling over a cliff.

* * *

It is late as I sit at my kitchen table, moonlight flooding through the window, a half-empty mug of chamomile tea in front of me. I close my eyes and run two fingers over my chest trying to feel what Nathan felt. Did he notice my scar? The skin feels thinner to me. Puckered. But I know it's there. My thoughts are so chaotic. I can't imagine how I'll sleep tonight.

"Stay," Nathan had begged.

"I can't." I had wriggled out of his grasp and called a taxi. Nathan had offered to drive but I insisted on a cab. I didn't want the awkwardness of feeling obliged to invite him in.

"It's not like you've got anyone to rush home to, is it?" He had frowned.

"No." I had nipped the soft flesh of my bottom lip between my teeth. I hadn't known what to say. I hadn't wanted the awkwardness of getting undressed. Questions about my scar, and besides, it's Callie's birthday tomorrow and I need to leave my flat early to get to Tom and Amanda's.

"I've got a day off on Monday," I said. "Are you owed any more hours?"

"Yes, Monday's good but what about this weekend too?"

"I've got plans. Sorry," I added as his face fell.

The taxi honked its arrival and Nathan had walked me to the car, and kissed me long and hard.

"Any chance of you getting in today, luv?" the driver had called and I climbed into the back of the car.

Now, as I rinse my cup at the sink I glance out of the window. Across the road, out of the blackness, a shadow moves. A figure. I stand motionless. My light is off so they shouldn't be able to see in but the hairs on the back of my neck prick up. They lean against the wall, staring up at my window. I can't properly see them in the darkness, and it's difficult to tell whether it's a man or a woman. My chest feels tight. Who is it? Can they see me? I force myself to look away. But my eyes are drawn back to the window. They're still there. I tell myself they've probably stepped out for a cigarette but I can't see a tell-tale red glow. My body is rigid. Muscles ache. But I remain standing, watching them watching me, until I blink and they're gone and I wonder if they were ever there at all. Vanessa said there is nothing to be scared of, but my heart races all the same.

CHAPTER THIRTY

It's drafty and the breeze lifts the hem of my skirt and I place my palms flat against the silk, smoothing it down. Marilyn Monroe may have carried off the effortlessly sexy windswept look but I don't want to expose my knickers to the whole of Paris, even if they are brand-new red silk—ooh la la. This is the second time we've been up the tower. We had stood in this exact spot earlier, freezing fingers wrapped around mugs brimming with thick hot chocolates bought at the café, marveling at the people scurrying past below us like ants, never glancing up. How long do you have to live in a city before you become immune to its beauty? If I lived here I'd never take it for granted, I'm sure. This is stunning though, even if I am cold. The lights splayed out before me; the moon casting a creamy glow on the river. It's even clear enough to see the stars. This is the singular most romantic evening of my life.

A boat glides along the water. Camera flashes pepper the sky like miniature fireworks and I wonder what time the last trip is and whether there's a bar on board. I shiver and you drape your suit jacket across my shoulders. You stand close behind me and wrap your arms tightly around my waist, and I try to memorize every tiny detail. There's such a buzz. The women so elegant with their tiny waists and pixie cuts. I finger the ends of my hair. It's been long for ages. There's a hairdresser in our hotel and I think tomorrow I'll have it cut short and perhaps dyed too.

I rest my head back against your chest. You clear your throat behind me and your body stiffens. I'm suddenly cold as you let me go, and I turn to ask if you're OK.

I can't comprehend what I'm seeing at first. You're in front of a spotlight, nothing but a giant shadow, and I think you might be hurt as you drop to one knee, but then I see it. The diamond sparkles brighter than Parisian evenings and I can't take my eyes off the box you're clutching in your hand.

"Marry me, baby?"

It is so unexpected I can't speak, and the other people who are up here with us fade away even though I can still hear them whispering. Waiting for an answer. The world seems to swirl around me, as though I've got vertigo, even though I'm not afraid of heights, and I feel I'm falling. You stretch out a hand and I take it, feeling safe once more. There's a click of a camera, a flash, and black dots dance in front of my eyes. I can't see but I can feel. I can feel what's in my heart, and it's you. It's always been you.

"Yes," I say and I can hardly believe how lucky I am to have you.

I'd trust you with my life.

CHAPTER THIRTY-ONE

It's silly, I know, but I pull a black and white striped top out of the wardrobe this morning. Dreaming about Paris last night has made me long for the effortless chic the Parisian women all seem to pull off, and if I feel good on the outside maybe I'll feel better on the inside. Ignoring my usual perfume, I spray Chanel N° 5 onto my wrists but the floral scent makes my stomach roll. I am so nervous about seeing Tom and Amanda today. How must they be feeling on the first of Callie's birthdays without her here?

As I apply my mascara there's a knock on the front door making me jump, and the wand slips, streaking my cheek with black that matches the shadows under my eyes. Last night I'd tossed and turned in bed for hours and every time I came close to dropping off anxiety nudged me awake, sending me skittering to the front door to check it was locked. That if there was anyone watching me they couldn't get in.

The knocking comes again and I hesitate before I answer but if I'm ever going to get over this Secondary Traumatic Stress I have to start somewhere, and it seems unimaginable that anything bad could happen with the sun streaming so brightly through the windows. I pull the door open as I rub at my cheek.

"Nathan!"

"Sorry." He doesn't smile. "I know I shouldn't just turn up unannounced and we weren't supposed to meet until Monday." He stares at his feet.

"Do you want to come in for a minute? I'm going out in half an hour but ..."

"Where did you say you were going today?" He steps over the threshold and I am uncomfortable at him standing in the hallway, in the place Sam once stood. I am not sure how I feel about him in the cold light of day. I don't know what's me and what's Callie anymore.

"Are you OK?" I study him, avoiding his question. "You look shattered." He hasn't shaved and the whites of his eyes are streaked red.

"I couldn't sleep."

He can't quite look at me, and after a beat I ask: "Is something wrong?"

"Last night." He clears his throat. "I hadn't planned on that happening. It felt right though. To me. But today ... well, today is a difficult day. It would have been Callie's birthday, and I can't help wondering if I'm a terrible person. I'd hate for her to think I was forgetting her. I like you, Jenna, I really do, but I feel so bloody guilty." His shoulders begin to shake, and I step forward and pull him into a hug, and we remain standing, arms wrapped around each other, hearts beating together, for the longest time. When we eventually pull apart he asks: "Can I have a glass of water?"

"Of course." I swivel and head toward the kitchen, Nathan trailing me, but as I approach the door I see Callie's face smiling down from my walls, the mind map on my fridge, and I stop so suddenly Nathan crashes into me. I turn, trying to block his view, but he is frowning and I don't know if it's too late. What has he seen?

"Why don't you wait in the lounge. It's a mess in here." I point down the hallway.

"Washing up everywhere is there? It's OK. We've all got bad habits, haven't we?" He sidesteps, trying to get past me, and I block him, take a step forward, forcing him to step back.

"Please," I say, putting my hands on his chest, and his eyes narrow as he looks over my shoulder, and I push him backward.

Nathan is sitting on the sofa in silence when I hand him his water, and I hope he doesn't notice how much my hand is trembling.

We don't speak, each of us lost to our own thoughts, but as he leaves the kiss he gives me on my cheek feels forced, or is it just my imagination?

* * *

"Come on in, Jenna," Tom says but his smile is fleeting, quickly replaced with an expression of unhappiness he can't hide. The lounge is stuffier than normal and it feels as though there is something tight squeezing my lungs as I cross the room to greet Joe and kiss Amanda hello.

"How did you get on at the cemetery?" I ask.

"There were silk flowers on Callie's grave," Amanda says. "She would have loved them. Nathan must have put them there. I'm so glad he hasn't forgotten her."

"I'll make some tea," Tom says.

"Why don't we go out? Have a bit of a walk?" I suggest, longing to escape the trapped, stale air.

"Out? Again?" Amanda looks stricken at the thought, and I squeeze her hand.

"We could go to the park?" Tom says. "Callie would have liked that."

"OK," she says.

"It's really warming up outside. You might want to change out of your jumper," I say, and Tom takes her upstairs to get ready.

When they leave the room, I turn to Joe. "Have you heard from Sophie today?"

"No," he says.

And it's the way his face sags that makes me blurt out: "I've been trying to find her."

"What? Why?"

The question throws me and I fall silent but he leans toward me and I know I have to explain. I speak, tentatively at first, explaining how much I want to help but I feel as though I've strayed on to shifting sands, watching his expression, gauging his reaction. Without meaning to I tell him about the pub, the police; the words falling from my lips as I stumble over sentences in a rush to get it all out before Tom and Amanda return. When I've finished, he leans back in his chair and rubs his hand across his face.

"I know you mean well," he says. "But that pub doesn't seem like the sort of place you should go. I'm surprised Sophie did, quite frankly. Neil sounds as though he could be quite dangerous. And this Sara at the dentist? She was sure that's where Sophie went? The one on Green Street? There's a Prince of Wales in West Creaton too. That one is nice and it would have been nearer for Sophie."

I hesitate. Had I got the wrong pub?

"Look, I'll go and check it out myself but ..."

But he doesn't get to finish his sentence before Tom sticks his head around the door and tells us they are ready to leave.

* * *

At the park Amanda is on edge, her eyes darting around. I can't imagine how overwhelming it must be to step out into the world after being cooped inside for months. The brightness. The noise. I wonder if it's too much for her. Tom raises his face to the sun. It's a glorious day. Multi-colored kites float against a backdrop of brilliant blue sky, their tails flapping in the breeze. The squeals of happy children blend with birdsong and the smell of freshly cut grass. Tom sneezes.

"Hay fever," he says, blowing his nose. "Sophie was the same. Always sniffing."

"Callie would have loved it here, wouldn't she, Thomas?" Amanda says.

"She would. She loved the outdoors," Tom tells me. "She always covered up though in long sleeves and skirts; she thought she was fat. I don't know why. She had a lovely figure. Sophie practically lived in a bikini in the summer. A beanpole, that one. Do you like the sun, Jenna?"

"Yes, although I have to be careful of my skin with the medication I'm on. I'm using plenty of sun cream."

"Remember the birthday picnics we had with the girls?" says Joe. "We always finished with ice cream. I'll go and get us some."

Tom and Joe head up the hill toward the pink van, giant ice-cream cone on its roof, and Amanda and I sit on a wrought iron bench overlooking the pond.

"It is warm, isn't it?" Amanda fans her hand in front of her face. "I wish I'd asked for a drink instead of an ice cream."

"Do you want some water?"

"Yes. Please."

I trudge toward Tom and Joe. They are engrossed in conversation at the back of a queue that snakes around a huge oak tree and I slip behind them, grateful for the shade. I am about to ask them about the water when I realize they are arguing. Tom snaps: "Stop it, Joe. We're brothers. You can't change the past...Jenna!" His voice softens to his usual tone as he notices me. "Is everything OK?"

"Amanda would like a bottle of water," I say.

"Of course. It's turning out to be a belter, isn't it?" He pulls his collar away from his neck. I walk back down the hill and as I turn around Tom and Joe aren't arguing anymore. They are standing stiffly. Arms folded. Not saying anything at all.

* * *

Shielding my eyes against the sun I watch ducks peck at soggy bread thrown by mums and toddlers.

"Callie used to love feeding the birds," Amanda says. "One year she wanted a swan princess party. I couldn't find a costume to buy and Tom was working all hours so Joe bought feathers from a craft shop and stuck them onto cardboard to make her some wings. I'll never forget her face." She breathes out, slow and deliberate, and I take her hand.

"Tell me about the party."

"It was—" She stops and clears her throat as though unused to the sound of her own voice. "It was at home. Pass the parcel. Traditional games. We didn't have much when they were small. A couple of years ago we took them to Fortnum & Mason for afternoon tea and then to a West End show. And last year we flew to Paris. I never spent my birthdays in England when I was young and I wanted them to experience the same thing. The excitement of spending your special day in a different country, but to be honest all they talked about were the parties they had as kids. The time Sophie tried to pin the tail on the donkey but stuck a drawing pin into Joe's thigh instead. I don't think it really hurt. She didn't push too hard but he'd hopped around on one leg, screaming, making the girls roar with laughter. I wanted to give them everything but it rained in Paris. We took a boat trip down the Seine and it was freezing. Not the memories I wanted to create. Callie must have liked it, I suppose. She went back there with Nathan a few weeks later."

"I think birthdays are always more exciting when you're young. The anticipation. We grow out of that, don't we?"

"Maybe but I felt I always let them down. I never gave them enough."

"All a child needs is a mother's love," I say, wincing at how trite the words sound.

"I have a bucket full of love, and no one to give it to." A film of tears glazes Amanda's eyes, and I slip my arm around her.

Peals of laughter pierce the air and we both look to our right. Playing tag on a patch of grass the color of wine bottles are two small girls, matching denim dresses, and I feel Amanda's shoulders rise as she sharply inhales. Her eyes follow them as they chase each other, but it's not them I'm watching. Behind them, on a bench shaded by trees, dappled sunlight obscuring his face, is a figure, black hood drawn over his head. I stare at him, and his head tilts to the side as if he knows I am looking at him but he doesn't move.

Tom and Joe return with half-melted ice cream trickling down the side of waffle cones, and Joe tries to make conversation but Tom and Amanda are transfixed by the girls, and I can't tear my eyes away from the figure. We finish our ice creams, and as we stand, he does too.

We walk toward the exit; Tom and Joe are discussing the fish in the lake, but I don't pay proper attention. I can't help looking over my shoulder: the girls are still playing, the man has disappeared, and I crane my neck, trying to see past the trees that flank the path, as though he might be hiding. Was he ever there at all?

"Are you OK, Jenna?" Joe asks.

"Fine, thanks," I say, but I'm not. In spite of Vanessa explaining Secondary Traumatic Stress to me, my fear is spreading like the ripples on the duck pond, and I can't seem to still it.

CHAPTER THIRTY-TWO

Harry isn't due to arrive at the vet's until ten to see the animals, but it's a little after nine when I arrive at the practice. I have been awake since first light trying to bury thoughts of Callie under a blanket of Sunday chores, but as I'd emptied the fridge, squeaking a damp dishcloth over its glass shelves, I found myself ruminating again. The walls of the kitchen seemed to inch forward, photos of Callie looming over me, until I'd grabbed my bag and keys and come here in an attempt to escape her, but her heart thump-thump-thumps inside my chest and I know that even if I take all her pictures down I will never be free of her. Not really.

The front door to the practice is unlocked and I instantly worry that I'd forgotten to lock up when I'd left but then I remember I haven't been here since Thursday. For once, I am not to blame, but that doesn't dispel the writhing feeling in the pit of my stomach. Who else could be here? I look over my shoulder. The car park is empty.

Pushing open the door I am surprised to see Rachel stooped over the computer.

"Rach?" I am hesitant as I cross reception. We haven't

really spoken since that awkward Wednesday evening at mine. "What are you doing here?"

"It is today, isn't it, that Harry is coming? I thought it would be nice to see him. To spend some time with you." The whites of her eyes are peppered with tiny red blood vessels.

"You look awful," I blurt out.

"Cheers, mate. I'll go home and crash soon. I've been stacking shelves all night in the supermarket. Trying to get the cash together for Liam's school trip."

"I didn't know you'd taken a second job?"

"It was my first night. And my last. I'm just looking online to see if there are any other part-time jobs."

"I can help." But by the time I have walked around the back of the desk she is powering down the computer.

"You can help by making me a strong coffee." She offers a tired smile, and I head toward the kitchen. It's the least I can do.

* * *

Harry bursts into the surgery clutching a Lego model. "It's an escape pod from Star Wars, Jenna."

I crouch down and examine it carefully before handing it back to him.

"Morning." I flash a smile at Kathy, Sam's mum. Even though we'd had that nice tea last week it still feels a little odd. I'm not sure how we fit together without Sam.

"Morning, Jenna. Thanks for doing this. He's talked of nothing else all week. Well, nearly nothing else." Her face darkens and I wonder whether Harry is still pestering Kathy to meet his dad.

"I've been looking forward to it. Do you want a drink?"

"If it's OK with you I'll nip to Tesco. Be back in a couple of hours?"

"No rush. We'll be fine, won't we, Harry?"

But he's already wandered out the back and I can hear him chattering to Rachel, and I say goodbye to Kathy and join them. Harry is kneeling on the floor dangling a stick with a feather on the end in front of a young black cat. She has a white stripe across her nose and is called Zebra. She hunches down, eyes following the toy and, as she pounces on it, Harry roars with delight. We don't usually board animals if their owners are going away but Zebra belongs to one of John and Linda's friends, and John is a soft touch when people ask for favors.

Harry plays with Zebra for most of the morning, and when the kitten is exhausted, Rachel scoops her up and places her back in her cage.

"Come see what's in here, Harry, but you have to be quiet." I take his hand and lead him into a small room. Harry walks with exaggerated steps toward the dog crate, on the tips of his toes, trying not to make a sound. He covers his mouth with both hands as he sees a small, black mongrel cowering on a once-white fleecy blanket.

Keeping my voice low I explain that the dog was brought in after being found in a garden. "We think she was hit by a car and we call her Lavender after the bush she was found in."

She isn't chipped and no one has claimed her yet. We'll keep her until her leg has healed and then we'll hand her over to the too-crowded animal shelter, where dogs tremble between bars as visitors scan the cages wanting the cutest, the cuddliest, or they bark incessantly, hurling themselves at the wire *pick me-pick me-pick me*.

"So no one loves her?" Tears well quickly and his voice is loud, and I put my hand on his arm to calm him.

"We don't know that yet, Harry. She might have a family

somewhere who are looking for her." I doubt this, looking at her matted fur and her visible ribs.

"I love her. I really love her. Can I keep her?"

We go through this with one animal or another each time Harry visits and sometimes I think it's too much for him, he gets so emotional, but Kathy says each time he leaves he says he's enjoyed it and begs to come back again.

"I think her family will come soon," I say diplomatically. I know Kathy isn't too keen on getting a dog.

"Mum says dogs are hard work. Children are hard work too but dogs are harder."

"That's right, Harry. They take lots of looking after."

"And walks and feeding. Do you think my dad has a dog?"

I'm thrown by the question and I busy myself filling Lavender's water bowl while I think of a reply.

"I don't know, Harry," is the best I can come up with.

"If Dad has a dog I could walk him, and I would love him and he would love me," Harry declares. "I'm going to meet Dad soon."

"Really?" I'm surprised. Kathy must have tracked him down.

"Yes. I've asked Mum. He will probably take me to the park. You know Debbie at school? I sit next to her. I don't like her though. She picks her nose and wipes her bogeys under the desk when she thinks no one's looking. Her dad sleeps at a different house now with someone called Auntie Sharon although she's not really Debbie's auntie. That's stupid, isn't it?" Harry's words stream so fast I have to stop what I'm doing and concentrate. "Her dad takes her out every Sunday. They can't stay at home and play video games as Auntie Sharon gets 'one of her heads' and the flat is too small and fresh air is best. They go to the park because her dad says he can't afford to take her anywhere good because her mum is 'bleeding him dry.' But I think the park is good. And if Auntie Sharon has one of her turns they have to stay out longer and eat McDonald's for tea." Harry takes a breath and I jump in.

"Has your dad been in touch, Harry?"

"Not yet but Mum says he'll turn up soon like a penny. How can you be like a penny, Jenna?"

Bad, I think, but I shrug my shoulders. "I don't know, Harry. Do you want to measure out some food for Lavender?"

The dog watches as Harry scoops dried food that smells of gravy into a measuring cup, before clattering the chunks into a stainless-steel bowl. Picking it up with two hands he walks carefully over to Lavender, who doesn't move but thumps her tail. Harry puts the food down, and she sniffs it and licks her lips before staring up at us beseechingly as if wanting permission to eat.

"Tuck in, girl." I scratch her behind the ear. "No one will hurt you here."

Lavender shuffles the biscuits around with her nose, sniffing hard, before wolfing the lot down.

"I'm going to the loo, Jenna," Harry says. "When I've finished you might want to give it five minutes." He wafts his hand in front of his nose as he speaks. "That's what Sam says in the mornings!" Peals of laughter follow Harry down the corridor. He closes the toilet door behind him, and I walk out into the courtyard. Rachel is sitting at the picnic table, her head in her hands.

"Are you OK?" I ask.

"Shattered. I'm going to head off soon. Can we talk for a sec?"

"Of course." I slide onto the bench opposite her. "What's up?"

"It's about those photos in your kitchen, the ones of Callie?"

My palms are flat on the table and they slide across the surface as I push myself up. A splinter embeds itself into the soft skin between my thumb and forefinger. I wince as a droplet of blood springs to the surface as I pick out the sliver of wood.

"Jenna, please. Sit."

"I thought I heard the bell on the door." I cock my head to one side but there's nothing to be heard except the birds twittering with delight as they swing from the green nets hanging from the feeder, pecking at fat balls.

"Kathy will find us. Listen. I know you want to help Callie's parents feel better in any way you can and I get that, I do. But I want to help you feel better, do you see?"

"I know." I sit down heavily and the bench shifts in the gravel with a crunch.

"I miss you."

"I'm still here."

"Physically you are, but mentally? You're so preoccupied with Callie, and I can't pretend to understand how it feels, having a piece of someone else inside you but—"

"I've been talking to Vanessa," I cut in. "I know my behavior has been a little ..." I'm loathe to use the word obsessive, "erratic but I've got to deal with this in my own way. In my own time."

"I'm so pleased you've talked to her. Did it help?"

"Yes," I admit. "I won't explain it all now when you're so tired but Vanessa's going to help me. Thanks for bearing with me, Rach. You're such a good friend. I know it hasn't been easy. I haven't been easy. I can't wait until my six-month check-up this week. When my medication is reduced, I hope I'll feel more like the old me again. Shift some of this weight I've gained at least." I place a hand over my stomach.

"You don't want to share this then?" She pulls a Mars Bar from her pocket.

"Do you really have to ask?" I raise my eyebrows and she smiles and peels back the wrapper and twists the chocolate into two. The caramel stretches before it snaps, and she hands me half. A truce of sorts.

*   *   *

"Jenna?" Kathy pokes her head out the back door.

"Hi." I stand licking my sticky fingers. "Harry's in the loo. He said he might be a while!"

"It's not easy living in a house of boys," Kathy sighs theatrically. "He'd better not be long. There's fish fingers defrosting in the boot."

I walk inside and tap on the toilet door. "Harry? Your mum's here."

Silence.

I knock again. Harder this time.

"Harry?"

I try the handle. The door opens into an empty room.

"Harry?" My feet slip-slide on the floor as I dash from room to room, sweat beading on my brow.

"Kathy…" I swallow hard. "I'm so sorry. He's gone. I can't find him anywhere." And it is only then I notice the scattered pieces of Lego on the floor.

CHAPTER THIRTY-THREE

Kathy's hand grips mine tightly as we sit in the back of the police car. The police have already checked the surrounding area but we still stare out of our respective windows, desperate for a sight of Harry. There are so many boys with dark brown hair and each time I spot one I feel a shard of hope that shatters into tiny pieces when I realize it's not him. Kathy hasn't shouted or screamed or done any of the things I'd probably do in her position but I know even if she were to fly at me, fists pummeling, punching out her rage, I couldn't feel any worse than I do right now. When the police asked if we'd heard anything, me and Rachel had exchanged a look, both remembering the way I'd stood in the courtyard, thinking I'd heard the bell on the door, but I'd sat down again and we'd eaten chocolate. The caramel and guilt rose in my stomach and I felt like I was going to vomit.

We're on our way back to Kathy's now. Her house has already been checked and we know Harry isn't there but it's early days we're told and statistically it's likely he'll just turn up. Children go missing all the time apparently but they're not Harry, are they? With his floppy brown fringe and infectious smile. It doesn't make sense he'd have wandered off. He never has before.

* * *

At Kathy's, a policewoman asks the same questions I've already answered.

There was nothing unusual in Harry's behavior. He gave no indication he was thinking of running away. We'd talked about the animals. About school. About Harry wanting to work for the Dogs Trust and rescue stray animals in a yellow van like in the adverts.

"And you didn't notice anyone suspicious outside the building at all?" The policewoman holds a mug of steaming coffee in front of me but when I stretch out my hand to take it I'm trembling so much she sets it on the table instead.

I hesitate before I answer this one. I'm not sure how to explain the sense of being followed. Being watched. I've nothing concrete to tell her, and anyway Vanessa thinks it's all in my head. Besides, even if it isn't, it can't be connected to Harry going missing, can it? And I didn't actually see anyone this morning.

"No."

"And there was nothing else?" The way she studies me is almost like she knows I'm holding something back.

"Well." I look at Kathy's white face. Her red-rimmed eyes. I don't want to upset her even more and yet there was one more thing we talked about, and I know this might be important. "Harry mentioned his dad. He really wanted to meet him and was wondering if he might have a pet dog."

A sob escapes Kathy and she clenches her hands into fists. "Harry's always asking for a dog. If he comes back, he can have anything he wants. Anything."

I shuffle closer to her and put my hands around her shoulders. She shrugs me off.

"And Harry's dad. Is he in the picture?"

Kathy shakes her head. "Owen? He's a waste of space. He's never had anything to do with Harry."

"Do you have contact details for him? A phone number? Address?"

Kathy wipes her nose and unlocks her phone. She scrolls through her contacts and relays his number. "He hasn't been answering any of my calls. He stopped paying maintenance months ago."

A flash of cherry red passes the window and rumbles into the driveway. Brakes squeak. Sam. I hold my breath as the front door bangs open and the thud of familiar footsteps pound the hallway. He's framed in the doorway, taking in the police, before he rushes to kneel in front of Kathy and he wraps his arms around her. "It's OK, Mum. We'll find him."

"They're asking about Owen. But he wouldn't have taken him, would he? He doesn't want anything to do with Harry. But what if he's fed up with paying for him every month? Oh God." She rocks back and forth. "He wouldn't hurt him, would he, Sam?"

"Of course not." Sam twists his head and addresses the policewoman. "What can I do?"

"Do you have a recent photo of Harry?"

Sam pulls out his phone and swipes through his photos. Over his shoulder I see pictures of Harry at the farm feeding goats; Harry in the garden playing with the hosepipe; Harry tearing wrapping paper from a large square box. His face shines with happiness from each one.

Sam settles on a recent shot of Harry at school: he's staring directly into the camera, beaming. Front tooth missing. Sam passes his phone over.

"And his dad? Owen, was it?" the policewoman asks.

Sam shakes his head. "I don't have a photo of him. Mum?"

Kathy wipes her cheeks with her sleeve. "There's one in Harry's baby book in the bottom drawer taken at the hospital. It was the only time Owen ever met Harry."

Sam pulls out a book and swipes through the pages. "Here." He points at a picture of Kathy: exhausted smile, dark circles under eyes, cradling Harry, while a dark-haired man stands to the side of her bed looking down at his son.

As I stare at Owen's face my chest burns as though the air has been sucked out of my lungs. Rain. Darkness. Blood. Images flash through my mind. It's as if I'm thundering through a tunnel on a train catching glimpses of posters I can't quite identify. Owen's face is so familiar. I know I've never met him but it's as if a bottle of champagne has been uncorked and fragmented memories froth and spill, and none of them are good. The fear builds and builds. A sense of helplessness. A thin film of sweat covers my body. What's happening to me? I press my hands against my ears trying to block out the muttering in my head.

CHAPTER THIRTY-FOUR

Oh my god. What have I done? What have I done? What have I done?

CHAPTER THIRTY-FIVE

"Jen?" I'm vaguely aware of Sam's voice and my mind begins to still. "Are you OK?"

I lower my hands from my ears. Everyone is staring at me and I'm caught between embarrassment and terror.

"You're sweating. Here." He pulls out a handkerchief from his pocket and dabs gently at my forehead, just like he used to do when I was sick. He pushes it into my hand and I curl my fingers around it. I know if I press it against my nose and inhale, it will smell of humbugs.

"Let's go outside and get some air," he says.

We sit on the back step. Our bodies in shadow, legs hot in the sun. The air is heavy with the smell of rosemary from Kathy's herb garden.

"What just happened, Jenna?"

I breathe in deeply through my nose. Puff air out of my mouth. It seems ages before I feel able to speak. "I've never met Owen, have I?" I confirm what I already know.

"No. Not that I know of. Why?"

How can I explain that as I looked at the photo I felt I'd seen those eyes before? There's a feeling deep in my gut that tells me something very, very bad has happened but it's like looking through murky water. Blurred shapes and movements. Instead, I say: "I'm so sorry. About Harry." I twist the corner of the handkerchief around in my fingers until it forms a point.

"It's not your fault," Sam says even though we both know that it is. "He's seven. He knows better than to wander off. We'll find him." There's a quiver in his voice. He runs his fingers through his hair and it sticks up at all angles, and I have to suppress the urge to smooth it down.

He stands and paces the small gray patio where we've spent endless summer days cremating sausages, caramelizing onions, blackened smoke drifting over next door's fence. "Sod what the police say. I can't sit here and do nothing. I'm going to Owen's."

"Does Harry even know where he lives?" I ask.

"Mum's got the address in her address book. It wouldn't be hard for Harry to find out. He's a smart lad."

"But surely Owen's will be the first place the police will check? They might be talking to him now?" I can see the policewoman in the kitchen, speaking into her radio.

"If Owen has taken him he's not likely to answer his phone, is he? They say they're doing everything they can but will checking Owen's be a priority? Are they even taking it seriously? It's not like he's a baby or there was any ... well, anything at the surgery."

He means blood, I think, and we fall silent for a moment.

"Why would he go now? Today?"

"Perhaps he's been waiting for a chance. He can't leave school without an adult picking him up and Mum watches him like a hawk at home. She still won't let him play out. Fuck it. I'm going." Sam's voice is firmer now. "Coming?" He stretches out a hand and I take it. As he pulls me to my feet I fall against his chest and he holds me, steadying me for a moment too long after I've found my footing.

* * *

Sam's engine roars to life and I can barely hear him as he says: "Sorry about the noise. There's a hole in the exhaust."

We sound as though we're part of the Grand Prix as we race toward Owen's house. Sam doesn't speak; his mouth is a thin line as he weaves in and out of the traffic, accelerating as lights turn to amber.

Owen's house isn't what I expected. Sam has such a low opinion of him I pictured him living in squalor. A bedsit, overrun with take-out containers and empty beer cans. We screech to a halt outside a small detached house. Weeds twist through the gaps in between the block paving at the front.

"Wait here." Sam flings open his door and races up the driveway, and the overwhelming panic I'd felt before when I saw the picture of Owen heats my blood and I struggle to control my breathing. I feel sick and I close my eyes. Thudding the door with my fists in the pouring rain. Crying. My heart feels it's going to beat its way out of my chest. Begging. Screaming through the letter box: "I just want to talk."

My trembling hand unclips my seatbelt and I push open my door and swing my legs out of the car. Standing, I put a hand on the hot car roof to steady myself before approaching the house. Sam has stopped knocking on the door and is making his way around the back. The front is locked. Blinds closed. I crouch and look through the letter box. Post is piled up against the door. Sam is rattling the patio doors as I pick my way through the back garden. Weeds and nettles snag my legs and grasp at the laces in my trainers. This garden hasn't been tended for a long, long time. I cup my hands over my eyes and press my face against the smeared glass.

I scan the lounge, the sofa, the coffee table, the fireplace. My eyes linger on the hearth; there's a dark stain.

From nowhere I hear a scream. I totter backward, almost falling. Not sure if it's in my head but there's no movement inside the house. Stretching out my hand I grasp Sam's arm. Reassure myself he is here. He is real.

"Did you hear that?" I whisper.

"Hear what?" he asks.

"Nothing," I say. What is happening to me? What happened to Callie? She knew Owen, of that I am sure, and what's more, she was scared of him.

* * *

Back at Kathy's, friends and neighbors arrive for the search. I keep busy, worried that if I stop moving, my surroundings will fragment and I'll be swathed in darkness once more. I make sandwiches that will sit and curl on the plate, lettuce wilting and egg congealing. No one is hungry. The TV flickers in the background and Kathy stares blankly at the screen but I know if I stand in front of it and ask her what she's watching she wouldn't have a clue.

Sam is pacing up and down the hallway, making call after call. No one has seen Harry but people want to help. He's told them all to come, and the printer whirrs out maps of the local area and he highlights places to search. My parents are on their way.

"We'll divide everyone into pairs when they turn up; we can cover more ground that way."

I rub my eyes, exhausted although it's not yet 4:00 p.m. I can't believe Harry has only been missing a few hours.

It feels like days. I can't settle. It's as if seeing the photo of Owen has unplugged something in my mind, sparking pulsing images that vanish before I can fully grasp them. It's like a game of telephone almost, and I've no idea how to interpret them.

At a loose end, I text Nathan to let him know what's going on. He offers to come and help but I hesitate, not sure I want my past and present in the same room.

"Jenna?" Sam says, and I put my phone away. He is a mantle of calm as he organizes a search, his voice steady, but he blinks twice as much as usual and I know how scared he is. "Can you cover the area near the vet's? You know it better than anyone."

A clipboard is being passed around and I scribble my mobile number onto the list of others; Sam's going to copy them so we can all contact each other with news. "When we've found him," Sam says and we all smile and nod. "Of course we'll find him."

I squeeze next to Kathy on the sofa while I wait for the list of phone numbers. "He'll be OK," I tell her but she's lost to another world. I pick up the remote, my finger poised to change the channel from the 24-hour news to something less depressing. But I'm drawn by the flurry of policemen swarming around a field. The reporter, face set in a serious expression, gestures with his hand to the yellow police tape behind him. The camera pans to a white tent before zooming in to the somber face of the policeman guarding the entrance. Legs splayed, hands clasped in front of him. I turn up the volume and lean closer to the set.

A woman's face fills the screen. Her cheeks are flushed, gray hair escapes under a black beanie.

"Could you tell us in your own words what happened?"

"Yes." The woman's eyes fill with tears and she rocks

from side to side. The shot pans out. The reporter puts a hand on her forearm, whether to comfort her or steady her, I don't know.

"I was walking Barnaby."

"Your dog?"

"Yes." She gestures to the King Charles spaniel leaping around her feet. "I got him from a rescue center. I let my granddaughter, Chloe, name him." Her mouth flicks into a quick smile as though she's just realized she's on TV. That Chloe might see her. But her face droops as she glances over her shoulder.

"That's where I found it." Her voice cracks and she pulls back and wipes her nose, but the reporter is thrusting the microphone into her face again.

"And what did you find?"

Tears spill and she shakes her head from side to side. "It was Barnaby really. He wouldn't stop digging. I tried to pull him away but he growled at me. That's not like him and I thought he must smell something good. A bone perhaps." Her pupils dilate as she stares into the distance.

"What happened next?"

She visibly jumps as the reporter's voice jars her back to the present moment. "Sorry. Yes. I grabbed Barnaby's collar and I tried to drag him away, and that's when I saw it." She screws her eyelids tight.

"It?"

"The hand. A human hand. I'm sorry. I can't..." She runs off and the camera zooms in to the reporter's face.

"Breaking news. A body has just been discovered by a dog walker at Burton Aerodrome. Stay tuned for live updates."

CHAPTER THIRTY-SIX

You fucking, fucking bastard.

CHAPTER THIRTY-SEVEN

At first I think it is Kathy that has spoken but she is sitting on the sofa, arms wrapped around herself, rocking gently back and forth. The police are quick to reassure her that the body isn't Harry but the "what-ifs" hang in the air and the mood has changed. As I look around the room the shock on everyone's face is apparent. Although no one says anything there's been a collective shift in our thinking. We've gone from hoping Harry's just wandered off to fearing the worst. People pull on shoes and zip up coats ready for the search. My head is reeling. Burton Aerodrome is the last place that Callie visited using her satnav but before I have time to think about it properly I hear a familiar voice call "Hello?" from the hallway. The lounge door is pushed open, and at the sight of Mum and Dad, standing shoulder to shoulder, a hot lump rises in my throat. I've been desperate for them to be in the same room. But not like this.

"Mum." I cross the room and kiss her powdered cheek. She smells of baking and as she tucks her hair behind her ear I notice she has flour and butter under her nails, and I am so touched she has dropped everything to come.

"Dad picked me up. I thought it would be quicker than

waiting for a taxi." Mum crouches down beside Kathy and pats her hands. "We'll find him. Don't worry."

"Hello, Sam." Dad shakes Sam's hand but there are no smiles. No "pleased to see you again." This is not a happy reunion.

"So he went missing at the vet's? Does Linda know?" Dad asks me.

"I'm sure the police will have spoken to Linda if they need to," snaps Mum.

"I didn't mean that I—" begins Dad.

"Stop it, you two. This isn't the time or place," I almost hiss and both my parents stare down at their shoes, and I feel our roles have been reversed.

We are heading out of the door when the police radio crackles and hisses and the policewoman holds her hand up as though she's stopping traffic, and we stop mid-stride as she slips outside. Please let him be OK. When she returns, minutes later, she's smiling.

"We've found him. He's fine and a car will bring him home shortly."

Kathy slumps back on the sofa—still and silent—and I step outside and pull out my mobile. There are several missed calls and texts from Nathan, all asking what's going on, but I have to ring Rachel before I do anything else. She's still at the practice, waiting for news.

"Rach? It's OK; he's been found," I blurt out before she can even say hello.

"Thank fuck for that." She exhales sharply. "I've been sitting here thinking how I'd feel if it were Liam. I think I've aged ten years this afternoon."

"Sorry. I owe you a stiff drink."

"You owe me more than that, Jenna McCauley! See you tomorrow at work."

In the lounge, we sit and chat in low voices as the hands on the clock seem to move at half speed. It feels like hours before there is the thrum of an engine, the slamming of doors, and Harry limps into the room, his pale face streaked with tears. Kathy envelops him into a hug and, for once, he doesn't try to wriggle away.

"Where was he?" Sam asks.

"Miller Road," says the policeman who drove him home. "A young mum spotted him crying outside her front window and came out to check. Not many would nowadays. He has twisted his ankle but we've given him a proper check over and he's fine. No harm done."

Kathy releases her grip on Harry although she doesn't break contact as though afraid he might disappear again. "What on earth were you doing there, Harry? We've been worried sick." Her voice rises in pitch as she speaks and Harry breaks into fresh sobs and the policeman talks instead.

"He said he came out the loo and went into reception looking for Jenna." I shift uncomfortably in my seat. "Harry saw someone outside in the car park. He waved and they waved back and Harry got this idea it might be his dad come to surprise him and so he slipped out of the unlocked"—I cringe again—"door and followed them but he couldn't keep up and tried to run but twisted his ankle."

"And this person," I say, "what did they look like?"

"He couldn't give a description beyond they were wearing jeans and a black hoodie, and that could be anyone, couldn't it?"

* * *

Over the next half an hour the lounge gradually empties of people and Dad asks if I want a lift home.

"Stay for a bit?" Sam says, and I nod and hug my parents goodbye. "Thanks for coming."

"I'm always here if you need me," Dad says but he's looking at Mum as he speaks. "Shall we make a move, Daph?"

"I can get a cab, Ken," she says.

"If I drive you, I could mow the lawn while I'm there, and afterward perhaps we could talk?"

She stares up at the sky as if seeking guidance before she answers. "Have you eaten?"

"Only a bowl of cornflakes."

"That's not a proper dinner. I've made a pie." Without looking at him she turns and walks stiffly out of the door and we watch from the window as she waits at the car. Dad opens the passenger door for her and, although she shrugs him off when he brushes her shoulder as he passes her the seatbelt, I think it might be the start of something.

* * *

As Sam drives me home his hand rustles inside a bag of humbugs and he pulls one out and fumbles to unwrap it as he steers. There was a time I'd have twisted off the plastic for him, popping it into his mouth, but that feels too intimate now. The engine thrums as we wait at the traffic lights, and I study the red-bricked cottage that doesn't quite fit in with the rest of the street we're on. Honeysuckle weaves in and out of the trellis either side of the front door and a pale pink clematis climbs to the dusky sky.

It all looks so achingly beautiful. So achingly normal. If something awful had happened to Harry today I know I'd never have been able to see the world in quite the same way again.

Sam's reached the chewy bit in the middle of his sweet now and his teeth grind together before he swallows.

"Jen, I've been wanting to talk to you."

I turn to look at him but his face is impassive as he watches the road ahead.

"It's about your . . . fixation with Callie."

"I don't have a fixation. I have Secondary Traumatic Stress Syndrome."

Sam twists his head to look at me and the surprise on his face is apparent.

"You've already talked to someone?"

"I went to see Vanessa on Friday. I know I've been a little bit . . . preoccupied."

"So you've taken them down, the pictures in your kitchen?"

"How do you know about those?" I try to keep the sharpness out of my voice.

"Rachel told me. She's so worried about you. We both are."

"You've been talking about me behind my back? Very bloody cozy." Jealousy bubbles like acid in my stomach. Rachel hadn't mentioned that earlier.

"It's not like she was gossiping. She was really upset after she'd seen them. She said it was like a shrine almost."

"It's not a bloody shrine. I'm interested in Callie, that's all. Who wouldn't be?"

"So you're not embroiling yourself into her family thinking you can somehow . . ."

"I'm not embroiling myself anywhere. They want to see me too."

"Rachel said you're trying to find out more about the night Callie died? I don't think . . ."

"Rachel's said a bloody lot, hasn't she?"

"You're lucky to have her, Jenna."

Before my surgery I'd probably have been described as

"honest," "loyal," "kind." Now I'm "lucky," "inspirational," or "courageous" and hearing this from Sam causes me to bristle.

"Don't tell me what I am," I snap.

"You seem to feel you owe these people." He's shouting now as well, and I'm not sure if it's the pent-up emotions of the day spilling out but I can't seem to calm down either.

"And you think I don't? They saved my life."

"It was their choice. You don't owe anyone, Jen."

"Not even you?"

He screeches to a halt on the double yellows outside the flat and we glare at each other.

"Yes actually, I do think you bloody owe me, now you come to mention it."

"And what? What do I owe you, Sam? The rest of my life?"

"A proper conversation at least. You seem to care more about a bunch of strangers than you do about me." The vein on his forehead pulses. "You pushed me away because of . . ."

"What if I didn't? What if I just didn't want to be with you anymore? You can't handle the thought of that, can you, Sam?"

"Maybe I don't want to be with you either, did you think of that? But there are things we should talk about."

"You probably want to be with Rachel so you can continue your cozy conversations." I can't seem to control my words, and a look of disgust flashes across his face.

"At least Rachel's happy to be alive. You're not dying, Jen, not today. Stop acting like every breath could be your last, because right now, I think you're wasting Callie's heart."

His words slam into my chest and I almost fall out of

the car, banging the door closed after me. I march toward my flat, not turning as the wheels on Sam's car squeal as he accelerates away.

My anger doesn't recede as I clump up the stairs to my flat. If I wasn't so lost in thought I might have heard it. A sound. The opening of the communal door. A creaking of the stair. Footsteps quietly creeping up behind me. But as it is, I am completely unaware that I'm not alone as I rummage through my bag for my keys until I inhale sharply in frustration, ready to huff out air, and I smell it. Oil. Stale smoke. And then it only takes a split second to feel the presence behind me. Breath hot and sour against my cheek. A scream builds inside my throat but there's already a hand clamped over my mouth, fingers knotted in my hair.

CHAPTER THIRTY-EIGHT

The person who attacked me is speaking. His voice is low, his words controlled but I can't hear anything beyond the blood hissing and pounding in my ear as I struggle to break free.

Terror gallops through my body and as I struggle I lose my footing and my body folds like a rag doll. I'm yanked upright by my hair and it feels like thousands of red-hot needles are pricking at my scalp. My mouth springs open, despite the hand covering my lips, and I bite down as hard as I can, my teeth a vise around his fingers.

"Fucking bitch."

I am pushed forward, falling heavily onto my knees, and banging my head against the floor. Dizzy, I scramble into the corner and shuffle around until my spine is pressed hard against the wall. My eyes dart around, looking for something, anything, I can use as a weapon. Neil from the Prince of Wales pub scowls at me through slitted eyes as he sucks his fingers.

"What do you want?" I force myself to stand up, clutching my bag against my chest like a shield, my fingers looped around the handle, ready to swing it at him if he steps closer.

"Where's Owen?" he growls, and I am momentarily thrown.

Why is he looking for Harry's dad? Why would he come to me? I rub the lump that's forming on the side of my head as though I can dislodge the fuzziness.

"Did you follow me home from the pub the other night? Why are you asking about Owen? Do you know Kathy and Harry?"

I'm babbling, I know. Asking too many questions, but I'm scared that if I stop I'll be the one expected to give answers, and I don't know anything about Owen. What will he do then?

From outside there's the sound of a car engine, and we wouldn't normally hear it here, if it wasn't for the hole in its exhaust.

"That's my boyfriend, Sam!" The words spill out in a rush of relief.

Neil hesitates before he peers out of the small, cracked window that overlooks the street.

"What sort of car does he have?"

"It's a Fiat. Red." I take long, juddering breaths as Neil spins and hurtles down the stairs, two at a time, and as the outer door bangs open I make my way over to the window. Sam is slotting his car into a space outside the florist's. I look up and down the street but I can't see Neil.

Sam has parked now but he doesn't cut the engine. Instead, I see him lower his forehead onto the steering wheel as if trying to decide what to do, and as I watch him I rest my forehead against the dirty glass willing him to come upstairs. Time seems elastic. It stretches and stretches. Neither of us moves. My breath fogs the glass and I pull my sleeve over the heel of my hand to wipe the window, and when I can see out onto the street again Sam's reverse lights are on. His car shifts and engine roars, and as he pulls away I whisper: "Don't go, please," but he can't hear me, of course, and I am alone.

Or am I?

There's a sound. It could be a floorboard shifting. It could be the wind against the letter box. It could be something. It could be nothing. But I yank my keys from my bag and run into my flat, locking the front door behind me and dragging the telephone table in front of it. Just in case.

* * *

I'm so tired. My mind map is a tangle of sweeping lines and as I struggle to focus my sleep-heavy eyes the colors seem to swarm on the page. But my exhaustion is tiny in comparison to the fear that has wrapped itself around me like ivy clinging to a tree ever since I visited Owen's house. I'm sure I've seen him before. I check my phone for the umpteenth time. I've set a Google Alert for Burton Aerodrome. There haven't been any updates and I can't stop thinking about the body they found there. Why had Callie been there? A sudden sound slices through the early morning stillness making me jump and for a split second I worry Neil has come back, and I wonder again whether I should have called the police but it's only a dog barking. Neil. Owen. Callie. Their faces zing round my mind and just as I feel my head might explode it comes to me. The grainy photo of Neil I'd found with the article online, accusing him of assault. The blurred image standing behind him. It was Owen. I'm sure it was, and it only takes a quick check to confirm I am right. Did Callie know Owen? Was she having an affair with him? Although I didn't know her it seems almost impossible to think of her with Neil. I'm so tired. I dig my hands in my hair and pull as though I can release some of the pressure inside my skull. My eyes are drooping now, and I drain my cup, but this time my eyes don't snap open and I cross my arms on the table in front of me and rest my head down. Just for a second. I'm so tired. But I won't go to sleep. It's not safe to sleep, but darkness folds itself around me anyway, burrowing into my subconscious, sparking a memory.

CHAPTER THIRTY-NINE

I strip off my dress and knickers and stuff them deep into the wicker laundry basket in the corner of the room. Tomorrow I'll throw them away. I can't bear to wear them again. My legs are shaking so much it's an effort to climb into the bath. I twist the dial on the shower to hot and sink to my knees. I don't feel I will ever be warm again. What have I done? I am motionless for so long goose flesh crawls along my arms. The plughole sucks away the cascading water and my tears. I reach up for the shower gel and wash mitt and I scrub at my skin until it's pink and raw but I still feel dirty on the outside. Dirty on the inside. An image springs to mind of the last bath we took together. Me leaning back against your chest as you gently shampooed my hair. Candles flickering. Lavender bubbles soothing. How can things have changed so much?

There's a tapping on the bathroom door. "I didn't hear you come home. Did you have a good night?" you ask, even though I know you're hurt whenever I go out without you.

Nausea swells and my whole body violently shakes. I try to reach the toilet in time but I can't and I heave and retch, splattering the contents of my stomach all over the bathroom floor in between my choking sobs.

"Are you sick, baby? Let me in," *you say, but I can't.*

I can't let you in. I've never been able to keep anything hidden from you. You've always said the only thing we need is each other. But that isn't true. Not anymore. And I don't know how to tell you, but I know that I must.

*** *** ***

"Cat got your tongue?" *you ask, and I shake my head.*

"Then say it. You need to promise me you won't tell anyone how you got this." *You lightly run your finger over my bruised cheek, and trace the swelling under my eye, and I shrink back into my chair.*

"Of course. I promised, didn't I?"

"I think I should take you," *you say, and I stand and take our breakfast things over to the sink, not quite meeting your eye.*

"I'm on a late schedule today. It will look odd if I arrive this early. You get to your meeting."

"I'm not sure ..."

"Look. You wanted things to be normal again?" *I touch my cheek and wonder how you possibly think I could forget.*

"OK."

You kiss me on the head and tell me you'll see me later. Your footsteps echo down the hallway and when the front door slams shut I scuttle into the lounge and peep out of the window, staying half-hidden behind the curtains. You disappear around the corner, beige mac looped over your arm, tan briefcase swinging in the opposite hand. I don't know how you can act so normal this morning, as if the screaming rage of last night never happened. I hardly dare breathe as I wait to see if you'll come back—surprise—but as seconds turn to minutes I feel myself beginning to relax. You're really gone.

It doesn't much matter what I wear and even though I've only just pulled myself away from the window I couldn't tell you what the weather is. Rain. Sunshine. I've no idea. I pull off my work uniform and wriggle into jeans and a T-shirt. My overnight bag is on the top of the huge oak wardrobe and I have to stand on tiptoes to yank it down. Dust motes fall onto my upturned face and I cough and cough.

There's no thought to what I'm stuffing into the bag. Clothes, underwear, toiletries. The essentials really. And when it's almost bursting I struggle to zip it closed.

I slip into my jacket and loop my handbag over my shoulder, flipping open my purse to check how much cash I have, but it is empty. I was sure I had two twenty pound notes. I'll need to stop at a bank, and I open up the Lloyds app on my iPhone to check how much money we have. I used to have my own account but now my wages are paid into a joint savings account each month. I wasn't keen at first but, as you said, if I'm left in charge of my own finances I overspend on clothes. I'm pleased now you're so meticulous with your spreadsheets and box for receipts. We have quite a nest egg. Punching in the passcode I tap my foot as I wait for the page to load and when it does my breath catches. There's nothing in the account.

Fear and frustration collaborate and tears bite at the back of my throat. I throw myself onto our bed and sob. How can I leave you now? I have nothing left.

CHAPTER FORTY

In my dream I was crying, and as I wake my cheeks are wet. At first I'm disorientated because I'm not in bed. My arms are pins-and-needles numb lying heavy on the kitchen table. I sit up and sharp pains shoot through my neck. The mind map is stuck to my cheek and I peel it from my skin and rub at the drool that has crusted around the corner of my mouth. Outside the sky is streaked with apricot and the glowing numbers on the hob tell me it is 6 a.m. I check my phone. There are no updates for Burton Aerodrome, but later, I'm picking at the scrambled eggs my tumbling stomach doesn't want, when my mobile beeps. I seize it from the table hoping for news. Instead it's a text from Nathan confirming he will pick me up from work at midday, and a flash of annoyance streaks through me. I can't go to work. I can't see Nathan. I've stuff to figure out here, but Owen's name leaps out at me from the mind map and I think if Callie knew him then Nathan must too. *Looking forward to seeing you,*" I reply but there's a dullness in my chest and my teeth are clamped together so hard my temples throb.

* * *

I look up as someone enters the practice and all I see is a pair of denim-clad legs and a lady's head, her body obscured by a huge wicker basket full of roses and lilies.

"Delivery for Jenna McCauley?"

"That's me!" I take the flowers, turning my head away from their overpowering fragrance. Setting them on reception I slice open the envelope and read the card—"THANKS SO MUCH FOR JOINING US FOR CALLIE'S BIRTHDAY. TOM AND AMANDA X"—and at their names the familiar clamp tightens around my chest.

At twelve I am pushing the door to leave when Kelly calls: "Don't forget your flowers, Jenna."

"I'll leave them here until tomorrow."

"Do you mind if you don't?" She pulls a face. "I have hay fever." She sniffs hard, and I swallow my irritation.

Petals fall on the floor as I snatch the flowers, and I don't pick them up.

* * *

Nathan is sitting waiting in his car. "They look expensive," he says, twisting around in his seat as I place the bouquet in the back. "Secret admirer?"

"They're from a grateful patient." The lie trips easily from my tongue.

"That's nice. Isn't there a card?" He peers among the flowers.

"No. They brought them in personally."

"They're a florist, are they, this patient?"

I am momentarily confused.

"It's just I saw the lady bring them in from her van." There's a beat before he continues: "Anyway, do you like art? There's an amateur exhibition in the church hall on Chiltern Road." But he doesn't wait for an answer, indicating left as he pulls out of the car park. His eyes fixed firmly on the road ahead.

* * *

There is a three pound entrance fee to get into the exhibition, which includes a piping hot drink in a thin Styrofoam cup that burns my fingers, and a custard cream. It's gloomy and chilly inside. A faint whiff of air freshener hangs in the air. Goosebumps blanket my skin as we wander around the hall. The art ranges from startlingly good to what-on earth-is-that?

"You're very quiet. Are you OK?" Nathan asks, and I feel the heat of his palm on the small of my back and there's a fluttering deep in my belly. I can't work out whether it's excitement or revulsion. The closeness we'd felt on Friday night has vanished and now I feel awkward in his company.

"I'm fine, just a little tired." I step closer to the painting of an orange cat shaped like a rectangle, so his hand falls away.

"We can go back to yours if you want to?"

"No!" The word rockets from my mouth louder than I intended, and I ignore the hurt that flashes across his face and walk over to the next display screen. A small beach scene catches my eye. Pastel beach huts strewn with bunting line up as though they're preparing to race toward the apple green sea. A lone pink bucket and spade sits on honeycomb-colored sand. It reminds me of the paintings Amanda used to do, the ones I'd seen on the wall in their house. It reminds me why I'm here with Nathan.

"Sorry." I reach out and touch his arm as he joins me. "I'm shattered. I didn't get much sleep last night after Harry going missing."

"That's understandable. I thought you were annoyed with me for turning up unannounced on Saturday. I could tell you were uncomfortable having me in your flat."

"It wasn't that, it's just I wasn't expecting visitors. I hadn't washed up."

"And you didn't want me to wander into the kitchen to see it?"

"It?" My stomach contracts into a tiny ball as I think of the mind map, but then I realize he's referring to the washing up and I keep talking. "Saturday must have been hard, being Callie's birthday."

"Every day is hard. Birthday or not." There's a sadness in his eyes.

"You must think about her all the time? About the night of the accident? If you want to talk . . ."

"Shall we move on?"

At first I think he means the conversation but he gestures to the next display board. I find I can't tear myself away from the beach painting and, on a whim, I find myself buying it for Amanda. It's the last day of the exhibition so the artist is happy to let me take it away, and while he wraps it in tissue paper Nathan asks me to hold his jacket so he can go to the loo. I pay for the painting and slip it into my bag and move toward the toilet door. Nathan's jacket is heavy in my hand; it swings against my leg and something hard and solid bumps into my thigh. His phone. I glance up at the toilet door. It's shut and I know I don't have long if I want to check Nathan's contacts. See if Owen is listed. Surely if Callie did know him, Nathan might too? My hand is trembling as I reach into the jacket pocket and pull out the phone. I touch the home button and the screen illuminates. A photo of Callie sitting cross-legged by a lake, gazing out into the distance, unaware she was being watched.

There's no passcode and I navigate the menu, scrolling down the contacts. There's a listing for an "Owen" but before I can open the contact to see if there's an address the handset slips from my grasp, hitting the floor with a clatter. I crouch and wrap my fingers around it, but before I can stand Nathan's shoes come to rest before me and I look up, aware that my face is flaming.

"What are you doing?" Nathan asks stretching, out his hand.

"Sorry. It fell out of your pocket."

I give him the phone and he glances at the screen before stuffing it into his trouser pocket, and he grasps both my wrists, pulling me to my feet. His grip is tight. Almost too tight and I can't quell the feeling of panic in my stomach. The smell of the air freshener wafting from the toilet as the door swings open again is sickening. My phone rings and Nathan releases me but as I delve into my bag for my handset I can still feel hands tight around my wrists, fingertips pressing into the soft flesh, crushing my bones. I feel hot. Dizzy. Faint. My screen is flashing "*unknown number,*" and I step away from Nathan as I accept the call.

"Hello?"

"Jenna. It's Joe. Callie's uncle. I hope you don't mind me calling; I got your number from Tom."

I glance at Nathan but he's engrossed in one of the paintings. "Not at all. Is everything OK?"

"Not really." His sigh comes down the phone so hard I can almost feel a puff of air against my ear. "Callie's birthday has really set Amanda back and Tom's really struggling. He tries to put a brave face on all the time but after the first birthday without her, and Sophie not being here too, it's pushed them over the edge. Amanda wouldn't get out of bed at all yesterday, or today."

"I'm so sorry. Is there anything I can do? I'd still like to help you find Sophie, if I can."

"You could help by spending some time with Amanda?"

His voice is quiet, drowned out by the squeaking of the tea trolley as it is pushed past me, and I turn to face the wall, pressing the heel of my hand against my right ear.

"It will give Tom a break. I help as often as I can but I'm on the road for the next few days. It worries me sick to see him so stressed, it's not good for his heart. It helped them both that you were there for Callie's birthday, I know it did. You're not family but there's a bond."

"I'll do what I can. I'll give Tom a ring and see when they're free. I've got something for Amanda anyway."

"Like they ever have plans! They're both at home now. I've just spoken to Tom."

"Oh. Right."

"Sorry, you're probably busy?" Joe asks, and I hesitate, but how can I refuse them? The family of my heart.

"No, I could go now," I reply.

"You're a star. Thanks so much."

I disconnect the call and swing around. Nathan is standing directly behind me.

"Who was that?" he asks, and I can't instantly think of an answer as I wonder how long he's been there. What he's overheard. Did I say Tom and Amanda or Callie or was it only Joe who mentioned them?

"Cat got your tongue?" Nathan says and he smiles.

But as he repeats exactly the same phrase from my dream last night sharp, jagged images spring to the forefront of my mind eclipsing my ability to answer: bruised face, missing money, feeling trapped. Nathan continues to stare at me, waiting for me to speak, and my whole body grows cold. He can't be the person Callie was scared of, can he? He was so tender when he made love to me, it doesn't seem possible.

"Jenna? Are you OK?"

"I'm so sorry. I have to go."

"Was it something I said?"

"No, no. It's just a ... it's a ... It's a friend. In need."

"Is it the person who sent you flowers?"

"No. It's ..." I trail off, unsure how to explain myself. "It's an emergency."

"I'll drive you," he says.

"It's a long way ..."

"I insist." He sounds pleasant but I think there's an icy undertone to his voice, the same as in my dream, or am I just imagining it?

We step out into the bright sunshine. Standing at the crossing I glance sideward at Nathan—did he hurt Callie? The beep-beep-beep of the green man tells me it is safe. But as Nathan grips my elbow, guiding me across the road, safe is the last thing I feel, and I wonder how I'm going to get away.

CHAPTER FORTY-ONE

"Thanks for the offer of a lift, Nathan. But I'm going to get a cab." I fight to keep my voice bright and breezy as I flag down a passing taxi. "I'll call you later."

"But what about..." he begins but I'm already climbing into the back seat and slamming the door behind me. As we pull away I swivel my head to look out of the back window, and the shock on Nathan's face is palpable.

Forty-five minutes later I arrive at Tom's. His face is pale as he opens the door but he hugs me hello and asks how I am.

"I'm fine. How's Amanda?" I keep my voice low as I step into the hallway.

Every line on his face is etched with worry. "She's getting worse. I don't know what to do."

"Why don't you have a break? Go for a walk. I'll stay with her."

He seems torn as he glances toward the stairs. "A walk would be nice, but..."

"She'll be fine, I promise. She probably won't even notice you've gone."

"Thanks. I won't be too long."

He is slipping on his shoes as I pad upstairs; I'm not sure if Amanda is awake. I stick my head around their bedroom door trying not to recoil from the sour smell of sweat and despair.

"Amanda?" I whisper. It's hard to see in the gloom and I tiptoe across the room toward the shape huddled in the bed. The duvet rises and falls as she gently snores, and I leave as quietly as I can. At the top of the stairs I hesitate. The spare room is to my right. The door is ajar. I can see the boxes containing Callie's things, and I glance downstairs. Tom could be gone for ages. Amanda is asleep. There'd be no harm in taking a quick look, would there?

* * *

I try to open the first box as quietly as I can but the cardboard flaps scrape against each other and I pause every few seconds, listening out for Amanda. The first box is full of clothes and I press down into the softness but I can't feel anything else and so I try another box. I lift out a tangle of wires and underneath there's an iPad. I open the magnetic case but the screen remains dark and I find the right lead and plug it into a socket. The battery symbol flashes red, but within a few minutes it shows it is charging and as it switches on I feel a rush of excitement as I press open Safari, but I'm not connected to the Internet and I have to create a hotspot from my phone before I can try again. Callie's search history is empty and, disappointed, I try her emails instead. Scrolling down I notice nothing of interest. Recipes Amanda has sent her, YouTube funny cat videos forwarded from Sara at work. I flick through her apps. *Words with Friends*, *Air Hockey*, *Tetris*. I press my finger against the icon for *Evernote*. There's a file for gardening. Notes on shrubs. And a folder marked "*flights*." I open this one and there's a weblink to a page of prices for two one-way tickets to Spain. Callie must have helped Sophie and her boyfriend with their travel arrangements, but I wonder why the tickets are one-way when Tom and Amanda seem to expect Sophie to return any day. There's another file and this one contains links to an application for a payday loan but before I can read any more there's a movement from Amanda's bedroom. I unplug the iPad and quietly place everything back where I had found it before slipping out of the room and tapping on Amanda's door.

She is lying on her back staring up at nothing. Her hands rest on top of the covers and her wrists look like twigs poking out of her sleeves; one wrong move and they'll snap.

"How are you, Amanda?"

"Tired," she whispers although she's only just woken.

"I've got something for you. Can I open the curtains?"

Her head barely moves but I think she nods. I skirt around the bedstead, and I part the curtains before cracking open the window. A warm honey glow fills the room. Already, it's less stuffy.

The mattress sags and squeaks as I perch on the edge of the bed. Amanda props herself up with a pillow while I pull open my bag and take out the painting.

Her hands shake and it takes her an age to take off the tissue paper. When the picture is unwrapped I'm shocked to see anguish streak her face as she stares at the picture, seeing more in the scene than I ever could.

"I'm so sorry. I didn't mean to upset you."

"You haven't. It was very kind of you to think of me."

"I bought it from an amateur art exhibition today. It reminded me of the ones you painted."

"We loved the beach. All of us. I was used to foreign holidays growing up. Guaranteed sunshine but Tom and I couldn't provide that for the girls. We went back to Owl Lodge Caravan Park at Newley-on-Sea, year after year, and the girls adored it. Even when rain splattered on the caravan roof so loudly I had to stuff cotton wool in their ears just so they could get to sleep. Callie and Sophie had a pink bucket just like this one." She traces the swirls the brush has made in the paint with her finger.

"Good memories to have."

"I didn't realize how lucky I was." Amanda bursts into tears.

I stand and contort my body so I am leaning over hugging her, and my T-shirt becomes damp with her grief. I hold her as her body shakes, ignoring the pins and needles in my hand, the aching in my back, until Tom comes home.

* * *

It's been such a long day and I'm exhausted, but as I push open the communal door that leads to my flat I instinctively feel something is wrong. There's a sickly sweet scent in the air. At first I put it down to nerves—after the experience with Neil yesterday I'm bound to feel apprehensive—but as I step inside I see them. Lilies and roses scattered over the stairs. The flowers I'd left in Nathan's car. The wicker basket they'd been delivered in is lying in pieces, broken and twisted, as though it has been stamped on. As I stand staring at it there is a rush of blood to my head and I wobble on my feet. I place one hand against the wall to steady myself. The door crashes shut behind me and my stomach constricts into a hard knot of fear. Reaching behind me I pull the door open again and let it slam shut as though I have left, and then I crouch in the shadows to the side of the staircase waiting for footsteps to pound down the stairs. I stay hidden, keeping myself as small as possible as the minutes tick by, until cramp forces me to my feet. I don't think there's anyone here.

Slowly. Quietly. I creep up the staircase, craning my neck, looking for the shift of a shadow, the shuffling of feet and, although there's nothing, my fear builds and builds until I reach the top of the stairs—and then I know.

My front door is cracked open.

Someone is in my flat.

CHAPTER FORTY-TWO

Clapping my hand over my mouth I hold myself perfectly still, ears straining for the sound of movement inside. There's nothing to hear except faint laughter from the flat above, the low hum of their TV, and I think about running upstairs but they've only just moved in and I haven't met them yet. Besides, I can't hear any noise coming from inside my flat.

Stretching out my arm, my fingertips lightly press on the door, and ever so gently I push. The hinges squeak and I drop my hand. Random images rush at me. A figure hiding behind the door, under my bed, in my wardrobe. I can't bring myself to go inside. Stepping backward I press my spine against the wall, half-expecting someone to charge toward me. I don't take my eyes off the door as I retreat downstairs, and once I am outside I sink to the curb, dropping my head between my knees, waiting for the feeling of weightlessness to pass. When it does and I feel able to speak, I pull my mobile out of my bag. There's a text from Nathan and my breath stalls in my lungs as I read *"Hope your friend is OK. I've left your bouquet on your step x."* A sense of unease slithers in the pit of my stomach as again I feel like I am being watched, and I look over both shoulders before I start to punch out numbers on my phone. "Nine." "Nine." I hesitate, my finger hovering over the keypad. The flowers might prove Nathan has been here but it doesn't necessarily mean he has been in my flat. That anyone has been in my flat. Did I lock my door when I left? Did I close it even? Sifting through my clouded mind doubt swallows me whole. I can't be sure. Think, Jenna.

Closing my eyes I picture my keys in my hand and I have a really strong feeling I pulled the door closed behind me. "We don't go on feelings, Miss McCauley." The way I'd been dismissed at the station still smarts and I don't want to call the police unless I'm sure someone has broken into the flat, and I'm not sure. I'm not sure at all. What now?

* * *

I'm still sitting on the curb when Sam arrives, my teeth chattering, but I don't feel cold. He screeches to a halt on the double yellows.

"Jen." Slamming his car door he reaches me in three strides, and as I stand I wobble, and he pulls me to his chest. The wool from his jumper is itchy against my cheek but I don't pull away.

"Are the police upstairs?" he asks.

"I haven't called them."

"Why not?" Holding my upper arms he steps back so he can scrutinize my face and I hope he doesn't see the guilt in my eyes and guess that I've slept with someone else.

"I'm not sure if I shut the door when I left. I had a lot on my mind," I eventually confess. "It's my biopsy tomorrow. I'm not thinking straight. I don't want to waste police time." I chew my bottom lip not wanting to tell him I'd visited the police station days before and am worried they won't believe me again. The things I keep hidden are beginning to outbalance the truths I tell—the scales are tipping, weighted with deceit.

He glances up at the window of the flat. "I'll go and check. You wait here."

Sam disappears through the communal door and it takes seconds for me to follow, tiptoeing behind him, but as he reaches the top of the stairs I stage-whisper: "Sam!"

He turns.

"Perhaps we should call the police. There could be someone inside."

Emotions slide across his face. "I won't let anyone hurt you," he says and he steps through the door before I can reply it's him I'm worried about, not me.

A gasp escapes me as I follow Sam through my door. Glancing to my right I can see the lounge is in disarray. Books pulled from the shelves, cushions on the floor.

"Go and wait outside." His voice is tense, but although I don't follow him as he pads down the hallway, I can't step away either. My stomach is a tight, hard knot and my feet are rooted to the floor. Sam disappears into each room before returning to me.

"There's no one here but we need to call the police."

Pushing past him I rush into the bedroom. "Don't touch anything, Jenna," he cries but it's too late. Stepping over drawers that have been pulled from the chest, contents spilled like paint, I drop to my knees in front of the open doors of my wardrobe and pick up the carved wooden box, upended and empty.

"Jenna?"

I hear Sam but I don't speak. I can't speak. I frantically rifle through the mess, locating everything that's lost, placing the items, one by one, back into the box, but they're all sullied now. A stranger has touched them, and I swallow the acid that has risen in my throat. There's the pair of lemon newborn baby socks, the cream floppy rabbit with ears that crinkle, the tiny Babygro imprinted with a curled and sleeping hedgehog. At first I can't find it, the scan picture, and although the image is scorched onto my heart panic wells until my fingers brush against the shiny paper and I pick up the print of the life that never got to live.

"You kept everything?" Sam murmurs and I feel a punch of raw emotion, deep in my stomach, and I fold into myself, my head on my knees.

All the things we've never properly talked about hang in the air like mist. I want to tell him how sorry I am that I lost our baby when my heart gave up trying but my apologies are stuck in my throat, along with my tears and my shame. Sam holds me as I rock, his thumb rhythmically stroking the back of my neck, and my stain of regret spreads.

* * *

It felt a little awkward, fetching Sam blankets and a pillow as though he is a guest. As though this was never his home, but I'm grateful to not be alone tonight. I lie in bed listening to the rain pitter-patter against the window. Staring so long at the street lamp outside the orange blurs and blends into the charcoal sky. I close my eyes. It's my six-month check-up tomorrow and I need to get some rest.

The toilet chain flushes and water whooshes through the pipes under the floorboard. The creaking tread of Sam's footsteps as he pads down the hallway is comforting, but instead of him coming into the bedroom and spooning behind me, the lounge door creaks open and the sofa springs squeak as he lies down.

He doesn't settle. The sofa creaks and groans under his

weight and I wonder whether he'll come and get into bed with me. I wonder whether I want him to.

Since the break-in, anxiety has pulsed through me in short, sharp bursts. I haven't called the police. Despite the mess, my paperwork strewn everywhere, my bills, my sketchbooks, nothing has been taken, and I can't face trying to explain everything, given that it's all so muddled in my head. Sam had been silent as he picked up the photos of Callie that had been pulled from the kitchen walls as he helped me tidy up, but I had seen the look of disbelief on his face as he'd examined the torn pieces of my mind map. I'd noticed the slight shake of his head as he studied my random thoughts. Would he still think it's all in my head if I hadn't rushed over to the fridge when we walked into the kitchen and stood in front of the door so he couldn't see what I saw? The magnetic letters had been rearranged into two words: "STOP DIGGING."

CHAPTER FORTY-THREE

"It's nothing." My hand flutters to my face, fingertips gently touching the swollen skin beneath my eye. "I fell down the stairs at home." It's been a long morning explaining myself, fielding off concerned questions and sympathetic smiles, but I can hardly tell the truth, can I? I was honest with you. Too honest and look where that's got me.

I'm longing to be alone and I watch the hands on the clock tick; seconds turning into minutes, minutes into hours, until at last it's lunchtime.

"I'm nipping out," I call as I race toward the door, craving some fresh air. Some time alone. Space to think.

The wind is icy and I lower my head, pushing against it as I cross the car park. There's a light smattering of rain and I think how exposed I'll be if I sit in the park and I think about popping in to see my parents even though I've promised you I won't see them. I won't see anyone. Not without you there.

I'm lost in thought, hardly seeing the drab, gray pavement as I hurry, when I see them. Shoes. Shiny black brogues. Your shoes. I raise my head and you're sitting on the wall. Briefcase at your feet.

"Mind if I join you for lunch?" you say, and my heart sinks.

CHAPTER FORTY-FOUR

My eyes snap open. Someone has a hold of my foot. I try to kick out, my body slick with sweat, but I can't move my legs. My heart leaps into my mouth until I realize it's only the sheets tangled around my ankles. Leaning forward, I pull myself free and I sit up, breathing in slowly and deeply until my pulse begins to slow. I'm OK. I'm safe. But there's a shuffling from the lounge and panic takes hold of me again until I remember he's still here. Sam.

There's a creaking on the other side of the wall as Sam shifts on the sofa again, and I slot my hand between the spindles on my headboard and press my palm against the cool plaster that separates us.

* * *

"Morning." Sam pads into the kitchen, feet bare and hair sticking up at all angles. He picks up the kettle and shakes it from side to side before taking it over to the sink and swooshing on the tap. I turn over the new mind map I have drawn, facedown on the table in front of me, and cradle my now cold mug of coffee. I've been up for hours, sifting through my suspicions. Too scared to fall back to sleep.

Who left the warning on my fridge? Will they come back? Caffeine jitters through my veins and I fidget in my seat.

"You look shattered." Sam pulls a chair out and I momentarily close my eyes as the legs screech against the floor. "Look, Jen. We need to talk. Properly." I stiffen at his words and stand up, and something flashes across his face that could be hurt or irritation.

"It's not the right time, Sam." Whether he wants to talk about the break-in or the baby I don't know. "I need to get ready for the hospital."

"How are you feeling about the biopsy today?" The look of sympathy in his face makes my throat grow hot.

"Fine." But my voice is too bright, and as I stand under the hot pins of the shower I turn the water pressure higher so he can't hear me cry.

* * *

I can't remember ever feeling quite so tired. There is a humming in my head and I probably shouldn't be at work, but Dad's not picking me up for the hospital until 11:30 a.m. After Sam left for work the flat felt dark and empty and I was jumping at the slightest sound and I didn't want to stay there alone. But now I'm here, it's a huge effort to smile at the customers, to reassure them their pets are going to be fine even though I don't always believe that. Bad things happen.

The surgery door pushes open and the sudden breeze lifts the papers from the reception desk. I slap one hand on top of them before they blow away. The delivery driver wedges the door open and hefts brown cardboard boxes from the back of his van, stacking them in the corner of the waiting room.

"That's the last one." The driver thrusts a clipboard under my nose and I scrawl my name on his delivery sheet.

"Goodness," Linda says. "What are all these?"

"The drug order." But I've never seen this much arrive before.

The boxes feel like lead weights as I force one exhausted foot in front of the other until we've carried them all through to the stockroom. Linda slices through packing tape with a pair of scissors and we kneel on the floor unpacking the contents. As we finish Linda sits back on her heels.

"Jenna, there's three times the amount we need here." Her voice is terse. "I really think you should consider taking some time off. I'm worried ..."

"I'm fine. It's probably a mistake at the warehouse. I'm sure I emailed through a repeat of last week's order." I scrunch my face up trying to remember, but my mind is full of dark holes. If I'm honest I don't even remember placing the order at all. "I'll fetch the delivery note from my desk."

In reception the phone is ringing, a dog is yapping, urine drips from a cat carrier, and the smell is strong and sour. I don't know what to do first. I'm barely holding it together.

"Jenna!" Mrs. Bainbridge's anguished cry jars me from my thoughts. She's staggered through the door. Tears torrenting down cheeks that are gray with worry. Casper is cradled in her arms. I shudder at the sight of the Jack Russell but he's still. Too still. Ignoring my rolling anxiety, I force myself to take him from her, and as I look down at his mouth lolling open, his pig pink tongue and needle-sharp teeth, he begins to swim out of focus.

"What's happened?"

Linda's voice snaps me from my daze and I gratefully pass Casper over to her. Despite being small he felt like a dead weight in my arms.

"He was like this in his basket this morning. The kitchen

was a mess. Covered in diarrhea. Is he going to die?" Her voice is tremulous.

"We'll do what we can."

I follow Linda into the treatment room and she lays him on the bench. "Are you OK for a minute? I need to finish up with the rabbit next door."

"I'll be fine," I say. I'm shattered but I function on automatic pilot as I insert a cannula into the vein in Casper's leg before hooking him up to a drip. I attach the plastic bag of fluids, squeezing gently until liquid travels down the tube. I call Mrs. Bainbridge through. Her lip quivers when she sees him.

"What's wrong with him?"

"We're not sure until we've run some tests. He's critical but stable now. As soon as you've signed the consent form we'll take some blood." Mrs. Bainbridge's hand trembles as she takes the pen I offer. Her signature is barely legible. I lead her back to reception. "It could take a while. You're probably better off waiting at home."

"I want to stay."

We are still waiting for the results of the tests nearly an hour later. I've made her three cups of milky tea that she sips while I hold her other hand, stroking the dry, liver-spotted skin with my thumb.

"It shouldn't be too much longer," I say, conscious that I need to go soon for my appointment. I'm worried about leaving her.

"Can I see him?"

"Let me check." I pat her hand.

In his kennel Casper is lying on his side, legs rigid, unseeing eyes glassy.

"Crash box!" I call, although I know from looking at him it is too late.

Footsteps pound into the room. When I turn around, Linda, Kelly, and Rachel are standing silently behind me.

"He..." I gesture toward the dog. "Poor Mrs. Bainbridge. Poor Casper." His beady eyes seem to watch me and I drape a sheet over his motionless body. As I stand up again I notice Kelly picking something up from behind the sink.

"Jenna?" says Kelly. Her cold, hard stare chills me.

"What?"

"I found these." She unclasps her hand and there are two empty vials of insulin. "You're the first person to use this room today. Did you spike Casper's drip? Cause him to fit?"

"Of course not." I swallow hard. Why is everyone glaring at me?

"It's no secret you're scared of him," Kelly says.

"I wouldn't do this." I gesture toward him with my hand.

I wait for Linda or Rachel to stick up for me, but they don't.

"We'll run some more blood," Linda says, frowning.

"It wasn't me." I'm stricken at the thought I could make such a stupid mistake. Except how can it be a mistake? There's no way insulin should have been anywhere near the drip. It was deliberate. I'm tired and confused but even factoring in the cloudiness my medication causes, I wouldn't have done this. I just wouldn't. I tally up the things that have gone wrong since I returned to work. Missing orders. Over orders. Wrong doses. Anger builds and I'm swathed in a fog of fury as suddenly everything falls into place.

"It was you." I jab Kelly in the chest with my finger and she staggers back. "Trying to make me look bad. Lose my job so you could have it. You...you fucking bitch." I shove her. Her head thwacks against the wall and her eyes widen with shock and pain. I spring toward her but Rachel grabs my arm, fingers digging hard into my wrist.

"Stop it, Jenna. Kelly wouldn't do that."

Shaking Rachel free I round on her. "Was it you then? You were on the computer on Sunday when I arrived. Have you been messing with my orders?" I'm out of control, I know, but I can't calm down. "It's no secret you're broke. With your drunk dad and brother to support. If I was sacked you'd get to keep the senior position's wages. Or is it Sam you're after? He's told me about your cozy conversations behind my back." Words pour from my lips, toxic and acerbic, as anger bubbles in my chest like acid.

"Thanks, friend. I've been the one covering up your mistakes."

I open my mouth to respond but Linda speaks. Low and quiet.

"I think it would be best if you went home, Jenna."

"Linda, you surely can't believe I've done this? You've known me for years."

"I don't know what to think, but I've a surgery full of patients, a dead dog to explain, and my nurses screaming at each other. I'll talk to you all when you've calmed down and we have Casper's blood results, but in the meantime, Jenna, in light of your attack on Kelly, I'd like you to leave."

"I want to be the one to break it to Mrs. Bainbridge." I know how upset she'll be.

Linda glances at Kelly. She's clutching the back of her skull with her hands. I didn't push her that hard.

"You can go out the back way," Linda says.

"Fine." I shove the door open. It bangs against the wall, and after grabbing my bag, I storm out of the fire door.

I walk briskly at first but gradually the waves of adrenaline recede and my pace slows. Have I lost my

job? Anxiety rises, harder and faster this time. Have I lost
Rachel? There's nothing as corrosive as suspicion. It's eating away at me from the inside out. Rachel wouldn't have
done this. Would she? But mistrust gnaws at the pit of my
stomach. Rachel didn't deny it, did she? But then another
thought occurs, slamming into my chest, stopping me in
my tracks. *What if it was me?* There's no denying how
many things have slipped my mind lately. I press the heels
of my hands against my forehead, fingertips digging into
my scalp as I try to reconstruct the last hour, but from the
moment Casper came in everything is hazy like it happened long ago. I'm sure there was just saline in Casper's
drip but I can't be absolutely certain. Right now I feel as
though I can't trust anyone. Not even myself.

CHAPTER FORTY-FIVE

I'm waiting on the corner at 11:30, out of sight of the surgery, when Dad's car pulls over. I'd thought Mum was meeting us at the hospital but she waves at me from the passenger seat and I'm touched they've set aside their differences to both support me today. I climb into the back, wrapping myself in the musty red plaid blanket Dad always carries "in case of emergency" and it's like wrapping myself in comfort. I could be small again, strapped in the back of the car, Dad crunching a sherbet lemon; Mum telling him he's going the wrong way.

We all walk into the hospital shoulder to shoulder and I feel a rush of gratitude there are two people I can still depend on. The waiting room is hot and quiet, save the distant rattle of a trolley. We pump antibacterial gel into our palms and I grimace as it stings the paper cut I've got. Perched on a hard orange seat I ignore the out-of-date magazines piled on the table and ask: "Well? Are you two..."

They glance at each other, and for a split second I wonder if I've got it wrong but Dad takes Mum's hand and says: "Yes. We had a good talk after all that business with Harry and we're trying again."

"That's brilliant," I say and I mean it.

"We've booked an appointment with a therapist like your Vanessa, to talk things through," he says.

"You're going to talk about your feelings with a stranger?" Dad can't even ask directions from a stranger when he's lost.

"Whatever it takes, Jen."

I burst into tears. Hot, noisy tears.

"Jenna? Darling. I thought you'd be pleased?" Mum fishes a tissue from her bag.

"I am." I blow my nose. "It's nice to hear of something good. It's just everything's been so awful lately, so hard, and I think . . . I think I've lost my job."

"Why?" Mum's voice is sharp.

"I've been making so many mistakes. Ordering too much stock. Giving out the wrong medication. There has been a complaint of me being rude to customers. I don't remember doing most of it. The medication makes my mind fuzzy sometimes. It's hard to concentrate. This morning . . ." I wipe my eyes. "Casper died and Kelly found a vial of insulin next to his drip. She accused me of spiking it deliberately."

"Oh, Jenna." Dad squeezes my hand. "I'm so sorry."

"But, Dad, I accused Kelly of doing it. I thought she was after my job and when she denied it . . . I accused Rachel. I said she wanted me sacked so she could take over the senior position for the money. I said some awful things about her family. God knows, it probably was me who mixed insulin with the saline. I'm so bloody tired. I really don't know what I'm doing at the moment."

"I don't think it was you for a second." Dad passes me a clean tissue.

"You don't know that. I completely forgot to call by your house the other day, didn't I, Dad, to pick those books

up for Linda? And I didn't ring you, Mum, like I'd promised. I'm forgetting things all the time. Messing up. Poor
Casper." I blow my nose.

Mum and Dad exchange a look.

"See even you two think I'm useless." A fresh bout of
tears washes over me.

"For God's sake, Ken. Tell her," Mum snaps.

"Tell me what?"

Dad stands and paces the corridor.

"If you don't, I will," Mum says.

"Jenna." Dad crouches down in front of me and takes my
hands in his, as though he's about to give me terrible news.

"When you were ill..." He swallows and looks away as
if ordering his words before he continues. "It was hard. For
everyone. I felt so helpless not being able to help you and I
needed someone to talk to. Linda has always been such a
good friend, but one night I made a massive, massive mistake." He bites his lower lip. "Let's just say Linda and I,
well, we got too friendly."

At first I don't realize what he's implying and I look
questioningly at Mum but she won't meet my eye. And then
I know. "You slept with Linda?" I yank my hands away.
"How could you? What about Mum? John? He's your
friend!" It explains why Dad stopped golfing with John so
suddenly.

"I'm not proud of what I did. The hurt I caused. It was
a moment of madness but, well...it got more complicated
than that. Linda wanted more. She hadn't been happy with
John for years. I told her she and I were a silly mistake. She
didn't like that, though she had to accept it, but she wanted
a clean break. No more us all being friends. She didn't want
to be around you."

"That's why you and Mum were against me going back.

You weren't worried about me getting an infection from the animals at all."

"Darling, we were. Of course we were," Mum says. "But..."

"And Linda. She's always asking if I'm up to working there. Telling me she'll understand if I leave."

"Of course she couldn't just sack you. How would she have explained that to John? And she wouldn't want to appear heartless in front of everyone. Not after your surgery. I think she's been doing these things out of spite. Hoping you'd leave or she'd have a proper reason to dismiss you."

"And you let me go back to work there?" I'm glaring at Mum now and she shifts uncomfortably in her seat. "Why didn't you tell me?" I can't believe this. How did Mum stand me working for her? But I think of the way she's tried to push me in different directions since my op, to gently persuade me to think of other things to do.

Mum expels a long juddering breath. "It was an extreme situation. Your Dad and Linda were a one-off. A mistake, and you'd lost so much already. Sam, the baby, your health. Your job was the one thing you were clinging onto. I couldn't be responsible for taking that away from you too."

"You've lied to me." I stand as the nurse approaches and, as much as I'm dreading what's to come, it's a relief to follow her down the winding corridors. I don't once look back at my parents.

* * *

I'm taken to change into a hospital gown and one of the ties at the back is missing and I hold it together as I shuffle forward, conscious that my bottom is visible for all to see. I'm glad I've worn my biggest pair of pants today.

Dr. Kapur is pleased to see me; he always greets me as though I'm his favorite patient and, despite knowing what's to come, it's good to see him too. He's become such a huge part of my life, it's almost like seeing an old friend. I climb onto the narrow trolley and cling on tightly as the nurse works her foot up and down on a pump. I rise higher and higher and each jerk upward makes my muscles tense as I try not to tumble to the floor.

I fall silent and try to quell my rising panic as Dr. Kapur fills the silence with tales of his twin daughters, who have recently started school. The first time I had a biopsy I thought it was a joke that a piece of my heart needed to be extracted and tested and I'd nervously laughed as Dr. Kapur told me this would take place under local anesthetic, not a general, but he was deadly serious. I had lain on the cold, hard trolley staring at the bright lights shining from the stark white ceiling and tried to relax. I had believed Dr. Kapur's soothing words that I would barely feel a thing. A catheter was threaded through the veins in my neck to reach my heart, and when the grabbing device extracted a piece of living tissue the slight tug he said I would feel was a sharp yank. Tears sprang to my eyes as a piece of my heart was snatched away and I felt as though I was falling down a rabbit hole.

This time I'm having an angiogram too. I screw my eyes tightly closed and try to transport myself somewhere else as my groin area is shaved and I tense as the sharp point of the needle enters this tender area. The background sound of the radio, the soft Irish lilt of the nurse, fades away and I'm breathing deeply. Forcing my body to relax until, despite being semi-aware of what's happening around me, I'm drifting, floating, soaring into a memory that instantly terrifies me.

CHAPTER FORTY-SIX

Jets of water pelt from the shower masking my voice as I press myself against the cold blue tiles in the bathroom, one hand clamped over my ear, as I strain to hear the voice on the other end of the phone. My voice, low at first, gets louder and louder as I fight to make myself heard.

The door handle rattles and I jump, pressing the phone to my chest. I wait.

Thump-thump-thump. The door judders in its frame and my pulse skyrockets.

"Who are you talking to?" Your voice is dark and angry.

"N...N...No one." I cut the call and twist the dial on the shower.

"I heard you speaking."

"I've hardly got someone here in with me, have I?" I retort. "And you've taken my mobile, haven't you, so I can't call anyone?" My heart is pounding so hard I'm surprised you can't hear it. I hope you don't remember the pay-as-you-go phone I bought a couple of years ago when I had to send my iPhone off for repair. If you take this too I don't know what I'll do.

The door handle rattles again. Harder this time and I place my palm against the tiles to steady myself.

"Unlock the door."

"I'm drying myself."

"I insist …"

"One sec, please …" I'm not wet, still fully dressed, and I yank off my clothes and wrap my towel around my body. Coughing as I open the mirrored bathroom cabinet to mask the sound I scoop my tampons out of the box and nestle my secret phone inside. I heap tampons back on top, shaking them to ensure the black plastic is covered. I put the box back in the cabinet and stack my Veet on its lid and shut the door.

I crouch and run my hands along the bottom of the bath and shake the droplets of water on my hands over my shoulders.

"Come. Out. Now." Your voice has an edge. That edge. And I take a deep breath before unlocking the door.

CHAPTER FORTY-SEVEN

Later, I'm on a day ward dunking a ginger nut into a cup of weak tea and as the sugar hits my system I start to feel a little less shaky. I reach over for my bag and delve inside for my mobile. I'm still angry with my parents but I want to let Mum know it went OK. She'll be worrying. I've a missed call from Linda and my jaw tightens as I see her name. She's left a voicemail and I unlock my phone, intending to delete it, but curiosity gets the better of me and I press play.

> "Jenna, it's me. Linda. Your dad has called and told me that you know about...well, that you know and I never meant to...I shouldn't have...Anyway, it wasn't you—Casper, I mean—or me. He was old and he was dead when I found him. I'll send you a copy of the reports so you can see if you want to. The vials were just...stupid. And the other stuff... Look, we've always been so fond of you, John and me. He's not well. Did you know that? He's having tests and can't be stressed. I'm hoping we can sort this out between ourselves. Call me. Please. If I can just have the chance to—"

She runs out of time and a mechanical voice offers me a list of options, and I choose to listen again and again as the ginger swirls in my stomach along with sadness. John and Linda have been part of my life for so long. My world has shrunk a little bit more.

* * *

I'm half-dozing when Dr. Kapur strides into my cubicle and swishes the curtain closed around me.

"How are you feeling, Jenna?" he asks in a loud voice. I'm sure he must think the flimsy material acts as soundproofing.

"Fine." I give the stock British response as though he has not just snipped off a piece of my heart to study.

"Nothing you want to tell me?" he questions, consulting his clipboard.

I shake my head and he scribbles a note before clicking the end of his ballpoint pen and tucking it into his pocket.

"I will be reducing your medication but I would like to see you again in a couple of weeks."

"A couple of weeks?" I instantly place my hand over my chest fearing the worst. "Is something wrong?"

"Physically, everything's looking good. Better than good." He smiles reassuringly. "But your side effects have been a little ... extreme. And I want to make sure the reduction in medication is alleviating them."

"Side effects?" There are so many, I wonder if he's referring to anything specific.

"Your paranoia."

"How do you know about that?" I don't remember telling him.

"Vanessa said ..."

"Vanessa?" I'm the one speaking too loudly now. "She's my therapist. She can't share ..."

"Vanessa works in very close conjunction with us. We were the ones who sent you to her. When she's concerned about one of our patients, as she has been with you, she's quite within her rights to—"

"What about my rights? It's a betrayal of confidence. I trusted her."

"You still can. I can reassure you she wouldn't discuss—" But his voice is silenced by the voice inside my head whispering: *Don't trust anyone*.

* * *

It's almost a disappointment when I am told I can leave and as the smiling nurse hands me my aftercare instructions, side effects to look out for, and list of numbers I should ring in an emergency, I almost ask her if I can stay. I don't relish the thought of seeing Mum or Dad, especially Dad, or going back to the flat. She asks who is picking me up and I tell her my parents are here somewhere, most likely in the cafeteria, and she offers to call them but I tell her I'll do it.

I take my time dressing, and when I can't avoid it any longer I pick up my phone. A text message has come in from an unknown number and when I open it I feel my chest tighten.

"Hope you got the message on your fridge yesterday? I'd hate for YOU to have an accident."

CHAPTER FORTY-EIGHT

"Take it."

"No."

"Open your mouth." You force your thumb between my lips and press down hard on my bottom teeth. I try to thrust my head backward but your fingers are gripping my chin. Tears well and I clutch your arm with both my hands and try to push you away, but I'm weak.

"Come on," you say. "It will make you feel better. You know it will."

Exhausted, I stop struggling and as you loosen your grip I slump back on my seat.

"Just one."

You loom toward me and I try to shake my head from side to side but I'm sick. Dizzy. Scared.

"For me." Your tone softens now.

I can't fight you anymore. I open my mouth. You pop the capsule on my tongue. It tastes bitter and you hold a glass of warm water to my lips and I swallow.

"Good girl," you say as you brush my hair away from my face, fingertips soothing my brow.

I close my eyes. Wait for the numbness to spread. Gradually, my muscles relax. I feel like I'm floating.

The next time you speak your voice sounds muffled as though you're coming from very far away. I think you say: "I only want to make you feel better," but I can't be sure of anything anymore.

* * *

I'm drifting in and out of consciousness. My limbs are heavy and I seem to have lost coordination. There's the sensation of movement. You're carrying me and I struggle to break free but my body feels as though it's made of lead.

"Shhhh," you say. Your arm is around me and my head fits perfectly into that space between your head and shoulder.

"Please," I try to say but my tongue is thick and I can't form the word properly. I'm falling back into blackness. It's a relief not to feel anymore. Not to think.

"I can't let you go, Callie," you whisper.

CHAPTER FORTY-NINE

I am still shaking when I wake up, stiff and uncomfortable, on the sofa. It has been two days since my biopsy and I haven't been to bed yet. Each time I sleep it seems I fall back into Callie's memories and I'm scared of what I might see when I close my eyes. I'm scared of the darkness of my dreams. The things I can't always remember as I wake, sweating and screaming. The finer details fading, slipping just outside my consciousness once more, and all I'm left with is a thick coating of fear.

"I'd hate for YOU to have an accident," the text to my phone had said, and I know if I take it to the police I will be dismissed again. There's no way of knowing who sent it and it's so carefully worded it may not be interpreted as a threat—but I know it is—and despite my incessant checks the front door is locked, the chain is across, the furniture I've dragged in front of the door hasn't moved; every little sound I hear, I convince myself someone is here with me.

I try to stay awake with perpetual cups of coffee, pacing the flat, studying my mind map, endlessly Googling. It's been days since the body was discovered at Burton Aerodrome—why haven't the police identified it yet?

Who was in my flat? The local news hasn't reported any other burglaries the past few days and I wonder whether mine could somehow be connected to Tom and Amanda's break-in. I go back to the day of Callie's funeral and check the archives around that time. It takes hours of reading until I find it. A small paragraph reporting the break-in and then days later a follow-up.

> Police have arrested two men in conjunction with the burglary at Chester Road. All items have been recovered except the cash taken from the safe and an unusual necklace, pictured below. Police ask if anyone has information about this item to contact them on the number below. It is believed the pair have been responsible for a spate of burglaries that have all taken place while the homeowners have been attending funerals.

Below is a photo of Amanda's ruby and diamond star necklace. Neither of the men named are Neil or Owen and I think Tom's break-in was probably unconnected to Callie, but what about mine? My mind keeps flicking to the message on my fridge.

"STOP DIGGING"

Oh God. I'm so scared.

As dawn begins to break I slump on the sofa, staring blankly at the TV glowing in the corner, the sound down low so I can hear if anyone tries to get into my flat again. Listening. I'm always listening.

One hundred and eighty-four days ago Callie's heart was transplanted into my body. Sometimes now I hate her, this girl who allowed me to live. I don't know what she wants. What she's trying to tell me. I don't know what's real anymore and what isn't, and there's no one I can talk to. No one I can trust.

Outside the window the sun rises gold but even in the
first twinges of daylight I still feel it. The prickling sensation of eyes on me. Watching me. Waiting. And I stalk
around the flat again. Checking inside the wardrobe,
behind doors, under the bed, but there isn't anyone there.
There never is.

There's a thickness in my throat as I swallow down
my medication. My nose is streaming and my forehead is
burning. *I'm dying.* The thought pops into my mind unbidden and I push it away. Of course I'm not. But what if I
am? What if my body is starting to reject Callie's heart
and I never find out what happened that night for Tom and
Amanda? I cradle my heavy head in my hands. Despite
the warnings I have received I have to try again but I don't
know which way to turn.

In the kitchen, I study the mind map, and as the sun
shifts in the sky it reflects in the silver of the fridge handle.
The dazzling brightness triggers a memory, mine this time,
of the first visit I made to Nathan's house, pulling the garden chair cushions from Nathan's shed, upsetting the flowerpot. That glint of silver before I ran from the spider. A
door key.

* * *

I step into Nathan's hallway and lock the front door behind
me, slipping the key inside my pocket. I'll put it back in the
shed before I leave. The house is still. Quiet. But I find the
silence oppressive rather than reassuring. Although I know
there's no one here, Nathan is at work, I only crack the
lounge door open a fraction before squeezing through and
I tiptoe toward the window. Dropping my bag, I hook back
the curtains and peep out onto the street. I count the ways
this could go wrong but although an air of unease hovers

over me, there are no neighbors pointing at the house, talking worriedly into mobile phones. I don't think anyone saw me come in, and after a few minutes I feel calm enough to move. I don't know what I hope to find here but I feel both excited and scared; my pulse is rapid and light.

I have never been upstairs before; we never made it from the sofa to the bed that night, and as I remember what we did, his hands on my body, I swallow down bile. On the landing there are three closed, glossy white doors in front of me and I push the first one slowly open. It's the bathroom, smelling faintly of bleach. I scan the room taking in the wicker laundry basket in the corner, the blue tiles around the bath. It's exactly as I had dreamed it and, if I had a smidgen of doubt before, I am now as certain as I am of my own name that my dreams are Callie's memories. I open the mirrored bathroom cabinet but there's no box of tampons, no Veet, just Nathan's lonely razor and some aftershave.

The bedroom is next; the tall oak wardrobe stands in the corner from where Callie pulled her overnight bag in my dream. So she did want to leave Nathan. I sit heavily on the end of the neatly made bed, quilted throw hanging even and straight, and think about the texts she sent to the unknown person. It seems likely she was having an affair, and Nathan found out and hit her, and I wonder if it was the first time or if he's beaten her before. He doesn't look like a violent man. "Attentive," Tom called him. But I think there's probably a fine line between being attentive and being controlling, and it seems Nathan crossed it. If he hadn't emptied their savings account she'd probably have left him sooner and the thought she might still be alive saddens me, conflicting with the knowledge that if she were still here, I probably wouldn't be.

She was probably on her way to meet her lover when she died, perhaps the payday loan she'd applied for had come through and she was dreaming of her happy every after. But I'm only speculating, and even if I had definite proof I know I can never tell Tom and Amanda their daughter was unhappy with Nathan, and I feel I've failed them somehow. My thoughts race and my head throbs. I press my hand against my forehead. It comes away hot. I should go home. I'm really not feeling well but I can't help wondering who Callie was sleeping with: if it was Owen, if he was a friend of Nathan's. I rummage through the wardrobe and chest of drawers, not quite sure what I'm hoping to find, but there's no clutter to sift through, just clothes crisply pressed and folded.

The third bedroom is just as neat. Orderly. Housing only a single bed and a wooden blanket box. I lift the lid and I'm greeted with an array of brown padded envelopes. I tip out the contents of the first one. It's a pile of Valentine's cards and *"I love you"* notes and I feel desperately sad as I read them. Callie and Nathan were happy once. The next envelope is bursting at the seams and as I look inside I am shocked to see bundles of cash bound together with elastic bands, and as I pull them out I see something else at the bottom of the envelope that glints in the light. It's a necklace: rubies and diamonds shaped like a star. It's the pendant that was stolen from Amanda during the burglary on the day of Callie's funeral. Why would Nathan have this? I remember Tom telling me Nathan didn't go to the wake, but surely he wouldn't have broken into Tom's house?

The next envelope is light, and at first I think it's empty but my hand pulls out three passports, and I flick to the photos in the back. There's one for Nathan, one for Callie, and one for Sophie. Sophie, who is supposed to be in Spain? How can she be there if her passport is here? Nathan must know she's not abroad. Why's he lying? Why hasn't she been in touch with her parents? A thought hits me hard. What if the body in the airfield is Sophie's? Is that what Callie has been trying to tell me? Just how dangerous is Nathan? There's a sick feeling in my stomach as I bundle the passports back into the envelope, and they slip from my fingers as I'm startled by a crashing sound. The garden gate. I scoop everything from the floor and shove it in the box and I hold my breath as I wait, hoping for the rattle of the letter box as junk mail is pushed through. A key scrapes the lock and a draft shoots upstairs as the front door opens. Nathan is home. I look around the room wildly. There's nowhere to hide. And then with a sinking feeling I remember.

I left my handbag in the lounge.

CHAPTER FIFTY

Panic stutters in my veins as I listen to Nathan's movements downstairs. There's the thump of his briefcase hitting the floor, his shoes thunking on the mat. *Please don't go into the lounge* spins around my mind like a mantra but then it strikes me that I don't want him to come upstairs either. I feel as though I'm made of stone, my muscles are so tight. I daren't move. Hardly dare breathe. A creak. The stairs. He's heading this way. I try to remember whether I've put everything back where I found it but I can't remember whether or not I closed the bathroom cabinet. Ever so quietly I take exaggerated steps over to the window and look outside, desperately searching for another exit but I know there isn't one. His footsteps come closer and closer. Sweat pools in the small of my back; my T-shirt is clinging to me. I'm surprised he can't hear the frantic pounding of my heart. There's a second of complete silence. Stillness. Why has he stopped moving? I rest my forehead against the door, picturing him standing on the other side, his hand reaching for the handle. I'm sure the doors were closed when I arrived. Now they are all ajar. He must know someone is here. What will he say if he finds me? What will he do? The shrill sound of a mobile slices through the air and I instantly delve into my pocket, but Nathan snaps: "Hello," and the ringing has stopped. It wasn't my phone and I breathe a sigh of relief and put mine onto silent.

"What the fuck do you want?" He sounds angry. Really angry. I've never heard him speak that way before.

There's a tickle in my throat and I swallow hard. Don't cough.

"I've told you to never contact me again." There's a beat. "I know. I saw. It's really not my problem, is it?"

A pause.

"Where are you?"

"Fuck!" He sounds furious and a whimper escapes and I clamp my hands over my mouth and crouch down, resting on my heels. My knees feel too rubbery to stand. "It's a dangerous game you're playing. OK, tomorrow night."

A pause.

"Around ten o'clock then, and then we're done. Understand? You never. Ever. Contact me again."

There's a slam and my shoulders jerk upward but seconds later water pitter-patters into the bath as the shower is switched on. I'm hesitant to move. Convinced he'll notice the bathroom cabinet is open and spring out at me as I try to leave. Seconds turn to minutes and I know I can't have long. I slip off my shoes and hold them in one hand and I reach for the door and slowly pull it toward me. It squeaks. I screw up my forehead but the water still runs. The bathroom door remains closed. The staircase seems endless as I take the stairs one at a time, pausing after every step, every creak, looking behind me, and when I've reached the bottom I retrieve my bag from the lounge and try to open the front door. It is locked. I am reaching into my back pocket for the key when I realize there's something different. The sound of the water has stopped. The bathroom door clicks open. I clamp my lips together to stop a sound escaping and I fumble to unlock the door as quickly as I can. The floorboards shift above me. The lock springs open. A shadow falls on the stair carpet. My fingers grip the handle. He's coming. I wrench open the door and I am outside, closing the door as quietly as I can behind me. And then I run.

* * *

The fury in Nathan's voice during his phone call snaps at my heels, and as I run I imagine his fingers grabbing my shoulders, tugging me backward, hot breath on my neck. The stitch in my side burns and I press my palm against my flesh, feet slowing, until I stop moving altogether. I stand with my back against a wall, hands on my knees, hunched over, grappling for breath, eyes fixed on the direction I have just come. My heart leaps into my mouth as a figure appears around the corner, but it's not Nathan. I wipe my forehead with my sleeve while I think of what to do. I'm exhausted. Nausea spins in my stomach and I know I can't make it home. Usually after a biopsy I rest for days, letting the energy the procedure has drained, physically and emotionally, seep back in.

I didn't bring my purse and there's no cash at my flat so I can't call a cab. Usually I'd ring Dad but I don't know what I'd say to him. He called this morning but I had let it go to voicemail and as he stuttered out yet another apology I'd pressed hard with my thumb, deleting the voice that used to soothe and calm. I swallow hard. My throat stings and anxiety pounces, grasping me tightly as all the horror stories I've heard about transplant patients picking up infections in hospitals circle like sharks in my mind. I grow hotter and hotter with every passing second until I've convinced myself I have a fever when I know it could be panic, and I try to remember the things Vanessa has taught me. Straighten my spine. Breathe in deeply, push my stomach out. After a few breaths I feel calmer. Cooler. I close my eyes and try to picture myself in a beautiful garden, but instead I see Nathan's angry face looming toward me. Did he hurt Sophie? Is it her body in the airfield? I snap my eyes open and force myself to carry on walking, pulling my phone out of my pocket and making the call I didn't want to.

* * *

It feels I've been sitting on the hard wrought-iron bench for ages and I've almost convinced myself he won't come. Cars whizz past, windows down, bass thudding. None of them are him. The smell of soaps and bath bombs wafting out of the propped open door of the shop behind me is overpowering. Strawberry mixed with sandalwood, citrus with lavender. A headache creeps behind my eyes.

At last he's here and a rush of relief lifts me to my feet as I step toward the curb and wave.

"Thanks for coming, Sam," I say as I climb into the passenger seat.

He's crunching a humbug and he's reached the chewy bit in the middle but he nods. I rest my head back as the indicator tick-tick-ticks and we pull into the traffic. As the engine thrums and music floats from the speakers there's comfort in the familiarity.

Sam keeps his eyes on the road. "You OK?"

"Feeling weak after my biopsy. I went for a walk and lost track of where I was. I shouldn't have ventured so far."

"Let's get you home then."

Home. He means the flat, I know, with its empty rooms

and almost bare fridge, but here, my body melded to the seat, the smell of mint, Ed Sheeran strumming his guitar, imploring "give me love," I feel more at home than ever. I feel safe, and it pains me to think Callie didn't have that too.

"Sam? Do you have time to take me somewhere first?"

* * *

The car crunches into the pub car park in Woodhaven. It seems a lifetime ago we stopped off here on our way back from the coast. As we judder over the rough surface a petal falls from the sunflowers on my lap that we had stopped at a BP garage to buy.

"I don't know why you want to come here," Sam says. "You're supposed to be moving on."

"I know. But I can't shake the feeling there is something I need to do, but maybe I've got it all wrong." I rub the fallen petal between my fingers. It feels like velvet. "Perhaps it is just that I need to see where Callie died and say goodbye to her properly. I think it's just up there." I shield my eyes from the sun and point up the road. "There's a crossroads, and beyond that, the tree. Why don't you get a drink and wait here?" I reach for the door handle.

"I'll come with you," Sam says, and I'm touched by his offer.

"Thanks," I say as we step out of the car. "But I want to be alone."

"Of course you do," he snaps and I balk.

"What's that supposed to mean?"

"You're pushing me away again. The way you do with everyone."

"I don't—"

"The way you have with Rachel," he says.

"You've been having cozy chats about me again, have you?"

"How could you accuse her of stitching you up at work, Jen?"

"I wasn't thinking straight. It was right before my biopsy and ... Anyway I know it wasn't her, Linda said—"

"It shouldn't have needed Linda to say."

"I know," I say quietly. "I am sorry."

"I'm not the one you should be apologizing to."

"I feel I owe everyone an apology at the moment. It's hard to know where to start. Look, Sam—"

"I can't do this anymore, Jen. This trying to be friends. It's too bloody hard." He looks down at his feet as he toes the gravel. "I'm sorry, Jen. I'm going to get a pint. Let me know when you've finished and I'll take you back to yours."

He strides away and despite everything that's been said it's his referring to our flat as "yours" that makes me want to cry.

* * *

The tree is an oak, large and solid; a tangle of dried grass and daisies pepper the dusty soil covering its roots. I run my fingers over its rough bark looking for the damage Callie's car must have caused, but there's only the slightest scuff. How quickly nature eradicates signs of life. It's almost as if she was never here at all.

I place both palms hard against the trunk and close my eyes. The ground seems to shift beneath my feet and I lose my footing, landing heavily against the tree as the truth hits me as hard and painful as a brick.

CHAPTER FIFTY-ONE

"Stop it, stop it, stop it!"

"NO!" you roar and although we've had some blazing rows recently I've never heard you quite so angry. I press myself close to the door and my fingers grip the cool metal handle. I wish I could jump out but you're driving way too fast.

Windscreen wipers swish-swish-swish as the rain hammers down, and the headlights barely pick out the road in front of us.

"Slow down," I almost whisper. The roads are treacherous. "Slow down. Please."

There's a rumbling as a lorry thunders past, its bright white headlights making the red sequins on my dress glisten like drops of blood. The vibrations cause the glovebox to fall open—the catch has never worked properly—and, as I start to push it shut again, I see it. My iPhone! The one you'd taken from me. No wonder I hadn't been able to find it when I searched the house. I glance sideward, your eyes are fixed on the road ahead, and I slip the phone into my bag. I had stupidly left the old pay-as-you-go one I had been using in my desk drawer today and I am massively relieved I am, once again, contactable.

I know you think you're doing the right thing, trying almost to pretend it didn't happen, but it did and we can't go back to the way we were before. I'm not the same person. And neither are you, not if you're honest. How could you be after what I have done?

The muscle in your cheek tics and you're clutching the steering wheel so tightly your shoulders almost touch your ears. You raise your left hand and tug the cravat from around your neck and as you toss it to the floor you knock your buttonhole. Petals tumble like tears.

"I thought tonight you were making an effort," you say. "But tonight wasn't about us returning to normality, was it? Be honest. Do you think things can ever be normal again?" There is so much heartbreak in your voice.

"I don't see how they can. I'm trying, but I can't forget. Every time I close my eyes I see..." I swallow hard and touch my still-tender cheek. "I had to lie to my parents. Telling them I walked into a cupboard. What a cliché. I'm lying to everyone. I can't do it anymore. I just can't. I have to leave. I'm sorry."

"You don't have to leave," you say. "You can make a choice, Callie. We can change jobs, move away, and start again. If you agree to break contact completely it can be a fresh start."

"Nathan," I say and your furious gaze meets mine. "I can't."

"But we were happy once. We can be again. You could choose me?"

"I'm so sorry." You turn to look at me and as our eyes

lock there's a split second where I catch a glimpse of the old us.

There's a horn, the squealing of brakes, the screeching of tires, and I clutch the door handle with both hands.

"Nathan!" I scream.

CHAPTER FIFTY-TWO

My senses roar back to life and I'm blinking in the brightness. Nathan was driving. My anger blazes as hot as the sun in the sky. Now I'm here, at the scene, the details are diamond sharp in my mind. The red sparkly dress Callie wore to the wedding reception. Nathan's lemon cravat.

That fucking bastard was driving. He crashed the car. I'd seen the anger on his face and felt Callie's fear as she screamed his name. Did he unclip her seatbelt? Deliberately kill her? He must have run off and left her dying in a ditch. What a fucking coward.

I stalk back to the pub. Sam is sitting in the car, fiddling with his phone. He doesn't speak as I climb in and fasten my seatbelt. He twists the key in the ignition and the wheels spin as we leave the car park in a cloud of dust. From the speakers Ed Sheeran and Taylor Swift tell us everything has changed, and Sam snaps off the stereo. But I don't fill the silence. My thoughts are toxic. Corrosive. Burning away at my gratitude, until all I feel, in this moment, is cold, hard hate. For all the people who have lied to me. For all the people who have saved me. Left me to live this half-life. Not quite mine. Not quite Callie's. I know now what Callie has been trying to tell me: Nathan killed her, and I don't think she'll rest until he pays.

God, I'm going to make him pay.

CHAPTER FIFTY-THREE

I had dozed fitfully on the sofa last night, convinced I wouldn't sleep at all, but as I wake, still furious with Nathan, I recalled an earlier dream I once had of him and Callie. It has birthed an idea. It's barely light as I unlock the door to the vet's practice, locking it behind me. I don't have long. Linda's always in early. The rising sun shines pale stripes through the slatted blinds but I don't open them. I dart to the box on the wall and disable the alarm, holding my breath as it beep-beep-beeps but the code hasn't been changed and the lights flash once, twice, three times. I'm in.

The stockroom is dark but I daren't switch on the fluorescent lights. They buzz long after they are switched off and I don't want anyone to know I've been here. Find out what I've taken. They won't miss anything until the next inventory. With shaking hands I unzip my bag and pull out my mobile and using the torch app I navigate my way across the room. The dangerous drugs cupboard is locked and I punch in the combination.

The bell rings as the front door opens.

Shit.

It closes.

A sneeze builds and I stick my hand over my nose to try to contain it.

There's the click-clack of Linda's heels in the corridor outside. I scrunch myself against the wall—please don't come in here for anything—she pauses.

My throat tickles and I swallow frantically trying to suppress a cough. There's the sound of heels again as Linda passes by and I hear the opening of her office door, and the slam as it swings shut behind her.

I quietly open the door of the cupboard and locate what I am looking for straight away. I drop the vials into my bag and inch by inch I open the door, my heart beating a tattoo. As quietly as I can I creep down the corridor and slip out of the fire exit, circling around the car park the long way so I am shadowed by the surrounding wall. I can't risk Linda seeing me. Would she call the police if she knew what I had taken? The vials barely weigh anything and yet my bag feels heavier than it did before, and as it slides down my shoulder I hitch it back up.

The exhaust fumes from a passing bus make my empty stomach contract as I sneak out onto the street. It's eight o'clock now and the road is busy. Cars speeding past, people walking to work, stifling yawns and staring at smartphones, but I feel the burn of their eyes on me. Watching me. Judging me. I half-expect someone to stop me and label me as the thief I am. I grip the strap on my bag a little tighter. Convinced everyone knows what it contains. What I am planning to do.

I keep my head down, eyes fixed on the pavement, and I move as quickly as I can, but my muscles are achy and I'm so, so hot. My breath is faster than the steps I take and I increase my speed.

The sound of my blood whooshing in my ears drowns

them out at first. The footsteps. Increasing in pace as I do. Someone is following me. I turn my head slightly and there's a flicker of movement in the corner of my vision. I sense rather than see someone reaching out to grab me.

Almost without thinking I dart across the road. There's a squeal of brakes and I'm frozen in terror in the path of an oncoming car. Seconds feel like minutes and I see every tiny detail as though the world is moving in slow motion. The driver's terrified face as he leans back in his seat, arms stretched straight. The gasp of bystanders. Blaring horns. The car swerves but doesn't mount the pavement, which is full of pedestrians; a lady pushing a pram, an elderly man leaning heavily on a walking stick. I'm still directly in the car's path. Still unable to move. There's the clatter of a bike as a cyclist falls to the ground as he tries to avoid the inevitable collision.

A scream.

I close my eyes and wait for the impact.

CHAPTER FIFTY-FOUR

My head jerks, twisting my neck, and sharp pains shoot through my upper back as I am yanked back onto the path from which I have just stepped. The car that almost hit me continues down the road, much slower now, and the cyclist stands and pats himself down as though checking for injuries. The tension in my muscles starts to dissipate and I begin to shake. It's only as my vision sharpens, and my hearing returns to normal, that I realize someone is still gripping my arm and I try to shake it free as I turn to face them, but their fingers dig a little deeper.

"Rach?" I swallow hard.

"What the fuck, Jenna? You just stepped out in front of a car?"

"I didn't see it."

Disbelief flashes in her eyes. "This is a main road. There are always cars. Are you OK? You look like shit. When was the last time you slept?"

I shrug.

"You weren't trying to ... you know. Hurt yourself?" she asks.

"God no. Who do you think I am?"

She studies me silently and I don't blame her for not answering. I don't know who I am anymore. She releases my arm and I shift my bag onto my other shoulder, conscious of the vials inside.

"What are you doing here?" she asks. "I thought it was you as I got off the bus. I tried to catch up to you."

"I can't believe you're still working for Linda..." I say and my tone is terser than I intended.

"I need the money. Did you come to apologize?"

"To her?"

"To me!"

"Oh right, sorry," I say but my apology sounds hollow, even to me. Distracted, I look past her up the road, toward the surgery. Worried Linda will have been drawn outside by the cacophony of car horns. "Rach, I have to go. We can catch up another time?"

"Sorry, Jenna." Her eyes glisten as she sadly shakes her head. "I don't think we can."

* * *

I am home before nine o'clock and I am still feeling shaky after the near miss with the car. It takes every ounce of strength I have to drag the telephone table in front of the door and, after I have ensured the chain is pulled across, once, twice, three times, I make my checks. There is no one lurking under the bed or hiding in the wardrobe. In the lounge I pull my sleeve over my hand and use the cuff to wipe my sopping brow before falling onto the sofa. There's hours to go before Nathan comes home from work. Before I need to leave. I wedge a cushion under my head and think about Callie. What I'm going to do. For her. I press my hand against my heart. For us.

My body is heavy. Hot. My muscles ache and my hair is

damp with sweat. I tell myself it's just a cold but I'm feeling progressively worse with every passing minute. Like I'd thought yesterday, I've probably picked up a bug at the hospital. My throat is scratchy.

It's just a cold.

But I'm all too aware that since the second this heart was implanted, my body has been conspiring to reject it. There's only so long the immunosuppressants can stop my body doing what it's supposed to do naturally and repel what it sees as a foreign body. As I think about my medication I remember I'd been in such a rush to leave this morning, in such a state, I'd completely forgotten to take my tablets. But one missed dose shouldn't hurt. It shouldn't make me feel this ill.

"*Hang on, Callie*," I tell the thump-thump-thump of my heart. Is it my imagination or is it growing slower? Weaker. No! *It's just a cold.* I try to push myself to sit up to fetch my pills but my body is too heavy and I slump backward, and I fight to keep my eyes open, but I can't.

CHAPTER FIFTY-FIVE

It's half past four when I wake drenched in sweat. The afternoon is dark and gloomy. Outside the lounge window, storm clouds are bunching together in the gunmetal sky. My throat is so raw it feels like I've swallowed a wire brush and I cough so hard my chest burns.

It's just a cold.

I roll onto my side and my mind drifts back into a memory that hurts: the first time I ever put an animal to sleep. There was a sour sting of bile at the back of my throat as Linda loaded the syringe. My hands shook violently as I stroked the coarse fur of Maud the golden retriever waiting patiently on the treatment table. My mouth was dry. Tongue thick, as I murmured to her: "It won't hurt, darling. It's for the best."

"You don't have to do this," John had said. Linda had stood silently next to him.

"I know." My voice was so quiet I could barely hear it. I had flattened my hand and when Linda placed the syringe in my palm I had closed my fingers around the cold plastic.

Linda liked all the veterinary nurses to be able to carry out euthanasia although they needed supervision to do it.

"It's not all kittens and puppies," she'd say. "If you're not up to the bad as well as the good, you're in the wrong job," and I'd nodded along, never letting on that my insides turned to liquid whenever I thought about witnessing those last breaths. Being responsible for those last breaths. But I did it anyway.

I push myself up. My borrowed time is running out. I feel progressively worse with every passing minute. Callie is leaving me. My body is rejecting her heart. I am aware of it with each weakening heartbeat but she's clinging on, and I want to make it right for her. We're almost the same person, Callie and I, and I know through my dreams that Nathan controlled her: He took away her phone and money and she was scared. Nathan was driving the car that night— he didn't get a taxi home alone like he had told Tom and Amanda. I'm absolutely sure of it, but what about proof? No one will take me seriously. But everything I saw, everything I felt when I had my fugue at the crash site, was so real. But what if I've got it wrong? The thought keeps coming and coming no matter how many times I bat it away.

It's quiet. So quiet. I wish I had someone to talk things through, but who? Vanessa didn't believe me, Rachel doesn't want to be friends anymore, and even Sam has given up on me. I have barely spoken to my parents since I found out about my dad and Linda. There is no one I can share this with. Even if I go through with my plan I won't be able to tell Amanda and Tom that Callie's death is absolved. But I will know, won't I? What I'm about to do is the right thing, the same as it was with Maud. *But what if I've got it wrong?*

I drag myself to the kitchen and splash cold water on my face before swallowing my medication down. I switch the radio on low to keep me company as I stand and stare at my mind map. At the printouts of Cellular Memory. Of the photos of Callie and her family I downloaded from Facebook. There's a picture of the old Amanda, face unlined, eyes crinkled with laughter, and I know that if it weren't for Nathan she'd still be that woman. Not the aged shell sitting in the same chair, day after day, grieving for the daughter she'll never see again.

The song changes on the radio. Ed Sheeran sings "Kiss Me." Mine and Sam's song, and for a split second I feel such a sharp, stabbing pain in my chest I double over, and I have to hold on to the edge of the chair to steady myself. I know it's not too late to call a cab to the hospital, to ask for treatment, but as I raise my head I catch sight of Amanda again, and I know without a shadow of a doubt I have to do this.

I have to kill Nathan.

CHAPTER FIFTY-SIX

Nathan's garden gate creaks as I push it open. My muscles are taut with tension as I rap the silver knocker. His shadow moves toward the opaque glass. Sweat beads on my temples. His keys jangle. My pulse gets faster and faster. The front door swings open. Nathan stands, shower wet, towel wrapped around his waist. Getting ready for whoever he spoke to on the phone and arranged to meet at ten, no doubt.

"Jenna?" He hesitates for a moment, confusion in his eyes. "Do you want to come in?"

Oh God. Can I really do this?

* * *

Nathan has gone to dress and I've told him I'll sort out some drinks. I know I don't have long before he comes back downstairs, but now I'm in his house I don't know if I can go through with it. In the kitchen I stand at the sink, looking out at the garden. The sky is streaked red as the fiery sun dips. I feel as though I could race toward it with my hand outstretched and touch it. The world is so beautiful. It's the people that make it ugly, and I want to curl in

a ball and howl with the unfairness of it all. The prisons
are packed full of rapists, murderers, child abusers—why
should they live, their hearts strong and steady, while my
life ebbs away? But if I kill Nathan, aren't I as bad as them?
I just don't know. I dig my fingers into my scalp as though
I can silence the voice in my head telling me not to do this,
and I think I should just go home, but the strains of Nathan
whistling as though he hasn't a care in the world drift down
the stairs and it causes a spike in my anger. I make my
decision.

Pulling two glasses and a bottle from the cupboard I
glug Jack Daniel's into one of the tumblers, sharp and sour.
I can't keep my hand steady and I try again and again to
pull the stopper from the vial I've stolen from work, and
the harder I try the more my hand sweats. The glass is slip-
pery and my grip is weak. I yank the tea towel from its
hook near the oven and try again. This time there's a loos-
ening, a give, and I tip the contents into the amber liquid
and swirl it around with my finger. I slosh apple juice into
my glass and for a second I am tempted to add a splash of
alcohol. It doesn't seem important anymore if I drink, as I
feel so awful I'm convinced I'm rejecting Callie's heart, but
I need a clear head. I pick up both drinks. It's an effort to
hold them. They feel the weight of bricks in my hands. I'm
really, really sick.

It's just a cold.

I'm ready.

* * *

In the lounge, I can't settle. Above me, the floorboards
shift as Nathan moves around his bedroom. In the photo,
over the mantelpiece, Callie's eyes appear to follow me as
I pace around the room. She looks so joyful, standing on

the bridge, laughing. There's nothing quite like that feeling of being utterly loved, utterly happy, and in that moment I bet she thought she'd feel that way forever. I think back to the last picture of her with her bruised and swollen face and think about the damage we do to each other when relationships crack and crumble. I pull out my mobile and text Sam, *"I'm so, so sorry for everything."* I'm not entirely sure if I'm apologizing for what I've done or what I'm about to do. My eyes sting with unshed tears but I can't cry. Not yet. Footsteps thump down the stairs; it isn't too late to change my mind, I know, but as Nathan walks into the room I cross the cream rug and hand him his glass.

"Thanks," he says. "You don't look good, Jenna." He presses his palm against my forehead. "You're burning up."

I move my head back to dislodge his hand and pain pulses behind my eyes. The urge to have someone take charge, look after me, is overwhelming, but I call to mind the dread my heart has known. I want Nathan to feel that. To know what it's like to feel helpless and terrified.

"It's a cold. It's nothing. Sorry I haven't answered your texts the past few days. I thought we could talk?"

"I'd love to but I don't have long. I'm going out tonight."

"Where?" I keep my tone casual.

"To meet a friend." Whoever he spoke to on the phone was certainly no friend but I shouldn't be surprised at the ease with which he lies, and suddenly I am icy calm.

"You've time for a drink, surely?"

"Yes, but I thought you meant tea. I'm going to be driving." He raises his tumbler to his nose and sniffs. "But I haven't had a Jack Daniel's for ages. I suppose one won't hurt." He raises the crystal to his lips, but then lowers the glass before he drinks and I swallow back my frustration.

"Something wrong?"

"Ice. Do you want some?"

I shake my head—my throat is too tight to speak. Nathan strides from the room and I hear the chink of ice cubes falling from the dispenser in the fridge, and I sink onto the sofa. My legs feel as though they are made of rubber.

"What are we drinking to?" Nathan asks as he returns.

"The truth." My voice is an octave higher than normal and I hope he doesn't notice.

"Truth?" He takes a mouthful of his drink and grimaces. "There's no water in this either—trying to kill me?" He takes another sip, smaller this time.

"Cheers." I down my apple juice in one and as the cool liquid hits my chest I splutter it back into my glass and tears stream as I cough and cough.

Nathan takes my glass and wraps his arm around my shoulders and I don't have the energy to shrug him off. He passes me a box of tissues and I take one and wipe my eyes. While I'm blowing my nose he fetches a blanket and tucks it around my legs. I wish he'd stop being so kind. A wolf in sheep's clothing—that's what Mum would call him, but what if he isn't?

What if I've got it wrong?

But he's already drained his glass, and I know it's too late.

CHAPTER FIFTY-SEVEN

I pass the time with stilted small talk until Nathan says: "Jenna. I'm not feeling good."

His pupils are dilating. He rests his head against the back of the sofa as though it's too heavy to hold up. "I think I've caught what you have."

"I can promise you, you haven't," I say. My tone is cool and clipped. I haven't time to get emotional. "Let's talk, Nathan. Let's talk about Callie."

"Callie?"

"Tell me." I slide his empty glass from his hand and slam it on the coffee table. "Tell me what you did to her."

"What I did to her? Jenna, you're not making sense. You're really not well."

"I'm not the one who's sick, Nathan." I lean toward him and whisper in his ear, "I know."

"Know what?"

"Know that you controlled her. Scared her." My face close to his. "Killed her."

"That's ridiculous," he snaps. His mask is finally slipping. "I loved Callie. I did nothing but protect her. Nothing. You didn't know her." His face becomes redder and redder and I'm not sure if that's his anger or the drug I've put in his whisky. "I think you'd better go." His words come slower now and he shakes his head as though trying to clear his thoughts.

"I'm not going anywhere. Not until you tell me the truth."

I stand over him. He pushes himself upright but then flops back onto the sofa, shakes his head, and tries again.

"Jenna. I feel really odd." His voice is slurred and he opens and closes his mouth once, twice, as if checking his jaw still works.

"That would be the pentobarbitone I put in your Jack Daniel's. It usually kills dogs pretty quickly but judging by the size of you, and the amount I put in your drink, you have at least twenty minutes. Give or take. It's hard to guess."

Nathan's eyes widen and he grips the edge of the sofa and tries to lever himself upright but his legs must be numb and he sprawls to the floor, his head missing the coffee table by millimeters. His hand snakes toward my ankle and I step back, out of his reach, and stare down at the man whose horrific, heartless actions inadvertently saved my life. I kick him sharply in the ribs to keep him awake. "Start talking."

CHAPTER FIFTY-EIGHT

Nathan lies on the floor, on his stomach, his body twitching as he tries to control his limbs. Tiny, helpless movements like a turtle on its back trying to right itself. He turns his face toward me, the veins in his neck protrude, and his eyes bulge with fright.

"What's happening to me?"

"Your body is shutting down, little by little. Organs start to fail. Speech is the last thing to go. Luckily for you it's relatively painless."

"Jenna—"

"Shut up and listen." Inside my bag is another vial and I pull it out and show him it. "This is the antidote. If you admit what you've done, I'll give it to you and you get to live out the rest of your miserable life in jail. Understand?"

"Yes, I—"

"Not yet."

I crouch down and dig my fingers into his shoulder and pull, once, twice, three times, but I can't roll him over onto his back. Sweat is pouring from me as I kneel and this time I place one palm against his shoulder, one against his thigh, and I push upward as hard as I can, and as he shifts slightly,

I wedge my knee under his bottom to stop him rolling back and I grit my teeth and push again. This time he flops over. I'm panting as I reach for my phone and I open the voice recorder app and place it on the coffee table.

"Now talk."

"Give me the antidote. Please."

"The faster you talk, the faster you'll get it. Don't worry. Despite how you feel, you're not about to die. Yet."

"I don't know what you want me to say. I haven't done anything wrong. Please, Jenna—" His eyes glisten with tears but they only fuel the anger inside me.

"Did you listen to Callie begging as you drove her to her death? Did you show her any compassion?"

"I honestly don't know what you think I've done. Me and Callie were happy. Don't let me die, Jenna."

"You took her phone away from her."

Nathan blinks rapidly. "How did you . . ."

"You emptied her bank account so you could control her."

"It was a joint account—"

"You followed her. Watched her. Didn't leave her alone for a second. She couldn't even get away from you at work, could she? When she came out for lunch you were there. Scared she would run off, were you? Admit it." I scream now. "She wanted to leave you, didn't she, Nathan?"

A single tear trickles down his cheek and I hold the recorder closer to his mouth as he whispers: "Yes."

CHAPTER FIFTY-NINE

"You couldn't let her leave, could you?"

"It wasn't what she really wanted, deep down."

"It was. She was scared of you."

"How the hell would you know?" His voice is marginally louder. "You didn't know her."

"No, but I feel her." I yank down my T-shirt and show him my scar. "I have her heart. Have you heard of Cellular Memory?"

"No. But please, Jenna, give me—"

"Some scientists call the heart 'the second brain,' and believe it can store memories, and when a heart is transplanted organ recipients can inherit the donor's memories. I've inherited Callie's memories. I've felt her fear."

"It wasn't me she was scared of. I can't believe you have drugged me."

"I got the idea from you. You forced her to take something, didn't you? Was that the night she died?"

"I've never..." He pauses. "Do you mean the sleeping tablet? A couple of nights before she died I encouraged her to take one of the tablets she had been prescribed after her dad's heart attack when she couldn't sleep. She'd been awake for days. She needed the rest. Anyway, how do you know that? What do you mean you've inherited her memories? That's ridiculous."

"How do you think I know all of this then? I dream about her. About you. About Sophie. You killed her. You killed them both." The random ideas that have been flashing through my mind finally take shape. "Callie wanted to leave you; Sophie was helping her. Were they going abroad?" I'm thinking out loud. "You hid their passports to stop them going and took away Callie's access to her phone, her money, but why did you break into Tom's house during Callie's wake?"

My head is thick and my forehead burns. It doesn't quite make sense. Time is running out. Why the hell isn't Nathan admitting what he's done?

"I didn't break into Tom's house during the wake. I came back here and drank myself into oblivion. I didn't hide anyone's passport. Jenna, I think you're delusional. I think you need help and I'll help you. I will. I promise. But you need to help me. I'm really not feeling good."

Nathan pales and his lips are tinged blue. I'm worried about how quickly he's going downhill.

"Amanda's necklace is upstairs, and the passports. I've seen them." I rub my hands across my tired eyes, as though trying to conjure up their image again. I had seen them, hadn't I?

"In the spare room?"

"Yes! You admit it." I'm not going mad. I knew it.

"Then you must have seen the list from the hospital?"

"What list?"

"Tom signed for Callie's belongings at the hospital and handed them to me with the list of her possessions. He didn't read it. No one could focus. They'd signed the transplant form and she'd slipped away and everything else blurred into the background. I brought everything home with me. She had the passports in her handbag along with the necklace and the money. She must have taken them the night we were at their house picking them up for the wedding. Tom and Amanda can't have used the safe in the days in between Callie's death and her funeral. It was only when the police asked them to list what had been taken in the burglary they noticed."

I hesitate. I'm not sure if he's lying but I have to find out. I reach into his pocket and pull out his mobile phone so he can't call for help. "Don't move," I say, but I don't think he can, and I make my way upstairs to the spare room and open the blanket box. I don't check inside the envelopes I looked in before Nathan came home and disturbed me, but as I dig toward the bottom of the box, I find an A4 piece of paper with the logo for St. Martin's Hospital embossed on the top of the page. It's a list of Callie's possessions dated the night she died, and as I scan through them I see Nathan was telling the truth. The necklace, money, and passports are all on the list.

Leaving the contents of the box strewn over the carpet I stand and black flecks flash in front of my eyes. I rest my palm against the wall to steady myself. *It's just a cold*.

On shaky legs I make my way back downstairs to ask Nathan more questions, but the lounge is empty. Nathan is gone. I cross to the rug and crouch down, rubbing my hands across the flattened fibers where his body lay as though I can make him materialize. The rug is still warm. Where is he?

From behind me, there's a noise.

CHAPTER SIXTY

I turn around as I hear the shuffling noise behind me. The door to Nathan's dining room is ajar and I creep over to it, and through the gap I see Nathan dragging himself forward on his elbows. And as he hears me approach he twists his head around and stares at me with bloodshot eyes.

"Jenna. Please call an ambulance. I don't want to die."

"Then tell me the truth." I hate the pleading tone in my voice. This isn't how I thought it would go.

"I don't know what you want me to say. Tell me what you want me to say. I'll say anything. Sign anything. But Callie did die in an accident. Nobody killed her."

I fetch my mobile, leaving Nathan's phone on the coffee table, and I begin to record again. "Callie was scared, wasn't she? I've felt it. I've seen things. The bruise on her face, did you do it?"

"No. I'd never have hurt her. I loved her."

"But you said 'promise you won't tell anyone where you got this' as you touched her cheek. If she had got the bruise falling it wouldn't have mattered who she told, would it? You wanted her to lie."

"How did you . . ."

"Cellular Memory. I told you I've been dreaming her memories." My throat is sore as I raise my voice.

"I didn't want her to leave. I thought if she stayed, if we carried on as normal, things would eventually go back to the way they were. We were so happy once. I suggested we could change our jobs and move away. Have a fresh start. She just needed some time to see it could work. That's why I took her phone and the money and stayed close to her all the time. To stop her leaving. But I think she was going anyway, that night."

"The night of the wedding?"

Nathan gives a faint nod.

"You were driving the car the night she died. I saw it."

His eyelids droop.

"Just admit it. Admit you were in the car the night she died. You argued, didn't you?"

"Yes. I asked her if she'd choose me and she said no. She should have chosen me." His voice is weak and I slide the mobile phone nearer, to be sure of picking up his words.

"Who should she have chosen you over, Nathan?"

His eyelids flicker and I know I'm running out of time. I push on: "You were driving?"

"Yes." His voice is growing fainter and I thrust my phone's microphone toward his mouth.

Finally, I hear what I am expecting, but it doesn't bring on the sudden rush of relief I hoped for.

He tries to say something else but his words are thick. Hard to understand. He licks his lips and I fetch some water from the kitchen and hold the glass to his mouth. Water dribbles down his chin and he chokes. When he stops coughing there is no rise and fall of his chest. His body is perfectly still. Perfectly silent.

CHAPTER SIXTY-ONE

"Nathan!" He can't be dead. Fear slices through me and I drop my ear to his chest and cry with relief when I hear his heart beating beneath his ribcage. My tears drip onto his chest. Soak into his shirt. I knew when I stood in Nathan's kitchen earlier, gazing at the setting sun, that I couldn't murder him. I just couldn't do it, no matter what he's done. I had stolen two different drugs from work; one that would kill Nathan, and one that wouldn't. It was the non-lethal one I had slipped into his drink. But the dose of ketamine I had given him was far too large judging by how quickly he's flaked out. The sealed vials of pentobarbitone, enough to kill a man, are still nestled inside my pocket. Linda will panic when she realizes they are unaccounted for. It will serve her right.

"Wake up." I shake his shoulders hard, and his eyes open, wild and staring, and he struggles to sit up but he can't. "Did you unclip her seatbelt? Did you crash on purpose?"

"I wasn't." His eyes close to slits again. "I wasn't driving when she crashed. We argued at the wedding and we were shouting at each other all the way home. It was awful.

When we got back I went to the toilet and when I came out she had taken the car and gone."

I sit back on my heels. My T-shirt is sodden with sweat, and I don't know what to do, and I'm so very tired. An uncomfortable feeling twists inside my gut and it's not just because of what I'm doing. I believe him. I think about his kindness, the way he'd fetched me water and looked after me, the bread he'd brought so I could feed the ducks. He told the truth about the necklace and the passports. Callie's dreams flash through my mind: *"I'd trust you with my life,"* she'd told him, and I have a deep-rooted feeling I should too.

"Nathan, you're not dying. You'll just sleep for a while but please try and stay awake. Callie needs me. Needs us to do something, I know it. I don't think I'll be free of her until it's done but I don't know what it is. I owe her. Tell me. Who did she choose instead of you? Who are you meeting tonight?"

Nathan's struggling to say something and I bring my face level with his. Smell the Jack Daniel's on his breath. "Sophie." His eyes are closed but he speaks again pushing the words out slowly. "She would want you to help Sophie."

"Sophie? Is she in trouble?" Could that be what Callie is trying to tell me?

Nathan barely moves his head but I think he's trying to nod.

"Is that who you are meeting tonight?"

"Yes. I wanted to keep them apart. Keep Callie safe. She should never have got involved."

"Involved in what?"

"I thought it was over but it isn't." His eyes are rolling now.

"Where is Sophie, Nathan?"

"She's at—" Speaking again seems to expel the last amount of energy he has and as his eyes close his dark lashes rest against his deathly pale skin. I shake him by the shoulders, hard and fast, but his head lolls to the side. His chest inflates and deflates with a juddering and a rumbling snore. I cradle my head in my hands. Nathan could be out for at least an hour. He's due to meet Sophie at ten and if I don't get to her before then she might disappear again. My heart swells like popcorn in my chest and I know my borrowed time is running out. If I call Dr. Kapur, I will be admitted to hospital, but I think it's too late for me and I owe Callie. I owe her parents. If Sophie's in danger, I have to help. I have to help now. I screw my hands into fists and press them into my eye sockets and the fog in my mind dissipates. Where is she?

Think. The background noise. The call I made from Callie's second handset: the one Sara gave me at the dentist. The number on there must have been Sophie's if Nathan was trying to keep them apart. What was the noise? I've heard it before. Think.

Suddenly I know what the sound was. It was the crashing waves of the ocean.

I know where Sophie is. I've seen it enough times in my dreams. Owl Lodge Caravan Park. I have to find her.

CHAPTER SIXTY-TWO

It's freezing. Fucking freezing, she thinks. Sophie's chest hurts as she inhales the damp. She wishes she had a blanket but instead she has to make do with tucking her coat around her shoulders and tugging the sleeves of her jumper down over her hands. There's the sound of scratching, sharp and relentless, and she curls herself into a ball, bringing to mind the rhyme Callie would chant when they were small and she'd crawl into Callie's bed in the dead of night, trembling with fear, convinced there was a monster in her room.

"It's not real,
It's all in your head,
There is no monster,
Under your bed.
You must go to sleep,
It is nearly day,
Think of all the fun we'll have,
And the games we'll play."

Sophie would snuggle against the person she loved most in the world, safe and warm, and in the morning when they woke Callie would never tell their parents Sophie had disturbed her sleep again. Sophie had never thought there would be a time her big sister wouldn't be there to protect her. Callie had stood hands on hips over Darren Patterson in the playground after she'd tripped him for calling Sophie a crybaby.

"You mess with my sister, you mess with me," Callie had said. She was always there for her, and Sophie needs her now, more than ever. But Callie can't help her anymore, can she?

Sophie's stomach growls in hunger, she hasn't eaten for hours, and she pulls a Snickers from her pocket. She had swiped it from the metal display rack next to the till as she'd queued to pay for her coffee, stuffing it in her pocket before the snotty girl behind the counter with faded red hair could spot her. Serves her right, silly cow. Sophie had noticed the look of disgust as she took in Sophie's matted hair, her dirty clothes. Sophie checks her phone again. The battery is flat now, not that she thinks anyone will ring, unless Nathan calls to tell her he's not coming. He'd bloody better come. She thinks he will. He would never ever want people to find out what Callie had done. Spoil the memory of his perfect girlfriend, not to mention the perfect daughter and the perfect sister. Sophie wipes her eyes with her sleeve. It's the dust in here that's making them stream, that's all. But she knows she's being unfair. Callie was her perfect sister and Sophie wishes she'd never dragged her into the mess she made. She misses Callie every single day.

It's pitch-black. A scream. The hairs on the back of Sophie's neck prick up but she tells herself it's just a fox. There's nothing here that can hurt her. But she knows that's not true. Monsters don't always live under your bed.

CHAPTER SIXTY-THREE

I have called a taxi. I'm not comfortable leaving Nathan on his own but I think he'll be OK. I grow cold as I think I could have killed him.

When he wakes I hope he understands that everything I've done, I've done for Callie. If only her message to me had been clearer. "You must listen," Fiona the medium had said. How could I have got it so wrong? It is Callie's love for her sister that is driving me forward. What kind of trouble is she in?

Nathan's face is pale but relaxed. I brush the fringe away from his forehead. He could be asleep. This could be like any other morning, and in different circumstances maybe I'd have a lifetime of his voice being the last thing I heard before I drifted to sleep, his face the first thing I saw when I woke. But he was never mine to love. Not really. I should never have slept with him.

I grasp Nathan's belt between my fingers and somehow manage to hoist him into the recovery position, grunting as I move him. His pulse is steady. He'll be OK. Please, God, let him be OK.

There are two sharp blasts of a horn outside the window

and I scoop back the curtains and peer out into the night. I signal to the driver I'm on my way and I grab my bag and slam the front door shut behind me.

It is starting to drizzle. I give the driver the address and rest my head back against the fabric seats that smell faintly of smoke, even though there's a red "NO SMOKING" sign on the window.

* * *

"We're here," the driver says. I'm already clutching two twenty pound notes in my hand, and I thrust these toward him. "Keep the change."

My face is wet with rain as I stand on the doorstep and thud my fist against the front door, and I think I should be cold but I am burning hot and I don't know how much longer I can keep going. I thump on the door again, my arms trembling with the effort, and when the door swings open I practically fall into Tom's arms.

"It's Sophie," I croak.

CHAPTER SIXTY-FOUR

Sophie angles her watch toward the moon so she can check the time again. It's past nine. She's not as convinced as she was that Nathan will come. What will she do if he doesn't? She can't stay here, but without cash and her passport there's nowhere she can go. There's no one left she can call without putting her family in danger, and she loves her family. She really does.

Tears slide down her cheeks and snot streams from her freezing nose. Once she starts crying, she can't stop. Sophie rocks backward and forward. The wailing that comes from her mouth is so unlike anything she's heard before, it takes a few minutes to register that it's her making that sound. More than anything, Sophie wants her dad. She wants him to stroke her hair and tell her that she's his princess, like he used to do. She wishes again that he could hold her now, tell her everything's going to be OK. But he can't. It isn't. And she knows she's not his little girl anymore. She hasn't been for years. Not since she met Owen. Despite all that's happened, when she thinks of him, her stomach still flip-flops.

Sophie met Owen three years ago. Her dad had just had

his second heart attack and everyone thought he might die. She was terrified. Callie had Nathan to lean on. Mum and Uncle Joe were permanently at the hospital, and Sophie was left alone to imagine the worst, and she did. Each time she closed her eyes she saw herself huddled under a black umbrella as rain splattered over her dad's coffin as it was lowered into the ground. Unable to shake the image that sprung at her time and time again she had tucked Dad's whisky under her coat and traipsed to the park. The first gulp of whisky she swallowed made her chest burn and acid rose in her throat. Why did people drink this stuff for fun? She sipped from the bottle as she spun slowly on the roundabout until it jerked to a stop and she had spluttered amber liquid over her white jeans.

"Hey!" Sophie had wiped her mouth with one hand and twisted her neck around. She had clutched the bottle a little tighter as she saw the man holding the roundabout still with both hands.

"Drinking alone? Are you OK?" he had asked and his concern encouraged Sophie to tell him the truth.

"No," she said.

"Do you want to talk about it?"

His head had tilted to the side as though he really wanted to listen, and Sophie had blurted out: "My dad's sick. I think he might die."

"Come and sit with me and tell everything," the man said. He was older than her. Not as old as her dad, but an adult all the same. A bit like one of the teachers at school, and Sophie had climbed off the roundabout and allowed herself to be led to a bench.

"I'm Owen," he had said as he sat a fraction too close.

"Sophie." She had swigged again from the bottle and when she had lowered it from her mouth he took it off her.

She thought she was in trouble, but he put it to his own lips and gulped greedily before handing it back to her.

"Are you old enough to drink?" he had asked.

"Seventeen," Sophie had said. "But everyone says I look older."

"You do." He had appraised her. "Tell me about your dad then?"

Sophie had sobbed into his black-leather-jacketed shoulder, her tears sliding down the shiny surface as she told him how scared she was. How alone she felt. They passed the bottle back and forth as he listened. *Really listened*, Sophie thought. And by the time he placed two fingers under her chin, tilting her face upward, and planted the first-ever kiss on her Johnnie Walker numb lips, Sophie had known she was in love.

CHAPTER SIXTY-FIVE

Tom half-carries me into the lounge and lays me on the sofa. I struggle to sit up.

"Jenna?" Amanda perches next to me and presses the back of her hand against my forehead. "You're burning up."

"I'll ring for an ambulance," Tom says.

"No." I push Amanda's hand away. "Sophie's in trouble."

"Sophie's in Spain," Tom says steadily. "With Owen."

"No. She's not." My tongue feels thick in my mouth and forming words is almost more than I can manage.

"You're not making sense, Jenna. You have a fever and I'm taking you to the hospital," says Tom.

"Look in my bag," I say desperately, gesturing to the floor.

Tom unzips my bag and tips the contents out onto the coffee table. Amanda grabs the passport. When she opens it the color drains from her cheeks.

"It's Sophie's," she whispers through her fingers. "Jenna." Her voice is louder now. "Where is she? Where's my baby girl?"

"Why have you got Sophie's passport? What's going on, Jenna?" Tom is staring at me as though he's never seen me before.

I sift through words that spin around my fevered head, trying to formulate an explanation that won't make me sound crazy, but I can't.

"There's something called Cellular Memory, where ..."

"The recipient inherits the donor's memories. I've heard of that. I spent hours researching transplants after Callie. I told you about it, Amanda, remember? The research that scientist was doing. What's that got to do with Sophie?"

Tom crosses the room and wraps his arms around Amanda as though my words are arrows that will wound her.

"I feel things. See things. Muddled images. Fragmented dreams. I think they are Callie's memories. She's been trying to tell me something but it all became so blurred, but now I know. Sophie is in danger. Nathan told me." I hold up my palm to stop their inevitable questions. I can't answer them. "He was going to meet her tonight. We need to find her."

Tom and Amanda fall silent as they try to process what I'm trying to explain. Will they trust me? I hope so. Callie's desperation has seeped into every single cell in my body. Tom walks toward the front door and for a horrible moment I think he's going to ask me to leave, but instead, he fetches his shoes from the doormat.

"Where is she?"

"I think—"

"You think? If she's here I need to know where. I'll call Nathan if he was meeting her." He picks up the landline.

"He won't answer," I say and Tom hesitates. "I know how it sounds but you have to trust me." There's a beat before he places the receiver back on the cradle.

"I've had lots of dreams of Callie and Sophie," I say. "But all in the same place. It's a place they both felt happy and safe and I think that's where she is."

"Where?" Amanda is wringing her hands together. She looks distraught.

"The caravan park you used to go to. Owl Lodge you said it was called, Amanda?"

"Newley-on-Sea? We used to go there when the girls were small. It shut down a couple of years ago."

"I'm sure that's where she is."

"I'll fetch my keys, and your shoes, Amanda." Tom thunders up the stairs, and I pull myself up and put my arm around Amanda's shoulders, partly to hold myself up and partly to comfort her.

"I thought she was in Spain. With Owen," Amanda says.

"Perhaps we should call the police? If she's in trouble?" I say.

"We don't know she's in trouble and we can hardly tell the police you've had a dream Sophie is at a caravan park that has been shut for years. They won't take us seriously. We need to find her ourselves."

"We will," I say with far more confidence than I feel.

Amanda looks at me, a worried expression on her face. "You must see a doctor, Jenna. You look terrible."

"I'm OK," I lie. I must see this through.

"I can't be responsible for you too. I'll phone an ambulance. You can't take any chances with Callie's heart."

Before I can answer Tom bursts into the room, talking loudly on his mobile phone: "I know, I know. It sounds mad. But we have to at least look though. I'll call you as soon as I know more."

He puts his phone into his pocket and hands Amanda her shoes. "Just filling Joe in," he explains. "Let's go then."

I take a step but Amanda places a hand on my arm. "Tom, I don't think Jenna should come, she's sick."

Tom glances at me. "You don't have to come."

"I want to," I say firmly.

"She wants to," echoes Tom. "Come on, no time to waste arguing about it. Sophie is our priority."

* * *

In the back of Tom's car, I press my hands against my chest. My heart beats out *Sophie-Sophie-Sophie* and I whisper to Callie that we'll help her sister, but I don't know how much longer I can hold on.

It's just a cold.

Except it's not, is it? All the lies I've told and, even now, I'm lying to myself.

My phone beeps. Nathan's name illuminates the screen: *"Where are you?"*

"Going to get Sophie," I reply. *"I'm sorry."*

I shudder when I think I could have killed him, and I wonder if I'll ever be the same after this. If there's to be an after this for me?

Housing estates are replaced by dark country roads and the wheels on the car spin faster and faster. We hare through the village of Woodhaven. Icy fingers of fear reach out and squeeze me as I think about the journey Callie made through here six months ago and how it ended for her.

I'm growing weaker, and weaker.

The weather is foul. Rain torrents from the invisible night clouds and the windscreen wipers swish-swish-swish and it's hypnotic.

I try and try but I just can't keep my eyes open anymore.

CHAPTER SIXTY-SIX

Up until last weekend Sophie had thought she was safe; she had gradually stopped looking over her shoulder all the time. These past few months Sophie had tried to build a new life moving from town to town, staying in hostels. She had picked up cash-in-hand work as a barmaid in pubs as putrid and soulless as the Prince of Wales.

Sophie will never forget the nerves that had gripped her belly the first time Owen took her to his local for lunch.

"Are you sure I look OK?" she had asked, hanging back as they reached the front door. Sophie had spent longer than usual lining her eyes with thick black kohl and gluing on fake lashes, desperate to try and look older than her seventeen years. She wanted to impress Owen's friends.

"You look great, babe." Owen's eyes had roamed her body and she had felt the delicious thrill of anticipation. "Just a tweak." He undid another button on her blouse and Sophie felt heat prickle her chest as she realized the black lacy bra he had bought her last week was now on show. "Stop worrying. You're my girl now and I'll take care of you. Besides, I'm mates with Steve, the landlord." Owen had kissed her hard before linking his fingers through hers.

They sauntered into the pub and the stale smell of beer and sweat pervaded her nostrils, eradicating the scent of hospitals that seemed to have penetrated her very being.

"This is my business partner, Neil." Owen introduced her to a man who stared so hard at her cleavage Sophie instinctively crossed her arms, blocking his view.

"Business partner?"

In the two weeks since she had met Owen she had done most of the talking, pouring out her fears about her dad dying. Telling him how, late at night, she heard the sound of her mum's muffled sobbing drifting through the paper-thin walls. The unpaid bills that were stacked on top of the microwave. How she'd overheard her mum on the phone telling her friend that without the income from the business they might lose their house. Where would they go? Sophie couldn't imagine. Worry after worry had tripped off her tongue. Sophie had felt a burst of shame as she had realized she hadn't given Owen a chance to talk. She didn't know much about him other than the way her insides softened as his warm tongue snaked into her mouth, and how the feel of his hand running up her bare leg momentarily tugged her away from all her problems. "What do you do?" Sophie asked Neil.

"This and that," he said. "Drink?" He pulled a wad of notes from his pocket and peeled off a twenty.

Sophie hesitated. She wanted to appear sophisticated but she had been so ill after that night drinking whisky in the park the thought of alcohol made her stomach roil. "A Coke, please."

Neil raised an inquiring eyebrow.

"I have to visit my dad in hospital later," Sophie had explained. "He's really sick and I don't want him to smell the alcohol on my breath." At the thought of her big, strong dad lying in the hospital bed, his face as white as his pillow, tears sprang to her eyes and she sniffed, conscious if she cried her makeup would run in rivulets down her cheeks.

"I can't imagine how hard it must be for you." Neil placed his hand on hers.

It had felt as heavy as the arm Owen had slung around her shoulders but as he looked into her eyes she had felt a sense of belonging and it didn't seem to matter so much that Mum and Uncle Joe were always at the hospital and she was largely ignored. That Callie had Nathan to comfort her. She had friends now of her own, didn't she? Someone to love her.

"Do you want something to take the edge off?" Neil had asked.

"What sort of something?"

"It will help relax you and won't leave a smell. Your dad will never know."

"I don't think . . ."

"Leave her alone, she's just a kid," Steve the landlord had said as he shot her an amused look and started to pour flat Coke from a bottle.

Sophie straightened her spine. "I'm not, it's just . . ."

"It's fine, Soph." Owen cupped her bottom with his hand and squeezed. "It's there if you need it. You know, if your dad dies and you can't cope. It'll get you through the funeral at least."

It was as though a huge weight had slammed into Sophie's chest. Her dad couldn't die. He just couldn't. But she pictured the machines, the wires, the beep-beep-beep that stayed in her head long after she had left the ward, and she raised her tear-glazed eyes to Owen's.

"OK. What have you got?"

CHAPTER SIXTY-SEVEN

My head jerks upright, and I wipe a trail of drool from my chin. I must have nodded off. I squint into the blackness trying to work out where we are. There are no landmarks, but outside, in the darkness, the ocean roars. I crack the window open and I can taste salt on my tongue.

"They've blocked off the lane leading to the main car park," Tom says, as the car slows and stops. "We'll have to drive around the other side and park in the beach car park." The engine throbs as he pushes the car into first and we are moving once more.

"I wonder where this leads?" Tom swings hard left onto a track and my already pounding head bangs against the window.

Grass grows where the road once was and, as the car lurches in and out of potholes, I grasp the door handle to steady myself. And there it is. Tom's headlights illuminate the owl, wings spread wide, beak open in a silent screech. Owl Lodge. Newley-on-Sea.

We're here.

CHAPTER SIXTY-EIGHT

It is freezing here at night. Sophie draws her knees up to her chest and wraps her arms around her shins. The seat she is sitting on smells of damp, and apricot foam pokes through holes where insects have burrowed. She remembers folding this seat out into the bed that she and Callie used to share on holiday, snuggled down in their matching pajamas. In the morning, they would shower in the communal bathroom, standing in cool, sandy water that had pooled in the shower tray from the person before. Callie would help Sophie wash her hair, never letting the frothy bubbles sting her eyes. Callie always helped her, and Sophie feels so many shades of regret as she thinks that if Callie hadn't helped her that night she would still be alive today.

It had been a foul night. Rain flung itself at the windows like handfuls of tiny gravel, but inside Owen's house they were warm and cozy, the radiators belting out heat.

"Come on, baby. You know what it does to you." Owen offered her the rolled-up note.

"I don't do that anymore. I thought you understood when we got back together. I'm staying clean."

"And I respect you for that. I really do. One last hit though. For old times' sake?"

Sophie hesitated. Longing for the rush. "This is the very last time." She bent over the coffee table and sniffed hard before wiping the white residue from underneath her nostrils and curling up on Owen's lap. She kissed him deeply as euphoria flooded her body. She was just sliding her hand inside his boxers when somebody banged on the front door.

"Ignore it," muttered Owen as she froze, and he had put his hand on hers, urging her to carry on.

The thumping came again, louder this time.

"They'll go away." Owen pinched her nipple hard and she had groaned.

The letter box rattled open. "I know you're in there," screamed a voice. Callie's voice, and Sophie had scrambled to her feet, straightening her top. "I just want to talk," Callie yelled.

"She won't go away until you answer," Sophie had said, and Owen muttered furiously as he zipped up his fly and swaggered down the hallway.

Callie strode into the lounge, dripping hair plastered to her skull, eyes blazing.

She grasped Sophie's arm. "We're going."

"No!" Sophie stood firm.

"She's not going anywhere." Owen stood in the doorway. "We were in the middle of something until you rudely interrupted." He grabbed his crotch and smirked.

"What the fuck do you see in this loser, Soph?"

"I love him." Sophie wished Callie would give Owen a chance and get to know him properly.

"This. Isn't. Love." Callie slapped her palm against her forehead in despair. Her diamond engagement ring glinted in the light, and all of a sudden, Sophie was sick of her perfect sister, with her perfect boyfriend and perfect life. She grabbed Callie by the shoulders and shook her hard. "Leave me alone. You're always trying to ruin things for me. I don't need you!" The words felt hot to Sophie as they spilled out of her mouth.

"You heard her." Owen stepped to the side and gestured to the hallway with his hand. "See yourself out. We've things to do." Owen's hand moved toward the zip on his trousers, and Callie sprang at him, pushing him backward.

"You fucking, fucking bastard."

"Get off, you mad bitch."

Owen shoved Callie hard, and she fell. There was a sickening thump as she hit her head on the coffee table and lay motionless on the stained carpet. For a split second Sophie thought she was dead and the pain was so physical she thought she might be sick. Sobs ripped through Sophie but Callie pushed herself up and Sophie rushed to her with relief. The side of Callie's face was red and puffy and her eye was almost shut; blood trickled from the corner of her mouth and Sophie wiped it away with her thumb.

"Oh God. Callie. This was an accident. Right, Owen? You didn't mean it, did you?"

" 'Course not," Owen said.

"Soph. Please come with me."

Sophie swallowed hard. She couldn't look her sister in the eye. "Mum and Dad are happy me and Owen are back together. Why can't you be too?"

"Mum and Dad don't know about this shit, that's why." Callie picked up a white plastic bag of powder from the table, and Owen laughed. But it was a cold, hollow laugh.

"I'll tell you a story about 'this shit,' shall I?" Owen yanked Callie to her feet and she whimpered and tried to pull her arm free, but Owen wouldn't let go.

Sophie could see Callie's skin indenting, could almost feel how hard he was pressing. Sophie was scared. Really scared about what might happen next and she knew she had to get Callie away from here. She picked up a bronze figurine of an intertwined couple she had bought Owen for their first-year anniversary and brought it crashing down as hard as she could on the back of his head.

CHAPTER SIXTY-NINE

The site is pitch-black. If it weren't for the moon it would be impossible to see anything.

"Where is she?" Amanda wails. She has wound the car window down as though that might make it easier to see. It doesn't. Tom stops the car and pulls out the key. The headlights grow dark and the engine tick-tick-ticks as it begins to cool.

"We're better off on foot," Tom says, and he pulls a torch out of his glove compartment and hands it to Amanda before we step out of the car.

The roar of the ocean is deafening, and cold salt air stings my lips.

"Let's try the van we always rented." Tom grabs Amanda's hand and strides forward. I lag behind, shining the torch of my mobile to light my path, but it's hard to keep up and my feet keep sinking into the soft earth. My limbs feel like they are made of marble. I am so, so tired but adrenaline keeps me moving forward. We squeeze between a gap in the metal barriers put up in a half-hearted attempt to keep out trespassers, and ignore the "WARNING GUARD DOGS" sign. This site has been derelict for years, looking at it, and anything worth stealing is probably long gone.

We wend our way through the abandoned fairground. A Ferris wheel rises out of the darkness, carriages creaking in the wind.

Crash.

We collectively freeze. Turn. A hot dog sign hangs forlornly from one chain, banging against the side of the wooden kiosk.

My feet crunch over the broken glass of a hundred fairy lights that once twisted around the outside of a rotting waltzer ride but now trail in the dirt.

The fairground is only small, although I imagine it felt enormous to the small children who holidayed here. In the distance, there are rows of static caravans looming out of the shadows.

"Wait." I hold on to the rotting wooden frame of the mini-golf hut. Splinters pierce my skin. "One second."

"You OK?" Tom edges forward, desperate to get going again, and I let the sea-salt air flood my lungs. Steel myself to carry on. "It's not far now."

I can do this.

It's just a cold.

CHAPTER SEVENTY

Light spears through the filthy plastic window and in the distance Sophie can hear the throb of an engine before it is once more dark. Silent.

Nathan must be here.

Thank fuck for that, Sophie thinks and she begins to stuff her things into her rucksack, and as she thrusts a shirt into the bottom of the bag her hand connects with something cold and metal. Owen's gun. It was one of the few things she had packed when she left. Sophie had been horrified when Owen swaggered into the house one day and showed it to her.

"Why have you got that?" Sophie had shrunk away from Owen as he aimed the gun toward his reflection in the mirror and mimicked pulling the trigger.

"Protection, babe. Want to hold it?"

"No. I am never touching it." She had shuddered at the time, but now she pulls it out of her bag and the weight of it in her hand is reassuring. She won't use it, of course, but she'll keep it with her, just in case. Sophie takes a last look around the van where she spent so many happy childhood

times with her sister. Fizzy pop and chocolate buttons.
Games of Snap!

"Bye, Callie," she whispers.

Sophie hefts her bag onto her shoulder, but before she's
crossed the van, the door swings open and she lets out a cry
as the gun is wrenched from her hand.

CHAPTER SEVENTY-ONE

All the caravans look the same to me but Tom and Amanda seem to know where they are heading as they turn left, right, stopping outside a large van.

"This is the one." The pale-yellow beam of the torch shines on the mold clinging to the plastic windows.

Tom pushes the door. It swings open easily.

"Sophie!" He steps inside. "She's not here."

Disappointment sours his voice, and I am beginning to think I've got it wrong, I really am going mad, when Amanda rushes forward with more energy than I've ever seen her expel and drops to her knees. "Look!"

She pulls a checked shirt out of a rucksack and waves it like a flag. "It's Sophie's. Callie bought her it for her last birthday. They went shopping together. I remember." She presses it to her face as though the smell will lead her to her daughter.

"She was here then? Where is she now?" says Tom.

And then there's a scream.

CHAPTER SEVENTY-TWO

"Faster."

Sophie can't take her eyes off the gun in his hand as they cross the old mini-golf course where she and Callie spent hours tapping golf balls into the mouths of dinosaurs and under bridges. Sophie trips and lands on something sharp that slices into her palm. Her screams are whipped away by the crashing waves.

He yanks her upright.

"Please," she begs, holding onto his hand with both of hers, trying to prize his fingers apart. The wind forces its way inside of her mouth and she shouts to make herself heard. "I'm sorry. Can't we just stop and talk about everything?"

On the beach, her feet sink into the soft sand.

She can't see the ocean but the spray lands on her cheeks and she knows the tide is in.

"Please." She's begging now. "I'm scared of water."

"I know," he says. "Shhhh. We're almost there. Hurry."

Sophie shivers and although it's freezing she knows it is fear that is making her teeth rattle together like castanets.

They had stood at this water's edge once, she and Callie.

Callie had held Sophie's hand tightly as waves lapped around their feet. Callie had crouched down and scooped water into Sophie's little pink bucket—they were making a sandcastle and needed water for a moat. A wave had caught Sophie off guard and she'd slipped and landed on her bottom in the water, but Callie had never once let go of her hand. She knew how terrified Sophie was of drowning. Is that how she's going to die today? After everything she's been through? Sophie flexes her fingers and imagines she can still feel Callie's warm hand in hers.

CHAPTER SEVENTY-THREE

"It came from over there, I think," says Tom as we stand outside the caravan, still as the wooden owl, and there it is again. A scream. In the daytime, you might mistake it for a seagull.

"It's coming from the beach," Tom says, springing forward.

I don't know how I manage to scramble up the sand dune, but when I reach the top, Amanda and Tom are already running across the beach toward two figures who are hurrying away. The circle of light from their torch gets fainter and fainter and I'm on my hands and knees, my fingers tangling in damp seaweed, panting and sweating. I can't get up.

It's just a cold.

I shine my smartphone torch onto the sand that looks almost black, and lick my salty lips.

I can do this. For Callie.

My shoes sink into the wet sand as I stagger to my feet.

"Sophie! Sophie!" Amanda's voice is faint and I bend my head against the wind and push forward.

Sweat is pouring off me. It feels as if I am on a treadmill, getting nowhere fast, but when I glance up I have caught up with Amanda and Tom, who come to rest in front of two figures. Sophie is recognizable from her photo, next to her is Joe; his arm dangles by his side, something silver glinting in his hand. A gun! My feet involuntarily shuffle backward.

"Sophie?" Amanda takes a step toward her, but Joe snaps: "Stay where you are."

I stand behind Amanda and shield my phone with my hand to dim the light, but in this hollow there's no signal. I can't call for help.

"Joe? What are you doing here? Is that a gun?" Tom stops in his tracks.

"Daddy." Sophie sobs and I feel a rush of love toward this girl I've never met. This sister of my heart.

"I thought you were in Spain, Sophie," Tom says. Tears are streaming down his face. "In Spain. With Owen. We've been waiting for you to come home. I don't understand what's going on here."

"Let her go, Joe." Amanda's voice is deathly calm. "Sophie, come to me."

"No!" Joe raises his arm. His hand is unsteady as he aims the gun toward us.

"I am so sorry, Tom," he says.

CHAPTER SEVENTY-FOUR

"Joe? Why have you got a gun?" Tom can't keep his eyes off his brother as he waits for an answer.

I glance behind me, trying to judge the distance back to the park but I'm weak. Slow. Even if I run I don't think I will be quick enough to hide in the shadows if Joe pulls the trigger. My teeth chatter together. After all I've been through, is this how I'm going to die?

"It's not my gun," Joe says almost imploringly, as though we should feel sorry for him, but he doesn't lower his arm.

The sand feels like sponge beneath my feet and I will my terrified knees not to give way. I see Amanda sag and I wrap my arm around her waist. I'm not strong enough to hold her up should she fall, but I can't imagine how scared she must be, and I want to offer some comfort. I can feel her whole body shaking, and I'm suddenly furious at Joe for putting Amanda through this after everything else she has endured this year.

"Whose gun is it?" I almost demand.

"It's hers." Joe gives Sophie's shoulder a shake. "I've taken it off her to stop her doing anything else stupid."

"Sophie? Is it your gun?" Tom asks, and I don't know how his voice is so controlled.

I can almost imagine the parent he was when the girls were small, trying to calmly find out who put their vegetables in the bin or who broke a toy.

"It's Owen's," Sophie says but she can't look her father in the eye. She can't look anyone in the eye.

"And why would Owen have a gun?" asks Tom.

Sophie stares beseechingly at her mum, her eyes shining as the moon glows brighter.

"Don't push her, Tom. She's obviously been through a horrible experience but she's back now. Our daughter is back," Amanda says firmly.

"What's going to happen now then?" Tom asks.

Joe lowers the gun and releases his grip on Sophie but she doesn't move.

"Oh God. I just can't cope with this anymore, I can't." I am shocked to see Joe begin to cry. "We have to leave before Owen comes."

"Let's get Sophie home," Amanda says, taking a step forward, but Tom puts out an arm to stop her.

"I want to hear about Owen now. Why should we leave before he comes? What is that boyfriend of yours involved in?"

For a moment all is still. Quiet. The ocean fades into the background. Nobody moves. The wind has dropped and the roaring waves become a gentle lap. I feel I'm barely breathing, but at last Sophie wipes her nose with her sleeve and begins to speak.

"When you had a heart attack I was so scared you were going to die, but you promised me it would all be OK and I believed you. But it wasn't OK, was it? You had another heart attack and the doctor told us you might not pull through. I was terrified. Mum and Uncle Joe spent all their time with you. Callie was with Nathan. I had no one. And then I met Owen and he listened to me. Really listened to me. And we fell in love. When he started giving me stuff to stop me worrying, I thought it was because he cared."

"Stuff?"

"Cocaine. I only meant to take it until you were OK again, but when you came out of hospital I found I couldn't stop. I didn't mean to, Dad. I'm so sorry."

"That fucking, fucking, bastard. Where is he?" Fury emanates from Tom's voice and I think if Owen is here he should be very, very afraid. "I'll fucking kill him."

"He's already dead," says Sophie.

CHAPTER SEVENTY-FIVE

"It was self-defense, Soph," Callie said. "The police will see that."

They sat on the sofa, both pretending everything would be OK, but Callie's skin took on a green tinge and she spoke in a monotone.

"I'm a murderer. I'm going to jail." Sophie wrapped her arms around her middle and rocked herself back and forth. Panic filled her throat.

"You won't," Callie said but Sophie had never heard her big sister sound so uncertain before.

"I will. I'm going to jail. I won't be able to cope." Sophie buried her face in her hands and sobs ripped through her body so intensely she felt her chest might split into two and her heart might tumble to the floor.

"I won't let you." Callie slid her arm around Sophie's shoulders. "We'll say I did it. We could say I called around looking for you but you weren't here. Owen attacked me. The police will believe that." Callie's hand fluttered to her swollen cheek. "I was protecting myself."

"But the wound is on the back of his head. That's not

self-defense. I can't let you take the blame. Oh God. I can't go to jail."

"If we explain to the police—"

"No." Sophie shook her head. She knew if the police got involved the secrets she had kept, the lies she had told, would all come out. Her family would be torn apart. They would hate her. Callie would hate her. "Please, Callie. You've got to help me." Sophie squeezed Callie's arm tightly.

"How?" Callie asked, her eyes flicking to Owen. Blood had seeped from his head and stained the hearth.

"We could get rid of his body. No one would know." Sophie felt a kernel of hope. "No one would miss him. Not really. He doesn't have a family." Sophie blocked out the thought of Owen's son, Harry. It wasn't like he ever saw him, was it? "His mates are all losers. Particularly Neil. Thinking he's something special when he's just a small-time crook. He would miss Owen for his money but no one would actually miss Owen as a person." No one but her. Sophie pushed that thought away. "It's the perfect solution."

"Sophie, I can't . . ."

"If you loved me you would."

Hurt flashed in Callie's eyes, and Sophie knew she wasn't being fair but desperation was inflating inside of her like a balloon, and she didn't know what else she could do. She pushed forward, ideas sparking now.

"We could bury him. Look." Sophie grabbed the free local newspaper off the coffee table and flicked through it until she found what she was looking for. "Burton Aerodrome." She jabbed her finger at the article. "They've declared it a conservation area. They'll never build on it. Never dig it up."

Callie rose to her feet and paced over to the window.

Sophie wished she knew what her sister was thinking. They had always been so close but now they felt a world apart. Sophie wrung her hands as she waited. The clock ticked loudly. Her blood pulsed in her ears. Finally, Callie turned around. Her face streaked with tears.

"OK. I'll help you."

* * *

Sophie wanted to move quickly before Callie had second thoughts and she went into the bedroom to fetch a sheet to wrap Owen in. As she stood at the foot of the bed where she had lost her virginity, she noticed Owen's watch on the bedside table. He would never need to know the time again. What had she done? She ran into the bathroom and her stomach muscles screamed as she vomited in the toilet bowl until there was nothing left inside of her. When she had finished she stuffed a few things into a rucksack. She was never coming back here.

When Sophie walked back into the lounge, sheet bundled in her arms and a sour taste in her mouth, Callie was tapping on her mobile phone.

"What are you doing?" Sophie's heart stuttered.

"I'm telling Nathan we're having a night out. He'll wonder where I am."

"I bet he'll love that." Sophie knew Nathan didn't like her and although she understood why—all the relapses, all the stress she'd put Callie through—it still rankled.

Callie bit her lip and, for a split second, Sophie thought Callie had changed her mind and she wished she hadn't said anything but Callie rose to her feet, took a deep breath, and said: "Let's do this."

* * *

Callie reversed her car right up to the front door. She clicked open her boot, and Sophie took out the gardening tools and the wheelbarrow Callie always used to tend to their parents' garden and put them on the back seat.

Rain was still teeming down and although blanketed by darkness Sophie looked around nervously, imagining eyes watching them.

In the lounge, the girls shoved the coffee table out of the way and spread out the sheet.

"Let's lift him onto it and wrap him up," Callie said but neither girl moved.

"After three," Callie said, bending down and sliding her hand under Owen's shoulders. "Grab his feet, Soph."

Sophie was glad her sister had taken charge. It felt like old times almost, and tears stung as she thought of all the ways their relationship would change after this.

Sophie shuddered as her hands closed around Owen's ankles. His jeans shifted and she caught a glimpse of the Mr. Grumpy socks she had bought him for his birthday. She began to shake uncontrollably.

"If you're not sure, it's not too late to change your mind?" Callie asked. "I could call the police?"

But the thought of the police digging into Sophie's past was worse than the thought of what they were about to do.

"I'm sure," she said. But she wasn't. Not really.

"One, two, three," Callie grunted as she strained to move Owen. "Bloody hell." She crouched on her heels as she folded the sheet around him. "I can't believe he's so heavy."

"How are we going to get him into the car?" Terror had lodged in Sophie's chest and her voice was unnaturally high.

"Wheelbarrow?" said Callie.

* * *

The journey to Burton Aerodrome was silent save the clipped tones of the voice on the satnav giving directions and the rhythmic swish of the windscreen wipers. The smell of cleaning products still clung to Sophie's nostrils but, despite a lingering stain on the hearth, Sophie was sure they had removed the blood splatters from the lounge. Her hands felt raw from the bleach she had used.

When they reached the airfield Callie's car juddered over the rough ground.

"Where do you think?" Sophie looked anxiously out of the window.

"I don't know everything," Callie snapped, and Sophie felt the jolt of her sister beginning to slip away from her. "How about near the bushes? It won't be obvious the ground has been disturbed if anyone comes?"

Callie turned her face toward Sophie's as she waited for an answer and, in the half-light, her skin had a waxy sheen and Sophie wondered how Callie would move on from this. How they both would.

"OK," Sophie said.

Callie accelerated again and as the engine thrummed louder she unclipped her seatbelt and twisted around to reach for her handbag that she always slung on the back seat when she drove.

"I've told you before not to do that." Sophie snatched the bag from Callie's hands. "It's dangerous. What do you want?"

"There's a packet of mints in there somewhere. I'm feeling sick."

They circled around the airfield, sucking on Extra Strongs, until Callie slowed again.

"Here. I think."

She parked and cut the engine, leaving the headlights slicing through the darkness, illuminating the rain.

Callie handed Sophie the fork and took the spade and, although the ground was wet, it took a long time to dig a hole deep enough. By the time they had finished, the muscles in Sophie's arms trembled and burned and she was covered in a clammy sweat. She looked at her sister and she wasn't sure whether Callie's face was wet with rain or tears.

* * *

"Come with me," Sophie had pleaded as they sat in the car park at the train station.

"I can't," Callie said. "I love Nathan."

"But you love me?" Sophie didn't think Callie could anymore. Not after everything she had put her through that night.

"Of course. You're my sister."

"Will you tell him? Nathan?"

Callie brushed her damp hair out of her eyes with a hand that still shook.

"I don't know, Soph. I've never kept anything from him before."

"He'll tell the police."

"He won't."

"You've got to act normal. If you're going back. At work. Everywhere. You won't be able to do that. I know you."

"I can't just leave my life." Callie had scrubbed at her wet cheeks with her sleeve. "Where will you go?"

"Dunno." Sophie shrugged. "I always fancied Spain. Shit. My passport is still at Mum and Dad's from when they took us to Paris."

"Shall we . . ."

"Could you get it, Callie? And some cash? Enough for a flight and a couple of months in a B&B while I find my feet? Please?"

"I suppose. I have to give the bank notice if I withdraw savings so it might take a few days. What about Mum and Dad?"

"I'll text them tomorrow and tell them I've gone on holiday with Owen. I'll figure out the rest later." Sophie clicked open the car door and climbed out, hefting her rucksack onto her shoulder. She felt very small. And very alone. "I'll text you and let you know where I am. Thanks, Callie. For everything." She began to turn.

"Wait," Callie called. "I will come with you. To Spain. Not forever. I don't want to leave Nathan. But until you're settled at least."

Sophie's throat closed and she couldn't speak. She nodded instead.

"I'll meet you in a few days when I've got some money and our passports. It will be OK, Soph. I promise."

CHAPTER SEVENTY-SIX

Tom covers his mouth with both hands, and Amanda drops to her knees as though her bones have turned to dust. She curls herself into a ball on the damp seaweed-covered sand.

No wonder I'd felt so scared when I saw the photo of Owen at Kathy's house. Thoughts hurtle through my mind: Callie *was* driving when she crashed. The pieces fall into place so quickly it's difficult to keep up. "The night of Callie's accident she was coming to meet you?" I say. "When her and Nathan picked up your parents to go to the wedding reception she got your passport and took the money and necklace from their safe."

"Who the fuck are you?" Sophie glares at me, noticing me for the first time, and I feel irrationally hurt that she doesn't know me when I feel intrinsically connected to her.

"I'm Jenna. I . . ."

"You killed someone, Sophie?" Tom cuts in. "No wonder you ran away."

"I don't want to go to prison, Dad."

"You won't," he says. "Owen hurt Callie. You were defending your sister. I'll help you. But you have to tell me everything. Have you told me everything, Sophie?"

Sophie looks away. "No."

Joe's shoulders slump like a man defeated. "I can't believe you killed him. I thought he must be here with you. You don't have to say anything else, Sophie."

"I do. I'm sick of the secrets. I'm sick of the lies." Sophie's voice rises in pitch, and Amanda stumbles to her feet.

"You're distressing her. Stop it. We can sort this out at home."

"No! I can't come home. They discovered Owen's body on Sunday. I'd pushed it all to the back of my mind and half-convinced myself it didn't really happen, but the 24-hour news channel they show in the pub I work in reported Owen had been found and I know it's only a matter of time until they identify him and come looking for me. I was going to leave the country once Nathan brought my passport and cash. I can't believe he rang you instead."

"Sophie, we can figure something out," Tom says. "Just tell me the truth. I'll help in any way I can."

"Tom, she doesn't . . ."

"Amanda. Let Sophie speak."

Sophie stares out into the blackness of the ocean. "Dad. Owen got the drugs he gave me from his mate, Neil, at the pub. He never asked me to pay and I thought it was a gift because he was my boyfriend, but one day Owen said I owed Neil money. A lot of money. And not just from what I'd had either; Neil was adding interest. The amount increased every day. I didn't know what to do. Owen said he'd try to protect me but Neil said him and some others from the pub would hurt me. Hurt Callie if I couldn't pay it back. Owen was distraught he had got me into such a mess. But he said he could sort it all out."

"Sort it out how?" Tom asks.

"By using the car parts business to smuggle in drugs. I'd told him it was losing money while you were so sick and he said he'd be able to clear my debt and make enough to pay our mortgage until you were better. He was helping."

"But we didn't import that often," Tom says, "and when we did there was mountains of paperwork. Import forms. How did Owen manage that without my signature?"

There's a beat before Sophie says: "You weren't the only one who could sign things. The business wasn't solely in your name, was it?"

"Amanda?" Tom says, and he stares at his wife as though he has never seen her before as she drops her face into her hands.

CHAPTER SEVENTY-SEVEN

"I didn't know what else to do," Amanda says, lowering her hands from her face.

Tom clutches his left shoulder. Even in the shadow of the moonlight I can see how deathly pale he's become.

"You were in hospital," Amanda says. "The doctor had said you might die. The bills were mounting up. The mortgage wasn't being paid. What was I supposed to do? Our daughters were being threatened, Tom."

"You could have told the police."

"Like they would have offered 24-hour protection to Callie and Sophie? I had to do something to protect them. I'm their mother. Owen made it sound so easy. Sign a few forms and Callie and Sophie would be safe and we'd have enough to live on. How else could I have got the sort of money this Neil was demanding? It was thousands of pounds."

"You involved Sophie in something illegal."

Amanda flinches from Tom's words. I've never heard him sound so hard.

"It was *because* of Sophie I had to do something illegal. I did it because I love her."

"But you knew our daughter was taking drugs and you didn't tell me?"

"I tried everything to get her to stop and as soon as you came out of hospital she wanted to. Do you remember how she took off for months and you thought she just needed a break after the stress of your illness? I'd paid for her to stay in a clinic."

"I can't take this in." Tom dips and I'm worried he'll collapse. He really doesn't look good. "Did you know about this, Joe?"

"Not at the time, I swear. When you were home and you told me that Amanda had persuaded you to retire for your health and you asked if I'd run the business, I found out what had gone on when I looked at the accounts. Your profits had shot up. I thought Amanda had made a mistake with the books but she told me about her arrangement with Owen. I was livid. I didn't tell you because the doctor said you must avoid stress but I didn't want anything to do with it. I didn't *have* anything to do with it."

"But it stopped? This arrangement. When Sophie's debt was paid, it stopped?"

"No," said Joe. "It didn't. I'm so sorry, Tom. I tried to get them to stop, I really did, but the best I could do was make sure you were kept out of it. You and Callie."

"All these months you've been apologizing, Joe, and I thought it was because the business folded after Callie died, as no one had the heart for it anymore. I never thought... this." Tom screws his face up as though he is in pain.

"I felt so bloody awful," Joe says. "I hoped you'd never find out. When Sophie disappeared after Callie died I thought she must be using again as a way of coping with her grief. When you called me tonight and said she might be here I thought she must be with Owen. I didn't want you to have a run-in with him if she was off her face. When I found her alone in the caravan my first thought was to get her away from here as quickly as possible. I thought Owen must be around somewhere. I never dreamed he was ... that she ..."

It is disconcerting to witness Joe's anguish as he begins to cry again.

"You know, when you appeared earlier, there was a split second when I thought about shooting Amanda for what she's done. Can you believe that?" Joe wipes his nose with the back of his hand. "I tried to talk her out of carrying on so many times. I probably should have told you. I'm sorry. But I love you. You're my brother and I didn't want to risk your health."

"Neither did I, Tom," Amanda cuts in. "I looked after you when you were sick. I made sure you didn't have to worry about the bills. You didn't once ask me if we were managing. Not once." Amanda is shouting now: "And I carried on because without Owen all I could see was a future of struggling to meet the mortgage payments every month. Never anything left over for treats. Growing up it was holidays in the Maldives, eating at Michelin star restaurants. You. You brought us here." Her voice is bitter. "I gave up everything for you, but you couldn't provide for us properly."

"I loved you."

"I love you, I do, but I just wanted the girls to experience what I had growing up. It was all for them. For us. For our family. It seemed easy. It was easy. Owen arranged everything and I just turned a blind eye. I didn't actually do anything other than sign a few forms. It wasn't masses of money, not enough to draw attention to us but enough to provide a good income. Owen was careful. You didn't have anything to worry about."

"You could have ended up in jail. We could all have ended up in jail." Tom's voice is steely cold. "Where would the girls have been then?"

"Owen said there was no risk. He knew what he was doing, Dad." Sophie's voice is faint. "I'd told him we might lose the house. He was looking after us all."

"And Callie? Did she know?" Tom is still clutching his shoulder.

"No. She knew Owen got me hooked on drugs but she didn't know about Mum, about the business. Owen was about to tell her everything that night, that's why I hit him. I panicked. If I hadn't, Callie might still be alive."

"No!" Amanda wrings her hands. "Don't say that. It's been almost impossible to live with myself as it is. No matter how much medication I take I feel terrible every second of every day, losing Callie and thinking we had lost you too, Sophie. I thought you couldn't bear to be around memories of Callie and that's why you had gone to Spain with Owen. I can't believe you . . . you killed him. I'm so sorry for what you went through, but we can sort this out, can't we? Between ourselves. We're a family."

"We are not all family," Sophie says and she grabs the gun from Joe's hand and points it at me. "I still don't know who the fuck you are but now you know an awful lot about me."

"Sophie!" Amanda tries to wrestle the gun from her.

There's a struggle. A bang.

Tom drops to the sand, clutching his heart.

Amanda screams but as I look at Tom in the moonlight I can't see an entry wound. I can't see any blood. And then I realize. Tom must have had a heart attack. He isn't the one who has been shot.

CHAPTER SEVENTY-EIGHT

Sophie is crumpled on the sand. Joe drops to his knees, fingers pressed to her neck searching for a pulse. My heart is screaming *no-no-no* and I try to silently back away, but my feet crunch into the shingle and Amanda's head jerks up. I am staring into the anguished eyes of a woman with nothing left to lose, except her freedom.

"We need an ambulance," Joe shouts.

The gun dangles from Amanda's hand. She is frozen to the spot. I don't know what she's planning to do but I can't take any chances. I've seen and heard everything.

Run.

Willing my sick body to move, adrenaline floods my system and I stagger toward the silent owl, a shadow in the distance. Amanda may be older than me but I'm weak. Slow. My best hope is finding somewhere to hide, reaching higher ground to try and get a signal and call for help.

It's dark. So dark. Clouds scud across the charcoal sky, blanketing the moon and stars. Dampness fills my lungs and as I draw a sharp breath nausea crashes over me in sickening waves.

Don't let me down, Callie, I think, as I try to sprint

toward safety but my feet are sinking and I feel like I'm moving in slow motion. My mouth opens as I gasp for air. The taste of salt and desperation on my tongue. I clamber up the sand dune, my heart almost bursting with the exertion, feet scrambling for traction in the soft sand. My fingers cling onto tufts of grass as I heft myself upward. My chest feels like it is on fire but I hear Amanda panting behind me and the survival instinct kicks in. The past few months I have spent wondering if I want to live, but this question is now obliterated from my mind. I'm terrified of dying.

I reach the top and steal a glance behind me. I can't see the top of Amanda's head appearing but she can't be far behind. There's a bump. And I think she's slipped back down.

My energy is fading fast.

"Jenna, wait, please. I need your phone," she shouts but her voice sounds too close, she's quickly catching up with me, and I look around wildly trying to regain my sense of direction. Work out where the car is. Where the road is.

"Jenna! Please. You've got it wrong. It was all for the girls. All of it."

I take a deep breath and furl and unfurl my fists before propelling myself forward once more, arms pumping by my sides. I look over my shoulder.

"Jenna! Stop. Please don't go. Don't call the police. Let me explain." But she doesn't sound remorseful. Fury pushes out her words and each one feels like a thump between my shoulder blades.

Run. I must not stop.

My trainers slap against the concrete and I don't think I can hear footsteps behind me anymore, but it's hard to tell over the howling wind. I've got no chance of outrunning her. My best hope is that she has gone the wrong way.

I steal a glance over my shoulder but my feet stray onto soft earth and I lose my footing and stumble, splaying out my hands to break my fall.

The side of my face hits something hard and solid that rips at my skin. My jaw snaps shut and my teeth slice into my tongue flooding my mouth with blood, and as I swallow it down, bile and fear rise in my throat.

Don't make a sound.

I'm scared. So scared. I don't know what she's capable of. How far she would go to stop me talking to the police.

I lie on my stomach. Still. Silent. Waiting. My palms are stinging. Cheek throbbing. Rotting leaves pervade my nostrils. My stomach roils as I slowly inch forward, digging my elbows into the wet soil for traction. Left. Right. Left. Right.

I'm in the undergrowth now. Thorns pierce my skin and catch on my clothes but I stay low, surrounded by trees, thinking I can't be seen, but the clouds part and in the moonlight I catch sight of the sleeve of my hoodie, which, unbelievably, is white despite the mud splatters. I curse myself. Stupid. Stupid. Stupid. I yank it off and stuff it under a bush. My teeth clatter together with cold, with fear, with fever. Where is she? To my left twigs snap underfoot and instinctively I push myself up and rock forward onto the balls of my feet, like a runner about to sprint. Over my heartbeat pounding in my ears I hear it. A cough. Amanda's cough. Behind me. Close. Too close.

Run.

I stumble forward.

I can do this, I tell myself, but it's a lie. I know I can't keep going for much longer.

"There's no point running," Amanda shouts. "I know this park like the back of my hand."

My legs are so weak. My head feels too heavy for my neck. *It's just a cold.*

Move.

The clouds roll across the sky again and the blackness is crushing. I momentarily slow, conscious I can't see where I'm putting my feet. The ground is full of potholes and I can't risk spraining my ankle, or worse. What would I do then? How could I get away? The wind gusts and the clouds are swept away and in my peripheral vision a shadow moves. I spin around and scream. Amanda is right behind me.

Run.

CHAPTER SEVENTY-NINE

I slow. I'm exhausted. The world is spinning and black flecks zigzag across my vision. She'll find me wherever I am. I'm sick. I'm dying. I can't outrun her and there's nowhere I can hide. Hot tears spill from my eyes, cooling on my cheeks. It's over. The life I've fought so hard to keep. Hopelessness washes over me and, as I slowly turn around, Amanda stops. Hunches forward and puts her hands on her knees, panting for breath.

I check my mobile. There's still no signal.

"Give me your phone," Amanda says and I shake my head.

"Please. Tom and Sophie need help."

I waiver. If she wanted to kill me surely she'd have done it by now.

"We can sort this out, can't we?" She straightens and walks toward me and the gun hanging from her right hand glints. I swallow hard. How does she think we can ever sort this out? I dread to think.

Move, Jenna, a voice whispers inside my head, and my toes twitch and all of a sudden I'm running again, weaving among the abandoned ice-cream kiosks and giant plastic animals, their paint chipped and faded.

"I'm not going to hurt you. You've got it all wrong. You can't hide!" Amanda cries but in an instant I know that I can.

Count to ten. I know just where I'm going.

The fairground is pitch-black but I see flashes of how it used to be: orange, yellow, green flashing lights. Music blaring. The smell of candyfloss. Small children tugging on the hands of parents. "Can I catch a duck?" "Can I go on the merry-go-round?"

I cut across the waltzer, my feet thudding against the wooden boards, almost feeling it spinning round and round, faster and faster, until the faces of the bystanders blur into one.

The large building with the faded food and drink sign is boarded up and I skirt around the edge, imagining I can smell hot, oily chips.

The hut is in front of me. The mini-golf sign hanging from rusted hinges, blowing in the wind. I drop to my knees and scramble around for the large loose footboard. It wobbles but the weeds have woven between the planks and I can't free it.

Snap. A twig breaks and I know she is close. I dig my nails in the tiny gap between the boards and yank as hard as I can. The nail on my index finger is ripped off and I bite back a scream. The gap is small. Big enough for a child, but I don't think I will fit and a lump of frustration lodges in my throat. I stick my hand through the gap and realize that, inside, the ground dips. If I can squeeze through there's enough space for me to hide.

My elbows dislodge dirt as I wriggle forward like a snake, and as I swallow dust an urge to cough grips me, but I hold my breath until the feeling passes. My head enters the dark, damp space, my shoulders, my torso. Something touches me, stopping me, and I freeze—thinking she has caught me—but it's just my bottom hitting the plank above and I have to twist and twist until I can fit it through.

I'm inside. A tight ball now, and I maneuver myself around, my muscles already screaming. I reach my hands through the gap and replace the board just as a slither of light appears around the corner of the canteen.

Amanda's torch.

My knees are digging into something hard and lumpy and my pins and needles feet are itching to move but I keep still, ignoring the pain.

I'm incredulous that she can't hear my galloping heart, my ragged breath, but she calls my name over and over and I hear the frustration in her voice. She doesn't know where I am.

I peek out of the slit between the boards and see her shoes. They are getting larger and larger as she approaches me, and I'm shaking with terror. Praying she won't find this place where Sophie used to hide from Callie so long ago.

There's a creak.

The door of the hut opens.

The stamping of feet above my head. Dust pours into my face. My eyes. My mouth. I know if I can just keep still, I'm safe. She'll go to look somewhere else.

And then my mobile rings.

CHAPTER EIGHTY

Whimpering like one of the injured animals I treat, I struggle to pull my phone from my pocket in the confined space. It's Sam.

"Jenna, I've just read your text and—"

"Help me," I garble into the handset. "She's going to kill me."

"Jenna? What's going on? Where are you?"

Amanda drops to her hands and knees and peers in through a knothole. I poke my thumb in her eye as hard as I can and she screams with pain. Her hands slap against the boards trying to find a way in, but she's on the wrong side of the hut.

"Jenna, please. I just want to talk. You owe me that much at least?" Amanda says.

"I'm at Owl Lodge Caravan Park in Newley-on-Sea. Please call the police and an ambulance. Sam? Sam?" I check my screen but the signal has dropped off again and I don't know if he heard me.

"Jenna. Please come out. Let's talk about this properly. I'm sorry. I really am. I know what I did was wrong but I did it for the right reasons. Please. Don't tell anyone. For

Tom? He doesn't deserve to be alone. I was trying to protect him. Protect the girls."

I hesitate. If she wanted me dead she'd have shot me by now. There must be some good in her.

"Please. Let's talk about what you're going to do. You don't want to tell anyone, do you? It's Tom who will suffer if I go to prison and you're fond of him, aren't you? He's very fond of you. We both are. Think about Callie's memory. You don't want everyone knowing she helped cover up a murder. She saved your life. You wouldn't be here without her. Without me. You owe us. Surely?"

Callie. I press my hands against my chest and a tear runs down my cheek. I don't know what to do and I'm so very, very tired.

It's just a cold.

But my heart is slowing and I know it's very nearly over.

The hut above me rocks and creaks as Amanda kicks the panels and there's the sound of splintering and I know I can't possibly make it out before she gets in, but I summon every last ounce of strength I have left. I have to try.

I push the loose footplate with both hands and crawl through the gap. My body is free, my legs are still inside, when I hit against something solid. I twist my neck and look up. Legs. Amanda's legs.

She puts both hands under my armpits and pulls, and I scream as I feel myself sliding across the dirt. I fumble around behind me with my hands trying to find something I can hang on to, but years of yoga have made her surprisingly strong. I'm almost out the gap and then I feel it. Something cool and metal. The thing I was kneeling on. A mini-golf club, and as she drags me out into the open, I manage to grasp the handle and tuck the club against my body.

The wind howls as she stands over me. We are both panting hard.

"Why can't you promise not to tell anyone?"

I can't take my eyes off the gun. It bumps against her leg as her hand shakes.

"Would you believe me if I did promise?"

It seems an age before she speaks. "When the girls were small they were having a cushion fight while I cooked dinner. I had told them a million times not to. There wasn't enough room to swing a cat in our lounge. A vase got smashed. It had belonged to my grandparents and was worth a fortune. I was furious and demanded to know what happened and Callie stepped forward straight away and said, 'It was me, Mum.' And that's what she was like. Honest and kind and you . . . you have her heart. You are the last part of her to live on and I want to trust you but . . . but you're not her."

"I feel what she felt. The holidays. Coming here with you and Tom when her and Sophie were small. She was so happy."

"I thought they'd be happier with more money."

"You were happier with more money."

"I wasn't though. Not really. It was a relief, of course. Tom wasn't well enough to work and I don't know what we'd have done otherwise. I hadn't worked for years and even if I could have got a job I couldn't have paid Sophie's debt. But I've paid the price. The ultimate price, and I can't go to prison. I really can't."

"I won't make that promise, Amanda." I'm dying anyway. My integrity is the last thing I have left.

"Please, Jenna. Don't make me hurt you. I really don't want to."

A click.

"You are making me do this," she says.

The gun is cocked.

"I'm so sorry, Jenna."

I push myself to kneeling, to standing, and I swing the club. It hits her shoulder and knocks her off balance but I haven't hit her hard enough and she rights herself and raises the gun.

I grip the handle of the club with two hands this time and somehow I muster the energy to swing it as hard as I can. This time it thwacks against the side of her head. She concertinas to the ground. There's a sickening crack as her head falls onto a rock.

Silence.

I try to move but my legs don't seem to work. My knees buckle, and I'm falling, lying on my back, the stars twinkling above me, and as the black sky rushes down toward me I wonder whether it will be the last thing I ever see.

CHAPTER EIGHTY-ONE

The beeping comes first, invading my ears, my skull. Pain throbs at my temples. Next is the feeling of warmth, uncomfortable and sticky. As I breathe in, I smell it. Disinfectant. I'm in hospital. I try to open my eyes but my lids feel heavy and it's too much effort. There's the sound of shuffling footsteps approaching the bed and I know I should speak, but my tongue is stuck to the roof of my mouth. There's a hand on my arm, fingertips on my skin, the feel of my pillow shifting beneath my head, and I surrender to the blackness tugging me under.

* * *

I don't know how much time has passed before my senses spark to life once more, but this time I force my eyes open. My room is cloaked in darkness but light shines in through the small glass window from the corridor outside, casting a rectangle on the floor. Two nurses talk outside, their voices low, and I try to reach the buzzer to let them know I am awake but the weight of the sheets on my body feels crushing. It takes all of my might to turn my head.

Curled up on a chair is Sam and I think I must be dreaming but, as if he realizes he is being watched, he stretches, yawns, and crosses to perch on the edge of my bed.

"Hello, beautiful." His lips graze my forehead, cool and soft, and I want to cry, but I don't have the energy.

"Thirsty." My mouth feels like it's been sanded, rough and dry. Sam presses the button by the side of my bed to summon the nurse and holds my hand until she pushes open the door. The room is flooded with brightness and I blink furiously as my eyes water.

"You're awake then? You gave us quite a fright. I'll buzz Dr. Kapur."

"Can she have some water?" Sam asks.

"A few sips—don't overdo it."

Sam cradles my head and holds the glass against my lips. The water is warm and musty but I've never tasted anything so good.

"Sophie?" It's an effort to speak.

Sam takes my hand. "I'm so sorry, Jen. She didn't make it."

Sadness swells and sleep tugs me under once more.

* * *

When I wake again I lie still at first, focusing on the thump-thump-thump inside my ribcage; it feels different somehow. Sorrow squeezes me tightly. Rolling onto my side, curling into a ball, I grapple for breath before I lock eyes with Sam. He's here. He's still here. The effect is instantly calming.

"Am I dying?" I whisper and even though I've been half-expecting my body to reject Callie's heart, I still feel an unimaginable sadness that this could be it. The end.

I'm not ready. And I berate myself for all the chances I never took. The life I never lived. Sam stretches out his hand—the hand I never should have let go—and our fingers entwine and every cell in my body weeps for the time I've wasted.

CHAPTER EIGHTY-TWO

Stars dot the inky black sky and waves lap against the shore. The swooshing sound lulls me as I sit and wait. I know you'll come. We once played hide-and-seek among these sand dunes. You'd clasp your small hands over your eyes and count to ten but as soon as I turned to race away you'd splay your fingers and peek. You thought I didn't know how you always found me straight away but I knew. I always knew.

I draw my knees up to my chest. The wind whips my hair and saltwater kisses my lips and I strain my eyes in the blackness wanting to catch the first glimpse of you.

The sky pales and a soft apricot glow tinges the clouds lavender as the sun rises. It's beautiful. The sky streaks purple, orange, red before settling on its usual self-conscious blue as if it could never be more than that. But we're all more than we think. Than we feel.

I see you now. Farther down the beach. Your movements are slow, uncertain, and I raise my hand to wave and your face lights up, shining more brilliantly than the sun.

I wrap my arms around you. It's been so long.

"You're here," you say as if I'd ever be anywhere else.

My fingers lace through yours and we turn and watch the waves crashing into white froth. Soon the beach will be full of chubby toddlers, ice cream dripping from chins. Racing dogs, tongues lolling to one side, and sisters playing just like we used to.

"Ready?" I ask, and you swallow hard and nod and together we walk into the light.

CHAPTER EIGHTY-THREE

When I wake again, the overhead hum of the fluorescent tubes is the first thing I hear. The room is too bright and I roll over to bury my face in the pillow, but the sheets catch the cannula that is taped to the back of my hand and I let out a small sound.

"Are you OK?"

Sam is still here and I wonder as I look at his wrinkled clothes, the shadow around his chin, when he last went home.

"I'm still alive?" It's more a question than a statement.

"You're going to be fine, Jenna," Sam says and I scan his face, looking for the tell-tale way he sometimes screws his eyes up if he's not being entirely truthful—of course your bum doesn't look big—but I can't see any sign of a lie.

I give a small shake of my head. "But . . ."

"You have a bacterial infection. If you hadn't got here when you did . . ." He squeezes my hand. "Dr. Kapur is pleased with the way you're responding to treatment. He'll tell you himself when he does his rounds. Trust me," he says, and I do. I'm not feeling quite as hot as I was. My muscles aren't as achy.

He sloshes water into a glass and cradles my head as I sip.

"I'll call your parents; they've nipped home for a shower and a change of clothes."

"You don't have to stay," I say when I have drained the glass.

"But I want to. Jen. I nearly lost you. Again."

My throat swells and eyes sting. "I'm sorry. For everything. I thought I was doing the right thing. After I lost the baby I felt I'd really let you down."

"It wasn't your fault. You could just as easily blame the doctor you saw after we had the flu who told you your lack of energy and dizziness was a normal symptom of the first trimester. He couldn't envisage what was to come and he was a doctor. It wasn't anyone's fault, Jen."

"I couldn't bear to look at myself. I didn't know how you could stand to look at me."

"I love you," Sam says. The simple truth.

I know I have to tell Sam about me and Nathan. But it's not the right time. Not here. Not now.

"I love you too, Sam." And at this moment it's the only truth that matters.

He strokes my arm with his thumb. "I'd best make some phone calls in a minute. Everyone has been worried about you."

"Everyone?"

"My mum's been frantic."

"Has she? I thought she'd never forgive me after Harry going missing."

"You might have some making up to do. But not for Harry going missing. She knows that wasn't your fault."

"What for then?" I can't think of what else I might have done.

"Because she was so relieved Harry was OK she caved and adopted that stray dog he kept wittering on about. Lavender. Mum is walking her twice a day. Grumbles, but I think she loves it really. She met a widower on the common yesterday with a boxer dog called Johnson. They're meeting again. He's got a son around Harry's age who is mad keen on Star Wars Lego too. Might be the start of something?"

Mr. Harvey from the vet's!

"Rachel will be here later too." Sam notices the look of surprise on my face. "She's resigned, you know. I think her exact words to Linda were 'go fuck yourself.'"

Sam fiddles with his phone before placing it on my bedside cabinet. "Kiss Me" streams from the speaker and, as Ed Sheeran sings, Sam swings his legs onto the bed and I shuffle toward the wall making space, and we lie together, his arm around my shoulders, my head on his chest, the rise and fall. I've missed this so much. It isn't until the song is over that Sam speaks.

"I was so scared when I got your phone call, Jen. I didn't know what was going on and the thought I might never see you again terrified me. This isn't the most romantic of settings. Again." His hand reaches into his pocket and pulls out a ring box. "But, marry me?" He flicks open the lid and there it is. His grandmother's ring, and my throat constricts.

"I can't pass it on."

"Pass what on?"

"The ring." I sniff hard. "You said your grandma wanted to keep the tradition going. I'll never have a granddaughter to pass it on to."

Sam pulls his arm from underneath me and rolls onto his side and stares deep into my eyes. "Jen, none of us know what's going to happen. How long we've got." He brushes a tear from my cheek with his thumb. "We might decide we want children, to adopt, to foster; we might not. But if you don't take this ring, it's not going anywhere. I love you. Only you."

There's a flutter in my chest and I wait to see if the feelings I thought I once had for Nathan resurface, but there's nothing, except a burning love for Sam that eclipses my doubts. I know that no matter what the future holds, he will be there by my side, and I'm determined to make the most of every single second I have left.

"Yes. I'll marry you," I say, my voice strong and certain, and Sam bends his neck so our foreheads touch.

And we stay that way until a trolley clatters into the room and Sam is offered a drink and a newspaper. He digs some change out of his pocket and buys two cups of tea.

"Not exactly champagne but do you want a strawberry to go with that?" He rolls open the drawer of my bedside cabinet and pulls out a punnet of fruit.

"Your mum brought them in. She said they are your new favorite thing?"

My stomach turns at the thought of the taste, the texture.

"Nope. Still hate them." I am so relieved.

Callie's gone and there's me. Just me.

And Sam.

Our own little family of two.

EPILOGUE

One year later

Light pushes its way through a crack in the curtains. I roll onto my back, sinking into the sunken mattress as I starfish my body, stretching out my aching muscles. My feet hang out of the end of my single bed and an early morning chill nips at my toes.

From down the hallway I can hear Mum clattering around the kitchen, the hard spray of water as Dad turns on the shower. You can hear everything in a bungalow.

I prop myself up on my elbows and my mouth stretches into a wide smile as I look at the oak wardrobe I've had since I was a child. It used to be my school uniform hanging from the smooth, round handle. Shirt starched, tie pressed. Today it's my wedding dress. Folds of cream silk and hand-stitched pearls that shine pale pink in the half-light. Happiness skips around my stomach as I think of Sam, and I wonder how he's feeling, waking up alone in our bed in our new three-bedroom house. It was a relief to move. Joe's face was full of shame as he told me it was him who had broken into the flat and sent me the text to deter me from my search for Sophie. Although I understood he was trying to stop me finding her, in case I found out what Amanda had done and told Tom, it never felt quite like home again. Harry has his own bedroom with us and he stays often. It took a whole weekend to hang Star Wars wallpaper onto the walls, smoothing out the bubbles, but it was worth it to see his face light up.

There's a little garden too, and I grow mint and rosemary for our potatoes. I often stand outside feeling the wind in my hair, the rain on my skin, the sun warming my bones, and I feel thankful for everything I have. Of course, it's impossible sometimes not to think of Amanda cooped up in a tiny cell, and I feel sorrow tempered with anger. Sadness mixed with hope. Despite the awful things she's done she took responsibility for everything and pleaded guilty to all her charges, leaving Tom and Joe free to start again. I am still aware that without her I wouldn't be here. I am still grateful to her. We all have our reasons for doing the things we do, don't we? The lies we tell. We are all a mixture of good and bad, and I don't think anyone is entirely one thing or the other. That's what I like to think, anyway.

There's a tap at the door. Mum places a steaming mug of coffee on my bedside table.

"How are you feeling?"

"Excited." And I am. My medication and my check-ups have been reduced and I am no longer seeing shadows in every corner, eyes watching my every move. I felt like any other bride-to-be as I'd tried on dress after dress, loving them all, as Mum watched, tears sliding down her cheeks. There must have been times she thought she'd never see this day.

"This is for you. I was under strict instructions not to give it to you until today." She places a cardboard box on top of the duvet, and she swishes back the curtains before she leaves the room.

I prop myself up with pillows and open the flaps of the box. There's something wrapped in tissue paper, a white envelope nestled on top. I slice it open and unfold the piece of paper and my heart lifts as I recognize Tom's handwriting.

Dear Jenna,

I am so sorry Joe and I can't be with you today but it's our first trout season in Scotland and we are hoping our fishing business makes us enough to live on through the winter. It can be bleak here, colder than I'd thought but more beautiful too. I thought I'd feel isolated but there's a steady stream of tourists and I feel content. The fresh air and exercise has done me the world of good. I've lost weight and am feeling fitter. Joe does all the manual stuff with the boats and I putter around with the rods and lines. It's a life that suits us both.

Anyway. You're getting married today! We are both delighted for you. I do think of you often, Jenna. I remember Callie fizzing with excitement when she told me she was engaged to Nathan (he's coming to visit soon by the way!). Callie never got as far as booking a venue or choosing a dress but she did buy this and I think she'd really like for you to have it.

Lots of love,
Tom xx

I gently unwrap the tissue paper, swallowing hard as I see the silver tiara Callie never got to wear. I cradle it in both hands. The sun streaks through the window, reflecting off the tiny diamonds, sending rainbows bouncing around my walls.

My door swings open.

"What are you doing still in bed?" Rachel yanks back the duvet. "You getting married in your pajamas or what? As bridesmaid, I order you to get your arse into gear."

I laugh. "You look great." My eyes sweep over her lemon dress. It's designer. She'd insisted on paying for it herself.

"I know!" She twirls. "Nothing but the best with the extortionate wages your dad pays me for being senior veterinary nurse."

"You deserve every penny." And she does. I work for Dad too now but only three days a week. In my spare time, I've taken up art classes and I've made the storage room in our new house a studio. I'm trying new things. "Living life to the full," Vanessa said. She was thrilled. It's different painting in oils to sketching and I haven't yet made the girls on the beach I paint come to life, but I will.

* * *

"Nervous?" Dad asks.

"A little." I peek my head around the door to the church. They are all there: Kathy holding hands with Mr. Harvey— I still can't get used to calling him Simon; Harry, one hand clutching Lavender's lead. She has a huge pink bow tied around her neck. Mum is dabbing her eyes already and, at the front, Sam. He turns and our eyes lock and my nerves melt away.

"Ready?" Dad asks, and I straighten Callie's tiara on my head before I loop my arm through his and we hover, waiting for the strains of the music to begin.

"I Have a Dream" by Abba begins to play.

And I step into the rest of my life.

A LETTER FROM LOUISE

Hello,

I do hope you have enjoyed reading Jenna's story. Cellular Memory is a theory more and more experts are supporting and it has endlessly fascinated me. I became utterly absorbed with my research, and in Jenna's discussions with Vanessa, most of the examples she gave are true. I have been stunned by the amount of transplant patients who have, to some degree, undergone changes after surgery. There are no rational explanations for these accounts. How can recipients have memories of a donor they never knew? Can science explain everything? It wasn't so long ago the heart was regarded as the center of wisdom and emotion. What do you think? I'd love to know.

Of course, ultimately, *The Gift* is a work of fiction and I have taken artistic license in my interpretation. In writing Jenna, I particularly wanted to explore the emotional impact dealing with such a drastic change of health can have, and I do hope I have approached the medical aspect sensitively, without trivializing the impact a transplant can have.

I cannot express how much admiration I have for donor families. My family and I have been on the register for as long as I can remember, and if you aren't please consider signing up. You really could save lives.

Finally, I love to hear from readers. You can contact me through my website or connect with me on Twitter and Facebook.

Thank you so much for taking time out of your day to spend with Jenna. If you have enjoyed *The Gift* I really would appreciate it if you could write a short review. It really does make such a difference.

Louise x

www.louisejensen.co.uk

 Fab_fiction

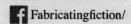 Fabricatingfiction/

READING GROUP GUIDE

1. Near the beginning of the book we discover Jenna has ended her relationship with Sam, as she feels she can no longer offer him the life he deserves. Was she right to do this? Are we ever justified in making a decision for someone if we feel it is for the best?

2. *The Gift* is about Cellular Memory, a theory that more and more experts are supporting. Can science explain everything? It wasn't so long ago the heart was regarded as the center of wisdom and emotion. What do you think?

3. Did your perception about the characters change from the beginning of the book until the end? How?

4. Jenna is partly driven by guilt that Callie died. Are some people more susceptible to guilt than others? Are her feelings justified?

5. Did you get a good sense of Callie throughout this story?

6. What did you assume about Callie and Nathan's relationship?

7. This novel is, in part, about secrets. Is it ever okay to keep a secret from a loved one? Is honesty always the best policy?

8. Were you satisfied with the end of the book? What alternative ending can you think of for this story?

9. Jenna concludes: "We all have our reasons for doing the things we do, don't we? The lies we tell. We are all a mixture of good and bad and I don't think anyone is entirely one thing or the other." Do you think this is true?

10. What do you think might happen to Jenna after the epilogue?

ACKNOWLEDGMENTS

It has taken a village to bring this book to life and I've so many people to thank: Bookouture, both the team behind the scenes, and the other authors, who are a constant source of support; my editor, Lydia Vassar-Smith; Henry Steadman, who has designed me another striking cover; and Rory Scarfe, whose belief in me as a writer has made an enormous difference.

I have met some lovely people in the writerly world, both online and offline this past year, and I'd especially like to thank all the book bloggers who work tirelessly. We are all united by our love of stories and I'm massively grateful for every single review.

It has been lovely to share the experience of being published with my virtual writing buddy, Sam Carrington, who spurs me on every day to sit down and just get on with it, and Tom Bale, who has been on hand to answer the endless questions I have had as I navigate my first year as a published writer.

Thanks to Leanne Laren for her input into police procedures—any mistakes are entirely my own. Sara Hammond for your listening ear and let's not forget THAT quote which will forever hang above my desk. Sarah Wade—thanks for always cheering me on. Symon Adamson—thanks for the early read. Bekkii Bridges for her insights into life as a veterinary nurse.

I am massively indebted to Emma Mitchell, Lucille Grant, and Mick Wynn, who generously gave their time and have really helped to shape *The Gift* into the story it is today. Your feedback has been invaluable.

My family for their love and support, particularly my mum, Diane Hockton, for bearing with me during this busy year, and my Aunty, Judy Kingston, for always championing me.

Karen Appleby—no one tells it quite like it is as much as a sister. I probably don't tell you I love you enough, but I do.

Callum, Kai, and Finley, my gorgeous boys, who inspire me to be the best version of myself I possibly can be. However big you grow, you are still my world.

I have come to the end of writing *The Gift* so grateful I still have a husband! Thanks, Tim, for picking up the slack at home and your unwavering belief that I could write a second book. You have been amazing.

And for Ian Hawley, of course, with all my love, always.

ABOUT THE AUTHOR

Louise Jensen has sold over a million English-language copies of her international #1 psychological thrillers *The Sister*, *The Gift*, *The Surrogate*, and *The Date*. Her novels have also been translated into twenty-five languages, as well as featured on the *USA Today* and *Wall Street Journal* bestseller lists.

The Sister earned her a nomination for the Goodreads Choice Awards Best Debut Author of 2016. *The Date* was nominated for the *Guardian*'s Not the Booker Prize 2018. *The Surrogate* was nominated for the best thriller of 2018 by Poland's online reading community We Like to Read (lubimyczytać.pl). *The Gift* has been optioned for a TV film.

Louise lives with her husband, children, madcap dog, and a rather naughty cat in Northamptonshire. She loves to hear from readers and writers.

For more information:
louisejensen.co.uk
Facebook.com/fabricatingfiction
Twitter @fab_fiction
Instagram @fabricating_fiction